Clare Willis is a primary school teacher who has taught in England, Scotland, Australia and now Singapore. Away from the classroom, she loves to travel and spends the school holidays exploring new places or relaxing back home in Cornwall. Clare loves to write uplifting, feel-good fiction filled with all her favourite ingredients: a touch of history, a dash of mystery, a bit of family drama, and a generous dose of romance. Her stories celebrate strong women, and centre on the relationships and challenges that define them. Clare lives in Singapore with her husband Chris and their labradoodle, Ruby.

CLARE WILLIS

The
SINGAPORE
SECRET

**HODDER &
STOUGHTON**

First published in Great Britain in 2026 by Hodder & Stoughton Limited
An Hachette UK company

The authorised representative in the EEA is Hachette Ireland,
8 Castlecourt Centre, Dublin 15, D15 XTP3, Ireland (email: info@hbgi.ie)

2

Copyright © Clare Willis 2026

The right of Clare Willis to be identified as the Author of the
Work has been asserted by her in accordance with the
Copyright, Designs and Patents Act 1988.

All rights reserved. No part of this publication may be reproduced, stored
in a retrieval system, or transmitted, in any form or by any means without
the prior written permission of the publisher, nor be otherwise circulated
in any form of binding or cover other than that in which it is published and
without a similar condition being imposed on the subsequent purchaser.

All characters in this publication are fictitious and any resemblance
to real persons, living or dead, is purely coincidental.

A CIP catalogue record for this title is available from the British Library

Paperback ISBN 9781399754101
ebook ISBN 9781399754118

Typeset in ITC Garamond Std by Manipal Technologies Limited

Printed and bound in Great Britain by Clays Ltd, Elcograf S.p.A.

Hodder & Stoughton policy is to use papers that are natural, renewable
and recyclable products and made from wood grown in sustainable forests.
The logging and manufacturing processes are expected to conform
to the environmental regulations of the country of origin.

Hodder & Stoughton Limited
Carmelite House
50 Victoria Embankment
London EC4Y 0DZ

www.hodder.co.uk

For Doris

PROLOGUE

She is back there again, reliving the moment for what must be the hundredth time. She stares, in wide-eyed terror, the scene unfolding before her as she knows it must; step by step, just as before. She cries out, but her cries make no sound. Each time she revisits it she is desperate for a different ending. What could she have done to have made things turn out differently? But the ending never changes. And the guilt never changes. It was her fault.

She opens her eyes as her body jolts her into heart-racing, sweat-soaked consciousness. The balmy heat and the lingering scent of frangipani of her memories fade away. Replacing them are darkness and the cool night air of the place she now calls home. She breathes deeply, regaining her composure. With shaking hands, she reaches for the glass of water on the bedside table. Moonlight spills in around the edges of the curtains and she can make out the gently swaying branches of the old oak tree in the garden. Before, it was the palm trees that swayed, but that was another time, another life. Somewhere, out there in the night, an owl hoots. It was just a dream, she reassures herself. Thank God, it was just a dream.

But still she cannot settle. She gets up and softly pads towards the door, avoiding the floorboard that creaks, and quietly opens it. Along the landing she creeps, compelled by instinct to check that all is as it should be. She pushes open another bedroom door and tiptoes towards the little bed. She smiles, watching the contented, innocent face of the sleeping child.

Feeling relieved, she makes her way back to her own room and climbs into bed. The steady breathing of the sleeping figure beside her reassures her that all is well. Nothing has changed. Nobody knows. Nobody must ever know. She has kept her promise and she knows that it was for the best. For now, her secret remains just so.

CHAPTER 1

Cornwall

SATURDAY 9TH MARCH, 2019

Annabel Penrose groaned as yet another tractor pulled out in front of her. She eased off the accelerator, looked at her watch and sighed. She couldn't be late, not today. Sleeping through her alarm had made for a bad start to the day, but she'd been so exhausted after a week of marking her students' dissertations that she had really needed the rest.

The argument with Luke hadn't helped, either. Her stomach sank as she thought back to it, remembering the anger etched all over his normally handsome face. She didn't think it had been unreasonable to ask her boyfriend of four years where he had been until 3 a.m. that morning or why he hadn't replied to any of her messages. But apparently it had been 'controlling and manipulative', and now she was driving to Cornwall alone. How had it all become so difficult?

The heavy traffic had been the icing on the cake and the journey from Bath to her grandmother's house on the north coast had taken over an hour longer than usual. The fine spring weather had encouraged everyone to escape to the coast and clog up the M5 motorway in doing so, and the local farmers were out making the most of the sunshine. She took a deep breath and turned up the radio, recognising the start of one of her favourite nineties boy band hits.

'Don't turn left. *Please* don't turn left,' she muttered as the tractor approached the next junction. A flicker of the indicator told her that it was going to do just that. Annabel groaned again, then followed in the wake of the giant machine as it turned off the main road and onto the narrow lane.

Her phone buzzed on the passenger seat and she stole a quick glance. Mum. For the third time.

> Where are you? PLEASE don't be late!

'Doing my best, Mum!' she said through gritted teeth.

The tractor slowed and indicated again. Sticking his head out of the cabin, the farmer gave her a cheerful wave and disappeared through a narrow gateway. She managed a smile and returned the wave; she couldn't really be cross with him. With a clear road ahead, she put her foot down, eating up the last couple of miles in a style of which Lewis Hamilton would have been proud. She really mustn't be late.

Annabel rounded the last bend and saw the black and white sign: Penrose Farm. She relaxed and felt a warm, fuzzy feeling: she was coming home. She drove between the stone pillars and followed the gravel drive through the trees. The lush, green lawn was a neat tapestry woven with delicate primroses and on either side of the track daffodils danced in the breeze. She had always loved this time of year in Cornwall. With spring flowers emerging and lambs frolicking in the fresh, green fields, it filled her heart with a renewed sense of hope. And she was needing some of that today.

Penrose Farm had felt like home for as long as Annabel could remember. Some of her earliest and fondest memories were here; rolling around on the lawn with her grandparents' Collie dogs, bottle feeding baby lambs or climbing trees in the woods with her older brother, William. She had never actually lived at the farmhouse full-time, but with her parents often posted overseas for her father's work, most of her boarding school holidays and exeats had been spent here, with Granny Dotty, as she and William called her. She had been their rock, Annabel mused, smiling to herself as she thought of their cheerful, white-haired grandmother.

At the front of the farmhouse was a sea of cars, lined up bumper to bumper, and it was a struggle to find a space. After squeezing between her brother's Audi and the farmer's mud-splattered Land Rover, Annabel applied a quick slash of lipstick, grabbed her overnight bag from the back seat and made her way to the front door. She ran a hand through her long, dark blonde hair in a bid to tame it and grinned at the gold helium balloons attached to the door handle. 'Happy 100th birthday!' they announced.

Her mother's radar was clearly on high alert as the door opened right as Annabel reached for the handle.

'Hi Mum! I'm—'

'Darling, what on earth happened?' Her mother cut her off. She kissed her cheek perfunctorily then continued with a furrowed brow, 'You look tired! I messaged you, but you didn't reply!' She looked out towards the sea of cars and asked, 'Where's Luke?'

'I was driving, Mum, I couldn't reply. And if I'd stopped to reply, I'd have been even later. Luke's not coming, he's not feeling well.'

Annabel took a deep breath and tried to stay calm. It wasn't exactly a lie; he wasn't feeling well. At that very moment, he was probably sprawled on the sofa nursing his hangover after last night's shenanigans. She groaned inwardly at the thought. Why hadn't he just told her where he had been?

Jeanette Penrose was a trim woman in her early seventies, but in her smart turquoise shift dress and matching jacket, with her silvery blonde hair elegantly styled into soft waves, she looked at least a decade younger. Retirement in the Algarve clearly agreed with her, and Annabel envied her year-round tan.

'Oh, I see.' she said. 'Well that's a shame, I hope he's feeling better soon. Do send him my love.'

How did her mother do it? Annabel had been there for less than a minute and every single comment that she had uttered so far had irritated her. Her making of fuss of Luke annoyed her at the best of times, but today it felt like something of a betrayal after he'd been a complete shit to her.

Jeanette had put Luke on a pedestal when they first got together and Annabel couldn't bear the way she fawned over him. She seemed to view him as some sort of knight in shining armour, nobly rescuing her daughter from a future of spinsterhood and maiden aunt status. What a hero. What an arse, more like. If only her mother knew the half of it.

'Anyway – ' Annabel forced a smile and followed her mother through the hallway and into the kitchen – 'I'm here now. How's the birthday girl?'

'Oh she's fine, you know Dotty; loving all the attention!' Jeanette gave a dramatic eye roll and Annabel swallowed down an irritated reply. 'She's in the conservatory, surrounded by her adoring fans! Everyone's been here since eleven, as per the invitation,' she added tartly.

Just for once, why couldn't her mother be nice to Dotty, today of all days? Annabel wondered. Maybe it was just the usual tension between daughters- and mothers-in-law, but it had always been this way and it was tedious; Jeanette playing the role of the perfect daughter-in-law, whilst making sneaky, barbed jibes behind the scenes. Dotty, for her part, always seemed to rise above it as far as Annabel could tell, which doubtless rankled Jeanette.

'It's been a busy morning, getting everything ready,' she continued. 'A helping hand wouldn't have gone amiss. Thankfully, William and Sarah got here before everyone else and helped finish setting up. They stayed with her sister near Exeter last night, so they didn't have far to come. She's so artistic; wait till you see the conservatory, she's done it beautifully!'

Annabel refused to rise to the bait. She forced a smile and agreed how fortunate it was that they'd been around to help put up the decorations. She loved her brother and sister-in-law dearly, but the Golden Couple treatment that they always got from their mother never failed to grind her gears.

The usually neat farmhouse kitchen had been invaded by multiple food containers and boxes from the local caterers. Two middle-aged ladies in matching company polo shirts looked up from the chaos with cheerful smiles as Jeanette and Annabel came in. Annabel tried to compensate for her mother completely ignoring them by greeting them warmly and thanking them for their efforts. Jeanette was on a mission: she made straight for the kettle, filled it, switched it on and glanced at her watch.

'Right, you have exactly twenty-three minutes to have a coffee and a shower, and get yourself ready.' Jeanette looked her daughter up and down, and wrinkled her brow at her T-shirt and jeans. 'Please tell me you've brought something to change into?'

Be nice . . . Be nice. It's Dotty's day, don't let her spoil it, Annabel told herself. She swallowed her frustration and managed an affirmative nod. She was thirty-five years old and a history lecturer at a university. She had a PhD, for goodness' sake, yet her mother still had a way of making her feel like a hopeless child. She took a deep breath and bent down to make a fuss of Monty, her granny's faithful old black Labrador, who was observing proceedings from the safety of his dog bed by the back door.

'The Lord Lieutenant's arriving at midday,' Jeanette continued, taking a mug from the cupboard and opening the jar of Nescafé. 'And he'll do the presentation first. That man from the press is here, it's going to be in the local papers, would you believe! Then we'll have the speeches; the Lord Lieut first, then your dad's going to say a few words.'

As if on cue, the tall figure of Noel Penrose appeared in the kitchen doorway. He was dressed smartly in a navy-blue suit. In his mid-seventies, he was still a handsome man with his dark features and year-round golfing tan, and the salt-and-pepper flecks in his black hair lent him a distinguished look.

'Annie, my darling girl!' he called, opening his arms to his daughter with a wide smile. Annabel grinned and rushed over to him, letting herself dissolve into his safe, pine-scented embrace.

Annabel and Dotty often joked that the phrase 'opposites attract' had been coined when Noel and Jeanette first met, back in the seventies. Whereas Jeanette was a bundle of highly strung energy, determination and drive, Noel was Mr Easy-Going, with a laid-back charm and relaxed sense of humour.

'I'm so glad you made it,' he said, rubbing her back as he hugged her close, 'How was the traffic?'

'Bloody awful! The motorway was bad, but the A30 was even worse! I'm so sorry I'm late, Dad,' she began. 'It's been the morning from hell!'

'Oh, bad luck!' He made a sympathetic face. 'No Luke?'

Annabel sighed and shook her head. 'I'll tell you later.'

Noel's blue eyes filled with concern for a moment, then brightened. 'Well lucky us, I say; we get you all to ourselves!' He gave her an encouraging wink, then lowered himself onto a stool at the breakfast bar with a grimace.

'You alright, Dad? Hip still giving you trouble?'

'Yes, damned thing! It was probably sitting cramped up in the plane that did it, plus the drive down from Heathrow. It just gets a bit stiff, I need to keep it moving. I'm booked in for the surgery, did Mum tell you? Getting it done in a couple of weeks, so that's a relief. Hopefully I'll be able to get back out on the golf course again soon!'

'Enough chit-chat, there'll be plenty of time for catching up later, you two!' Jeanette cut them off as she handed the coffee mug to her daughter. 'Noel, you need to practise your speech, and Annabel' – she glanced at her watch again – 'twenty-one minutes and counting!'

CHAPTER 2

Cornwall

SATURDAY 9TH MARCH, 2019

Dotty Penrose beamed out at the sea of familiar faces from her 'throne', as she'd dubbed the chair of honour at the far end of the conservatory. The royal blue of her dress matched her eyes, which at that moment were sparkling with excitement. Beside her, Annabel squeezed her hand and felt a lump form in her throat. She was so proud of her granny and it was a joy to see so many friends and neighbours come and pay tribute to her on her special day. Dotty had been delighted to see everyone, but confided in her granddaughter that she didn't know what all the fuss was about, 'Honestly, all these people making all this effort for this old biddy!'

Dotty was something of a local treasure in the Cornish village of Wincastle, where she had lived for over seventy years. She knew everybody and everybody knew her. To the locals, she was a second granny and she was never short of a friend to take her for a trip out, for a coffee or a meal. Annabel often teased that her social life was busier than her own, but was relieved that she was still able to keep busy and enjoy company. So many people became so isolated in old age, but Dotty seemed determined to keep going and stay interested in the world around her.

She had been blessed with remarkably good health, she admitted, never having broken a bone or needed a trip to hospital. Hearing her contemporaries discuss their medication and various ailments was always a tedious experience for her, not to mention a conversation in which she could not join. For at the ripe old age of one hundred, Dotty was, amazingly, medication free. She still managed to live independently in her beloved farmhouse, even managing the stairs to her bedroom and pooh-poohing Noel's suggestion of setting up a downstairs bedroom. He had briefly floated the idea of sheltered housing a couple of years ago, but such was the dressing-down from his mother that he never dared mention it again.

However, they had reached a compromise, with Noel arranging for a 'cleaner' to pop in every day, under the guise of doing the tedious jobs, such as vacuuming and doing the laundry and washing up. But really, she was there to keep an eye on things for Noel, who felt horribly torn between his golfing retirement in the sun and his dear old ma back home. Dotty had resented the daily intrusion at first, but had eventually warmed to Lizzie, the cheerful retired nurse who was in her late fifties. Noel felt relief the first time Dotty mentioned having had a cup of coffee with Lizzie after she'd finished her chores.

Every day, come rain or shine, Dotty walked the half mile to the village post office to buy her newspaper and have a chat with Pam, the postmistress. She liked to keep up to date with the news and do the daily crossword, but, more importantly, the routine and the company kept her going. 'The day I stop moving is the day this old body will pack up!' she had told Annabel.

Such was Dotty's popularity that today it was standing room only in the conservatory. Several guests had spilled out onto the patio beyond, where trestle tables had been set up for the buffet lunch later. Annabel looked out and smiled. She never tired of the view from the house and today it was nothing short of spectacular. There wasn't a cloud in the azure sky, and fluffy white lambs skipped and jumped in the fields that led down to the sea, sparkling in the distance. It was a perfect Cornish spring day.

The Lord Lieutenant of Cornwall, Colonel Edward Tremayne, arrived at 12 p.m. on the dot. He was a handsome man in his late sixties, with silver-grey hair and piercing blue eyes. Dressed in his full military regalia and with a charming greeting for everyone, he set a few elderly pulses racing. 'I suppose this is the OAP's equivalent of ordering a stripper for a twenty-first!' William whispered to Annabel as the colonel stood up to address the audience, causing her to snort and earn a reproachful look from their mother.

Congratulations were given and snippets of Dotty's life story (provided to him by Noel, via email) were shared, then it was the moment they had all been waiting for: the birthday card from the Queen. It had arrived in the mail a couple of days earlier and Dotty had been under strict instructions not to open it, but to wait until the official presentation.

A hush fell as Colonel Tremayne handed the white envelope to Dotty with due pomp and ceremony and said, 'Mrs Dotty Penrose, it is my very great honour to be here with you and your loved ones today. I have been instructed by Her Majesty Queen Elizabeth, to wish you a very happy birthday!' There was a round of applause and Annabel looked up to see a wall of cameras and mobile phones; everyone wanted to capture the special moment.

Annabel had never seen her grandmother lost for words before, but receiving personal correspondence from Her Majesty left her in a kind of awed silence. There wasn't a dry eye in the house as her nearest and dearest watched her gaze at the photograph on the front of the card. Annabel heard her whisper, 'Well I never!'

Then she opened it and read the message aloud:

I am so pleased to know that you are celebrating your one hundredth birthday on 9th March, 2019. I send my congratulations and best wishes to you on such a special occasion. Elizabeth R.

'Well, thank you very much, Your Majesty; it was very good of you to remember!' she quipped, earning a burst of laughter and another round of applause as she held the card up for everyone to see.

'Speech!' came a voice from the back of the room, which Annabel recognised to be that of Neil Polkerris, the farmer who leased the Penrose farmland. Everyone laughed again and Dotty let herself be talked into it.

'I'm not one for speeches, but I would just like to say a few words,' she began and then paused as she looked around the room. Sitting next to her, Annabel squeezed her hand encouragingly.

'I'd just like to say thank you so much to you all for coming today, it really does mean an awful lot to me. I'm a very fortunate old woman! Lots of you have asked me the secret to reaching this ripe old age. I'm not sure what the answer is, maybe it's the little glass of sherry I have every evening – purely for medicinal reasons, you understand!' More laughter. Annabel felt a surge of pride as she watched her grandmother captivate her audience.

'But in all seriousness,' she continued, 'I think it's love.' A sigh echoed around the room. 'I've had a long life filled with a lot of love, for which I thank my lucky stars every day. I was blessed with the most wonderful husband. He loved me and took care of me from the moment we met, until the day he died. And we were blessed with the best son we could have ever wished for, our dear Noel. I could never have asked for a kinder, more loving son. Thank you, darling.' She looked over to where Noel was standing and blew him a kiss.

'What about us, Nanny Dotty?' came the small voice of William's eldest, six-year-old Lucy, from the corner of the room. Everyone laughed and Dotty wiped away trickles of laughter.

'And you too, darling, I was saving the most important till last! I am so fortunate to have my wonderful grandchildren and great-grandchildren here; my dearest Annabel, William and his Sarah, and their cheeky little monkeys, Lucy and Aiden. I love you all, thank you for being my family.' Dotty smiled out at her guests and gave a slight bow to show that she had finished, prompting rapturous applause and cheers from around the room.

Noel stepped forward next and motioned for quiet. 'How to follow that?' he joked. He started by echoing Dotty's thanks to everyone for coming, to the Lord Lieutenant for making it such a special occasion and to the caterers, who were now busy setting up the buffet on the patio.

'And now comes the hard part, how on earth can I do justice to a hundred years of my wonderful mum in just a few minutes?' An encouraging chuckle murmured around the room.

'All I can say is thank you, Ma. You have been our family's rock and mainstay through the years, through all the ups and downs. And not just for us, but here in the village you have been a stalwart of the community. Never one to let the grass grow under your feet, you've always got involved, whether it was the bowling club, the WI, the church rotas, the keep-fit club or the Cancer Research committee. I know from all the cards you've received today – as well as all the guests here – that you are very much loved and very much appreciated.'

Dotty's eyes glistened with pride as a murmur of agreement echoed around the room. Several voices called out, 'Hear, hear!'

'Ma, you've made our family what it is. You talked about love, but it was you who showed us how to love. You and Pa – God rest his soul – have been the best parents I could have ever wished for. I am truly blessed to call you my mum. A mere "thank you" seems so inadequate, but I mean it with all my heart.'

Dotty's eyes welled up again and she reached up to take his hand in hers. Noel raised it to his lips and kissed it tenderly.

'Ladies and gentlemen,' Noel continued, dabbing at his own unshed tears, 'Please raise your glasses. To my wonderful Ma . . . To Dotty!'

'To Dotty!' cheered the guests as they toasted the birthday girl.

At that moment, Jeanette made her way through the crowd with the birthday cake. Annabel moved a side table in front of Dotty, as per her mother's instructions, and took the cigarette lighter from the pocket in her dress. The cake was covered in perfect, snow-white icing, with 'Happy Birthday Dotty!' piped in cheerful yellow lettering. Delicate yellow flowers decorated the top and a matching ribbon was tied around the outside. Springtime yellow was the perfect choice, Annabel mused, pleased with her mum's decision. It was bright and cheerful, just like Dotty.

Annabel lit the candle that stood in the middle of the cake and, as it flickered into life, Noel led the guests in singing 'Happy Birthday'. The beaming birthday girl leaned forward in her chair, ready to blow out the candle.

'Make a wish!' called out one of the guests.

Instead of the full complement to match her age, there was just a single '100' candle standing in the centre. Dotty closed her eyes and smiled as she made her wish, then took a deep breath and blew. The candle was soon extinguished and the guests began to clap. But then it flickered and came alive again, much to Dotty's bemusement.

Encouraging shouts of 'Blow harder, Dotty!' and 'Give it some welly, girl!' came from around the room. Dotty looked puzzled, but took another deep breath and had another go.

After the fourth attempt, the penny dropped and Dotty chuckled, realising that she'd been had. 'Oh, you rascals!' she said, slightly out of puff. 'Is this one of those fancy candles that won't go out?' she asked, causing much amusement around the room. 'Fine way to finish an old biddy off on her birthday!'

"Sorry, Dotty!" Annabel clutched her hand and gave a wry smile. "Blame William, it was his bright idea!"

Dotty looked across to see William grinning at her. He gave her a wink and she wagged a finger at him, but couldn't keep the smile from her face.

The last of the visitors had made their farewells by late afternoon and the family moved through to the comfy chairs in the sitting room. Jeanette directed the catering staff in their tidying up and Sarah set off to make tea for everyone, while Annabel helped her grandmother into her favourite chair beside the fireplace. Monty joined her, sitting loyally at her feet with his head on her knee.

'Well, that was a big success!' Annabel sighed contentedly, slipping off her shoes and curling up on the sofa. 'Did you have a nice time, Dotty?'

'Oh, I'm exhausted!' the old lady puffed. 'But it was marvellous! I had a wonderful time. It was so kind of everyone to come. And all these lovely cards!' She pointed to the sideboard, which was a sea of birthday jollity. 'I was very touched.'

'And the old colonel was a bit of alright too, wasn't he Dotty?' William quipped from the hearthrug, where he was getting out the Lego to keep his children entertained. He waggled his eyebrows suggestively at his granny, making her giggle like a schoolgirl.

'You never change, William Penrose, you cheeky boy! But it's been wonderful to have you all here together.' Dotty beamed at them all. 'I know it's a long way for you all to come. Especially for you, Noel, having to fly all that way! I do appreciate you making the effort.'

'It's no effort, Ma, it's only Portugal; just a few hours on the plane. It's an easy journey, very doable. You know we'd love you to come out and stay with us for a while. Maybe later in the summer, after I've had my hip done? I think you'd enjoy it; it'd be a nice change.'

Dotty appeared to mull it over for a moment, then shook her head. 'It's very kind of you, dear, but it would be awfully hot. You know I can't stand the heat. In one hundred years, I've never had a foreign holiday yet, and I'm afraid I don't intend to start now!'

'But that can't be right,' Noel's brow creased in confusion. 'We went on that holiday when I was very small. Don't you remember?' Noel asked. 'It was one of my very first memories as a child, I must have been about two or three. Surely you remember, Ma? I've no idea where it was, but it was incredibly hot and humid! I've a memory of someone doing that old nursery rhyme 'Round and Round the Garden' on my hand, and sitting on a wooden box with no clothes on, being fed soup from a bowl!'

Everyone chuckled at the unlikely image he'd painted, but Annabel noticed the flicker of a shadow pass across her grandmother's face. It was for the briefest of moments, then her smile was back, but Annabel had seen it. Had Dotty really forgotten? Her mental agility had been so sharp for so long, was she worrying now that her memory was starting to fade?

'Why would you eat hot soup in a hot country?' little Lucy, piped up. 'That would just make you hotter. Ice cream would have been better.' Everyone laughed at the comment.

'And you shouldn't go out in the sun with no clothes on, Grandad,' chided four-year-old Aiden, not wanting to be outdone by his big sister. 'You'll get all sunburnt with no clothes on, that's what Mummy says.'

'What do I say?' asked Sarah on cue, as she came back into the room with the tea tray. She put a plate of biscuits on the coffee table and handed out mugs of tea.

'That nude sunbathing is off limits, apparently!' quipped Annabel.

Later that evening, while William and Sarah were putting the children to bed and her parents were tidying up, Annabel sat and enjoyed a moment of calm with her grandmother.

Dotty smiled, looking at the card from Buckingham Palace. She pointed to the photo of the Queen. 'It's a lovely snap of her, isn't it? I do like her in lavender, don't you? I think it's her best colour.'

'I'll be sure to let Her Majesty know you approve of her colour choice.' Annabel teased good-naturedly. 'So tell me, dearest Ancient Relic, how are you feeling?'

'Old!' Dotty quipped without missing a beat. They both laughed. 'Oh, I can't really complain. The old bones are a nuisance, but the marbles are still present and correct,' she tapped the side of her head, 'And that's the important bit! But never mind me, how are you, sweetheart? You look tired, is everything alright?'

The tenderness in her grandmother's eyes made Annabel well up. She knew her so well, she always had done. She recognised every shade and nuance on her granddaughter's face, far better than Jeanette had ever done. It was Dotty to whom Annabel had turned for comfort and advice when she was growing up, whom she would call if she had a problem at school or needed cooking advice while away at university. And that would never change. Despite her granny's advancing years, she always seemed to understand and to strike the right balance between providing a listening ear and offering useful advice.

'It's Luke,' she sighed.

'Ah,' Dotty nodded her understanding. 'Things not going well?'

'I just don't know where we're going.' She shrugged. 'We'll have been together for five years in August, but instead of growing closer together, it feels like we're drifting further apart. He's been acting so differently lately; we used to socialise together, but these days he's only interested in nights out with the football lads. And when we do have time together, he just seems to want to veg in front of the TV.'

'Have you spoken to him about it, told him how you're feeling?'

'I've tried. But he gets so defensive and somehow always manages to turn it around and put the blame on me, like I'm the one with the problem.'

'Gaslighting.' Dotty nodded sagely.

Annabel couldn't help but burst out laughing at hearing her centenarian grandmother utter such a twenty-first century colloquialism. 'Where on earth did you pick that up?' she asked.

'My friend Pam in the post office.' She chuckled. 'Her Wendy's boyfriend does it to her all the time, apparently. Not a pleasant fellow, by all accounts. But it's a term from my era, would you believe? It comes from a film from the forties with Charles Boyer and the beautiful Ingrid Bergman, it's very good! But I digress, sorry; do go on,' she smiled.

'I suppose I'm just wondering if we've actually got a future together or if it's time to call it quits. I'll be thirty-six next birthday and I do want to get married and have a family. And, as Mum never tires of reminding me, my biological clock is ticking.' Annabel rolled her eyes at this. 'I guess I just don't want to waste any more time if he's not the one I'm meant to be with. What should I do?'

Dotty reached over and took her granddaughter's hand in hers. 'You need to tell him, darling. Hard as it might be, you need to be sharing this with him.'

'But how, when he stays out till all hours and refuses to tell me where he's been?'

'Well,' Dotty replied carefully, 'if that's the case, maybe you've answered your own question.'

Tears welled in Annabel's eyes and she sighed. 'But the thought of ending things and starting out again feels completely terrifying!'

'You are one of the strongest women I know, my love. I like Luke, but you mustn't stay with him if he isn't making you happy anymore. Please, darling, you deserve so much more than that. You are perfectly capable of standing on your own two feet and living an independent life until Mr Right comes along.

And these days, there are so many modern ways to meet someone. There's Tinder and Grindr, for a start . . .'

'Woah, woah, woah!' Annabel laughed and held up a hand to stop her granny. 'Is this Pam again? I need to have a word with her! What ideas has she been putting in your head?'

Dotty's eyes twinkled mischievously, 'I do love Pam and her stories, she keeps me up to date on all sorts of things!'

'I can only imagine!' Annabel raised an eyebrow in mock horror. 'But in all seriousness, those dating apps sound awful! My friend Jenny at work uses them and you should hear some of the tales she tells me. She'll spend a couple of weeks chatting online with some guy who's perfect on paper, only to meet him and find out that his profile picture is about ten years out of date. Or he's used someone else's picture. Or he's only after one thing. It all just sounds exhausting.' Annabel sighed at the thought.

'We may have come a long way on the technology front,' she continued, 'but I'd much rather go back in time and meet someone the old-fashioned way, like how you and Grandpa met.' Annabel looked over at the ornate frame on the mantelpiece, showing her grandparents on their silver wedding anniversary.

'It was at a dance, wasn't it? In London, during the war?' Annabel turned back to her grandmother and she saw that look again; as if a cloud was passing across Dotty's face as she, too, gazed at the photograph.

Dotty had never shared much about her younger years, which had always been a huge disappointment to Annabel, the historian. She would have loved to have heard about her wartime experiences in London, but Dotty had always brushed it off, with a glib, 'Oh you don't want to hear about all that; no great heroics, we all just did our bit,' and would then change the subject. Annabel had put it down to her avoiding painful memories, having lost both her parents during the war and her brother, Thomas, a few years later.

'Dotty?' she probed.

'Sorry my love, I was miles away!' she resumed. 'Oh, he was a good man; the very best of men. I knew he'd always take care of me. And Noel, too. We were very lucky. It wasn't a bed of roses all the time, you understand, but we shared the same values and wanted the same things. And we tried every day to make each other happy.'

'You must miss him very much. We all do.' Annabel smiled sadly at her grandmother. 'Dear Grandpa.'

'Every day for seventeen years.' Dorothy sighed. 'But that's life, I'm afraid. Nothing lasts forever, good or bad, remember that. And there's no need to rush into anything new.' Dotty patted her hand. 'Maybe you just need a bit of time apart from Luke, a bit of space to think about things. A little break somewhere nice and a bit of "you" time to see how you really feel. You've got Easter holidays coming up soon, haven't you?' Dotty asked. 'Why don't you take yourself off somewhere nice for a change of scenery?'

'Yes, that's a good idea. I asked Luke if he fancied having a few days away somewhere, but he said he's too busy at work.' She sighed again and looked out of the window.

The evening sunlight was making the patio daffodils glow and the sea sparkle a perfect shade of turquoise in the distance. She suddenly felt an overwhelming sense of calm and an idea formed.

'Dotty, can I come and stay here with you?'

CHAPTER 3

Bath

Friday 22nd March, 2019

The last day of term arrived and Annabel was at work in the university history department, making a coffee in the little kitchen near her office. She had a busy day ahead, preparing for her lecture on Roman architecture and going through her tutor group's essays on the Greco-Persian wars. She yawned and ran a hand through her hair, wishing she'd got more sleep.

'Morning!' came the cheerful Yorkshire accent of her colleague, Jenny. 'Happy almost end of term!'

Annabel turned and mustered a smile for her friend. 'Hallelujah! We're nearly there!'

Jenny's eyes widened as she stared at her friend. 'You alright? You look terrible!'

'Thanks a bunch!' Annabel scoffed. 'I'm definitely ready for a holiday! Too much marking and not enough sleep. And things with Luke aren't exactly helping either. Fancy a coffee?'

'Go on then,' Jenny replied. She sat down at the little bistro table and her brow furrowed in concern. 'Still being a dick, is he?'

Annabel sighed as she spooned instant coffee into two mugs, added the water and stirred. 'Yep, sure is.'

'How did he take the news of you heading down to your granny's for the holidays?' Jenny asked.

Annabel put the coffee mugs on the table and sat down opposite her friend.

'He was remarkably unfazed by it. I was only going to go for a week, then try to book a couple of days for us to go away together. But he told me that he's going to be so busy with work that he can't do that, and suggested I spend the whole holiday at Dotty's.'

'Oh!' Jenny said, surprised. 'That's a bit rubbish!'

'It certainly is.' Annabel gave a helpless shrug. 'They're working on their proposal for that Ashton House project, you know that old Victorian place near Bristol?'

Jenny rolled her eyes as she recalled the project. 'It's a crying shame that that beautiful stately home is being converted into flats!'

Annabel nodded. 'My sentiments exactly! Where's the National Trust when you need them?'

'Exactly!' Jenny agreed, shaking her head.

'Don't get me wrong,' Annabel continued, 'I love my independence. And I'd hate for him to tell me that I *couldn't* go to Dotty's, but part of me wanted him *not* to be OK about us spending so much time apart. Part of me wanted him to actually want me to be around.' She sighed and leaned her elbows on the table and rested her chin in her upturned palms. 'Pathetic, hey?'

Jenny's brow furrowed. 'Not at all!' She thought for a moment, choosing her next words carefully. 'Don't hate me for putting this out there, but . . . ' She paused. 'Is there any chance he's seeing someone else?'

'It crossed my mind, but I've never ever worried about his loyalty. His dad cheated on his mum when he was little and he has always been so completely and utterly against guys who do that. But he's been funny for a couple of months now.' She sighed.

'But we're going out for dinner tonight, before I head to Cornwall, so that's something. Hopefully we can have a chat and I can figure out what's going on.'

'Well that's good,' Jenny said, rubbing her friend's arm affectionately. 'Don't lose heart just yet. Maybe a bit of time apart will do you both good, have a bit of a space and see where you are. And all that lovely Cornish sea air is just what you need to recharge the batteries!'

'Yes, exactly. Let's hope it's a case of absence making the heart grow fonder, rather than being out of sight and out of mind!' Annabel quipped as she spooned sugar into her coffee. 'Plus, it'll be good to spend some time with Dotty and I can make a start on my writing.'

'Sounds like a plan! What's happening with the book?'

'Not much!' Annabel sighed. 'Hence the need to make some time for it.'

She glanced at her watch then glugged down the hot, sweet coffee. 'Time to get cracking, this lecture isn't going to write itself!'

Several hours later, Annabel was all dressed up and ready for her dinner date with Luke, but there was no sign of him. She had been pleased when he'd suggested going out for dinner tonight; not to mention a little relieved. He had booked a table at Salvatore's, their favourite restaurant in the early days when they had first got together. They hadn't been there for ages.

Wanting to make an effort, Annabel had spent longer than her usual ten minutes getting ready. She'd had a long, relaxing bubble bath, spent time on her make-up and deliberated over her outfit. Sensible little black dress or flirty red strapless number? Annabel had held them up against herself alternately as she looked in the mirror and opted for the latter. She rummaged in the back of her underwear drawer and dug out the matching red lingerie set Luke had bought her for Valentine's Day a couple of years ago. It was time to inject a bit more passion into the relationship, she had decided; she wanted to give him something to remember while she was away.

But now there was nothing to do but wait for him. She had tried calling his mobile but he hadn't answered. She had texted, asking where he was, but no reply. She tried to stay calm and not worry, but her mind was taking her in all sorts of directions. In the end, she switched on the television and tried to distract herself with a mindless reality show.

'Annie, I'm so sorry!' he called, when the front door finally opened at half past eight. 'My phone died and I'd lent the stupid charger to Phil and he'd taken it home! Work was crazy today.'

He stopped talking as he reached the open doorway and saw her, sitting on the sofa. 'Wow! Look at you, you look gorgeous!' He dropped to his knees on the carpet in front of her and took her hands in his. 'And I'm a complete shit. I'm sorry.' He brushed her lips with his and Annabel caught a slight waft of alcohol.

She rolled her eyes dramatically but managed a smile. 'Yes, you are,' she said teasingly, but only half joking. 'But I'm starving and spent ages getting ready, so go and get changed, let's go!'

He got back up to his feet and looked at his watch doubtfully. 'You still want to go?'

'Of course! I'm starving and there's nothing in the fridge. I rang Salvatore's and managed to push the table back an hour.' She stood up. 'Go and get ready and I'll book a cab. We should just make it.' She smiled up at him, determined to try to make the best of this evening despite his lateness.

He gave a long sigh. 'To be honest, babe, I'm knackered. Can we just get a takeaway?'

Annabel's heart sank. She had been looking forward to an evening out together before she went to Cornwall, but she didn't want to risk rocking the boat by pushing back. 'Sure,' she said, forcing a smile. She went upstairs and changed back into her jeans and sweater, then dialled the number for the local pizza place.

'You OK?' she asked later, as they settled in front of the television. She opened the pizza box as he poured them each a glass of red wine.

'Just tired,' he replied with a sigh. 'It's been a long week. And I guess I felt a bit pressured that you wanted to go out tonight.'

Annabel screamed inside. 'But it was your idea? I just thought it would be nice to have a date night before I went away,' she said quietly. 'But I'm sorry for pushing it when you weren't in the mood.'

'No, don't apologise, it's not you,' he said, instantly backing down. He took a long swig of red wine. 'I'm sorry. I'm just tired.'

He put on an action movie that he'd been wanting to watch. An uneasy silence filled the room as they ate.

'Luke, is everything OK?' she tried again, as the movie credits began to roll a couple of hours later. 'I'm worried about you; I'm worried about us. What's going on?' she asked, her eyes filling with tears. 'And please don't tell me it's nothing, or that I'm imagining it,' she added gently. 'Things have felt different for a while and I don't think you're happy. Is it me?'

His eyes shot up to meet hers. 'God, no! Annie, please don't think that!' He sighed and reached across to hold her hand. Then he reached for his wine glass again.

'I don't know,' he continued. 'I'm just feeling under pressure.' He paused again, struggling to find the words. 'Like there's this weight of expectation hanging over me.' He ran his hand through his wavy brown hair. 'It's been almost five years and I love being with you. But with every birthday, Christmas or Valentine's Day that passes, I feel this pressure from everyone around us that I should propose. My parents drop hints, your parents drop hints, our friends, neighbours, everyone!'

'But not me!' she countered, her brow furrowing. 'I'm not dropping hints!'

'No, babe, you're not.' He paused. 'But it's there, below the surface. This feeling that I'm disappointing you the more time that passes. But I don't feel ready for it. And, to be honest, I'm not sure if I'll ever feel ready for it. I suppose I'm feeling a bit . . . ' he paused, looking uncomfortable, 'trapped.'

'Trapped?' she repeated, stunned.

He sighed. 'Stuff like you wanting to know where I am all the time; who I'm with, what I'm doing. I guess I'm not ready to give up my freedom and settle down.' He used his fingers to make air quotes on the last two words.

There was a long pause while they both considered his words. Annabel could hear her pulse start to thump in her ears.

'I just don't know if I'm cut out for the whole marriage-and-kids thing,' he eventually managed. 'I'm sorry, babe, I know that's not what you want to hear. You've always wanted the white wedding and the two point four kids, but I don't know if that's what I want.'

'So where does that leave us?' she asked quietly.

He shrugged. 'I don't know. Maybe we should use this time apart to think about what we both really want. I don't want to hurt you, Annie, I love you.'

'And I love you too.' She smiled through unshed tears. 'And that's enough, Luke. All that other stuff, the wedding, the kids – none of it matters, I just want to be with you.'

He smiled back sadly. 'Oh, but it *will* matter, Annie, one day. You'll end up resenting me for stopping you from having all of that. And that's not fair, on me or on you.'

She cleared away the pizza boxes and washed the wine glasses. Then she went upstairs, telling Luke that she was tired. He said he'd follow her up shortly, but as she reached the landing, she heard the clink of the whisky bottle. She got undressed and dropped the red lingerie into the laundry bin. So much for a night of passion.

When he finally came to bed later, he rolled over to her side and spooned himself around her. He kissed the back of her neck and whispered, 'I do love you, Annie.'

She let the silent tears trickle down her cheek and onto the pillow and pretended to be asleep. Tomorrow, she was heading to Dotty's and she couldn't wait. She was sure that things would feel better after a good dose of fresh air, bracing beach walks and Cornish cream teas with her dear granny.

*

Luke was up before her the next morning and on his best behaviour, it seemed. He busied around the kitchen, making fresh coffee and her favourite bacon and poached eggs on toast. Annabel did her best to match his cheerfulness, fighting the dull ache that she felt inside.

'Send Dotty my love, won't you,' he said when it was time for her to leave. Annabel managed a smile and a nod, then gave him a brief kiss on the lips.

'Good luck with work,' she told him. 'I hope you get it all finished on time.' Her eyes suddenly filled with tears now that the moment of parting was upon them.

'Oh, you soppy thing!' he teased. 'Come here!' With that, he pulled her into his arms and enveloped her in a bear hug. She breathed in his scent and enjoyed the feeling of fitting perfectly against his body, his chin resting on the top of her head. He rubbed her back, kissing her hair.

'It's only Cornwall, Annie, not Antarctica!' he joked, making her laugh. 'And it's only three weeks; you'll be back before you know it. And don't worry, we'll figure everything out.'

Unlike the previous trip, the roads were quiet this morning and Annabel made good progress. She let herself cry as she left the city and headed up through Lansdown towards the M4, and it felt good to get it out of her system. Despite trying to carry on as normal this morning, she was still feeling crushed by Luke's news last night. Did they have a future together, or was this the beginning of the end? She felt like he was pulling the rug from under their safe, happy life and it made her feel anxious.

The journey passed quickly, with a couple of stops for coffee near Taunton and fuel near Exeter. Soon, she found herself turning into the familiar driveway to Penrose Farm. Annabel smiled and felt the usual, soothing sense of calm. She had made the right decision to come here. A bit of time apart from Luke was exactly what they both needed to re-evaluate things. Part of her hoped that she would return from this trip to his loving, open arms and his declaration that he had missed her so much that he couldn't imagine a future without her. But the other, more pragmatic part of her knew that ignoring the fact that they wanted different things out of life would just prolong the inevitable.

As soon as she opened the car door, she heard a dog barking; an urgent, frantic sound. Annabel knew instantly that something was wrong. She took out her keys and let herself in through the front door. Monty bounded up to her, clearly upset and agitated.

'Dotty?' Annabel called, a sense of panic rising in her. She waited a moment for a response, but there was none. Quickly, she checked the hallway and sitting room before making her way into the kitchen.

There, on the tiled floor, was the crumpled figure of her dear grandmother.

CHAPTER 4

Cornwall

SATURDAY 23RD MARCH, 2019

Annabel sat at the side of the hospital bed, gently stroking her grandmother's hand. She was so deeply asleep and looked so tiny and fragile that, at first, Annabel had feared the worst. But the steady beeping of the monitor in the background reassured her otherwise.

There was something fundamentally wrong about seeing Dotty like this. She had always been so vital, so alive, that her current, diminished state made no sense to Annabel. With her left wrist in a plaster cast, she reminded her of a little sparrow she'd once found in her garden. It had a broken wing and couldn't fly, so Annabel had put it safely in a cardboard box in the shed and had taken care of it until it was strong enough to take off again. She hoped and prayed that she could nurse Dotty back to full strength, too.

The nurse had explained that Dotty had broken her wrist and cracked a rib when she fell. They were giving her morphine for the pain and it was giving her 'a good sleep'. The nurse was a kindly lady in her fifties, with short blonde curly hair and a round, smiling face. She'd introduced herself as Sue and patted Annabel's arm sympathetically, telling her not to worry. The kind gesture nearly had her in tears. 'People don't make it to a hundred without a bit of fighting spirit,' Sue had said in her lilting Cornish accent. 'Your granny's a fighter, my love, and I'm sure she'll be awake again soon and glad to see your pretty face!'

As she sat there, sipping a vending-machine coffee and chatting to the sleeping Dotty as Nurse Sue had suggested, Annabel's mind went back to those awful moments after her arrival. She had made her grandmother as comfortable as possible and telephoned for an ambulance. After that, she had called Dotty's friend, Pam in the post office, to let her know what had happened and to ask her to take care of Monty.

'I *knew* something wasn't quite right,' Pam had said on the phone, sounding worried. 'Eleven o'clock and there'd been no sign of her. You can set your watch by your granny; she comes in every day at ten thirty on the dot for her newspaper, come hell or high water! I tried the house phone first and when there was no answer I knew something must be up. So I was going to ask my Paul to keep an eye on the shop when he got back, so I could go up and check, but he was running late! Thank goodness you arrived when you did, Annabel!'

And now it was a waiting game. There was nothing else to do but stroke her beloved grandmother's hand as she prayed for her recovery. She wasn't naive enough to think that Dotty would live forever. She thanked her lucky stars that she'd had her in her life until now; most of her friends had few, if any, grandparents still living. But the thought of her not being around anymore filled Annabel with an overwhelming sense of dread.

Needing some comfort and the sound of a friendly voice, she stepped out of the ward and went outside into the hospital car park to ring Luke. Regardless of what issues were going on between them, he knew how much Dotty meant to her, and he was always a source of reassurance and support when times were tough. But his phone was switched off. Her stomach gave an anxious somersault and she felt the icy chill of being alone. Was this a premonition of things to come? Instead, she rang her dad, needing to hear his comforting voice and reassure herself that he was alright after his hip surgery. At the sound of his voice, she dissolved into tears.

'Oh, Annie, I'm so sorry! How awful, poor Ma.' His deep voice had been filled with concern, for both Dotty and Annabel. 'I can't tell you how glad I am that you're there with her, thank you. I'm afraid I'm not much use at the moment, still stuck in hospital myself!' he scoffed. 'Are you alright to hold the fort? I'll ring William, maybe he can get down to help out, too.'

'No, it's alright, Dad,' she reassured him, using the end of her sleeve to dry her eyes. 'Don't disturb Will, it's a long way to come and there's not much point until we know what's going to happen next. I'll be fine, honestly. Just a bit tired.'

'Well, if you're sure? Thanks so much, darling. And remember, I'm only at the end of the phone; ring me any time. Keep in touch.'

Annabel bought another coffee and a chocolate bar then returned to the ward. Caffeine and sugar were going to get her through today. There was no change when she got back to Dotty's bedside, the old lady was still sleeping peacefully. *Please wake up*, Annabel silently willed her grandmother as she held her hand, *please don't leave me, Dotty, not yet*.

A tap on the shoulder startled her and she looked up into Nurse Sue's kind green eyes. The doctor wanted to see her, she said, then led her down the corridor and into a consulting room.

'Ah, Ms Penrose, I'm Stephanie Underwood, one of the doctors here. Please' – she gestured to the chair opposite her – 'have a seat.'

Dr Underwood was an efficient-looking woman in her early forties. She had neat black hair in a bob and a clipped, well-spoken accent. Annabel thanked her and told her to use her first name.

'Is she going to be alright?' she asked.

The doctor smiled before replying, 'Yes, I should think so. She'll be rather sore for a while with the broken wrist, and the rib will take a bit of time to heal. But it's not the injuries from the fall that I'm concerned about.'

'Oh?' Annabel was surprised. 'Do you think she's not safe at home anymore? Is it time for a nursing home, do you think?'

'No, no; nothing like that. She'll need more help while she recovers from the injuries, obviously, and you'll probably want to think about arranging carers, if she chooses to stay in her own home, that is. But that's not my main concern.'

The doctor paused for a moment as she referred to the papers on her desk.

'I see on your grandmother's notes that you and your brother William are named as her next of kin while your father is out of the country.'

Annabel nodded in agreement.

'In that case, I can share more with you and give you the full picture.'

Another pause.

'We did a scan when your grandmother came in; standard procedure when the patient's had a fall. It showed a cyst.'

Annabel looked confused. 'A cyst?' she repeated.

'Yes, but not just any cyst. It was the biggest cyst that any of us here had ever seen.' The doctor's brow furrowed. 'To give you some idea of scale, it was around the size of a rugby ball.'

Annabel's mouth dropped open.

'Did your grandmother ever complain of being in any pain? Any breathlessness or stomach pain ever?'

Annabel cast her mind back to the last time she had seen Dotty, on her birthday weekend. She racked her brain but couldn't think of anything, so mutely shook her head.

'Incredible! That generation really was made of stern stuff!' The doctor's eyes widened, as if in admiration, then she continued, 'The cyst looks ovarian in origin and it has been pressing on all her major organs for quite some time. It's a wonder that she hasn't been suffering from it.'

Annabel pictured her dainty grandmother and imagined the size of a rugby ball. She winced. It didn't bear thinking about.

'The scan also showed a malformation of the uterus; "uterine septum" is the technical term. Strange really, it doesn't rule out conception, but I'd say nine times out of ten it would make carrying a foetus to full term almost impossible. Your mother or father wasn't adopted?' the doctor asked in a clipped, business-like tone.

'My father,' Annabel clarified. 'And no . . . ' She paused, her brow furrowed in confusion. 'He wasn't adopted, he's her son.'

'Ah, there we are then.' Dr Underwood gave a tight smile. 'Your grandmother was obviously the lucky one!' She looked a little uncomfortable, then moved on quickly to explain how they would take care of Dotty. At her age, surgery to remove the cyst could result in further complications, so unless the family felt strongly, they would leave it alone and focus on keeping her as comfortable as possible.

A few minutes later, Annabel escaped the disinfectant-scented corridors of the hospital for some fresh air. The consultation had left her feeling confused and emotional and she needed time to process what she had just heard. The sun was emerging from a cloudy sky as she found a bench in the small hospital garden. She took a deep breath and closed her eyes, tilting her face up to enjoy the sun's warm rays.

There was something about the way the doctor had raised the question of adoption that had left her feeling unsettled. The look in her eye as she'd said that Dotty must have been the 'lucky one' had unnerved Annabel. Never in her life had she questioned her father's parentage; why would she? But the conversation with the doctor had introduced an element of doubt which Annabel was now struggling to shake off.

She leaned back against the bench and gave a sigh. It was the first time she had stopped today and she felt exhausted. After the conversation with Luke the previous evening, she had struggled to sleep and the drive had tired her out. Her stomach rumbled and she made a mental note to find something more substantial than hospital coffee and chocolate bars later on. The staff seemed confident that Dotty would be alright, but it had shaken Annabel. Dotty had been her rock her whole life and this was a very real reminder that she wasn't going to be around forever. Tears began to flow as she spent a moment imagining a world without her grandmother. She couldn't face the thought of losing her. And what if she lost Luke as well? She had to stop that thought process, she would just torment herself.

The door to the garden opened and she heard the excited voice of a small child. She turned to see a young boy of five or six, dressed in jeans, a blue dinosaur sweatshirt and a woolly hat, kicking a ball out into the open lawn of the garden. 'Come on, Daddy, come on!' he called as his father trotted obediently behind. The mother appeared last and, not joining in with the impromptu football game, came over to the bench.

'Mind if I join you?' She gave a faint smile and Annabel noticed her red-rimmed eyes.

'Not at all, please.' Annabel smiled back and indicated the space next to her. 'He's a little bundle of energy!' She chuckled, nodding over to the little boy who was lining up to take a penalty against his dad.

'Today's a good day,' the mum said, nodding. Then her face creased and the tears started flowing again. 'I'm sorry.' She looked embarrassed. 'I must stop doing this.'

'Oh, please don't worry! I was doing the same thing before you arrived,' Annabel confessed with a chuckle. She handed the woman a tissue from the packet in her bag. 'Are you alright?'

The mum wiped her eyes and took a deep breath to steady herself. 'It's his chemo in a few minutes.' She checked her watch. 'It gets me every time. It's a bit fifty-fifty, you see; the doctors can't make any promises.' She blew her nose. 'You?'

'I'm so sorry, that must be so hard for you all.' Annabel's face turned grave with concern and she instinctively reached out to touch the woman on the arm. She gave a sad smile. 'It's my granny. She had a fall this morning and hasn't woken up yet.'

'Oh, I'm sorry to hear that. It's hard to watch someone you love suffering and be powerless to do anything about it. I'd do anything – literally anything – for my little Sam. I would have the cancer in his place if I could; he's my world. He's such a little fighter, bless him; spends more time worrying about me than about himself!' She gave a rueful laugh.

It wasn't the right order of things, Annabel mused as she sat watching Sam and his dad having fun in the garden. It wasn't right that a parent should face losing a child, especially such a young one with his whole life ahead of him. Much as she couldn't bear the thought of losing her dear granny, at least

Dotty had had a life well lived and well loved. There would be nothing tragic about her passing, unlike little Sam, should the worst happen. It certainly put things in perspective.

'Goal!' yelled Sam as the ball sailed past his dad. He ran around with his arms in the air, copying the goal celebrations of his footballing heroes while his dad cheered. 'Mummy, Mummy, did you see?' Sam looked over to her on the bench, an enormous smile lighting up his little face.

'Well done, Sammy! I think you're going to be a footballer when you're older!' His mum beamed proudly through her tears and gave her son a double thumbs up.

Annabel's heart ached for her. A mother's love really was the deepest kind there was; it could bring such joy and such pain. But despite the terrible sadness of the woman's situation, Annabel found herself envying her. She wanted to know that feeling of unconditional love, of someone being her world. She wanted a little one to look at her in the same way Sam had looked at his mum, with total devotion and adoration. Sitting there in the hospital garden, Annabel realised that she had told Luke a big fat lie the night before. It *did* matter to her, the marriage and children part, and she had been foolish to pretend otherwise. The realisation came with conflicting emotions: she felt a small flicker of hope at what the future might hold, but also an engulfing sorrow as she wondered where it left her and Luke.

They watched father and son in companionable silence for a few minutes, each silently appreciating the other's presence on the bench. After a while, Annabel got up to leave.

'Best of luck with everything,' she said, touching the woman's shoulder. 'I really hope Sam will be alright, he's a lovely little lad. He must make you very proud.'

'Here she is! I told you she wouldn't be long!' Nurse Sue's sing-song voice rang out as Annabel walked through the ward towards Dotty's bed. Her face lit up as she saw that her grandmother's eyes were open. Dotty took a moment to focus, then managed a faint smile of recognition.

'Hello, my darling,' she said, her normally strong voice sounding weak and breathy.

'Dotty! You're awake, thank goodness!' Annabel sat beside her and took her hand in her own. 'How are you feeling?'

'Oh I'm alright, don't worry about me,' she scoffed. 'I'm still here! Blasted nuisance about this,' she said, nodding towards the plaster cast, 'but I suppose it could have been worse!'

'Everyone sends their love,' Annabel said. 'Dad's so sorry he can't be here. He would have come straight over, but he's still in hospital after getting his hip done. Apparently, Mum offered to come in his place, if you need extra help.' She grinned as her granny raised an eyebrow to refute this suggestion. 'But I promised them that I could hold the fort for now!'

'Thank you, my dear. Please tell Jeanette that it's very kind of her to offer' – she nodded magnanimously – 'but I'd much rather just have you here for now.' She patted her granddaughter's hand. 'Is Monty alright?'

Annabel reassured her that her four-legged friend was being taken care of, then shared all the latest news from Bath and tales from her work at the university. While they chatted, the conversation with the doctor kept coming back to Annabel, gnawing at her like an itchy mosquito bite. Her grandmother was quick to spot that there was something bothering her.

'Darling, what is it?' The old lady's brow furrowed in concern.

'It's nothing, Dotty.' Annabel tried to force a smile. 'You just gave us all a bit of a fright, that's all. I'm just so glad you're alright now.'

Dotty raised her eyebrows, clearly not accepting her granddaughter's excuse. 'I can see that something's on your mind. Spit it out, my love, you'll feel better for it.'

Annabel sighed, her emotions conflicting. It didn't seem fair to quiz her dear granny on such a personal, sensitive topic, especially after such a stressful day. But as she looked into the old lady's eyes, she was reminded that Dotty had always encouraged honesty in the family; she had never been one to flinch from awkward conversations. She took a deep breath.

'It's just something that Dr Underwood said earlier about the scans they did. Something came up that was a bit unexpected and I didn't know what to make of it.' Annabel smiled brightly. 'But honestly, Dotty, we don't need to talk about it now.'

Dotty sank back into her pillows and closed her eyes. After a long pause, she opened them again and replied, her voice barely more than a whisper.

'She told you that I couldn't have children?'

Annabel took her granny's good hand in hers and gently stroked it. 'Something like that.' She ached inside to see her grandmother looking so tiny and frail in the hospital bed.

Dotty was just opening her mouth to reply when Nurse Sue reappeared, shattering the sombre moment with her broad smile and cheerful voice. She advised that it was time for Dotty to get some rest and that Annabel should come back again in the morning.

'And don't you worry about your granny,' she reassured Annabel with a squeeze of her shoulder. 'We'll take good care of her for you, I promise!'

Annabel stood up to leave, but bent down to kiss her grandmother's forehead before doing so. She smiled at her, telling her not to worry about anything and she would see her tomorrow.

Concern showed in Dotty's normally brilliant blue eyes. 'We'll talk then, my darling. There are . . . things I need to tell you. Things you should know.'

Confusion coursed through Annabel as she wondered what bombshell her grandmother might be about to drop, but she forced a bright smile and reassured her that everything would be alright. The old lady's eyes were closing as Annabel gave her a final kiss.

The drive to Penrose Farm was a sombre one. Annabel tried to distract herself by listening to the cheerful presenters on the local radio station, but her mind was racing with everything that had happened in the past twenty-four hours. It was early evening when she reached Wincastle and, suddenly hungry, she stopped at the chip shop on the high street. Her mouth watered as she took the salt and vinegar scented bundle back to the car, but she stopped herself from tearing it open and took it home.

Annabel couldn't recall a time at the farmhouse without Dotty being there. It was ominously quiet, with only the sound of the grandfather clock for company, and it didn't feel right. Everything was just as her granny had left it that morning; the makings of breakfast still stood on the kitchen table and a cereal bowl and coffee cup were in the sink, waiting to be washed.

She took one of her granny's bottles of cider from the fridge and carried it, together with the steaming paper bundle and a bottle of ketchup, out onto the patio. She didn't bother with a plate or cutlery, but ate straight from the wrapper, just as she and William had always done with Dotty and Grandpa. 'It's the only way to do it!' Grandpa had always said.

It had always been something of a family tradition to start the school holidays with fish and chips. Dotty and Grandpa would meet them off the train in Bodmin and stop at the chip shop on their way home to the farm. Depending on their father Noel's work, their parents would join them in the holidays when they could, or whisk them off abroad or to wherever they were living at the time. But Annabel had always been perfectly happy with her grandparents in Cornwall. She loved driving home from Bodmin Parkway station through the narrow, leafy lanes in the back of Grandpa's old Land Rover, one of their dogs usually curled up between her and William on the back seat.

Their grandparents were always so happy to see them. They were always interested in all their news and the holidays were always full of adventures. Penrose Farm really was a perfect holiday idyll, with animals to take care of, farm machinery to play on and acres of countryside to explore. Then there was the beach, the golden stretch of sand with rock pools to investigate and caves to explore. It wasn't a private beach, but the only access to it was down the cliff steps at the end of the Penrose Farm land. There was a public right of way along the clifftop path, but with no available parking for miles in either direction, it was a quiet spot and the beach was usually deserted.

The sun was low in the sky as Annabel finished the last few chips, casting a golden glow across the sea in the distance. She briefly considered walking down to the beach, but was feeling so full after wolfing down her supper that she decided against it. Instead, it was time to make some phone calls.

She started by calling her mum with an update on Dotty. She was going to ring her dad, but wasn't sure she could tell him the doctor's news without straying into the difficult territory of what the scan had highlighted. Next, she called Luke. His phone rang and rang, but there was no answer. She had texted him earlier in the afternoon, telling him about Dotty's accident and saying that she'd had to go straight down to the hospital. She could see that he'd been online recently, but the delivery ticks were still grey, meaning 'unread'. Something didn't feel right.

The air grew cooler as the sun made its descent. Annabel cleared the empty chip wrapper and went inside to make herself a mug of tea and fetch a jacket. She went back out and sat nursing her mug as she watched the sun set, an explosion of oranges and yellows out over the sea. How often she and William had sat at this same table with their grandparents, she thought, enjoying breakfasts of orange juice and bacon rolls or summer picnic lunches. She thought of the last time she'd sat here with her grandfather, with him in his wheelchair, a rug over his knees to keep warm on that crisp autumn morning. Annabel had been nineteen years old at the time and they had played cards and chatted out here for hours. He had been such a kind and gentle man. She missed him.

At last, the sky darkened and, on feeling the first few drops of rain, Annabel took herself back inside the old stone farmhouse and settled in for the night. She closed the curtains, turned the lights on and switched on the TV for company. The eerie quiet of the room was replaced by the raucous laughter of a Saturday night entertainment show. It reminded her of cosy nights on the sofa with William when they were children, cuddled up in their dressing gowns, watching TV with their grandparents. It had always felt so cosy and safe.

Feeling an overwhelming nostalgia for the old days at the farm, she went over to the bookcase in the corner of the room, behind Dotty's fireside wingback chair. On the top stood a collection of photo frames, proudly displaying a selection of family photos through the years.

There were her parents on their wedding day in the late 1970s, Jeanette with big hair and an even bigger meringue of a dress. Next to it was an old black-and-white photo of a young Noel at the beach with Dotty. He must have been around five or six years old and the image never failed to make her smile; the look of pure delight on their faces as they paddled in the shallow water, holding hands and grinning at Grandpa behind the camera. There was another wedding photo, William and Sarah this time, then baby photos of Aiden and Lucy, and a picture of herself on her PhD graduation day at Oxford University. Dotty had been so proud, she recalled with a smile.

Annabel knelt down to look at the lowest shelf of the bookcase, where the family photo albums stood to attention like soldiers, Dotty's spidery handwriting on the spines. She slid out the earliest album: 1946–50.

She put the album on the coffee table and made herself comfortable on the sofa. She smiled as she flicked through the black-and-white images of her grandparents in their younger years. They had made a handsome couple, with Dotty's sparkling blue eyes and wide smile, and Grandpa's tall, lean figure and mop of shaggy hair. The young Noel Penrose featured in many of the photos and she smiled as she recognised her father's cheerful grin.

Annabel worked her way right through the album, enjoying the photos of the happy family – on the farm, with the animals, visiting friends, celebrating birthdays and relaxing on the beach.

It was only when she got to the end that something occurred to her: she hadn't yet seen any baby photos of her father. She looked through the other albums to make sure, but they were all in date order and Noel Penrose just grew older through each one.

She did the maths and figured that he would have been five years old in 1946, and that matched the pictures in the first album she had opened. But there was no album dated before 1946. Had the albums been lost during the war, maybe? That would explain it, Annabel mused. Poor Dotty had lost so much in the war. But she couldn't recall her grandmother ever mentioning losing their belongings. Maybe they had gone missing during the move from London to Cornwall?

A little niggling doubt crept in and made Annabel check the albums again. But no, she hadn't missed anything. The conversation with Dr Underwood replayed in her mind and her heart began to race. Where were her father's baby photos?

CHAPTER 5

Cornwall

Sunday 24th March, 2019

The sun streaming around the edge of the curtains woke Annabel from a long, deep sleep. For a moment, she wondered where she was. It was so quiet and all she could hear was the tweeting of birds and the bleating of lambs in the field.

She blinked open her eyes and the pretty English rose wallpaper reminded her that she was at Dotty's. This had been her bedroom for as long as she could remember and she loved it; it always made her feel like she was home. She had shared it with William for a while when they were younger, before he had moved to a box room further along the corridor.

Annabel reached for her mobile phone which was charging on the bedside table. The clock showed 8.09 a.m. She was surprised she'd slept so late, but was feeling so much better for it. The phone notifications showed messages from the three men in her life: two this morning from her dad and brother, and a very late-night – or early-morning – one from Luke.

She clicked on Luke's message first. 2.37 a.m.

> Sorry to hear about Dotty, hope she's OK. Let me know if you need anything x

Like bees, questions started buzzing around her head. Where had he been last night? Why had he been out so late? Who had he been with? She hated herself for feeling so suspicious, but why had he ignored her message for so long and taken almost twelve hours to reply? He'd never been one for long-winded text conversations, but was that really the best he could manage? She sighed.

The other messages made her feel better – gentle reassurance and gratitude from her dad, and light-hearted banter from William.

> Hey sis, hope you're doing OK, I'll be down in a couple of days to help out. Don't want you burning the house down while Dotty's away! X

She smiled at the in-joke. He had never let her forget the time when she was nine and they were toasting marshmallows on the fire in the sitting room. She had held hers too close to the flames and panicked when it caught alight, dropping it on the hearth rug. Grandpa had been quick off the mark and his well-aimed pint of beer had prevented the rug going up in smoke. Annabel had been so anxious about spoiling the rug and upsetting her granny, but had got away with a small black singe mark being the only telltale sign. And with Dotty busy doing the dishes in the kitchen at the time, Grandpa had given her a reassuring wink; the secret was safe with him.

Annabel replied to the messages, telling Luke that she'd ring him in the evening, then made a call to the hospital. The ward manager reassured her that Dotty had had a good night and was 'on fine form' this morning. Visiting hours would start at 11 a.m. and Dotty was looking forward to seeing her. Relief flooded through Annabel. She got out of bed and opened the curtains onto a perfect, blue-sky morning. Her favourite thing about her bedroom here was the view, which today looked across lush, green fields and out to the shimmering sea beyond.

She had just showered and was getting dressed when there was a loud knocking at the front door. She zipped up her jeans, pulled on a crisp white T-shirt and headed downstairs.

As she opened the door, she was greeted by the wet nose and wagging tail of an excited black ball of fur. 'Monty!' She exclaimed, grinning as she rubbed her granny's faithful companion behind the ears.

'Morning, lovey!' Pam beamed up from unclipping Monty's lead. 'He was homesick and wanted to come and see you!' She chuckled. 'But I can keep him longer, if you need me to?'

Annabel crouched down to make a fuss of the old Labrador, who had rolled over onto his back on the doormat, inviting her to rub his tummy.

'Oh no, it's nice to have him back; it felt strange, him not being here.' She got to her feet again and Monty continued to fuss around her, eager for her attention. 'Thanks so much for having him yesterday, Pam, that was a big help.'

'No problem at all!' She smiled. 'Now then, this is for you.' Pam changed tack, handing over the wicker basket she'd been holding. 'I wasn't sure what Dotty had in the cupboards, so I've brought a few bits to keep you going.' The basket was full of provisions from the village shop and Annabel felt quite touched.

'Oh Pam, that's so kind of you! Thanks very much.'

The older lady brushed off the compliment and declined the invitation to come in, saying, 'Never mind all that, I mustn't hold you up. But most importantly, how's Dotty getting on? Any news?'

'Yes, she's alright.' Annabel gave a reassuring smile. 'I spoke to the hospital and they said that she's on pain relief for the broken rib, but is comfortable and doing as well as can be expected.'

'Oh, well that's something. I am glad.' Pam sighed in relief. 'Do send her my love, won't you? I can't get down there today, it's our Wendy's birthday so there's a bit of a family do. But I'm heading down Bodmin way tomorrow so could visit in the afternoon, if that's allowed?'

'Absolutely!' Annabel smiled. 'I know she'd love to see you.'

Pam gave Annabel a big, comforting hug and reassured her that everything would be alright. Then she patted Monty's head before she left, chuckling as she told Annabel, 'You've got a new best friend there!'

The house phone started ringing after Pam drove off; the news of Dotty's accident had spread around the village and her friends wanted to know how she was. The vicar, Reverend Pascoe, was the first to call, followed by Isabel Polkerris, the farmer's wife, and then Catherine, Dotty's friend from her bowling club days. Annabel was touched by their concern and offers of help, and was reminded of what a well-loved member of the community her granny was.

After coffee on the patio, accompanied by home-made jam on a still-warm baguette, Annabel put on her fleece and trainers. She looked down at Monty, who had not left her side since he'd come home – even insisting on following her to the bathroom – and grinned at him as she whispered his favourite word: 'Walkies!' She was always amazed how the old dog, greying around the muzzle and in his senior years, suddenly transformed into a puppy again with the utterance of a single word. She laughed as he bounced around the patio, full of energy and desperate to head off adventuring.

There was plenty of time before Annabel had to leave for the hospital and she wanted to stretch her legs and make the most of the glorious sunshine. She locked the back door and they set off across the field, Monty on his lead just in case he got over-excited by the lambs. The little white fluff balls stood stock still as he approached, staring at the oncoming big black monster, and a couple of ewes objected noisily to his presence. Safely through the field, Annabel closed the gate behind them and let Monty off the lead as they came to the clifftop path.

They turned right and made their way along the dirt track. On either side, the hedges were a profusion of sweet-scented gorse, golden and glowing in the morning sun. Annabel breathed in deeply – she had always loved its coconutty aroma. Monty weaved his way in and out of the bushes, scaring himself when he eventually chased out a couple of chiffchaffs. It was a steep drop down to the left, where the cliffs cut away to the beach below, so Annabel kept him close. But after his initial burst of energy, the old dog was happy to trot along beside her.

Apart from the sound of Monty's panting and the waves crashing below, the morning air was silent. There was no one else around and Annabel was enjoying the solitude. Her mind wandered back to previous visits to the beach, always such fun times with the whole family coming down for a swim, a picnic or a game of beach cricket. There was something magical about having the beach right on their doorstep and it had been the setting of so many family gatherings and happy memories. She thought of coming here as a young child with William and their grandparents, with Grandpa teaching them to swim. Then later with William's own children. A memory resurfaced of a private skinny-dipping session here with Luke a few years ago. She smiled at the thought then felt a slight tug in her stomach.

After about a hundred yards, the track split, with the left-hand fork leading to steps down to the beach. It was so familiar that even Monty knew where they were going and instinctively turned left. Annabel paused at the top of the steps and smiled as she took in the view. The tide was coming in, but there remained a wide expanse of pure, unadulterated sand; not a footprint in sight. The water was a luxurious turquoise, the sort of colour one expected in the Maldives or the Caribbean. Shimmering in the warm morning light, it looked spectacular.

The beach was called Smugglers Cove, doubtless due to the nefarious actions that had taken place here in years gone by. It was a perfect spot for smugglers, Annabel mused, safely tucked away off the main coastline with a series of caves and a network of tunnels. It was also a good spot for swimming, and Dotty had been coming down here to bathe until she was well into her eighties. Shaped like a horseshoe, the water here was usually calm, with the rocky outcrops at either end protecting it from the lively currents of the Atlantic Ocean further out.

They made their way down the steps and when they reached the sand Annabel took off her shoes and socks. Monty trotted off ahead, barking noisily at the seagulls that hovered above. She rolled up her jeans and followed him towards the water. How good it felt to have the warm sand between her toes and the sea breeze on her face.

She felt a million miles away from the lecture hall, where most of the students spent most of the time gazing at their mobile phones, or the daily grind of rush hour in Bath, where she usually ended up stuck in a traffic jam. Yes, she had been ready for a break and the peace and solitude of Penrose Farm was just what she needed.

Annabel reached the edge of the sand and gasped as the cool water licked at her toes. It was mid-spring and it would be another couple of months before the sea reached a comfortable temperature for swimming. She thought of the magazine article she had read recently on the benefits of wild swimming, which had become quite the thing lately. A couple of her friends went every weekend and swore by it. 'So invigorating!' they always said. She'd thought she was too much of a softie, but maybe she would try it while she was here. Perhaps it was time to try something new, shake things up a little? She stepped further in, until she was ankle deep. There was something strangely satisfying about adjusting to the cool temperature and a sense of achievement came from overcoming the initial fear. With her face tilted up towards the sun, she closed her eyes and took in a few deep breaths. The refreshing tang of salt water and seaweed met her nostrils and she breathed it in keenly, enjoying its restorative effects as a sense of calm washed over her.

She thought back to the photographs from last night and the black-and-white image of Noel and his parents in this same spot, almost seventy years ago. His parents, yes. Without doubt they were his parents. But were they biologically related? The doctor had planted a seed of doubt that had taken root and sprouted overnight, especially after Annabel had failed to locate any baby photos of her dad. Dotty's photo albums were fastidiously organised, with everything clearly labelled and dated; they were a pictorial archive of the Penrose family history. It seemed incredible to Annabel that Dotty hadn't catalogued a single baby photo of her beloved son.

Could there be any truth in what the doctor had suggested? That Noel had been adopted? Stranger things had happened. One of Annabel's boarding school friends hadn't found out until she was in her twenties that she was adopted, but had never suspected a thing as there had never been any reason to. Would it change anything if it turned out that Noel was *not* Dotty's biological son? Of course not, Annabel thought. Mother and son were so close and so devoted to one another that the simple fact that they did not share DNA would not break their bond, she felt sure of it. The secrecy of it might be hard to deal with at first, but her grandparents had given Noel such a loving family and happy upbringing that, if they *had* adopted him, he couldn't be anything but grateful. She pictured her dark-haired father with his year-round tan. Was there any family resemblance to her grandparents? It was hard to tell. From the photos she had seen, Dotty and her grandfather had both been fairer in their younger years. And Noel wasn't as tall or as lean as her grandfather, but no two generations were ever exactly the same, were they? Annabel paddled along the waterline to the far end of the bay, mulling it all over and wondering what to do. How could she find out for sure? She didn't want to bother her dad with her suspicions, there would be no point telling him unless something was confirmed. Could she ask Dotty? She wondered. Her eye was caught by some pretty shells in the sand. As a little girl, she had always brought the best ones home for her granny, who had dutifully displayed them in a glass bowl in the porch. The old memory made her smile and she pocketed a couple of perfectly formed rose-pink scallop shells. Monty had given up chasing seagulls and was showing his age as he trudged along beside her. They made their way back across the beach, stopping for Annabel to collect her shoes and socks, then climbed the steps towards home.

As soon as she was near the farmhouse and within range of the phone signal, her mobile started ringing. It was the hospital. Annabel's stomach lurched.

'Oh Annabel, thank goodness!' came a worried voice. 'I'm glad I've finally got you. It's Sue here, Nurse Sue from the hospital. I'm sorry to say that your grandmother has taken a turn for the worse. She's slipping in and out of consciousness. Can you come straight down? The doctor doesn't think she's got very long, my love. I'm so sorry.'

Tears blinded Annabel as she ended the call. She wiped them away and ran the rest of the way back to the house.

There was a brief moment of fear when Annabel reached the ward and saw that Dotty's bed was empty. But Nurse Sue was on hand to tell that she had been moved to a private room and took Annabel to it. It was the cyst that had caused the decline, the kind nurse explained. It was pressing on Dotty's vital organs and making her breathing difficult.

The blinds were closed to keep out the morning sun and it was silent, but for the faint sound of Dotty's shallow breathing and the reassuring beeping of the monitors. Propped up on the white hospital pillows, Dotty looked even smaller and thinner than she had the previous day. Her eyes were closed and her breathing sounded laboured.

'Hello Dotty, I'm here,' Annabel said quietly as she sat by the bed and held her granny's hand. 'Can you hear me?'

The old lady's eyes slowly opened and they took a moment to focus. 'Annabel, my darling,' she whispered and a smile spread across her pale face. 'You're such a good girl.' Her voice was coming in breathy stops and starts. 'Always taking care of me. Are you alright? Is everything alright at the house?'

'Everything's fine, don't you worry,' Annabel soothed. 'Pam came round this morning, she brought Monty home. I took him down to the beach, you should have seen him chasing those seagulls! He loved it! I had a bit of a paddle, but it was pretty nippy! I don't know how you managed your daily swims down at Smugglers Cove, the water is freezing!'

Annabel kept her voice bright and cheerful as she followed Nurse Sue's advice, chatting about normal, everyday things. Dotty's eyes closed again, but Annabel could tell that she was still listening.

'I brought you some daffodils from the garden. I know you always love their scent. Thought they might cheer this place up a bit before we get you home!' But even as Annabel said it, she knew that the chances of Dotty coming back to Penrose Farm were slipping away.

Dotty's eyes opened briefly and she gave a small smile as she took in the cheerful yellow blooms that Annabel was showing her.

'Thank you, darling. I need to tell you something, Annie.' Her words were coming in breathy gasps now. Annabel felt sure that she was about to explain what the doctor had alluded to and she was eager to hear it. But she shut down her curiosity; it felt wrong to expect her grandmother to share anything in her current condition.

'Shh, don't worry about anything, Dotty. Everything's alright.' Annabel stroked her granny's hand. The skin was veiny and paper thin, but she smiled as she noticed her nails were still painted pink from her birthday party.

'But it's important, Annie. Tell Noel . . . ' She gave a little gasp and there was a long pause before she continued. Annabel leaned in closer so she could hear her grandmother's whisper. 'Tell him I'm sorry. I have loved him so much. And I kept my promise.'

She stopped talking and became very still for a few minutes. Annabel wanted to know more, to ask what promise. But it was too late for that.

'Look, Arthur is here.' Dotty's whisper eventually broke the silence, a faint smile on her lips. She looked so peaceful as she took her final breaths.

'Goodbye, darling Dotty,' Annabel managed, holding back the torrent of unshed tears as she kissed her beloved grandmother on the forehead. 'Go with Grandpa Arthur now.'

Everyone was very kind, especially Sue. Although Dotty's hospital stay had been short, the nurse had grown fond of the old lady. 'She was a very special lady,' she said as she comforted Annabel, tears in her own eyes, 'not to mention a very brave one at that!'

It was all very efficient; procedures were followed and routines explained, forms were signed and phone calls were made. Annabel's heart ached, but with the help of the grainy hospital coffee and some chocolate biscuits that Sue kept 'for times like these', she somehow held it together and got through it.

As she left the hospital building later, Annabel reached into her pocket and her fingers met the cold hardness of the pink sea shells. She'd never be able to give them to Dotty now. And with this realisation, the tears began to flow.

CHAPTER 6

Cornwall

Monday 25th March, 2019

After a night of fitful sleep, Annabel awoke to the squawking of seagulls. For one blissful moment, just before she opened her eyes, all was as it should be. Then she remembered and her peace was shattered. She allowed herself a few moments to wallow in her sadness, before snapping out of it as she remembered that Monty was waiting for her downstairs. She quickly dressed and went down to let him out.

The old Labrador knew. There was a sadness in his eyes that told her he was fully aware that his mistress would not be coming home again. The bereft look on his old face sparked fresh tears in Annabel and she knelt down to wrap her arms around him, burying her face in his dark fur.

Her phone rang and she pulled it out of her jeans pocket to answer it, opening the back door for Monty as she did so.

'Morning, darling,' her father's deep voice soothed Annabel. With the phone to her ear, she curled up in the battered old leather armchair beside the range. 'Did you get much sleep?' he asked.

'Hi Dad. A bit, thanks. How about you?'

'I suppose I should be grateful for these hospital drugs, I was out like a light I'm afraid!'

Despite the sombre mood, Annabel couldn't help chuckling.

'That's my girl,' Noel replied. 'It's good to hear you laugh. Oh Annie.' He sighed, 'yesterday must have been such a difficult day for you to deal with, I'm so sorry. I'm even more sorry that you had to go through it on your own.'

'It's OK Dad, don't worry,' she began.

'But one thing I'm *not* sorry about is that you were there with Dotty; that she wasn't alone. I'm so glad that you were with her at the end. She thought the world of you, darling, she really did. Thank you for being there.'

Hot tears slid silently down Annabel's cheeks. 'I'm glad I was there, too,' she said, reaching for a tissue to wipe them away.

'On a more practical note, Annie, we need to start thinking about the funeral. The doctors here have said I won't be able to fly for a couple of weeks with this new hip, so I'm afraid we'll have to hang fire for a while.'

'Don't worry, Dad, that's fine.' She blew her nose and set her mind to practical thinking. 'It'll give us more time to get everything ready. I had a chat with William last night and he's coming down in a couple of days. I'm sure we can start sorting things out between us. Just please don't rush, Dad, I know what you're like; please don't persuade the doctors to let you travel before the new hip is ready for it.'

'Thanks darling, I appreciate that. I'm glad William is coming down, I hate to think of you being there on your own.' There was a brief pause and Annabel feared that he might ask about things with Luke. She was relieved when he didn't. 'I'll have a chat with your mum about travel dates after I've seen the specialist this morning. Then we'll ring Reverend Pascoe and see when it can be arranged. But if you want to keep busy and make a start, I know that Dotty had an envelope in the bureau with her funeral requests in it. Favourite readings and hymns, that sort of thing. Do you mind looking it out?'

'Typical Dotty.' Annabel smiled. 'So organised, right up until the very end!'

After breakfast, she replied to a text from Luke, telling him that she was OK. She had called him from the hospital the previous day and he had offered to come down to be with her for moral support, but it had felt more than a little half-hearted. 'Just say if you want me to come down, Annie,' he had said. 'I can probably rearrange a few things and make the time, if you need me to.'

'If you want me to . . . If you need me to . . . ' It was all a bit half-arsed, Annabel now reflected. If he truly loved her, surely he should *want* to be there for her, not just come down because she wanted him to. After the bombshell conversation from a couple of nights ago, everything seemed so uncertain. It felt like the grains of sand of their relationship were slowly trickling through her fingers.

She sighed and took a mug of coffee through to the study. Monty followed dutifully and settled himself on the sheepskin rug by the fireplace. The room faced east and the sun's early-morning rays were already streaming in. Her grandmother's old oak bureau stood in the corner of the room and Annabel felt strange as she sat on the chair in front of it. It felt wrong to be opening Dotty's desk, to intrude on her personal belongings. But she took a deep breath and lowered the lid, which folded down to form a writing desk in front of her.

Inside the bureau, Dotty's characteristic organisation was on display. Colourful notebooks and journals stood smartly alongside pigeon holes arranged with an assortment of stationery. Shelves were neatly labelled in Dotty's familiar hand, 'Bills', 'Documents' and 'Personal'. Annabel felt a twist of emotions.

She smiled as she remembered watching her granny in full 'admin mode' sitting in this very spot, yet felt guilty to be invading her inner sanctum.

Carefully, she flicked through the papers on the shelves. She bypassed the bills section and sifted through the documents and personal papers, hoping to unearth the envelope her father had mentioned. There were letters, medical documents, Dotty's birth certificate and driving licence, but nothing obviously marked 'Funeral'.

'How strange,' Annabel mused, thinking how unlike her grandmother this was. 'It must be in here somewhere,' she thought aloud, before taking out all the papers from the bills shelf and sorting through them on her lap. Still nothing.

As she was putting them back, her eye was drawn to the shiny brass handle of the little drawer at the top of the bureau. It was only small, measuring about 10cm wide, and Annabel nearly overlooked it, assuming that the envelope she was searching for would be much bigger than that. She slid the little drawer open and gave a smile of satisfaction as there, right in front of her, she saw a small green envelope labelled in Dotty's neat, cursive script 'Funeral.'

Annabel sat back in the desk chair and took a deep breath before carefully opening the envelope. She thought of her granny – her vibrant, full-of-life granny – sitting right here, committing her funeral requests to paper and sealing them shut inside this envelope. It seemed rather morbid, but Dotty had been a practical woman with legendary organisational skills. Of course she wanted to have a hand in her last hurrah.

Annabel still found it hard to believe that her granny had gone; it had all been so sudden that she half expected the old lady to come into the room at any moment and tell her off for going through her things. If only she would.

Inside the envelope were three pieces of paper. The first was a note to Noel which brought tears to Annabel's eyes as she read,

Darling Noel, you have been the most wonderful son. Thank you for everything and for doing this one last thing for me. Be happy. All my love, Mum x

The second was a list of Dotty's favourite hymns and pieces of music. Annabel sighed sadly as she saw that the hymns – 'How Great Thou Art' and 'Guide Me, O Thou Great Redeemer' – were the same two that they had sung at her grandfather's funeral seventeen years earlier. For the entrance Dotty had chosen the beautiful 'Pie Jesu' and Annabel couldn't help but smile at the exit music, Glenn Miller's upbeat dancehall tune 'In the Mood'. Dotty had always loved it and Annabel remembered watching her grandparents dancing as it played on the record player when she was a little girl. It had been played at their wedding reception, her grandfather had explained as he twirled his grinning, rosy-cheeked wife around the sitting room. Annabel smiled through her tears at the happy memory.

The last insert was a cutting taken from a newspaper. It was a poem called 'She is Gone' that had been read at the Queen Mother's funeral. The words were poignant, asking the reader not to mourn the passing of their loved one, but to celebrate the happy times and smile at the joyful memories. Dotty had obviously approved of the sentiment to have added it to the envelope and Annabel thought it was perfect. Noel had asked her to do a reading at the funeral and this would be spot on.

She slid the contents back inside the envelope and stood up to close the bureau. As she was about to slide the little drawer closed again, a flash of silver caught her eye. Tucked in the corner of the drawer she saw a tiny key, the sort used for a little padlock. She took it out and examined it. It had no tag nor any clue to identify its use. Annabel frowned and cast her mind back to the times when she had seen her grandmother working at her desk, but was unable to recall her using a key to open anything.

From its hidey-hole in the little drawer, it made sense to Annabel that the key should open something inside the bureau. She looked around for a keyhole, but to no avail. She was just about to give up when she remembered something from a murder mystery she'd watched years ago – an Agatha Christie maybe? – where the killer had hidden the weapon in the secret compartment of his desk. She renewed her search, this time carefully pressing, tapping and feeling her way around the drawers and shelves, hoping for some sort of clue.

Suddenly, she found it. On the panel beneath the bottom shelf in the far right corner, her fingers made contact with a sliding cover. It was made of the same material as the panel and almost impossible to tell that it was a separate piece. It was only a few centimetres wide, but slid – if a little stiffly – both left and right, revealing a tiny keyhole. Annabel could see now that the plain-looking panel was actually a secret drawer, about a foot wide and a few inches deep. She put the little key in the lock and held her breath as she tried it. It turned easily and the secret drawer clicked open.

'Bingo!' Annabel said, waking Monty and startling him into action. The old dog got up from the hearth rug and came to rest his muzzle on Annabel's leg, eager to find out what was going on. 'Well, Monty' – she rubbed his ears affectionately – 'I think we're in. What on earth has Dotty been hiding in here?'

She paused for a moment, that uncomfortable feeling in her stomach again. It was one thing poking around her grandmother's desk to find her funeral requests, but quite another to nose around her personal things. But something drove her on. Was it her historian's instinct or her recent doubt over her father's parentage? She wasn't sure, but she suddenly felt an overwhelming need to find out what her grandmother had been keeping secret.

Annabel slid the drawer open and carefully lifted out several brown A4-sized envelopes. The only marking on each one was a number written in Dotty's hand. She opened the top one first, labelled '2010,' and slid out the contents: a collection of old, sepia photographs, held together by a large paperclip, and a short, handwritten letter.

She removed the paperclip and thumbed through the photos. She was surprised to see that they were of Dotty. But not Dotty as Annabel knew her or had ever seen her before. This was a much younger and much more beautiful Dotty in a very different setting. This was no London scene, where Dotty had grown up, or even rural English countryside, it was distinctly foreign.

In the photos, the gardens were lush and tropical, with palm trees and voluminous blooms. Even the people were different. There was a family portrait – Annabel recognised the images of her great-grandparents, the Templetons, with their children, Dotty and her brother Thomas – but with them were several Chinese people in traditional dress. Had the family gone on holiday when she was younger? Dotty had always been so adamant that she had never travelled and never wanted to, that this made no sense to Annabel.

She turned to the last photo and her heart almost stopped beating. There, outside an elegant white church, was the same young woman in a wedding dress. Standing next to her, their arms linked, was the same Chinese-looking lady from the other photographs, wearing a traditional Chinese outfit. They were both smiling at the camera, looking a little nervous. They were obviously close.

Annabel turned the photograph over and saw it had been labelled on the back '*With Mrs Llewellyn on her wedding day, St Andrew's Cathedral, May 1940.*' She stared again. The bride in the photograph was the spitting image of her grandmother, but it couldn't be her. Could it? Annabel's mind started to whirr: who was Mrs Llewellyn and why had Dotty locked away her photograph? If it *was* Dotty in the photo, she must have been married before meeting Annabel's grandfather. But surely Dotty would have told her if this was the case? It all seemed so unlikely.

She picked up the letter and began to read, hoping to find some sort of clue.

*Singapore,
October 2010*

*Dear Mrs Penrose,
I am very sorry to be the bearer of sad news, but I am writing to inform you that my grandmother, Ah Ling Wong, passed away last month after a short illness. She was 93.
She wished me to return these photographs to you and to offer you her deep gratitude for your unfailing friendship over the years. She talked of you often and loved to reminisce about the happy times you shared during your time in Singapore.
Yours sincerely,
Julia Chan (Mrs)*

Singapore? Dotty? What on earth was going on? None of this was making any sense.

At that moment, Annabel's mobile started ringing, startling Monty who was comfortably snoozing with his chin resting on her leg. It was her brother. After a brief hello, she jumped straight in.

'Will, did you ever hear Dotty mention anything about Singapore?'

CHAPTER 7

Singapore
June 1938

Dorothy Templeton never wanted to leave London. She was nineteen years old and perfectly happy with her life when her father announced the news. Her best friend Daisy, whom she had known since they were babies in their mothers' arms, lived on the same street – Queensmill Road – and the two were quite inseparable. They spent their free time going to the pictures, playing tennis together, shopping on Oxford Street or catching the number thirty tram to go dancing at the Hammersmith Palais. The two families were close too, regularly getting together for Sunday dinner and a good old sing-song with Daisy at the piano. Life for Dorothy was good.

She had recently enrolled in a secretarial course near the family home in Fulham and, according to the teacher, was showing real promise with her typing and shorthand. It was the first step to achieving her dream: to work for a newspaper agency. She was an intelligent and curious young woman, and the thought of being one of the first to find out the latest goings on in the world thrilled her. The news that the Templetons were relocating to South East Asia had, therefore, come as a rather unwelcome interruption.

The driving force behind the move had been her mother. Olivia Templeton wore the proverbial trousers in her marriage and had aspirations for her gentle, easy-going husband and his career in the rubber industry. The idea of mixing among the colonial elite of Singapore made her bright blue eyes brim with excitement.

'Oh, we simply must go, Anthony!' she had told him, 'This is how you will make a name for yourself in the company! And think of the advantages; the people we will meet, the circles we will mix in! It will be such an opportunity for Dorothy to find a husband, can you imagine? I don't know why you even need to think about it!'

Like his daughter, Anthony Templeton had also been perfectly happy right where he was. He was an easy-going man who loved his family and worked hard in his role in the London office of McKinley's Rubber Company. The company had headquarters in London, India and Malaya, and as the rubber industry was expanding at a rate of knots, they needed to increase their presence in the latter. Anthony had been selected to oversee the expansion. In the end, he had to agree with his wife; it was too good an opportunity to turn down. The company would provide a house, a car and servants. 'We are certainly moving up in the world!' Olivia had gushed, revelling in the prospect.

'Don't worry, my little Dodo,' Anthony had reassured his daughter. 'It's only for a couple of years, just while we set things up over there. We'll have some fun, see a bit of the world, then come home again in time for tea!' Dorothy had hoped that would be true.

Three months later, having bid a tearful farewell to Daisy, Dorothy found herself standing on the deck of SS *Naldera* as it dropped anchor in Singapore harbour. She squinted into the blinding midday light and gazed out at the city landmarks. A series of grand buildings lined the waterfront, many with ornamental turrets and towers. The imposing facade of the General Post Office was the one that really stood out, with its elegant pillars and lofty portico. Dorothy was not sure what she had been expecting, but found herself impressed by what she saw.

They had left her older brother, Thomas, behind in England. He was studying to become a doctor at Cambridge and had just finished his second year. Dorothy was missing him already. Yes, he would come out to spend holidays with them, but it wouldn't be the same. Until now, he had managed to come home for regular visits. It felt strange for Dorothy to be on her own with her parents.

The temperature had been rising steadily ever since they had left Marseilles, but this was a different kind of heat. Just two degrees north of the equator, it was humid and oppressive; a solid wall that smothered her. Her white cotton dress stuck to her damp back and sweat trickled down her legs. She longed for a cool drink. How would she ever get accustomed to this heat? She had attempted to stay cool in her cabin, lying in just her underwear beneath the ceiling fan with a damp flannel on her forehead. But taking her eye off the horizon, even for just a few minutes, had resulted in terrible seasickness. They had spent weeks at sea, with only brief respite in Marseilles, Bombay and Colombo, and she couldn't wait to set foot back on dry land.

After what seemed like hours, they disembarked and made their way through the shiny white building of Customs House. It was a relief to escape the unforgiving heat and she stood for a few moments beneath a ceiling fan, enjoying the sensation as it cooled her clammy skin.

The family was met by a clerk from her father's company, Mr Kent, a polite young man in a cream linen suit, who shepherded them out into the glaring sun towards a smart black sedan.

The scene along the waterfront was unlike anything Dorothy had ever witnessed; a veritable hive of activity with sailors, tradesmen, hawkers and locals all moving around the quayside, carrying out their business as if in some well-practised dance. It fascinated and terrified her in equal measure, with foreign sights, sounds and smells overloading her senses. Rickshaws weaved in and out of motor cars and trams, and she marvelled at the resilience of the Chinese workers who pulled them, trotting along in the full glare of the afternoon sun.

They left the bustling Collyer Quay and drove along a palm-lined avenue, past shops and office buildings, as they headed out of the town. Dorothy felt her eyelids grow heavy with the rolling motion of the motor car and her head drooped onto her father's shoulder.

When she awoke, with a foggy head and beads of sweat on her upper lip, they were pulling up outside a beautiful two-storey villa surrounded by greenery. 'A bungalow, as we call them here,' Mr Kent explained. 'And your new home! Welcome!'

Dorothy stepped out of the car and gazed at her new surroundings. The house was painted a bright white with black timber beams and black and white blinds. It appeared to be on stilts, with a covered veranda circling the ground floor. The house was surrounded by tall green trees and lush vegetation, reminding her of a school trip to Kew Gardens some years before. It felt like they were in the jungle and she couldn't wait to go exploring. Once she'd had a rest and had cooled down a little, naturally. She wiped the back of her hand across her damp forehead, then followed her parents as they made their way towards the house. Pretty green bushes with trailing stems of pink and purple flowers lined the path. 'Bougainvillea,' Mr Kent explained when her mother asked.

In front of the house was a neat lawn, in the middle of which stood a line of Chinese servants, waiting to meet their new employers. They were dressed in the traditional samfu, with white tops and black trousers, that looked, to Dorothy, a bit like pyjamas. One of them stepped forward, offering glasses of iced water which the Templetons accepted gratefully. Dorothy pressed her glass to her forehead and closed her eyes for a moment, enjoying the icy coolness, before gulping it down. She looked up and saw a maid step forward with a jug, ready to re-fill her glass. 'Thank you.' Dorothy smiled. 'What's your name?'

'Ah Ling, Miss.' The maid gave a shy smile, then made a slight bow before returning to the line.

Mr Kent introduced the servants as the cook, two house-maids, houseboy and syce. The latter would drive for the family and tend the gardens. They welcomed their new employers with a series of shy smiles and bows before getting back to work; the cook and the housemaids back into the kitchen to prepare dinner, and the houseboy and syce to unload the luggage from the motor car.

'Well, Templetons, I'll let you all settle in,' Mr Kent said. 'You must be in need of a good rest after the journey. The servants will take care of you, but if you need anything at all, here is my telephone number.' He handed Dorothy's father a folded piece of paper, then told him that he would be back to collect him the next morning. 'A word of warning: some of the neighbours will doubtless pop in to say hello. Having new blood arriving here is always a source of excitement! Are they being neighbourly or nosey? Well, you can decide that later!' He chuckled as he made his exit and gave a hearty wave. 'Cheerio for now.'

They had just finished their tour of the house and were in the process of selecting their bedrooms from the four on offer, when there came an enthusiastic halloo-ing from downstairs. They all looked down from the first-floor gallery to see a tall, dark-haired woman in a floral cotton dress step across the threshold. She was followed by a younger version of herself who looked cool and prim in a blue blouse and white A-line skirt, her dark brown hair pulled neatly back in a ponytail.

'You made it! Welcome to Singapore!' the woman began in a tinkling Home Counties accent. 'Marion Davies,' she introduced herself. 'We're just along the road from you; we thought we'd come and be neighbourly! My husband is Walter, he's in banking. And this is my youngest, Clara.' Marion nodded towards her daughter, then put the wicker basket she'd been carrying on the hall table and removed the cover. 'Just a few little treats to welcome you: some pineapple tarts and some fresh mangoes from the garden.'

Though travel weary, Olivia Templeton smiled and switched into hostess mode, calling one of the housemaids and ordering cold drinks in the drawing room. Dorothy felt proud of her mother's undaunted resolve to make the most of every opportunity. She had noticed her flushed face and the damp patches in the armpits of her dress; she was also struggling in this heat. Nevertheless, she welcomed the visitors, just as she would have done back home in Fulham. She led Marion through to the drawing room and suggested that Dorothy show Clara around.

The girls only got as far as the comfy rattan chairs on the shaded veranda, where a ceiling fan whirred overhead. Ah Ling appeared moments later with a fresh jug of lime squash and two glasses. Dorothy felt immense gratitude to the housemaid and wondered if she had read her mind.

'I'm afraid you're not seeing me at my best today.' Dorothy gave a rueful smile as she handed Clara a glass of squash. The girl looked so cool and poised that Dorothy, soaked in perspiration and with her hair sticking out in all directions, felt completely hopeless. 'Seasickness and overheating aren't exactly a winning combination! I think I'm going to spend my days here spread-eagled beneath a fan,' she joked, in an attempt to break the ice. 'How do you ever get used to it?'

Dorothy was relieved when Clara leaned back on the chair and laughed easily, shattering the perfect, prim first impression she had made. 'Oh, I remember that feeling! The journey is bloody awful. I always get so seasick and I still feel like I'm swaying days after we dock!'

Dorothy put her hands out, pretending to steady herself, and joked, 'Oh yes, definitely still swaying!'

Clara laughed again and Dorothy felt herself relax. 'It just takes a bit of time to adjust to the heat,' she continued, taking a sip of her drink. 'We've been here five years now and I find I don't notice it half as much as I did when we first arrived; it really is unbearable in the beginning. But there are electric fans everywhere these days and there's talk of the new air conditioning machines being installed in more places. Apparently the Alhambra cinema down by Raffles is getting it soon; it will be bliss!'

Dorothy's eyes widened at the prospect and she felt her spirits rise.

'Do you like the pictures?' Clara asked.

'Like it? I love it!'

'Then we'll have to go some time.' Clara smiled.

'What else is there to do?' Dorothy asked.

Clara laughed. 'Oh don't worry, there's plenty to keep you busy! Do you play tennis?' Dorothy nodded. 'Well I expect your parents will join one of the clubs. Then there's the beach as well. The Botanic Gardens are rather lovely, they're close by, too. Oh, and the Singapore Zoo is fun, it has over two hundred animals, including free-roaming chimpanzees. Anyway, what's the plan for you while you're here? Are your parents thinking like mine and hoping to marry you off to a "nice young man"?' Clara asked, rolling her eyes dramatically.

'Well' – Dorothy's forehead creased – 'I'm a bit worried that might be the case. I'd actually just started my secretarial training back in London and I'd like to see it through and get a job. I doubt I'll be able to continue with that here, though, or be allowed to,' she added, a disappointed edge to her voice.

'You really do think you've come to the back of beyond, don't you?' Clara raised her eyebrows at her new friend. 'We do have secretarial training here too, you know! Don't worry, you can still keep learning your typing and shorthand! What do you want them for anyway?'

'Oh really?' Dorothy exclaimed. 'I want to work for a newspaper, that's my dream.'

'Aha,' said Clara, nodding approvingly. 'I'm fairly sure that Daddy knows a few people who could help with that.'

Dorothy grinned, then suddenly leapt out of her chair with a cry as a small creature scuttled up the pillar in front of her. 'What on earth is that?' she shrieked.

Clara chuckled softly. 'It's only a gecko! Don't worry, they're perfectly harmless. In fact, we like the geckos as they eat the mosquitoes!'

'Oh!' Dorothy felt herself blushing as she took her seat again.

'It'll all just take a bit of getting used to,' Clara said kindly. 'I suppose you don't have geckos or lizards or monkeys back in Fulham? But don't worry, Singapore is a super place to live; you'll soon get used to it, I promise.'

'Thanks.' Dorothy gave her new friend a smile.

'And another thing, we're perfectly safe here, that's what Daddy says. There's talk of war brewing in Europe, but everyone says that Singapore is impenetrable. Like I said, it's a good place to be.'

'Well, that's something.' Dorothy smiled again. Then her face fell. 'Although I do worry about my brother, Thomas. He's back home in England.'

'I'm sure everything will work out!' Clara smiled. 'That's what the politicians are for! Now, what else can I tell you about Singapore?'

'You mentioned that the cinema was near Raffles. Is that the hotel? Can we go there too? I saw pictures of it in a magazine and it looked splendid!'

'Oh, absolutely! Once you've finished clacking away on your typewriter, we'll go dancing there and I'll introduce you to the Singapore Sling; it's divine!'

After a dinner of noodles with chicken in a ginger sauce, Dorothy was ready for bed. Never in her life had she felt so exhausted, but sleep evaded her. She tossed and turned beneath her mosquito net, her tangled sheets growing damp with sweat.

Night had fallen so quickly. Being so close to the equator, there was no long sunset, just a sudden splash of colour before the sky was plunged into darkness. She lay in the dark, listening to the unfamiliar sounds outside her window. The jungle chorus was in full flow, an orchestra of clacking crickets, croaking frogs and cawing birds. It all felt so alive and it fascinated her.

It felt like she had only been asleep for a few moments when an almighty crash woke her again. Her heart pounded in her chest and adrenaline pumped through her veins. Crash, it came again. It took her a moment to realise that it was thunder. Then, within seconds, rain began lashing hard against the window panes and lightning cracked, illuminating the pitch-black sky. A storm! She got out of bed and went over to open the window. The air outside felt so different; it was cooler now and had a sweet, earthy scent. She stuck her arms out of the window, enjoying the sensation of the rain against her warm skin.

It had been quite a day. Everything here was so foreign; so different from her life back in Fulham. But instead of the apprehension she had initially felt on coming here, she was surprised to feel invigorated by the newness and excitement of it all. She had a beautiful new home, a friend to show her around and the possibility of continuing her secretarial training. Maybe Singapore wouldn't be so bad after all.

Feeling cooler now, Dorothy got back into bed and fell into a deep sleep.

CHAPTER 8

Cornwall

TUESDAY 26TH MARCH, 2019

William arrived the next morning, by which time Annabel had gone over the letters from the secret drawer so many times that she almost knew the words by heart.

'Woah, sis, slow down!' he said with a grin as she bombarded him with snippets of information while he got out of the car. He gave her one of the big bear hugs that she loved and said, 'Let me get my things in, then you can start from the beginning.'

A short while later, they sat on the patio enjoying the morning sun. A plate of scones lay on the table between them, together with a jar of home-made strawberry jam and a pot of clotted cream, all courtesy of Pam. Monty sat obediently next to the table, eyes focusing on their every move, hoping a bit of scone might come his way. Annabel poured tea from Dotty's spotty red teapot and, after adding a splash of milk, raised her teacup in a toast.

'To Dotty,' Annabel said, mustering a sad smile.

William clinked his cup against hers and smiled back. 'Dear old Dotty. I still can't believe she's gone.'

Annabel's eyes shone with tears and William reached across the table to cover her hand with his. 'So come on then, what's all this stuff you've found out about Singapore?'

Annabel told her brother about the letter from Julia Chan, telling Dotty that her grandmother, Ah Ling, had passed away. She told him about the photographs of Dotty with Ah Ling and the friendship the young women had shared.

'But I don't get it.' William's brow furrowed. 'Dotty spent time in Singapore? How did we know nothing about this?'

'Well, brace yourself because there's more.' Annabel raised an eyebrow mysteriously. 'In one of the other envelopes, there was a whole batch of letters from Ah Ling to Dotty; they'd been writing to each other on and off for years! The first letter was from 1946, can you believe it? The letters stopped coming in 2010, which makes sense because that was the year Julia wrote to say that Ah Ling had died.'

Annabel paused in her narration and sliced open two scones, then put one on each of their plates. She pulled a face as her brother reached straight for the cream and barked with mock severity, 'William Penrose, don't you dare! I don't care how your wife does it, she's from Devon. You know full well that here in Cornwall it's jam first! Honestly, Dotty would give you what for if she saw you doing that!'

Her laugh turned into a sob and tears sprang unbidden as it dawned on her that Dotty wasn't here to give William her oft-threatened 'what for'. And never again would they hear her famous 'jam first' rant.

William smiled fondly and put up his hands in a placatory manner. 'Alright, alright, I promise I'll do it properly.' He reached across and squeezed her hand. 'You OK, Annie?'

She tried to smile through damp eyes and looked down when she felt a warm weight on her thigh. Monty was resting his muzzle there, gazing up at her with such concern and devotion. She rubbed the old dog's head affectionately with her free hand.

'I'm better now you're here, thanks for coming, Will.' She squeezed his hand back. 'It just doesn't seem real. It's so weird being here without her, I miss her so much. I keep thinking of things to tell her that would make her smile. And I keep expecting her to walk in and ask who fancies a cup of tea?'

'I know.' William nodded as he spread jam on his scone, followed by a generous dollop of clotted cream. 'It's going to take some time to get used to. She was such a constant in our lives. I knew she wouldn't last forever, but I suppose I just wasn't ready to say goodbye yet. To be honest, I'm not sure I ever would have been.'

There was a pause as Annabel sipped her tea and William started on his scone. The sombre mood was suddenly broken as, eyes closed, he moaned with dramatic pleasure then mumbled through a mouthful of jam and cream, 'God, this is good! That Pam sure can bake!'

Annabel burst out laughing and reached into her pocket for a tissue to dab her streaming eyes and running nose. Her brother always knew how to cheer her up and his larking about and general sense of impropriety never failed to make her giggle.

Once he'd finished eating, William got back to the business at hand. 'So, back to the Chinese woman: who was she and how did Dotty meet her? I *never* heard her mention travelling anywhere, never mind to the Far East! She was such a stay-at-home old thing, the idea just seems so ludicrous!'

Annabel nodded as she topped up her teacup. 'Well, incredible as it seems, it turns out that Dotty and her parents lived in Singapore for a while, in the late thirties. The letters don't go into much detail about how or why, but Ah Ling did refer to Dotty's father working for a company out there.'

William frowned, shaking his head. 'I knew her father worked for a rubber company, but Dotty only ever mentioned him working in London. How strange.'

'Maybe he was posted overseas?' Annabel shrugged, having had more time than William to process the information. 'Think about it, it was just before the Second World War and rubber was becoming a valuable commodity. Ah Ling was a housemaid in Singapore, she worked for Dotty's family and they became close. I think they were of a similar age. Here, have a look at these, they're amazing.'

Annabel opened the envelope and started laying out the photographs on the table.

'Wow, you're not wrong!' William studied the collection of old sepia photos, taking in every detail and turning each one over to read the descriptions on the back. 'It's like another world! The splendour of the old colonial days, hey? It all looks so tropical and luxurious. Look at the gardens!'

'I know, it's amazing,' Annabel agreed, picking up the Templeton family photo in front of the beautiful black and white villa. Even though the old photo lacked any colour, the lushness of the garden was clear to see.

William read the back of another photo, a picture of Dotty's parents dressed in their evening finery, standing in front of a Christmas tree. '"*Raffles Hotel, 1938*", it says. It's crazy to think that war was just around the corner, but they look like they didn't have a care in the world!' He shook his head, marvelling at the pictures.

'How blissfully unaware they were of what was to come.' Annabel mused. 'Everyone thought Singapore was undefeatable, but how wrong they were!'

William arched a quizzical eyebrow. 'You're going to have to remind me what happened, Dr Penrose. We mere mortals don't have quite the same capacity for nerdy military trivia as you history buffs!'

She scoffed at her brother's teasing, knowing he meant no harm by it.

'Well, Churchill and co. knew that the Japanese had their eye on Singapore; its position made it too useful an opportunity to miss. But they were expecting a naval attack. They pointed their cannons out to sea and were surprised to find out that the Japanese were actually advancing down the Malayan Peninsula instead. It was rough terrain, but the enemy had been trained in jungle warfare so were ready for it. It was a swift, surprise attack and it completely overwhelmed the Allies. They outnumbered the invaders by about three to one, but in just a couple of months the Brits were forced to surrender.'

William nodded slowly. 'But Dotty and her family must have moved back home again when the war started?' he asked. 'I remember her telling us about wartime London.'

'Yes, I remember those stories, too,' Annabel agreed.

'Are these all the photos?' William looked up and caught her eye.

'Yes, the other envelopes just had letters in them.' Annabel busied herself with putting the photos away again, feeling a pang of guilt at the white lie she had just told.

Safely tucked in her pocket was the one photograph that she wanted to keep secret for now, until she could figure out what it would mean to her family. It was Mrs Llewellyn on her wedding day. As an historian, Annabel knew all too well the importance of careful research and detailed fact-finding, and until she was sure of the story behind the photo, she was not going to share it with her family. She didn't like keeping secrets from her brother, but for the time being she felt an overwhelming need to keep the wedding photo and Ah Ling's very first letter to herself.

The letter, hidden in her suitcase upstairs, was dated 1946 and seemed to be Ah Ling's first contact since they had last seen each other several years earlier. How frustrating it was to only have one side of the conversation; she would have given anything to be able to read Dotty's letters as well. Goodness only knew what her grandmother had written in her first letter, but Ah Ling's reply referenced 'the horrors of war' and, several times, told Dotty how brave she had been. A spark of connection flickered here as Annabel remembered that somebody else had recently called Dotty brave. Who was it? She racked her tired brain but couldn't remember.

'Have you told Dad any of this?' William's question brought her back to the present.

'No.' Annabel shook her head. 'Much as I would love to ask him about all this, he's got enough to be getting on with, recovering from his operation, not to mention losing Dotty.'

William nodded. 'Yes, that's true. Probably best to see what else we can find out before telling him about it. Anyway, how are things with Luke? Has he been in touch?'

Annabel ran her hand through her hair. 'Not really. He offered to come down if I needed him, but that was a couple of days ago and I haven't spoken to him since. I've tried calling but seem to keep missing him. I've just had the occasional message.' She sighed. 'I really don't know what's going on or where we are. This time apart was meant to help us figure things out, to find out what we really wanted, but that's all been pushed to one side, for me at least.'

Her phone buzzed.

'Speak of the devil!' She raised her eyebrows and picked up the phone, frowning as she read the text message aloud,

> Heading up to Birmingham today for a new project, home at the weekend. Hope you're OK. Lx

She sighed again. 'See what I mean?' Then she frowned. 'And that's weird, he said he was going to be busy on the Bristol project.' She stood up and started to clear the table.

'Hmm, yes,' William replied, his own frown forming. 'It's pretty disappointing, to be honest. I'm sorry, sis. I thought better of Luke, that he'd be more of a support when you needed him.'

'I'm tired of it, Will. It all just feels like an effort. Is this the beginning of the end?' Her brother didn't have an answer, but his warm hug made her feel a little better.

William stayed for the night and Annabel enjoyed having her brother all to herself. They laughed, they cried, they reminisced over happy memories and shared funny stories. Together, they made arrangements with the undertakers and discussed a provisional funeral date with Reverend Pascoe. And they paid their darling grandmother one final visit in the Chapel of Rest.

They also made a start on going through Dotty's things; William focusing on categorising the contents of the garden sheds into 'keep', 'recycle' and 'bin', and Annabel going through boxes in the attic. She was itching to find further clues about Dotty's time in Singapore; her secret life, as they now thought of it. But how secret had it actually been? Had their grandfather known about it? She went through the photo albums again, just in case Annabel had missed anything, and rifled through documents and papers in the study chest of drawers. But it was a fruitless search. The only evidence of Dotty Penrose's life in Singapore had been the letters and photographs in the locked drawer of the bureau.

It was a sad parting when it was time for William to leave. He enveloped his sister in his usual bear hug and promised he'd be back again soon. Annabel promised to do a bit more digging around Dotty's letters and share her findings with her brother when she knew more.

The next day, she awoke feeling out of sorts with a gnawing sense of loss. She missed William and she missed Luke and, now that she was alone again, the absence of her grandmother felt even harder to bear. The grey, overcast sky matched her mood as she took Monty for an early-morning walk along the clifftop. The old dog seemed to sense her pain and stayed close to her, offering comfort as only a four-legged friend could.

Mid-morning, Annabel made a mug of coffee and took it through to the conservatory. She curled up in a comfortable armchair with her book, but after staring at the same page for several minutes, decided to call her father instead.

Noel answered after the third ring, but it took him a moment to realise that it was a video call and Annabel chuckled at the close-up view of his ear.

'That's better!' She smiled, when his face finally appeared. Noel was propped up on a mountain of pillows on his bed at home in Portugal, resting his newly replaced hip. He looked tired, she thought, but that was hardly surprising having recently undergone major surgery. He felt so far away and she wished that she could give him a hug.

'So you've been up and about then?' Annabel asked, pleased to see that he was dressed for the day.

'Yes, I've been up, doing my exercises, but I'm under doctor's orders to rest up and not overdo it.' He rolled his eyes. 'Although, between you and me,' he added, lowering his voice to a whisper as he looked over towards the bedroom door, checking the coast was clear, 'the doctor's orders are a breeze, compared to your mother's!'

Annabel laughed and shook her head fondly. 'Quite right, too!' she said. 'We want you fit and well and back on your feet as soon as possible. I hope you're behaving yourself?'

Noel grinned and gave her a mock salute. 'Aye aye, Captain!'

They chatted about various things, from the arrangements that Annabel and William had made for Dotty's funeral, to her mother's latest plans for a new pergola in the garden.

It was so good to see her father and feel the warmth of his easy company. A wave of loneliness suddenly rose up in Annabel. 'I can come over, you know, Dad; I can fly from Bristol very easily. I can come and help take care of you.'

Her father sensed the shift in her mood and smiled. 'Oh, that's so kind of you, my darling. And you know you are always welcome here, and we would love to see you.' He glanced towards the bedroom door and lowered his voice again. 'But you know what your mother's like; she's got everything mapped out for the next couple of weeks, and you know she's not good when plans get changed.'

'Good point,' Annabel said, mustering a smile.

'But we'll be coming over very soon and I'm so looking forward to seeing you, Annie! It must be tough holding the fort at Mum's, but don't feel you have to stay. I'm sure her friend Pam would take care of Monty and you could head home. Or better yet, take yourself off for a change of scenery for a few days; it is meant to be your holiday, after all!'

'Dad,' she began. 'I've been thinking.' She paused, choosing her next words carefully. 'I only really knew her as a grandmother, but was Dotty a good mother?'

A broad smile spread across Noel's handsome face and his eyes suddenly glistened. 'She was the very best!'

His expression changed to a look of confusion as he continued, 'Why do you ask?'

'Oh, I don't know.' She sighed. 'I suppose all of this has made me think about our family and where we all come from. I don't think I've ever really heard much about your childhood, when you were very little. You were born during the war; what was it like?'

Noel blew out, as he considered his answer. 'Well, I can't remember the very beginning, obviously.' He chuckled. 'I was born in London, but I suppose my first real memories were in Cornwall, at the farm. We moved there after the war. Halcyon days of sunshine, sandcastles, baby lambs and Mum's baking!'

'It sounds idyllic.' Annabel smiled.

Noel nodded. 'It was indeed. I had a wonderful childhood, I was very lucky.'

Annabel thought back to Dr Underwood's question in the hospital before Dotty's death: '*Your mother or father wasn't adopted?*'

She felt an uncomfortable knot in her stomach. Was Noel hiding something or was he blissfully unaware? There was no way she could ask him outright, what if she had got it all wrong? It would be an unkind thing to do while he was grieving the loss of his much-loved mother.

'And Dotty?' she asked, changing tack. 'Where did she live when she was younger? Before she married Grandad, I mean?'

'London, too. Fulham, actually. It was quite a modest terraced house back then, but these days I gather it's become quite a flash area.'

'She never moved anywhere else? Never lived abroad or anything like that?'

Noel laughed at the suggestion. 'Mum? Live abroad? Hardly! She hated travelling, she never wanted to go anywhere. You know what she was like, always said she was perfectly happy at home!'

'But you mentioned a holiday somewhere hot, remember? At Dotty's birthday party?'

Noel's brow creased. 'Oh yes, that was a funny one. But Mum was quite adamant that we didn't go abroad, so we couldn't have.' He shrugged. 'She thought I was probably remembering a camping trip to Dorset in 1947. There was a tremendous heatwave that summer, apparently, and she thought that was probably it.'

Annabel nodded, but something wasn't adding up. Her eye fell on the pile of letters and old sepia photographs on the coffee table beside her. She was itching to ask her father about them, but it seemed that he was none the wiser. Again, she felt it wasn't fair to burden him with half-baked theories while he was recovering from surgery and mourning Dotty's passing. She needed to find more conclusive evidence before potentially shattering the idyllic story of his childhood.

The rest of the morning was punctuated by a series of rings – doorbell and telephone – as various well-wishers offered their condolences and volunteered offers of help. In between, Annabel pottered about, feeling unsettled and confused. Although William had done sterling work on sorting the impersonal contents of the shed, she could not bring herself to start sorting the house; she would be happy to leave it to her sensible, pragmatic mother in a few weeks' time. Her mind was on overdrive, trying to piece together and make sense of the snippets of information she'd gleaned from the photos and letters. But she just couldn't figure it out.

Later that afternoon, Annabel decided to follow her father's advice and head home. She couldn't face the thought of staying at the farm on her own for another fortnight until her parents arrived and she felt a yearning for the comfort and security of her own four walls. Luke would be away for another couple of nights, so she would be able to please herself. She felt exhausted after the emotional turmoil of the last few days and welcomed the thought of a long bubble bath and a lazy evening on the sofa in charge of the remote control.

The only fly in the ointment was the guilt she felt about leaving Monty. The loyal old dog looked up at her with such love and devotion that she could have sworn he could see into her soul. She hugged him tight before dropping him off at Pam's, promising that she would be back to see him again soon.

It was such a spontaneous decision to head home and, knowing that he would be busy away with work, Annabel hadn't bothered to message Luke. She would text him later that evening, once she had had time to relax and unwind, and was feeling less prickly towards him.

She did, however, text Jenny. She lived nearby and Annabel was eager to get her take on Dotty's Singapore letters. Her friend loved a good mystery and would help her hatch a plan on how best to proceed. She was pleased to see Jenny's reply when she stopped for petrol at the M5 services.

'Sounds intriguing! Come round for a drink when you're back, I've got something to share with you, too.' She texted back, making a plan to go round when she got home. She was curious to find out what was on Jenny's mind.

It felt strange going home to a cold, dark and empty house that evening. Annabel put the lights on and boiled the kettle for a cup of tea. She sighed as she took in the state of the kitchen; Luke had many qualities, she reminded herself, but he did not keep a tidy house. She turned on the radio and started removing the dirty dishes from the sink, stacking them neatly in the dishwasher instead. She added a bar of detergent and was about to press the start button on the machine when she spotted the used wine glasses. Two wine glasses. And one had a telltale red lipstick mark on it.

Annabel's stomach sank and a shiver of unease ran through her as she went upstairs. The bedroom was a mess, the bed still unmade with the duvet in a tangled heap. Tears pricked as she saw the dent in her pillow where another woman's head had lain. Instinctively, she picked up the duvet and shook it out to straighten it. That was when she saw the bright pink thong hidden in the bed sheets. The unease turned into anger. How dare he?

Annabel sighed as she went downstairs again, a heavy weight pressing on her heart. For some time she had been fooling herself, she realised. It was time to take matters into her own hands and make a decision about her future without Luke.

CHAPTER 9

Singapore
JUNE 1938

After a restless night of unfamiliar noises in her new surroundings, Dorothy woke to see Ah Ling bringing her a glass of chilled water. For a moment, she forgot where she was and was puzzled by the gentle, Chinese face. She soon recovered herself and gave the maid a thankful smile. The night was over and it was a new day, with new adventures ahead. She gulped down the water, got out of bed and stretched.

Dorothy was expecting to see gloomy, grey clouds after the previous night's downpour, but the storm had blown over. She opened the shutters and looked out at a perfect blue sky. The garden had been rejuvenated by the rain and everything bloomed in a deep, lush green. It was all so beautiful.

'Good morning, darling!' her mother called up to her from the garden below, where she was eating breakfast with her husband. 'Morning, Dodo!' her father echoed. They were sitting at a table in the shade of the trees, her mother in a thin cotton house robe and her father ready for work in a smart, light cream suit.

'Do come and join us, it's lovely out here!' Dorothy was pleased to see her mother refreshed and back to her usual cheerful form. 'There's fresh pineapple juice, bacon and eggs, coffee and even toast and marmalade!'

The mention of breakfast made Dorothy's stomach rumble, so she quickly washed, using the jug and basin that Ah Ling had brought up for her, put on a loose cotton dress and went down to join her parents.

Later that morning, Mr Kent arrived to take her father, Anthony, to visit the McKinley's office and meet the staff. 'Nothing too strenuous,' he had assured him, clapping him on the shoulder. 'Just a quick social call to introduce you to a few of the troops – they're all dying to meet you – then we'll have lunch at the club and we'll have you back here in time for a mid-afternoon siesta!'

Once the men had left, Olivia sat down with the cook and the housemaids to discuss the family's routines and meal preferences. Dorothy took herself off to sort out her room. The family had never had servants before and it felt strange that the housemaids, Ah Ling and Mei Mei, had unpacked her trunk for her. They'd had Mrs Collins the char lady who had come to their house in Fulham three mornings a week, but having live-in staff, who were on hand to anticipate and meet their every need, was quite different.

Her clothes had been hung in the large wooden wardrobe or folded and placed neatly in the chest of drawers beside the bed. In the bottom drawer, she found what she was looking for: a fabric bundle tied with string. She unwrapped it and took out three silver photo frames. Relieved that the glass had survived the journey, she stood all three on the bookcase by the window.

The first frame showed a family portrait, taken just before they had set sail for Singapore. She smiled as she looked at her brother Thomas's uncomfortable expression and remembered how he had complained that his tie was strangling him. She missed having him around and felt a bit left behind, ever since he had left home and headed off to university. The siblings had always been close and she looked forward to him coming out to visit.

The second photograph was of her parents on their wedding day, outside All Saints Church in Fulham. They looked so young and carefree and it always warmed Dorothy's heart to see the pure joy on their faces. The third picture was of her and her best friend Daisy. They were on the beach at Eastbourne, wearing their bathing suits and laughing at something the photographer – Daisy's father – had said. It was one of many outings the friends had shared. Dorothy found it strange that, for the first time in her entire life, she was embarking on this new adventure alone, unable to share it with her best friend.

She was still holding the photo, her eyes misty as a wave of homesickness came over her, when she felt a presence beside her. She looked up into the kind face of Ah Ling. It was hard to gauge how old the housemaid was, but Dorothy estimated she was a few years older than herself, probably in her early twenties.

'Oh Miss, you sad? What you need?' she asked, her soft voice full of concern.

Dorothy managed a watery smile and wiped her eyes. 'It's OK, Ah Ling, I'm just a little homesick.'

Ah Ling pointed to the photo and smiled. 'Your sister, Miss?'

'No, I don't have a sister, just a brother.' She pointed to the picture of Thomas. Then she pointed to Daisy. 'This is Daisy, my best friend, but I suppose she is like a sister to me. She's back in England and I miss her.'

'Ah, I understand, Miss. I also miss my brother. He in Hainan, China. All my family there.' She put a hand on her heart, as if to indicate that a part of it remained there with them. 'You be alright, Miss. You make new friends and everything be tip top.'

Dorothy smiled at the unlikely expression, presumably picked up from Ah Ling's previous employers. The housemaid smiled back and reached down to touch Dorothy on the shoulder. Feeling grateful for the silent gesture of support, Dorothy covered Ah Ling's hand with her own. And in that moment, with that kind touch, a bond was formed.

A few hours later, Dorothy was enjoying an afternoon nap beneath the whirr of her bedroom ceiling fan when her mother woke her. Her voice brimmed with excitement as she told her daughter that Marion Davies had called again, this time issuing an invitation.

'They're taking us to the Raffles Hotel for dinner tomorrow night, darling! The whole family is going, so you can spend time with Clara and meet her cousin, Matthew, as well. He's staying with them for a while, apparently. I think Clara will be a good friend for you, she can show you around and help you meet the right sort of people.'

'That sounds lovely, Mummy, but what on earth am I going to wear?' Dorothy's face fell. 'None of the frocks I brought with me will be suitable, they'll all be far too hot!'

'Don't worry about that, darling,' her mother said, fanning her face at the mere mention of the heat, 'I asked Marion where we could find something and she recommended John Little department store in Raffles Place. Apparently, it's very popular among the British community and reasonably priced. They have tailors and dressmakers there, even a silverware department and a beauty salon, would you believe! Anyway, chop chop,' she continued, patting her daughter's leg. 'Your father will be home soon and we should be downstairs to welcome him.'

Later that afternoon, once her father was home from a successful visit to his new office, Dorothy and her mother set off in the black family sedan, their syce was a gentle, middle-aged man and his English was excellent. Encouraged by Dorothy, he was happy to play tour guide and tell them about the interesting things they passed. They left the lush tranquillity of Nassim Road and drove along the bustling Orchard Road, before eventually arriving in Raffles Place.

Named after Singapore's 'founding father', according to Amir, Raffles Place was the city's commercial and banking centre. Lines of European-style buildings made up two sides of the square, dominated by the imposing facades of the Mercantile Bank at one end and the Chartered Bank Chambers, with its striking dome, at the other. The centre of the square was lined with parked cars and rickshaw drivers waiting for customers. It was a busy spot, with all different kinds of people going about their business.

Their destination, John Little department store, was next to the Chartered Bank, 'The oldest department store in Singapore,' Amir informed them in his softly-spoken voice. It was an impressive white building, several storeys high, decorated with shuttered windows and an arched colonnade to provide shoppers shade from the hot Singapore sun.

'Look at the architecture!' Olivia observed as Amir opened the car door and helped her out. 'It's all so wonderfully modern!' She beamed, looking around the square. 'We could be in London!'

'Apart from the weather!' Dorothy laughed, feeling the full force of the afternoon sun as she stepped out of the car.

Amir escorted them to the entrance of the department store then returned to wait with the car. The ladies made their way into the cool interior and were greeted by a doorman in a smart uniform. He welcomed them, then pointed them in the direction of the grand wooden staircase, informing them that ladieswear was on the second floor.

They reached the department and were ably assisted by a smart young man who introduced himself as Harry. He spoke excellent English with a hint of a Chinese accent. With time being of the essence, they opted for off-the-rack outfits that they could take home with them, but promised Harry that they would return for some tailored garments at a later date. He guided them through racks of pretty day dresses and elegant evening wear and Dorothy was spoilt for choice. They deferred to his local knowledge on what would be most suitable for an evening at the Raffles Hotel, then also chose a couple of day dresses each that would help keep them cool in the sticky, tropical heat.

'An excellent choice, ladies! I trust you will be very happy here in Singapore. Please come and see us again soon. And, if I may be so bold, may I suggest our tearoom on the second floor? Many of our customers enjoy a visit when they have finished making their purchases. I am sure you will also enjoy.' With a smart bow, Harry bade them farewell and moved on to his next customer.

Clasping their shopping bags, mother and daughter made their way back towards the central staircase and went up to the next floor. With its wood panelling, ornate chairs and white tablecloths, the tearoom reminded Dorothy of going out for tea in London. Dorothy felt tired and ready for a nap, but the tea and fruit cake lifted her spirits and she felt excited at the thought of wearing her new dress on her first night out in Singapore.

The Dan Hopkins Orchestra was in full swing when Dorothy and her parents arrived at the Raffles Hotel the following evening. Dressed in her new turquoise evening gown with her hair clipped up in an elegant chignon, Dorothy was pleased with how she looked on the outside. But on the inside, her stomach was full of butterflies, fluttering a mixture of nerves and excitement about the night ahead.

She was looking forward to seeing Clara again and to meeting her cousin, and she couldn't wait to experience the hotel. She had seen photographs but nothing had prepared her for the reality of the place which had been dubbed the 'Jewel of the East'. Its magnificent white facade glowing in the early dusk, reminded her of a three-tiered wedding cake. A large extension came off the front of the building, from which the sound of laughter, chatter and rousing Dixieland jazz was coming.

The Templetons made their way to the hotel lobby and were shown through to the ballroom. The music was louder as they entered and the dance floor was packed. Around the edge of the room were wicker tables where guests were dining. Dorothy gazed around, taking it all in, then spotted Clara in the distance, standing up and waving them over.

'You made it!' Clara called over the noise of the band, hugging her new friend in welcome. 'And you look divine!' She stepped back, admiring Dorothy's outfit. 'Where did you get that dress? I love it!'

Introductions between the two families were made and they all settled around a large corner table, the parents at one end and 'youngsters' at the other. Dorothy looked at her surroundings; the sights and sounds were overwhelming, but in a good way. The music never stopped, with the band members – looking smart in their white dinner jackets and bow ties – giving the crowd exactly what they wanted: jazz, jazz and a bit more jazz. Waiters weaved expertly in and out of the crowd as they made their way around the outside of the room, delivering trays of exotic-looking drinks and plates of delicious food to the guests.

The conversation flowed as easily as the wine, with Walter Davies, Clara's father, proving to be a congenial host. He was a good-humoured chap with a round, animated face and seemed most interested in whether or not Anthony Templeton played cricket. His eyes lit up when Anthony confirmed that he did.

'I say, I don't suppose you're free on Saturday next and could help us out of a hole? One of our chaps has broken his ankle so we're a man down. Just a club match, down on the Padang, nothing too serious, but it's always a bit of fun!'

Olivia was thrilled by the invitation for her husband to join the cricket team and, for a moment, reminded Dorothy of an over-eager puppy. She discreetly laid a hand on her mother's arm in a subtle bid to calm her. Her mother had had such great hopes for their exciting new life in Singapore and seemed delighted to be made to feel so welcome so quickly. But Dorothy didn't want her eagerness to come across as off-putting to their new friends.

Clara's cousin, Matthew, was easy-going with a ready smile. He was twenty-one years old and was spending six months in Singapore with his aunt and uncle after completing his undergraduate degree in England. Although he wasn't her usual type to look at, with his tall, wiry physique and strawberry blonde hair, Dorothy found herself enjoying his company enormously.

'I'm a banker, or at least I'm training to be one,' he told her with a coy smile. 'I know . . . ' he sighed, 'it doesn't sound like the most exciting job in the world, but I'm afraid I'm a bit of a numbers man. And the chance to come out here and do some work experience with Uncle Walter's bank was just too good an offer to turn down!'

Dorothy was glad when dinner arrived; the wine was starting to go to her head. With such efficient waiters, her glass had never been empty for long and she needed something to soak up the alcohol. She was pleased to see some old favourites on the menu and devoured the roast beef and vegetables.

After dinner – all six courses of it – Dorothy asked Clara where the ladies' room was. 'Come on, I'll show you,' she replied, 'and let's stretch our legs while we're at it; time for a tour!'

The girls excused themselves and made their way through the cool expanse of the hotel lobby. They stopped at the ladies' powder room, then Clara led the way out into the garden. Night had fallen and the tall outlines of the palm trees were silhouetted against the dark, cloudy sky. The sound of the now-familiar clicking of cicadas filled the garden. The air was cooler now and fragrant with the sweet scent of jasmine. Dorothy paused and breathed in deeply. But they were not stopping; Clara led the way through the garden and out onto the road at the front of the hotel.

'Where are we going?' Dorothy asked.

'Time to cool off! You can't have an evening at Raffles without a quick paddle!'

On the other side of the road – eponymously named Beach Road – was the seashore. Dorothy followed Clara's lead when they reached the sand and slipped off her shoes. They wandered down to the water and she revelled in the sensation of the coolness lapping against her skin. It had been so hot in the ballroom that it was blissful to come outside and cool off. They weren't alone; several other hotel guests had had the same idea, including a few couples who were enjoying the romantic setting.

Clara found an area of dry sand and sat down, then rummaged in her clutch bag. Dorothy followed suit and sat beside her, but declined the cigarette she was offered. Clara lit hers and soft puffs of smoke floated in the air. In the distance, a crescent moon shone down, lighting up the horizon and the ships out at sea. Away from their parents and the noise of the ballroom, the girls chatted more easily, sharing details of their former lives back in England, movies and music they both liked, and tales of past romances.

'I was seeing a nice chap back in Fulham. Bertie, he was called.' Dorothy smiled wistfully. 'He was very sweet to me and we had a lot of fun. And he was very good looking; tall, dark and handsome, just how I like them! But my mother made it clear that he was "not suitable marriage material".' She mimicked her mother's clipped tones on this last part and rolled her eyes.

'That's mothers for you!' Clara chuckled. 'Mine's exactly the same; fixated on me making the "right sort of match". But I'm resisting for as long as is humanly possible! Honestly, the chaps she thinks of as being "suitable" are so unutterably dull that I would lose my mind through boredom within a matter of days! And anyway, I plan to work and support myself. I truly resent the idea that we have to chain ourselves to a man and hope that he'll take care of us. Times are changing and I feel perfectly sure that I can take care of myself!'

On that decisive note, Clara stubbed out her cigarette and got to her feet, 'Right, come on, time to go. Next stop on the tour: The Long Bar! Make sure you brush all the sand off that gorgeous dress.'

They crossed the road back to the hotel and made their way to the rear of the building. Inside, the Long Bar was cool, dark and inviting. The palm-shaped fans provided a welcome breeze and guests relaxed in wicker chairs. The girls crunched their way across the empty peanut husks that littered the floor – as per tradition, Clara explained – and were shown to a table near the bar. The waiter took their order, this time for a couple of sensible soft drinks. Clara signed the chit to her father's account then looked around, waving to a couple of friends and pointing out a few others to Dorothy.

'That is the local femme fatale, Maria da Costa,' she whispered as a stunning, dark-haired woman in a jet black dress breezed past them. Her expression was haughty and her eyes dark and fierce. 'Italian and highly strung. Used to getting what she wants.'

Dorothy watched as Maria da Costa paused briefly at the door on her way out of the bar. She exchanged a few words with a man who was coming in. Dorothy couldn't hear what was said, but she could tell from the woman's face that the words were not pleasant.

Maria swept out of the room and the man turned and looked in their direction. Seeing him properly now, Dorothy gasped. He was tall and dashingly handsome. With dark hair, smiling eyes and a neat moustache, he reminded her of Clark Gable.

Feeling at ease with Clara and bolder than usual after all the drinks, Dorothy whispered, 'Golly! Who is *that*?' The man walked past their table and headed over to the bar.

Clara followed her gaze. 'Ah, Douglas. Or, should I say, Dangerous Douglas! Yes, he's devilishly good looking, but equally devilish with the ladies, if you know what I mean!'

Clara's brow furrowed as she continued, 'That's interesting,' she muttered, almost to herself. 'They're playing their roles very well, I must say!'

'Playing their what?'

'Oh, sorry, I should explain. It's highly unusual to see Douglas on his own, he normally has at least one adoring female in tow. It was Maria da Costa for an awfully long time, but rumour has it that she's now engaged to be married to stuffy old Bernard Pemberton, who's at least ten years older than she is and looks like a fish!'

Dorothy giggled at the description.

'But Fish Face Pemberton is loaded,' Clara continued, 'and set to inherit a title and a big old castle back in Berkshire.' She shrugged, as if this explained everything.

'So I suppose they've had to call it off. Or, at least, make it look as if they have.' Clara added the last part almost under her breath.

'He's so handsome; like a movie star!' Dorothy whispered. She was still gazing at the side profile of the gorgeous Douglas when he looked over, a drink in each hand, and made his way out of the bar. Their eyes met for a brief moment and he gave her an amused nod.

Dorothy's cheeks flamed instantly and she turned away. 'Oh, what a fool I must have looked, staring at him like that!' she muttered.

Clara laughed. 'I wouldn't worry about it. He's used to having women staring at him.' Then her tone became more serious. 'But will you promise me one thing, Dorothy?'

'What's that?'

'I know he fits your tall-dark-and-handsome criteria, but please stay away from that one; he's dangerous with a capital D!' Then she brightened again. 'Anyway, you know what time it is?'

'No, I don't.' Dorothy started to look at her wristwatch, causing Clara to burst out laughing.

'Oh sweetie, you are funny! It's time for . . . ' and she tapped her fingers on the edge of the table to create a drumroll, 'the Singapore Sling!' She waved to a passing waiter, who came straight over and took their order.

While they waited for the drinks to arrive, Clara explained the origin of the drink. 'So the story goes that women were not allowed to drink alcohol when they came to the hotel – another example of female oppression, if ever there was one!' Clara made a disparaging face. 'Then a few years ago, the head barman here came up with the clever plan of making a cocktail for the ladies that looked like a fruit juice. You'll see, it's pink and fruity; it looks completely innocent! So that's how the ladies got round the stupid archaic rules. Oh, and here they are now.'

The waiter appeared and placed the fruity, pink drinks on the table in front of them.

'Cheers!' said Clara as they clinked glasses. 'Here's to you, to us, and to having a bloody good time in Singapore!'

The room was swaying as Dorothy followed Clara back to their table a while later. She squinted over towards their group, trying to bring everything into focus, and saw that her father was deep in conversation with a young man seated next to him. Her stomach sank when she saw that it was a handsome young man with movie-star looks.

'Ah, girls, there you are! Dodo, do come and meet one of my new work associates; Douglas. Douglas, may I present my daughter, Dorothy.'

Clark Gable stood and took her hand in his, before lifting it to his lips. He gave her that same, slightly amused smile and in her tipsy state she wondered if he was laughing at her.

'Dorothy, a pleasure!' he said, his deep voice as smooth as silk. She felt her face flush as she stared up at him. He was even more handsome up close and she felt girlishly tongue-tied and awkward.

The crowd clapped as the musicians brought their number to a close and Douglas, still holding her hand, nodded in the direction of the dance floor. 'May I have the next dance?'

Amid her parents' approving murmurings, Dorothy nodded mutely and let him lead her out into the hot, sweaty throng of dancers. The band soon started up again with a rousing rendition of 'I Got Rhythm' and Douglas took her in his arms. She stared up into his dark eyes and breathed in his scent, a mix of alcohol, tobacco and strong cologne. It was overwhelming to be so close to this handsome man and her insides were doing strange things. Just breathe, she told herself, realising that she was so tense that he must feel like he was dancing with a wooden broom.

He smiled down at her, as if sensing her tension. 'Relax Dorothy, I don't bite. Well, not too hard, anyway.' He winked at her and for a moment she was consumed by a heady mixture of exhilaration and terror. She took another deep breath and arched an eyebrow at him, trying the sophisticated 'Down, boy!' look she had seen Daisy use on over-enthusiastic suitors back home in London. She wasn't sure it had the desired effect as he burst out laughing, carefree and easily.

'Oh, Dorothy, something tells me that you and I are going to have some fun!' He winked again. 'So tell me, how are you enjoying Singapore so far?' he asked conversationally as he twirled her around the dance floor.

But the whirling was too much for Dorothy and she never managed a reply. The heat, the noise and the alcohol – not to mention the closeness of Douglas and his handsome looks – all came together in a billowing wave that rose up inside her. With a look of utter panic, she stepped out of his embrace and fled from the ballroom. She made it out to the garden just in time for the contents of her stomach to reappear all over one of the perfectly manicured flower beds.

CHAPTER 10

Singapore

Sunday 31st March, 2019

'Excuse me, Madam!' Annabel was roused from sleep by a sing-song voice and a gentle hand on her shoulder. She raised her eye mask and blinked a couple of times before opening her eyes, momentarily confused by her surroundings. Her neck was sore from an awkward sleeping position and she rubbed it as she sat up.

'Could you just pop your seat up while we're serving?' the smiling air stewardess asked in an overly bright voice.

'Yes, of course,' Annabel managed, before reaching for the lever. Then she wiped the sleep from her eyes, the dribble from the corner of her mouth and stretched to ease her aching back. She glanced at her watch, it was 8 a.m. But that was still UK time. She turned on the TV screen in front of her for more information and felt that nervous knot in her stomach again when she saw that they would be landing in just under two hours.

'Would you like the chicken rice or the vegetarian omelette?' The stewardess was back a few minutes later. Annabel opted for the chicken, then spent the next five minutes playing chess with the various dishes on the tiny meal tray, trying not to drop anything or spill her drink.

For about the one hundredth time that day – though, to be honest, she didn't know which day it was anymore – she wondered if she was doing the right thing. She was exhausted and emotional after recent events, she now wondered if it had been such a great idea to jet off to unknown, distant shores.

It had been an impulse decision and quite out of character, Annabel now thought. She smiled to herself as she remembered the look of shock on Jenny's face when she had told her the plan.

Dear Jenny, she had been an absolute rock when Annabel had turned up on her doorstep, hurt and angry over Luke's deception. Annabel winced at the memory. She had known that things had changed, that everything had felt different between them, but she hadn't expected Luke to jump into bed with someone new as soon as her back was turned.

Jenny had offered a glass of wine and a sympathetic ear, but she had not been surprised by the news of Luke's philandering. That had been what she had needed to tell Annabel; that her cheating boyfriend had started swiping on the same dating app that Jenny used as soon as Annabel had left for Cornwall. He had come up in Jenny's list of matches and, although he had done his best to disguise his identity – using a far-off photo of him on a beach in a baseball cap and sunglasses – Jenny had recognised him instantly. She had shown Annabel the screenshot she had taken of his dating profile picture.

'Look, this is from your holiday to Mallorca, Annie; I recognised your red dress. I'm so sorry, hon.'

Annabel had stared at the photo, noticing her pretty red dress at the very edge of the picture, where he had cropped her out.

With Dotty's passing, Jenny admitted that she had not known what to do. She said she had been stuck between a rock and a hard place, wondering when would be the best time to break the news to her friend. She seemed relieved that the secret was now out.

Annabel hadn't cried that evening. After losing her beloved grandmother she felt like she didn't have any tears left. She just ached inside. No more Dotty, no more Luke. It felt like her foundations had been shaken and everything had shifted. But Jenny had been there for her, providing a listening ear and distracting her by turning the conversation to Dotty's secret letters.

Once they had chatted it all through, Annabel had announced her plan. 'I'm going to go to Singapore,' she had said, nodding decisively for emphasis. 'I'm going to go and find this Julia woman. She's the one who'll be able to tell me all about it. Dad was saying I should head off somewhere new, it is the holidays after all!'

A few days later, the plan was in place, the tickets were booked and Annabel had set off to Heathrow. Jenny had helped her out by putting her in touch with her cousin, Emma, who had moved to Singapore the previous year when her husband got a transfer with his bank. Emma was a music teacher at an international school out there and Jenny had often voiced her 'Facebook envy' whenever Emma shared photos of her new life, usually involving rooftop bars, pool parties or exotic beaches.

Annabel had met Emma a few years earlier, at Jenny's fortieth birthday party in Bath, and they had got on well. Jenny had put them in touch, messages had been exchanged and Emma had kindly offered Annabel a place to stay.

Before she knew it, Annabel was tidying away her hand luggage under the seat in front of her and fastening her seatbelt in preparation for landing. Through the window, she could see the coast of Singapore, a long, straight stretch where the turquoise waters fringed an endless line of tall, modern buildings. The late afternoon sun was casting a golden glow and the sky was turning a deep shade of indigo. Along the coastline, lights flickered on the ships. She was surprised to see so many along the bay, then remembered reading somewhere that it was one of the busiest ports in the world. The island itself, however, was tiny, measuring just thirty-one miles by seventeen.

It had been a smooth flight and the landing at Changi Airport was much the same. Within minutes, the plane was at the gate and Annabel was gathering her belongings to disembark. That knot of anxiety formed in her stomach again, but everything was fine as she made her way through immigration and baggage claim, and out to find a taxi. Emma had mentioned in her texts how well organised the airport was and Annabel was impressed. Even the taxi queue was smooth and efficient, with uniformed staff directing vehicles and passengers.

Stepping outside the cool airport building, however, had given her an introduction to the tropical Singapore climate. The sun had set quickly but despite its absence, the air was humid and sticky. Annabel longed to change into something cooler.

Within minutes, she was sitting in the back of one of the many blue and white taxis, enjoying the air conditioning as they drove away from the airport along a busy, three-laned highway. She marvelled at the never-ending mass of pink and purple flowers decorating the central reservation and the tunnel of trees through which they drove. Annabel was exhausted, but she felt herself relax a little; it all looked so beautiful and, for the first time, it occurred to her that she might actually enjoy her time here.

'You on holiday, ma'am?' the driver asked, his English punctuated by a strong Chinese-sounding accent. He caught her eye in the rear-view mirror, the wrinkles around his smiling eyes suggesting that he must be in his sixties.

'Yes.' Annabel returned the smile, deciding not to explain her real reason. 'I've come to uncover the secret former life of my recently-deceased grandmother and find out what on earth she was doing here in the 1930s,' probably wasn't an appropriate response, so she went with, 'I'm visiting some friends who live here. It's my first time, it looks so lovely!' Through the palm trees that lined the highway she caught sight of a long stretch of sandy beach beyond.

'You have good time here.' He nodded sagely. 'Singapore very safe for tourist. But remember, low crime does not mean no crime. Always stay safe. And drink a lot of water; is very hot.'

Annabel nodded and thanked him for his advice, and was pleased when he slipped into tour guide mode, recommending places to visit during her stay.

'And this big thing: Marina Bay Sands.' He pointed at the enormous, futuristic building ahead of them. It rose up like a ship on top of three huge towers, overlooking the bay. 'Is hotel, restaurants, shops, casino. Very big, very expensive. Fifty-five floor.'

'Wow!' She sighed, impressed. She had seen pictures of it, but the reality was something else. She remembered reading how it had been built on reclaimed land, that the only way the tiny island of Singapore could cater to its growing population was to extend its boundaries out into the ocean. 'It's amazing; it's all so modern.'

'Singapore change a lot.' The driver nodded in agreement, 'Is modern now. But before, many farms and kampongs –

villages – here. Mr Lee Kuan Yew, he change all that; he make it modern.'

Annabel had read about Singapore's history and recalled how Stamford Raffles had transformed the sleepy Malayan backwater into a thriving British trading post in the early 1800s. Then, under Prime Minister Lee Kuan Yew's forward-thinking leadership, it had become independent in 1965. Since then, it had gone from strength to strength, becoming one of the most important financial hubs in Asia.

They passed the endless skyscrapers of the downtown area and the driver's commentary continued as they headed out towards Emma's apartment complex in West Coast. Annabel's eyelids were feeling heavy and she was glad when they eventually stopped at the entrance to Blue Ocean Condominium. They passed through the security gate and the driver pulled up outside the first block, informing her that they had arrived.

Annabel got out of the taxi and felt the muggy warmth of the evening envelop her. She looked around, taking it all in. Blue Ocean was a collection of tall white apartment blocks that formed a horseshoe around lush green gardens. In the centre was the crowning glory: a beautiful swimming pool. The sky was completely dark now, but the walkways were illuminated by pretty lights.

The taxi driver took her case over to the lobby entrance. 'You have good time, ma'am!' he said with a smile. Annabel thanked him and handed over the fare, plus a little extra for a tip. She wasn't sure if she had got the currency conversion right – was it two Singapore dollars to a pound, or two pounds to a dollar? – she'd have to check with Emma.

Beside the entrance was a large screen with a series of buttons. Annabel's brain felt like cotton wool, she was so tired.

But she dug out her phone and reread Emma's message with the entry instructions. Relief flooded through her when, after pressing a series of buttons, a friendly voice came through the intercom. 'Hi Annabel! Come on up; level 10.' She shouldered her tote bag, dragged her suitcase and weary body into the lift, and pressed the button.

Seconds later, the door pinged open and there was Emma, a wide smile on her face and her bright eyes twinkling. In her late thirties, she was younger than her cousin Jenny, but there was a clear family resemblance in their shared dark colouring and mischievous smiles. Annabel loved their positivity and the fact that they always looked as if they were up to something. Wearing a long, floaty dress with her hair in loose waves around her shoulders, she was the epitome of summer chic. Annabel, in contrast, was anything but. Still in her travelling outfit of yoga pants, trainers and hoodie she felt hot, grimy and disgusting by comparison.

'You made it! Welcome to Singapore!' Emma wrapped her in a big, floral-scented hug and Annabel felt herself relax into it. She was so exhausted and had come so far that this little act of welcoming kindness made a lump form in her throat. She swallowed it down and returned the greeting.

'It's so good to see you again, Emma!' she said. 'And thanks ever so much for having me!'

'Oh gosh, no problem at all! I was delighted when I heard you were coming! Here, let me take that,' she continued, reaching for the suitcase. 'Now come on in!' She led the way across the hall and into the apartment.

They stepped into a softly lit open-plan area and Annabel followed Emma's lead and slipped off her shoes. The apartment was modern and shiny, with a lounge off to one side and a dining area on the other. Sizzling sounds and delicious scents wafted through from the slightly open kitchen door beside the hallway. A corridor led off the lounge area to doors beyond, which Annabel presumed to be the bedrooms.

It was much cooler inside, thanks to the gently humming air conditioning units, and she enjoyed the cool feeling of the tiled floor against her bare feet.

'Right,' Emma began after parking the suitcase, 'what do you need first? You must be shattered! Drink? Shower? Food? Sleep?!'

Annabel stifled a yawn and quipped, 'All of the above! I'm just not sure in which order!'

Emma chuckled and with a 'Come on in!' pushed open the door to the kitchen. 'Gloria,' she addressed the older Filipino lady with long, dark hair who was stirring a pan on the stove. 'This is our friend Annabel. Annabel, this is Gloria, our lovely helper. We'd be lost without her!'

Gloria turned and smiled, still stirring. She gave a slight nod of her head and said, 'Pleased to meet you, ma'am!'

Annabel smiled in reply.

'Let's get you some water. Warm or cold?' Emma asked, taking a glass from the cupboard. She saw Annabel's confusion and explained, 'Ah, well the water in the tap is always lukewarm, you see; the air temperature here rarely drops much below thirty degrees so the pipes are always warm.' Annabel asked for cold and Emma reached into the fridge for the water jug. She filled the glass and handed it to Annabel, explaining, 'Just top up the jug from the tap if it's ever running low.'

Annabel gulped down the icy-cold water while Emma checked with Gloria when dinner would be ready.

'OK then.' She checked her watch. 'We'll eat in about half an hour, if that's OK with you? Tom should be home by then.' She smiled at her guest. 'Glass of wine? Or fancy a cuppa?'

Annabel couldn't help but chuckle. Although her accent was much more neutral than her cousin's, Emma's northern background revealed itself on this last question. 'Gosh, you just sounded so much like Jenny just then! Yes please, a cuppa would be lovely.'

'Ha! I'll take that as a compliment . . . I think!' She grinned impishly and went to fill the kettle. 'Go and make yourself comfy on the sofa and get ready to fill me in on my cousin's latest shenanigans!'

Annabel made her way through to the lounge, enjoying the tranquil ambience of the place. The lamplight cast a soft glow and mellow tunes were coming through the TV speakers. She curled up in the corner of the sofa, nestled among a collection of soft cushions, and breathed in the scent of the nearby candles.

The apartment was elegant and stylish, with little evidence of Emma's young twins apart from a collection of framed family photos on the sideboard. Daniel and Leila were six years old and had recently started kindergarten in the same international school where Emma worked as a music teacher. Annabel had never met them, but saw from the photos that they were mini versions of Emma and her husband, Tom. Gap-toothed and grinning in the pictures with their proud parents, they looked like such happy children.

'I don't know how you do it,' Annabel said as Emma appeared, a mug in each hand. 'Most of my friends who have kids live in a state of general chaos, with toys permanently decorating the carpet! This place is amazing!'

Emma raised a wry eyebrow, 'It's all for your benefit, you know; you should have seen the place half an hour ago – frantic tidying up before sending them off to bed just before you arrived!' She grinned at Annabel. 'Here you go, madam; one builder's tea with milk. Cheers!' Annabel took her mug and clinked it against her host's.

'Cheers! It's so good to finally stop!' she said, closing her eyes for a moment. 'The flight seemed to last forever. I honestly don't know how you can fly back and forth like you do.'

'Well, it's not much fun and it'll take you a few days to get over the jet lag, but just make yourself at home here and take your time. You'll probably nod off fine at bedtime, but most likely end up wide awake in the wee small hours! I've got some melatonin if you want to try it; it's natural and will help you get back to sleep.'

They chatted as they drank their tea, with Emma asking Annabel all about life in Bath and enjoying hearing the titbits about her cousin Jenny's recent dating adventures. She roared with laughter as Annabel regaled her with the tale of Jenny accidentally matching with one of her students.

Emma's phone pinged and she reached for it to read the message. 'That's Tom. He's bringing our friend James home for dinner, I hope that's OK?' She frowned in concern, but Annabel smiled and nodded.

'They've been out watching the rugby this afternoon,' Emma continued. 'James has had a tough time recently; nasty separation.' She pulled a pained face. 'It was a long time coming, though, and, to be honest, he *is* better off without her. But she's just taken their daughter back to live in the UK, so it's all a bit raw for him, poor guy. Honestly though, you must be shattered; do just make yourself at home and don't feel you need to be polite. Have some food and then go and pass out whenever you need to!'

They finished their tea and Emma helped Annabel with her luggage and showed her to her room. There was just enough time for a shower in the en suite bathroom before dinner, and Annabel stood for a long while under the rainfall shower head, luxuriating in the feeling of the hot water on her weary body. It took all her efforts to get out and dry off, and she fought against the temptation to get straight into bed.

As she dressed, in a long, pale blue, cotton dress, she heard male voices: Tom and his friend had arrived. She ran a brush through her towel-dried hair, gave herself a quick spritz of perfume and a dash of lip gloss, and with a deep breath she went out to say hello.

'Here she is!' Tom stood up from the sofa, whisky glass in hand, and beamed at Annabel. 'It's so lovely to finally meet you, Annabel! I've only ever heard good things about you!'

Tom was a couple of inches taller than her and had a round, jovial face. He was a good-looking man with his shaggy, dark blonde hair and dimpled cheeks. Dressed in a bright pink polo shirt and cream shorts, he looked relaxed and a few drinks into being rather merry. He came over and kissed her politely on both cheeks.

'Right back at you, Tom!' She smiled brightly, warming to him instantly, as Jenny had said she would. 'And thanks so much for having me stay, it's so kind of you both.'

Out in the hallway, a toilet flushed and a door opened and closed. They had just sat down on the sofa and were talking about Annabel's journey when a taller figure came into the room.

'Annabel, this is our friend . . . ' Tom began.

Annabel looked up at the handsome, dark-haired newcomer and gave a small gasp. 'James!' she finished for him.

His brow furrowed as he gazed down at her. There was a long pause before he replied, 'Annabel? Annabel Penrose?'

She looked up at him. 'Yes! Wow, long time no see!'

'You two old friends?' Tom beamed, leaning back on the sofa, clearly enjoying the surprise reunion.

'Yes!' Annabel said.

'Not really,' James said at the exact same time. 'Well,' he continued, a little awkwardly, 'we knew each other a long time ago.'

'We were both at Trinity, at Oxford,' Annabel explained. She stood up and stepped forward to greet him. She leaned in to kiss his cheek but instantly felt clumsy when he offered his hand instead. She moved back and shook it, horribly aware of the awkwardness between them.

It had always been like this with James, all those years ago in Oxford. She had never figured out how to be around him or what she had ever done to make him so ill-at-ease. Fourteen years had passed since they had left university and nothing had changed. She forced a smile and mumbled something about it being good to see him again, but inside her stomach sank. It was going to be a long evening.

Emma reappeared, announcing that dinner was ready and they moved across the room to the dining table. Gloria had cooked a beef noodle stir fry and it was delicious. Annabel thought how lucky Emma and Tom were to have a domestic helper who not only seemed lovely and friendly, but was also a great cook. What a different way of life it was, being an expat out here. Back home, only wealthy families could afford full-time, live-in domestic help, but here, Emma had explained, it was the norm.

Their hosts were good company and the wine and the conversation both flowed easily. Emma chatted about her teaching role at the international school and how the twins were getting on in their first year of kindergarten, and Tom regaled them with tales from a recent stag weekend in Bangkok with some of his work colleagues. Annabel found herself wide-eyed and roaring with laughter as she heard about a late-night visit to a 'ping pong bar' in the red light district and the various talents of the scantily-clad performers. She laughed even harder at Tom's attempts to defend himself against Emma's raised eyebrow of mock disapproval. 'What was I meant to do, darling?' he asked his wife. 'I *had* to go with them, my love, I didn't have a choice!'

In contrast, James was a closed book. He resisted Annabel's attempts to draw him into conversation, giving short answers when she asked him where he worked – the British High Commission – and how long he'd been here – five years. He asked nothing in return. She noticed that he talked a little more freely with their hosts, but there was still a certain level of restraint. In the end, she gave up worrying; Emma had said that he'd been through a tough time recently, so maybe he just had things on his mind and it was nothing personal. She relaxed and focused her attention on the meal and her hosts. She would have loved to have taken Tom up on his multiple offers to top up her wine glass, but feared that any more alcohol would have her nodding off face down in her noodles.

'So, Annabel, I'm intrigued to hear more about this family research you're doing,' Tom said over dessert of tropical fruit. 'Emma told me your grandmother lived here before the war?'

'Yes, it's all been a bit of a surprise to be honest. Dotty – that's my granny – passed away recently. When I was going through her things, I found out that when she was younger she lived here in Singapore. It was before she married my grandfather and none of us knew anything about it. There's a lady I'd like to meet to find out more, her grandmother worked as a housemaid at Dotty's family home and they kept in touch for years. The grandmother passed away, but I have a feeling that her granddaughter – Julia – will be able to tell me more about it. The trouble is, I don't have an address for her and the usual online searches haven't been much help. I thought I might start at a public library, see if I can look at the census records or something?'

'Oh, don't worry about any of that!' Tom grinned confidently, 'If you want to find someone in Singapore, James here is your man!' He turned to his friend. 'You must have a contact through the High Com who could help with a bit of detective work?'

'Well, I'm not sure . . . ' James began uneasily.

'I wouldn't want to . . . ' Annabel said at the same time.

Emma looked between the two of them, a curious expression on her face. Her eyes narrowed, as if sensing the unease between them. 'It would be great if you could, James,' she said. 'I'm sure Annabel would be grateful. What do we know about this Julia woman, Annie?' She smiled encouragingly at her guest.

A lump formed again in Annabel's throat. Emma's use of the word 'we' and the pet version of her name showed a new bond that she suddenly felt grateful for. Every fibre of her body was exhausted and she was feeling a very long way from home and everything that was familiar to her.

She smiled. 'Julia Chan. Her grandmother was called Ah Ling Wong and she lived somewhere called . . . ' she paused, trying to remember it, 'Ang Mo Kio?' The others all nodded, recognising the name of a local residential district.

'Ah Ling was 93 in 2010, which made her two years older than Dotty. So, given that our grandmothers were a similar age, Julia can't be too far off my age, maybe a bit older?'

'She'll definitely be older.' Annabel was surprised to hear James speak up. Given his standoffish manner this evening, she was surprised that he'd been listening to her at all, never mind helping figure out ages. 'Typically, Asian women had children younger than Europeans, so she'll be older,' he added, his tone matter-of-fact.

'See?' Tom grinned at Annabel in a told-you-say way, 'I told you James would be the one to help!'

'I can't make any promises, but I'll see what I can do,' James muttered in reply.

Annabel was relieved when Emma got up to clear the table soon after – Gloria having finished her duties for the evening – and announced it was time to call it a night; they all had work the next day. James fiddled with his phone for a minute, then announced that his taxi was on its way. He shook Tom's hand, kissed Emma's cheek and gave Annabel a brief nod, saying that it had been nice to see her again. Then he was gone.

Annabel stood up and started collecting the glasses, but was soon stopped by Emma. 'Go to bed! You must be exhausted. And here, take these,' she handed her a glass of chilled water and a plastic container of melatonin tablets. 'We'll try to be quiet in the morning; I just hope the kids don't disturb you too much! Gloria will be around, so she can help if you want to do anything or go anywhere. And you've got my number, just message me if you need anything. Sleep well!' Emma hugged her tight and Annabel wished her good night.

As she made her way to her room, Annabel heard the conversation continue as Emma and Tom cleared the last few things from the table. 'What was up with James tonight?' she heard Emma ask her husband. 'I've never known him so quiet; he wasn't himself at all.' But then their voices became muffled as they disappeared into the kitchen and Annabel didn't catch the reply.

She sighed, wondering if her presence had affected James. She couldn't recall ever doing anything to offend him, so just didn't understand why he was – and always had been – so on edge around her? But the wondering didn't last long. As soon as her head hit the pillow, Annabel felt herself sucked into a deep and dreamless sleep.

CHAPTER II

Singapore

June 1938

'You did *what*?' Clara shrieked. It was the day after the Raffles Hotel dinner and the girls were in Dorothy's bedroom. Still feeling fragile, Dorothy was lying prone beneath the ceiling fan, a damp flannel on her forehead.

She winced; partly in mortification at the memory of the previous evening and partly because of the throbbing pain in her head. She was not used to drinking such strong cocktails and this hangover was the worst she had ever had. She closed her eyes and sighed. 'You heard me! Please don't make me say it again; I've never been so embarrassed in my life!'

Clara burst out laughing, then regained her composure as she saw the crestfallen look on her friend's face. 'Oh, you poor thing!' She leaned across and rubbed Dorothy's shoulder, giving her a sympathetic smile. 'But did you have fun? I saw you dancing with Douglas.' She raised her eyebrows briefly at this. 'Then Mummy had one of her headaches and dragged us all home! Honestly, I don't know why she couldn't just let me stay and get a lift home with you. Mothers!' She shook her head in frustration.

Dorothy sat up and took a sip of water. 'I barely had time to have any fun.' She screwed up her eyes and rubbed her temples. 'But before I made my hasty exit and redecorated the flowerbed, Douglas *was* very nice to me,' she continued cautiously. 'He's a wonderful dancer. And he's so handsome.' She looked up and saw disapproval etched all over her friend's face. 'I know you don't like him, Clara, but don't worry; I doubt he'll ever want to talk to me ever again after what happened. He's so grown-up and, well . . . sophisticated, I suppose. He'll never want to dance with a stupid girl who can't even hold a conversation, let alone her drink!' She hid her face in her hands and moaned.

'Oh, Dorothy!' Clara soothed. 'Don't worry, I'm sure it will soon be forgotten. And it's not that I don't like Douglas, exactly.' She sighed. 'I've just heard things about him that . . . Well, let's just say things that have earned him his nickname of Dangerous. Just be careful, that's all I'm saying.'

Dorothy fell asleep after Clara left. She awoke to find Ah Ling gently touching her shoulder.

'Miss,' she began as Dorothy blinked her eyes open. 'You have visitor.' The maid's face widened in a bright smile. 'He handsome man, miss! He bring you flower. Come now, put on nice dress.' Ah Ling held up the new royal blue tea dress she had already picked out.

Dorothy screwed up her face. She couldn't face seeing anyone, never mind a handsome man bringing her flowers. Who could it be? Matthew maybe? It couldn't possibly be Douglas. 'Oh, Ah Ling, I feel dreadful and I look an absolute mess! Can you make an excuse? Tell him I'm ill?'

'You so beautiful, miss, no need worry. I help you. Come, come!' The maid encouraged her out of bed and sat her in front of the dressing table.

'First, you drink this,' Ah Ling said, handing Dorothy a small glass containing an amber coloured liquid.

Dorothy took the glass and wrinkled her nose as she sniffed the hot drink. It was an intriguing mix of sweet and sour, with a tang of an unfamiliar spice.

'What is this?' she asked. She looked closely. 'It's got bits floating in it!'

'Salted plum and ginger tea, Miss. I make it for you,' Ah Ling said with a nod. 'It traditional Chinese cure, it make you better.'

Dorothy raised her eyebrows. 'Thanks, Ah Ling, that's very kind of you. The way I'm feeling today, I'm willing to try anything!'

'Bottoms up!' the housemaid said as Dorothy sipped the tea. Dorothy narrowly avoided spilling it everywhere, amused by another of Ah Ling's unexpected British phrases.

A few minutes later, wearing her new dress and with her hair pinned up, Dorothy pasted on a smile and slowly descended the stairs. She wasn't sure exactly what Ah Ling had brewed in the traditional remedy, but for the first time that day, she was finally feeling some relief from the nausea and headache. The housemaid was an absolute godsend.

Male voices were coming from the drawing room, talking and laughing, but fell silent when Dorothy entered.

'Ah, here she is! Hello Dodo!' Her father came over to kiss her on the cheek. She cringed at his use of her family pet name when she saw who was in the room, it sounded so childish. Dangerous Douglas stood up from his chair by the window and also made his way over to her.

He was looking dazzlingly handsome; clean shaven, fresh faced and smelling divine. He was dressed in smart linen trousers and a crisp, white short-sleeved shirt. He held out a bunch of pure white orchids.

'A little something for the patient.' He smiled down at Dorothy and gave her a wink. 'I was sorry you were unwell last night. I do hope you're feeling better today?'

Dorothy thanked him and her father muttered that it must have been something she'd eaten. 'I'm much better today,' she said. 'Thank you for asking.' She smiled up at him.

'Well, that is good news,' he continued. 'Because I was wondering if you might fancy a bit of fresh air? I need to take my motor out for a run and I was thinking about a drive along the coast. We could head out east towards Changi Point. There's a delightful little café by the beach where we could stop for refreshments.' He turned to Anthony and asked, 'If that's alright with you, sir?'

Her father cheerfully gave his consent and, before Dorothy knew it, Ah Ling was handing her a headscarf and she was on her way out to Douglas's car. It was a beautiful machine, polished chrome with immaculate white bodywork. With the roof folded down, the smart red leather interior was glowing in the sunshine.

Douglas opened the door for her. Her heart raced as she tied her headscarf and slid on her sunglasses. She caught a glimpse of her reflection in the mirror and was pleased with what she saw. Alongside the handsome Douglas, she really did look the part; a perfect Joan Crawford to his Clark Gable, just like in the movie *Love on the Run*.

They set off at a steady pace along the residential roads. When they reached the highway, Douglas opened up the throttle. It was another hot, sunny day and Dorothy loved the feel of the cool breeze on her face and the pure thrill of it as they sped along. Douglas was a skilled driver, manoeuvring the motorcar with deft precision as they followed the road through the town and out along the coast.

They left the city behind, then passed through rural kampongs and plantations before eventually reaching Changi, a small fishing village at the far eastern end of the island. It was a busy spot with locals going about their business and street hawkers calling out, offering cold drinks and freshly cooked fish. Dorothy was fascinated, it was unlike anything she had seen before. She made a fuss of the children who came to say hello, delighting in their smiles and ignoring their grubby faces.

Douglas was less delighted, especially when dirty little fingers began poring over the car's bodywork. He shooed the children away, then gave instructions to a nearby hawker and handed over some notes from his wallet. He was obviously entrusting the man with the safekeeping of the sedan. Then Douglas put on his Panama hat, offered Dorothy his arm and escorted her the short distance to the café.

'Oh, this is charming!' Dorothy gushed when the owner showed them out to the back of the building and onto the terrace. From the road, the café hadn't looked anything special, a simple, rustic building with a tin roof. But the view from the back, out across emerald-green waters to the islands in the distance, was spectacular. The tables were covered in black-and-white-checked fabric with vases of bright pink ginger flowers in the centre.

Douglas ordered tea for them, as well as something Dorothy had never heard of before. 'They're called *kueh*,' Douglas explained as the waiter brought over a plate of brightly coloured little desserts. 'Local Malay sweets, made from pandan, coconut, rice and tapioca. Not exactly your classic Victoria sponge, but they're not too bad.'

Dorothy tucked in and found herself enjoying the flavours, even if the glutinous texture was a little rubbery. She sipped the black tea and sat back in her chair. She was enjoying the feeling of being out exploring in a new country, eating new food with a very handsome new man. Douglas was easy company and conversation flowed effortlessly from their upbringings back home in England – hers in London and his on his family estate in rural Wiltshire – to their musical tastes, hobbies and passions.

'So tell me, what brought you out here?' she asked, curious to learn more about him.

'Ambition, I suppose.' He shrugged with a wry smile. 'I wanted to make a name for myself, not just live off my parents' money. And, much as I loved growing up at Highcliffe Manor, after I finished at Oxford I just couldn't wait to get away from home and see a bit of the world. I started working at McKinley's in London a couple of years ago and when the chance of promotion and foreign travel came up last year, well, I jumped at it!'

After a while, he glanced at his watch and waved to the café owner for the bill. 'I wish we could stay longer, but I'm afraid I've got a couple of things I need to attend to this evening,' he explained.

'Oh, please don't apologise, it has been so lovely. Thank you for inviting me.' She smiled at him then finished the rest of her tea.

'Thank *you* for coming. An afternoon with a delightful young lady; the pleasure is all mine, I assure you.'

He took one of the pink flowers from the vase on the table and presented it to her with mock formality. 'A pretty flower for a pretty lady.' Dorothy grinned and felt a warm glow inside as she took it from him.

'Gosh, after I made such a fool of myself last night, I'm surprised you even wanted to talk to me again, never mind invite me out for tea and pay me compliments!'

He studied her for a moment and she instantly regretted her candour. She should try to be more grown-up, more sophisticated, surely that was what a man like Douglas liked. Casting her mind back to the exquisite hauteur of his former flame, Maria da Costa, Dorothy suddenly felt horribly child-like and gauche. She felt her colour rising and suddenly wanted to go home.

Douglas seemed to sense her unease and reached across the table. With his index finger, he slowly traced the outline of her cheek. 'But you are, you know; very pretty indeed.' His touch felt like a bolt of electricity and Dorothy felt herself back away. Awkwardly, she stood up from the table, a nervous smile on her face. She had no experience of men like Douglas and had felt on much safer ground discussing their favourite authors and movies than with him flirting and flattering her.

They got back to the car and Douglas nodded his thanks to the hawker. He was about to open the door for Dorothy when he looked down and noticed that she was still carrying the flower he had given her.

'You brought it with you?' He seemed amused. 'Oh, Dorothy, you are such a sweet one! I don't know quite what to do with you. So young and innocent; so utterly adorable!' He bent down and, without warning, brushed his lips against hers. She closed her eyes, but the kiss was over before she knew it and Douglas was opening the car door for her. Dorothy got in, pulse racing, desperately wanting more.

CHAPTER 12

Singapore

MONDAY 1ST APRIL, 2019

It was nearly lunchtime when Annabel finally awoke the next day. Her mouth was dry and her nose was feeling stuffy from the air conditioning. There was a fresh glass of water on the bedside table – presumably thanks to Gloria – and she gulped it down.

As predicted, jet lag had played havoc with her system and she'd spent most of the early hours tossing and turning. Despite her exhaustion, sleep had proved elusive. She had eventually nodded off again at around 6 a.m., with the help of Emma's magic tablets, and had slept soundly through the rigmarole of the family's morning routine.

Her head felt fuzzy and she reached for her handbag in search of painkillers. Then she checked her phone. There were several messages, one from Emma, checking that everything was alright, one from Jenny, another from her brother and a couple from Luke. She sighed at Luke's tone as she read these last ones. It started off conciliatory then seemed to grow frustrated as the hours had passed and she hadn't replied. Maybe she should have told him that she was out of the country. But then she stopped herself: was it really any of his business anymore?

A wave of homesickness suddenly swept through her, making her stomach sink. What was she doing here? Was it really Dotty's history that had brought her, or had it just been a convenient excuse to run away? It suddenly felt daunting being so far away from home, but the thought of returning to Bath and resetting her life without Luke and Dotty was equally stomach-churning. She felt as if she were in limbo.

Annabel enjoyed a long, refreshing shower, then dressed and padded through the silent apartment to the kitchen. She still felt exhausted and was glad of the peace and quiet. As she opened the fridge in search of cold water, another door opened into the kitchen and Gloria emerged from her room, smiling and wishing her good morning.

Annabel was soon settled at the dining table with cereal, orange juice and a much-needed coffee. There was something comforting about the gentle presence of the lovely Gloria, who felt like something of a grandmother figure in the family. Steady and efficient, she quietly got on with the business of running the home and keeping everything ticking along behind the scenes.

'How long have you been in Singapore, Gloria?' Annabel asked when the older lady reappeared with a platter of fruit.

'Twenty year, ma'am.'

Annabel was shocked. 'Gosh, you've been away from home a long time! Do you have a family?'

'Yes, ma'am, three children, ma'am; all in Philippines. All grown up, have their own children now. My sister, she take care of them when they are little.'

Annabel tried not to let her shock register on her face. 'You must miss them very much. It must have been hard for you to have been away from them for so long.'

'Yes and no, ma'am,' Gloria replied, after briefly considering the question. 'No job in Philippines. Is good money working here. I pay for my children go to university, give them good future, ma'am. And very happy here with Mrs Emma, she very kind boss.' Her face broke into a wide smile. 'She pay for me go visit my family twice a year, is very nice. Some of my friends here, their boss not nice' – her brow furrowed at this – 'but I have second family here, ma'am, I'm very lucky.'

Gloria smiled and, with a parting nod, returned to the kitchen, leaving Annabel mulling over what she had said. What a price to pay to give your children a head start in life, to leave them behind in someone else's care and move overseas to look after a stranger's family. She had warmed to Gloria immediately, but respected her all the more after hearing her story. She felt glad that she'd found such a lovely home among Emma's family. Her mind wandered to Ah Ling and the way she had played a similar role in Dotty's family. Had she had to make sacrifices like Gloria had? Annabel was eager to find out more.

Annabel finished her breakfast and replied to her messages from her friends and her brother. She had no desire to reply to Luke and found herself deleting his last few texts.

It was another beautiful day and Annabel decided to spend some time down by the swimming pool. She was looking forward to a dip and some lazy sunlounger time with her book. She was keen to make the most of her time in Singapore and do some sightseeing, and had marked several sights in her new guidebook during the flight. But that could wait for another day; today she was tired and just needed to relax and recharge her batteries. Gloria gave her a pool towel, a bottle of water and a key card so that she could let herself back into the building, then tucked a banana and a home-made cookie in her bag as she left. The woman really was a marvel.

Annabel went down in the lift, crossed the foyer and stepped out into the condo gardens. The early-afternoon heat met her like a solid wall and beads of sweat gathered on her lip within moments. How anyone ever got used to living in this, she couldn't fathom. She took her time following the winding path through the lush greenery, admiring the tall palm trees and exotic flowers along the way. She passed flame-orange birds of paradise and bright pink ginger, and delighted in the scent of the delicate white jasmine and soft yellow frangipani. It was a sensory overload, the sights and scents were a heady mix. She smiled and said hello to a couple of staff who were out working, pruning the bougainvillea bushes and sweeping the paths.

It was a relief to reach the pool and escape the direct heat of the sun underneath an umbrella. She put down her bag and stripped off her dress, flip-flops and sunglasses. After a quick spray of sunscreen for her face and shoulders, she straightened her cornflower-blue bikini and slid straight into the water.

In contrast to the sun's powerful rays, the water felt chilly and she swam a full length of the pool to acclimatise. It was a quiet afternoon in the condo and, apart from one mum with an excited toddler in the shallow end, she had the pool to herself. It felt good to cool down and shake off the lethargy of the jet lag, and she swam a full ten lengths before climbing out.

Annabel dried herself off with the warm towel, had a long drink of water then stretched out on the sunlounger, enjoying the shade of the umbrella. She thought of her little house in Bath and how different her life was from Emma and Tom's. Apartment living had never appealed to Annabel and she enjoyed having her own space. But having tropical gardens and a pool like this on her doorstep could help her change her mind, she thought, smiling to herself. It must feel like being on holiday all the time.

She took out her book and relaxed. The sunlounger was comfortable and she was feeling all warm and cosy. Three pages in, her eyelids became heavy and sleep took over.

An enormous crack of lightning woke Annabel with a jolt a while later, her heart racing as she resurfaced from the depths of a foggy, jet-lagged nap. It was followed by a low, menacing rumble and what sounded like rapid gunfire. She sat up, trying to make sense of the scene around her. Gone was the beautiful blue sky from earlier, replaced by stormy black rain clouds and a torrential downpour. The heavens had well and truly opened and rain was bouncing off the ground and splashing all around her.

The sky crackled again, spurring her into action. Heart still racing, she quickly gathered her belongings and shoved them back in her bag before throwing her dress over her still-damp bikini. She slid her feet into her flip-flops and, carrying the towel over her head in lieu of an umbrella, she ran along the path back to Emma's apartment block. Deep puddles had formed and it was soon apparent that the flip-flops were useless. She kicked them off and scooped them up with her free hand, then splashed barefoot along the rest of the flooded pathway and into the safety of the entrance lobby.

Annabel had never seen anything like it; this ferocious deluge had come out of nowhere. She had been asleep for less than twenty minutes, yet in that time the weather had done a complete one-eighty. She wasn't scared of thunderstorms, but she didn't exactly love them either. She was glad to be safely back inside.

Gloria had a towel and a sympathetic smile ready for her when she came in.

'You OK, ma'am? The weather change very quick here. Always take umbrella!'

Annabel thanked Gloria and locked away that little nugget of information for future outings.

Half an hour later, Annabel had dried off and was curled up on the sofa with her book and a cup of tea. Gloria was ironing in the dining area and the radio played softly in the background. Annabel had spent a good few minutes watching the lightning storm from the safety of the living-room balcony, absolutely fascinated. Still, the rain continued to machine-gun down outside.

Just after half past three, a key turned in the lock and the door burst open noisily as Emma and the twins tumbled in.

'We're home!' Emma called cheerfully, as she steered the children through the routine of depositing school bags and removing wet shoes.

'Sorry we're a bit late, it took forever to get a cab! Always does when it's raining.'

Annabel got up from the sofa and went over to say hello. She was given a warm hug from Emma and curious glances from the twins, who were dressed in their school uniform of green polo shirt and black shorts. Annabel bent down to their level and introduced herself. They smiled at her and said a shy hello.

'Thank you, Leila, for letting me stay in your bedroom. It's very kind of you to share with your brother so I can sleep in there. I brought you a little something from England to say thank you.' The little girl's face lit up and Annabel brought out a gift bag from the toy shop back in Bath.

'Here you go, I hope you like Lego?' Annabel smiled as she handed Leila a dinosaur kit from the bag. Leila gasped in delight and thanked her new friend with a wide beam. Her brother watched on, pleased for his sister, but Annabel spotted a slight hint of envy on his young face.

'And Daniel . . .' She paused dramatically. 'Thank you for putting up with your sister invading your bedroom while I'm here!' She winked at the young boy and pulled out a second Lego race car kit. His face turned into a broad grin. He had Tom's cheerful round face and the same dimples when he smiled.

'Thank you, Annabel, I love Lego! Mummy, can we do it now? Pleeease?' Emma nodded and with a celebratory 'Yes!' Daniel took his gift over to the dining area. He showed it to Gloria, who helped him open the packet then sat down with him to offer a helping hand.

Feeling bolder now, Leila said, 'I came to see you this morning but you were still asleep. You were snoring quite loudly. Thank you for my lovely present.' With a front tooth missing, she beamed a gappy six-year-old smile then, blonde pigtails swinging, she followed her brother over to the table. Annabel chuckled and Emma rolled her eyes in embarrassment.

'Let's leave this mad house and go out tonight!' Emma said. 'Fancy a cocktail or three? I reckon it's time to give you a proper Singapore welcome!'

CHAPTER 13

Singapore
NOVEMBER 1938

Dorothy had never been happier. She was completely infatuated with Douglas and couldn't believe her luck that he was interested in her. For the next few months, he took her out once a week in a gentle, steady courtship. They explored the island together, driving in his car or going for walks in the Botanical Gardens or on one of the beaches. They went to the movies, played tennis and had dinner in smart restaurants.

Her favourite nights were when he took her dancing, either at the Tanglin Club or at Raffles Hotel. After a couple of cocktails (she had learned to hold her drink better after that first, fateful night), she loved nothing more than getting lost in the music as she whirled around the dance floor in Douglas's strong arms. They drew curious glances wherever they went and their names were often the subject of whispered gossip. Not that Dorothy either heard or cared; so swept up was she in Douglas's attention.

For their part, Dorothy's parents were delighted that her daughter had the attention of such a handsome and successful young man, and wondered how long it would be before an announcement would be made.

Dorothy was desperately happy, falling head over heels in love with her gorgeous man. But, secretly, she wondered if something was missing. She longed for Douglas to take her in his arms and kiss her passionately, like they did in the movies, but the most she had got was a bit of hand holding and a chaste farewell kiss at the end of each outing. He was full of compliments, but from the words he used – dear, pretty, little, sweet, adorable – she worried he saw her as a child, and not as the hot-blooded woman she was fast becoming, fighting to keep a lid on her increasing passion and desire.

Dorothy longed to talk to Clara about it and ask for her friend's advice. She was far more experienced when it came to men, but from the outset, Clara had shown little enthusiasm about her and Douglas's burgeoning relationship. It had even become a source of tension between the pair. From time to time, Clara tried to warn her off him, but Dorothy refused to listen.

'All I'm saying is be careful, Dorothy. There's talk, you know. People are saying that Douglas and Maria—'

'Oh for goodness' sake,' Dorothy had interrupted angrily. 'Why are you listening to gossip, Clara? What do they know? I know that it's *me* Douglas is interested in; *me* that Douglas is courting. Maria da Costa is engaged to another man, it's over between them.' Her forehead creased in an angry frown. 'I don't understand why you're being so unkind. Are you jealous, Clara, is that it?'

'No Dorothy, don't be so ridiculous,' Clara had snapped back. 'I'm your friend and I just don't want to see you get hurt. I don't trust Douglas and I don't think you should, either.'

'Enough, Clara! Please stop. I don't want to hear malicious gossip about the man I love.' Dorothy closed her eyes and took a deep breath to calm herself. Then she opened her eyes and pasted a smile on her lips. 'Now, let's change the subject, please, I don't want us to fall out.'

Five blissful months passed, during which time Dorothy did her best to ignore the occasional mutterings that she heard about Douglas. She also tried hard to ignore the niggling worry about the lack of passion in their courtship. Douglas was just being gentlemanly, she reassured herself. It would be different when they were married. And he *was* going to propose, she was sure of it. They were in love with each other and nothing could persuade her otherwise.

It was the night of the St Andrew's ball and Douglas had invited Dorothy to go as his date. Unfortunately, she had been forced to let him down at the last minute, after coming down with a rotten headache in the afternoon. She had given up the idea of dancing the night away with her handsome man and gone to bed feeling rather sorry for herself instead.

Shortly afterwards, Ah Ling had tiptoed into the room carrying a tray bearing a glass of muddy brown liquid.

Dorothy raised her eyebrows questioningly, but knew enough about Ah Ling's ancient remedies to trust her.

Ah Ling smiled as she handed her the glass. 'It called Chuan Xiong Cha Tiao San. I make it for you, make head feel better.'

Yet again, Ah Ling's magical cure did the trick and when Dorothy woke from her nap, just before eight o'clock, she was feeling completely better. She saw her new dress hanging on the wardrobe door and felt a pang of disappointment that she was missing all the fun. Moments later, she was out of bed and calling for Ah Ling to help her get ready. She couldn't wait to see Douglas at the club and smiled to herself as she pictured the surprise on his face.

Less than an hour later, Dorothy stepped out of the car and into the lobby of the Tanglin Club. She spotted her friend Rebecca Dalziel there with her beau, Jeremy, cooling off with a long glass of something on ice. Rebecca smiled as she came in and complimented her on her new dress.

'You haven't seen Douglas, have you?' Dorothy asked.

'Yes.' Rebecca's brow creased in thought. 'Just a few minutes ago, actually. He was heading outside, in the direction of the tennis—'

Jeremy cut her off, his normally cheerful face turning suddenly serious. 'But come and get a drink first, Dorothy. I'm sure Douglas will be back in a minute. He's probably gone for a smoke, you know what he's like. Come on.'

He took her elbow and made to steer her towards the bar. Dorothy wondered why he was so serious tonight; this wasn't the usual, jolly Jeremy she knew. But she didn't spend long pondering it. Instead, she thanked them, slipped out of Jeremy's grasp and rushed out into the dark.

Dorothy grinned as she made her way along the lamplit path towards the tennis courts. She couldn't wait to see Douglas's reaction at her arrival. Past the terrace she hurried, then down the hill. The lights ended here and it took her eyes a moment to adjust to the darkness. She could hear a male voice up ahead and stopped to listen. Yes, it was Douglas.

Dorothy followed the direction of the sound and it led her all the way to him. He was in the equipment store at the side of the tennis court. She pushed the door open and was surprised that it was dark inside. But she could tell that he was not alone. Dorothy's face twisted in confusion as she tried to make sense of what she saw. A tangled mess of red satin fabric and black evening dress. Among this, the moonlight highlighted bare flesh, as arms and legs writhed together.

Hot and sweaty, moaning and panting; there could be no misinterpretation of the scene. She heard a startled cry and realised it had come from her. The movement stopped and she found herself staring into the dark, sultry eyes of Maria da Costa.

Clara took no pleasure in having been right. She consoled her friend as best she could, reassuring her that she was better off without the cheating Douglas. But Dorothy was bereft. He called at her home several times but she stayed in her bedroom and refused to see him. She instructed Ah Ling to send him away and return the stream of messages, cards and flowers that followed.

Dorothy's parents were disappointed that the courtship had ended, but she did not elaborate on the reason. Despite the way he had treated her, she was not a spiteful person and, given that Douglas worked with her father, she did not wish to ruin his opinion of him.

Over the next few months, Dorothy's life in Singapore found a gentler rhythm. She avoided the parties and clubs where she might bump into Douglas. Instead, she applied herself to her dream of working for a newspaper and enrolled in a secretarial course. She spent time quietly at home, practising her typing and shorthand, or with the new girlfriends she had met on the course. It was a relief to make new friends away from the social scene in which Douglas was involved.

Despite the earlier unpleasantness over Douglas, Dorothy was glad that Clara remained a close friend. The two would go shopping together, or spend time sunbathing by the pool in Clara's garden. From time to time, Clara's cousin Matthew would join them when he came home from work, and Dorothy found herself looking forward to these occasions more and more.

Matthew's gentle, steady manner was exactly what she needed after the rollercoaster of emotions she had experienced with Douglas. There was no great fuss or fanfare with him, no flattery or great charm offensive; Matthew was kind, gentle and honest. He treated Dorothy with nothing but the utmost respect. Little by little, she recovered from the whirlwind of Douglas's romantic attentions and felt she had grown wiser from the experience.

Time ticked by and a whole year in Singapore had passed. Dorothy spent her days helping her mother with her various charities and practising her secretarial skills. She was achieving excellent marks in her tests and, as hoped, Clara's father, Walter Davies, had managed to pull some strings and arrange some work experience for her at a local newspaper.

Dorothy was feeling content. She felt busy and useful, not to mention safe in this quieter, steadier post-Douglas life. She had a devoted friend in Matthew and felt entirely comfortable with him. After his initial six months of training at the bank, he had extended his stay in Singapore indefinitely and that had made Dorothy very happy. She enjoyed their conversations and his easy company, and, little by little, he helped her feel more like her old self again.

Despite Clara's gentle teasing to the contrary, Dorothy was adamant that her friendship with Matthew was just that; a friendship. After her experience with Douglas, she was not ready for any more romance. But maybe, one day, that might change. Dorothy hoped it would.

CHAPTER 14

Singapore

Monday 1st April, 2019

A couple of hours later, Emma and Annabel were getting ready to go out. Emma had suggested a rooftop bar in the downtown Marina Bay area of the city. Tom was working late, on a conference call with his company's US office, so it would just be the two of them. They had an early dinner with the children, after which Annabel read them a story while Emma sorted a few things for work, then they left the children's bedtime routine in Gloria's capable hands.

The rain stopped as quickly as it had started and, within half an hour, the storm had blown over and the flooded pavements and roads had cleared. The air had lost its earlier mugginess and now had a fresh, earthy scent. To Annabel's relief, it felt much cooler as they stepped outside and got in the taxi to head downtown.

The sun had set by the time they reached the CBD and Annabel recognised some of the sights from the taxi ride the previous evening. She gazed up at the brightly lit skyscrapers and felt the thrum of the city. The roads were busy with early-evening traffic and the pavements were buzzing; a mix of locals, expats, tourists and office workers. Office lights were still on and people were still working. What time did they finish? According to Emma, many didn't. With so many international businesses, like Tom's, working across different time zones, this really was a city that didn't sleep. Annabel thought of her lovely Bath and how quiet and provincial it seemed in comparison; by around 2 a.m. everything was closed up for the night and the lights were all off. Here, it all felt so alive, so vibrant.

'OK, so we're going to one of my favourite visitor spots! It's a bar on the rooftop of the National Gallery,' Emma explained. 'It has the most amazing view and the cocktails are delicious!'

The taxi dropped them outside the long, columned building of the gallery and they took the lift right to the top. They went through the bar, a stylish and modern place with mellow jazz music and low lighting, and Annabel gasped as the waiter led them out to their table on the balcony.

'Wow! You weren't wrong about the view!' Open-mouthed, she gazed out at the panorama. 'It's fantastic!'

Ahead of them was the large, green Padang, where Annabel spotted a floodlit cricket match taking place. The Padang had been the site of parades and ceremonies over the years, Emma explained, but was now mainly used as a sporting venue, with the Singapore Cricket Club at one end and Recreation Club at the other. Beyond the Padang, she could see the sparkling water of the bay, reflecting the lights of the skyscrapers and the little tourist 'bumboats' as they made their way around the bay and up the river. A pair of domed, spiky-roofed buildings sat off to the left, the Esplanade Theatres, Emma told her, designed to look like the local fruit, the spiky durian. Her friend also pointed out the large Ferris wheel attraction known as the Singapore Flyer and the quirky, lotus-shaped ArtScience building.

But the icing on the cake was straight ahead of them, across the water: the fabulous, glittering skyline of Marina Bay Sands.

The iconic landmark looked even more spectacular lit up at night. Annabel got her phone out to take photos while Emma ordered a couple of Singapore Slings.

'When in Rome! Or, rather, Singapore!' she quipped to Annabel when the long, pink drinks arrived and they raised them in a toast. 'Cheers!'

'And thanks again for having me!' Annabel smiled back before taking her first sip. 'Ooh, that is delicious! Well, I've only been here just over twenty-four hours, but I'm definitely enjoying it so far. Life is pretty good, I can see why you like living here!'

Emma laughed. 'It's not bad, hey? Sometimes I get stuck in the daily grind of work and kids, and forget to come down and enjoy all this.' She raised her glass and indicated the beautiful view. 'So it's great to have you here to remind me how lovely it is!'

'And having Gloria must make things so much easier, she's amazing!' Annabel said, before taking another sip of her cocktail. The fruity drink was delicious and was slipping down far too easily.

'I know! I wasn't joking when I said we'd be lost without her! She's so good with the kids and keeps the apartment and all of us on track. And it's so easy to go out when we have a live-in babysitter. I honestly don't know what we'll do when we have to move home again one day!' She pulled a horrified face and Annabel laughed.

'Hmm, you'll have to do what the rest of us mere mortals do and do your own washing up and cleaning!' She grinned mischievously at her friend.

'Let's not think about that!' Emma screwed her eyes closed in a bid to make the unwelcome thought disappear. Then she opened them again and smiled. 'We'll just enjoy it for now, the kids are happy at school and it's all so safe for them here. And now they're a bit older, hopefully we can start doing a bit more travelling with them and see the area a bit more. There are so many great places nearby, all within just a couple of hours' flight; Malaysia, Indonesia, Thailand, Cambodia, Vietnam' – she held up her fingers, counting them off – 'and the flights are pretty cheap.' An idea hit her and her face lit up. 'Come for longer next time and we can go and do a bit of exploring! Ooh, and bring Jenny, that would be even more fun!'

Annabel grinned at the idea and nodded. Midweek cocktails were right up Jenny's street and she knew she would love this place.

They worked their way through another couple of cocktails on the menu and Annabel felt herself relax. There was a gentle breeze out on the balcony which made the balmy temperature perfect. The venue was fabulous, the view amazing and the company fun. She found herself opening up when Emma asked her about recent events with Dotty and Luke and it felt good to talk. Emma was a good listener and, now that a bit of time had passed, Annabel was finding it helpful to talk things through.

After a while, Emma checked her watch and pulled a face; she had work in the morning and they should make a move. They took the lift down and were just arriving at the taxi rank when a vacant cab pulled up.

Emma had just opened the door and was telling the driver their destination, when Annabel gasped.

'Oh my goodness! The white church!' she interrupted, grabbing her friend's arm. She pointed at a building across the road. 'Can we have a quick look?'

'St Andrew's?' Emma asked, following her gaze. She apologised to the cab driver, closed the car door and followed Annabel across the road. Annabel seemed drawn like a magnet to the snow-white, Gothic structure that was glowing in the floodlights.

'Yes!' Annabel said, a smile of recognition spreading across her face as Emma caught up with her. They stopped at the railings that bordered the cathedral gardens. 'This is it; the church from the wedding photo! This is where Dotty became Mrs Llewellyn in 1939! But I guess finding it was the easy bit.' She sighed. 'Next, I need to find out *who* she married.' She screwed her face up as she looked at Emma. 'It's been baffling me since I saw the photo: who the hell was her *Mr* Llewellyn?'

CHAPTER 15

Singapore
May 1940

Dorothy stood in the shade of the Saga tree outside St Andrew's Cathedral and took a deep breath. Her heart was racing and, as she looked down at her bouquet of pink roses, she saw that her hands were trembling. The last couple of months had been such a whirlwind and she had been swept along by the romance and excitement of it all. But was she doing the right thing? She closed her eyes and concentrated on taking slow, steady breaths.

Her first two years in Singapore had flown by and so much had changed. She had completed her training and now had a part-time position working as a secretary for the women's page at a local newspaper, the *Straits Times*. She loved the sense of purpose that she got from going out to work, not to mention the independence of earning her own money and not always relying on her parents.

Despite her initial misgivings about leaving London, Dorothy had adjusted to life in South East Asia relatively smoothly, largely thanks to her close friendship with Clara. Her new friend didn't have Daisy's musical talents or dress-making skills, but she was always so much fun to be around and had introduced Dorothy to an exciting new set of friends. Life had taken on a pleasant routine of cinema outings, shopping trips, tennis at the Tanglin Club, family picnics at the cricket on the Padang, and cocktails and dancing at the Raffles Hotel.

Slowly but surely, Dorothy had grown accustomed to the heat and had fallen in love with the lush tropical greenery of the island. She spent much of her time at home outdoors, either on the veranda or in the garden, where these days not even the resident monitor lizard or monkeys could bother her. She loved her family's beautiful black and white home on Nassim Road and the kind, gentle staff who took care of them there. She had grown close to Ah Ling, who had become something of a big sister and confidante to her. It was an unlikely friendship, and one which her mother disapproved of, but Dorothy valued it greatly.

Part of her, however, still missed her old life in London and, now that England was at war with Germany, she worried terribly about her loved ones back home. Life had not changed in Singapore; they were so far removed from the horrors of war and she felt guilty to be living in such a bubble of privileged safety. But the newspapers were full of the relentless bombing attacks on the capital and the reports filled her with dread. In Daisy's most recent letter, she had written that a bomb had landed just three streets away, destroying a terrace of four houses. Their school friend Maisie Brown and her whole family had been killed that night. Dorothy prayed that they had all been asleep and had known nothing about it.

Daisy's news wasn't all bleak and Dorothy loved hearing about her new beau, Bert, as well as her new job as a seamstress at Barkers of Kensington department store. She was so proud of her friend and the steadfast way in which she was just getting on with it all. On top of working a full-time job, she had also started volunteering for fire-watching duties at night. How did Daisy find the energy to do it all? Despite the danger, part of Dorothy wished that she was still in London with her, going through the highs and lows of wartime together. She missed her so much and wished with all her heart that she could have been here with her today. But what would her childhood friend have made of it all? She had written to tell her the news, but the post took so long to cross the thousands of miles between them that she had not yet received a reply. Part of her knew that Daisy's cautious nature would probably have advised differently. But then she reminded herself, despite being the closest of friends, they had very different characters.

One big relief to Dorothy was that her brother, Thomas, *had* made it to Singapore in time. He had recently finished his medical training, it having been expedited due to the onset of war. On his return to London after the wedding, he would be due to start his military training, having been exempted from conscription while completing his studies. Doctors were in high demand during wartime and he would, doubtless, soon be whisked off to patch up wounded soldiers in some far-flung danger zone. She was so proud, but terrified about what might happen to him.

Dorothy loved having her brother here, even if they had argued terribly yesterday. Dear Thomas, he was always looking out for her, but this time he had taken the 'big brother' responsibility too far. It was time for him to accept she was a grown woman who could make her own decisions. But was it the right decision? She hoped with all her heart that it was. And that meant hoping that her brother had been wrong.

'Dorothy? Are you ready?' her father's voice broke into her thoughts.

She opened her eyes and looked up into his, hoping for some sort of guidance. But there was none. He glanced quickly at his wristwatch and tried to mask the sigh that followed. It was twenty minutes after the appointed hour. Anthony Templeton loved his daughter, but he hated tardiness.

'I . . . ' she began, but was interrupted by the photographer asking her to smile with her father. She obeyed, then watched her father move closer to the open door; a subtle hint that it was time to get the show on the road.

Ah Ling came over to smooth down her dress and spread it out on the ground behind her. Then she reached up to give her hair one final adjustment. She looked deep into Dorothy's eyes and seemed to sense her churning emotions. She leaned in close, pretending to fix a hairclip.

'Miss Dorothy, you no need do this,' she whispered quickly. 'You change mind if you no want do. Is no problem, I help you, will be OK.'

Mr Templeton looked over and cleared his throat, and the maid, suddenly a picture of innocence, tucked a wayward strand of hair behind Dorothy's ear.

'And a photograph of you on your own please, Miss Templeton,' the photographer called. He had been adjusting his equipment and was ready again.

Dorothy forced a nervous smile and pulled Ah Ling to her side before replying, 'I'd like one with Ah Ling, please.'

The photographer raised his eyebrows at this, evidently finding this a little unusual, but followed the instruction and set up for the shot.

Dorothy wrapped her free hand around Ah Ling's waist and they both smiled for the camera.

'Cheese!' Ah Ling said, making Dorothy smile at her knowledge of yet another unexpected Western practice. She was full of surprises.

Dorothy found such reassurance in Ah Ling's presence. Hearing her offer – so devotedly and bravely – to help her find a way out had made her realise that she *did* want to go through with it. She had given her word and she would not go back on it; she would not let her family down. And if she could put all her doubts to one side and quell the nagging thoughts in her head, she *was* excited. She *did* love him, she felt sure of that. She could make it work and they could be happy together, she was sure. Sometimes, she thought to herself, you just had to take a leap of faith.

She gave Ah Ling a determined smile and nod before walking over to her father and taking hold of his arm. They stepped into the cool interior of the cathedral and the organ music began.

The church was packed. Despite their relatively short time on the island, the Templetons had made many friends and connections, and her mother had seen today as the perfect occasion to cement the family into Singapore society.

Her father squeezed her hand as they reached the front of the church and smiled down at her before stepping away. She turned and looked up into her groom's shining eyes and all her earlier doubts floated away. In his dark morning suit with his hair neatly coiffed, she had never seen Douglas Llewellyn more handsome.

The wedding service passed in a blur. Later, all she would recall was the sound of the congregation as they sang out the hymns her mother had chosen, the racing of her heart as she made her vows and the delicious, weak-at-the-knees scent of Douglas's cologne.

They made their way back down the aisle to the strains of Mendelssohn's 'Wedding March' as Mr and Mrs Llewellyn. She had done it. There was no going back now. The thought thrilled her and she was glad that she had managed to silence her nerves just in time. Arm in arm with her new husband, Dorothy beamed as they passed rows of smiling faces in the congregation; their neighbours, her mother's friends, Clara and her parents, their household staff, Douglas's cricket mates, her father's colleagues, some of her friends from the newspaper and then . . . Dorothy's smile faltered. Her. Why did she have to be here?

Dressed in an eye-catching, scarlet red swing dress and looking utterly gorgeous, Maria da Costa – now Pemberton – gave a wide smile as they passed. But Dorothy noticed at the last moment that it was not for her; Maria's eyes were locked onto Douglas's. Her stomach sank as the niggling doubts returned. Could she ever really trust her new husband with this woman?

Dorothy had hoped that Maria's marriage would have changed things between them. But she and Bernard Pemberton had been married for just three months and the Singapore rumour-mill was already reporting that the marriage was not a happy one. Her new husband was regularly away on business, leaving Maria twiddling her thumbs in the opulent elegance of her new marital home. Dorothy swallowed down the annoyance and put her smile back in place, determined not to let it spoil her wedding day. Douglas was hers now.

The wedding breakfast was held across town in the Goodwood Park Hotel. In the lobby, Dorothy's parents stood alongside the new Mr and Mrs Llewellyn and greeted the guests as they arrived. With Europe at war, Douglas explained that his parents had, unfortunately, decided against risking the journey. They were older than the Templetons, in their late seventies, and were safely tucked up in their country house, Highcliffe Manor, in Wiltshire. Douglas had painted a beautiful picture of it as he described it to Dorothy and promised her that, as soon as the war was over, he would take her to meet her new in-laws.

A steady line of guests made their way in and Dorothy's face was starting to ache from all the pleasantries. She relaxed as she saw her friend approach.

'You look gorgeous, darling! Congratulations!' Clara smiled and kissed her on the cheek. She took her friend's hand and led her a couple of steps away from Douglas. 'Matthew sends his best wishes, he was sorry he couldn't be here but, well . . .' Her voice tailed off and she shrugged with a sad smile.

Dorothy screwed up her face. 'Matthew has absolutely nothing to be sorry about,' she whispered, pulling her friend to the side. 'It's me, I'm the one who's sorry. It was all so sudden, I had no idea . . . I mean, if I'd known, maybe I could have . . .'

Clara shook her head and put a hand on her arm to stop her. 'He'll be alright. He's up in Kuala Lumpur for a few days. He just needs some time away to lick his wounds; you know what men are like with their silly pride! Don't worry.'

But Dorothy did worry. Matthew was one of the kindest, most decent people she knew and it hurt to think that she had caused him pain. Their friendship had started off as just that: friendship. But over time, they had grown close and had shared an occasional kiss after an evening at the cinema or night out at the theatre. Dorothy had felt so safe with him, he had been the perfect antidote to Douglas. And after the emotional turmoil of finding Douglas in the arms of another woman – and not just any woman, but *that* woman – Matthew's steady, gentle manner had been exactly what she needed.

But despite all that, when Douglas had appeared out of the blue one rainy Sunday afternoon in May, with a bouquet of orchids and a diamond ring, Dorothy had been powerless to resist. Eighteen months had passed since she had ended things, during which time she had barely seen him. But with his movie-star good looks and devastating charm, he still had such a powerful magnetism that she felt hopelessly drawn to him, like the proverbial moth to his flame. She would lose herself in the depths of his chocolate-brown eyes when he looked at her, overcome by the delicious scent of him. He made her insides feel strange in a way that she had never experienced before; a hot, melting feeling in the pit of her stomach. She had never known such stirrings of desire; they overwhelmed and confused her, and threw all common sense and reason out of the window.

Douglas was a changed man; he had vowed that his 'friendship' with Maria was over. She was married and it was time for him to marry, too. And he could think of no one he wanted to spend his life with more than 'the adorable Dorothy Templeton'. She had been flattered by his words and, floating on a heady mix of romance and optimism, she had accepted. Her parents had been a little surprised but pleased and had given the match their blessing. Her mother was easily won over by Douglas's easy charm and her father, impressed by his work at McKinley's, was sure that he had a promising future ahead of him and would take care of his daughter.

It was a couple of weeks later, after the engagement had been announced in the *Straits Times*, when Clara confided to Dorothy that her cousin – dear, kind, dependable Matthew – had also been planning to propose to her. But Douglas had beaten him to it. Would she have accepted Matthew if Douglas hadn't got there first? She had spent a long time pondering and was confused when she realised that yes, she probably would have. She couldn't have picked two more different men: Douglas was dark and Matthew was fair, Douglas ambitious and Matthew easy-going, Douglas was all charisma and passion, while Matthew offered safety and stability. She hoped with all her heart she had made the right decision.

After the meal and the wedding toasts, the band struck up and the newlyweds took to the dance floor. Dorothy beamed as she glided around in Douglas's arms. She was a little merry after the champagne and had never felt happier. She beamed up at her handsome new husband, feeling like the luckiest girl in the world.

'Well, Mrs Llewellyn, I must say you look very lovely,' Douglas said, his lips brushing so close to her ear that it gave her goosebumps. 'Happy?'

She thought her heart would burst. 'Yes, Douglas, so happy!' She grinned up at him. 'It's been the most wonderful day.' She paused here and her smile slipped. He looked down, noticing the change in her expression.

'I know that look, my little darling; what's on your mind?'

Dorothy pondered whether this was the right moment to share what was bothering her. But she'd rather air it now than when they got home later and had, well, other things to occupy their attention.

'I was just wondering . . . I mean, I wasn't sure why . . .'
She paused and screwed up her face, unable to find the right words.

Douglas laughed. 'Spit it out, my dear!'

She took a deep breath and did just that, the words suddenly tumbling out in a rush. 'Why was Maria da Costa – I mean Pemberton – at the church?'

As soon as she saw the look in his eye, she realised she had made a mistake. For the briefest of moments, he paused in his steps, pulling slightly away from her as his muscles tensed. Dorothy felt the shift in him and she wished she could take her words back. Then he fixed a smile in place and continued, in a voice that seemed too calm, 'She's an old friend, that's all. It would have been strange not to invite her.'

'And that's all it is?' she probed, thinking back to what her brother had told her the day before. It was him reporting seeing Douglas and Maria together 'looking close' that had caused the siblings to argue the day before the wedding. 'It's only that Thomas—'

'That's all it is, my dear,' he said, cutting her off firmly. 'And we don't need to talk about this again.'

His grip felt firmer on her waist and she saw his jaw tense as they danced on. She hated the feeling that she had already managed to upset her new husband, that he thought she didn't trust him, and vowed at that moment never to mention her concerns about Maria da Costa Pemberton ever again.

It was late when they finally left the hotel and drove to their new house in York Road. With only a couple of months between the proposal and the wedding, there had not been much time to find a new home for the newlyweds. Together, they had viewed a few options, but Dorothy had fallen in love with the beautiful veranda and garden of their new bungalow, as well as its sweeping mahogany staircase. 'It's so grand,' she had said the first time she had walked down it, sliding her hand along the smooth banister. 'I feel like Scarlett O'Hara in *Gone with the Wind*!'

Douglas had moved into the house the week before the wedding and, with Ah Ling's help, had overseen its redecoration. The maid was now standing on the steps with the other members of staff, waiting to greet them. Dorothy was tired and felt glad to see a familiar face.

Douglas looked more than a little the worse for wear as they stepped into the harsh light of the entrance hall. His tie was undone and the six o'clock shadow on his face gave him a rather rakish air. Dorothy smelled the alcohol on him as he leaned down and kissed her full on the lips.

'Darling, you go on up and get ready, I'll follow you up shortly. I'm just going to have a smoke and one more for the road.' He winked at her before going through to the study.

Dorothy followed Ah Ling upstairs and into her new bedroom. It was a pretty room, overlooking the garden and decorated to Dorothy's taste in a soft, lemon yellow. Ah Ling had already unpacked her clothes and personal items and she was pleased to see her picture frames on the dressing table alongside a vase of fragrant yellow roses. The room was softly lamplit and there was a comfortable armchair by the window, next to a bookcase containing Dorothy's favourite novels. A large potted palm stood in the opposite corner, beside a tall chest of drawers. But the highlight was the air conditioning unit above the bed, which her parents had paid for as a wedding present. It felt so wonderfully cool in here and she felt at home straight away.

Dorothy went over to Ah Ling and squeezed her hand. 'Thank you,' she said, 'for all of this.' She smiled as she waved a hand around the room. 'You've done such a marvellous job, I love it!' Dorothy suddenly felt immensely grateful to her parents for letting Ah Ling leave their employment and come with her on this new adventure. Exciting as it was, setting up and running her own home for the first time, and managing the staff also felt a little daunting to Dorothy. Having Ah Ling by her side, in her new, elevated position as housekeeper, would be a great support.

Ah Ling helped Dorothy out of her wedding dress and into her satin nightgown and proceeded to brush her long hair, as she had done every night since the Templetons had arrived in Singapore. Dorothy yawned, despite the butterflies that were dancing around her stomach; Douglas would be coming up any time now. She felt a heady mix of excitement and nervousness and just hoped that she wouldn't disappoint her new husband. She said goodnight to Ah Ling, got into bed and waited.

The midnight chimes of the grandfather clock in the hall woke her a while later. The bedside lamp was still on but there was no sign of Douglas. What was he doing? Had he fallen asleep downstairs? After the amount he'd drunk, it would hardly be surprising.

The house was silent, but for the ticking of the clock, as Dorothy tiptoed down the staircase in her nightgown. As she reached the bottom step, she heard voices coming from the study and crept closer to listen. It was Douglas and he sounded angry. The other voice was much softer and Dorothy strained to hear. Someone was crying, their voice muffled with a handkerchief. It was a woman. Who had come here at this time of night? Was one of the servants in trouble? She didn't want to intrude, especially dressed in nothing but her pink wedding negligee, so she crept closer to peer through the gap in the door. As she did so, her blood turned to ice. Inside the study, she saw the unmistakable blood-red dress of Maria da Costa Pemberton.

CHAPTER 16

Singapore
Tuesday 2nd April, 2019

The next afternoon was another wet one. The rain lashed against the window panes as Annabel engaged in her favourite pastime: travelling back in time. She was in the National Archives office, where she had spent several hours scanning through the 1940 marriage records on an old desktop computer. The staff had been helpful and had shown her what to do, but it was a long and painstaking process. It seemed that every man and his dog had got married in 1940; there were so many records to scroll through. But as the next page appeared, Annabel gave a gasp of delight. 'Bingo!'

She traced the details on the screen with her finger, whispering the words out loud to herself, '"Mr Douglas Llewellyn and Miss Dorothy Templeton, daughter of Mr and Mrs Anthony Templeton of London, married at St Andrew's Cathedral, Singapore, Saturday 15th May, 1940." Yes!' she cheered.

'Found something useful?'

The voice startled her and she turned to see James, a curious expression on his face.

'James! Thanks for coming.' She smiled at him. 'I hope Emma didn't twist your arm too much to come and help me with this? And yes, I've just hit the jackpot and found Dotty's marriage record!'

'Oh, well done!' He gave her the ghost of a smile. 'That's a good start.'

He was dressed more smartly than when she had last seen him at dinner. He was wearing navy-blue chinos, tan leather shoes and a pale blue shirt, open at the neck. He had a black satchel slung casually over one shoulder. Clean shaven and tanned, he looked good, Annabel thought.

He came closer and bent down in her direction. Surprised by his approach and feeling unsure what to do, Annabel threw her arms around him and pulled him into a bear hug.

For the briefest of moments, he relaxed into her arms. He smelt good, she noted. But then, as quickly as he had relaxed, he stiffened and pulled away, clearing his throat.

'I, um, was actually just trying to read what you've got there on the computer screen,' he said, pointing at it awkwardly. 'The, um, marriage record, I mean.'

Mortified, Annabel's face turned beetroot red. James was so awkward around her at the best of times, but the boot was on the other foot now and she felt like a prize idiot. 'Oh! I'm so sorry . . . ' she mumbled, her usual eloquence momentarily lost.

He seemed to sense her discomfort and, after reading the details on the screen, turned back to her and relaxed his face into a grin. 'But thanks for the hug. Shall we get a coffee?'

For all Annabel's embarrassment, the accidental hug seemed to have broken the ice and the atmosphere between them felt lighter. James was a hard nut to crack, she mused; was this what it took to get through to him, making a fool of herself for his entertainment?

'It's good of you to help me with this, James,' she began as they found a table in a nearby café. James put down the tray of drinks and handed her a cappuccino.

'No problem at all. I might be able to dig out some useful contacts for you. I put out some feelers this morning to ask about Julia Chan. If we can find her, hopefully she'll be able to tell you what you want to know. I'm sure her grandmother would have told her stories of her time working in the big house for the English family. Let's hope Julia remembers some of them.' He paused and lifted his cup to take a sip.

Annabel smiled at him. 'Thanks, James, I really appreciate it. It's been a long time since our uni days and I know we moved in different circles and weren't exactly close, but it's good to see you again.'

'Yes, likewise.' He seemed a little stiff and focused on his coffee cup for a moment. Then he continued with a wry smile, 'And yes, they certainly were different social circles, you were very much part of the "cool" gang, if my memory serves correctly.'

She wrinkled her nose as he made quotation marks with his fingers for the word 'cool'.

'You were always with that Archie chap and his entourage of "beautiful people" as we called them,' he continued, raising an eyebrow teasingly.

Annabel tried unsuccessfully to stifle her snort of surprise, 'Cool? I was a complete and utter history geek! Gosh, I think you got the wrong end of the stick there, James! But yes, I did spend a lot of time with Archie. We'd been friends at school so naturally gravitated towards each other at uni, I suppose.'

'And didn't you date his friend, Hugo something-or-other, for a while?'

Annabel noticed James's jaw tighten as he mentioned her ex and she felt a wave of shame wash over her at the memory. Hugo Sotheby-Waugh was the best looking guy in her year, not to mention the coolest. She had been completely infatuated and had, briefly, joined his circle of sycophants. However, the more she got to know him, the more Annabel had realised that he was actually a self-involved narcissist with a penchant for unkindness and nasty comments. They had only dated for a few weeks, but it had been a few weeks too many. She shuddered inwardly at the memory.

'Don't remind me,' she muttered. 'Anyway, you were in your own "cool" gang with the swimming team,' she said, copying his air quotes. 'You lot were always so damn fit and healthy; you put the rest of us mere mortals to shame! Always going off to competitions and always back with yet more silverware for the trophy cabinet . . .'

'Always watching our diet, never being allowed to drink and always missing socials because we had to get up ridiculously early for training? Yes, we were *really* cool!' He rolled his eyes dramatically, making her chuckle.

'Anyway, it was a long time ago,' he said, then cleared his throat. 'It is good to see you again and I'm happy to help out with this; it's an interesting story. And, to be honest, I'm at a bit of a loose end at the moment. I've had some stuff going on lately and the office suggested I take some leave.' He shook his head. 'But the truth is, I'd much rather keep busy. So I'm happy to help.'

'Emma told me you've had a rough time lately. I was sorry to hear that.' Annabel gave him a sympathetic smile.

'You're not going to hug me again, are you?' He raised an eyebrow to show that he was in jest. Annabel laughed, then screwed up a paper napkin and threw it in his direction. She'd never seen this light-hearted side of him before and found herself enjoying the brief moments when he let it show.

'Just one of those things, I suppose.' He shrugged. 'Expat life can take its toll on relationships and any little cracks can end up becoming gaping wide chasms.' He stared into space, as if lost in his thoughts.

'Relationships are hard enough at home,' Annabel began softly. 'I can't imagine the added pressure of being away from all that's familiar. But I suppose if it's meant to be, you'll find a way to make it work. And if it isn't, then you won't. And if one of you has a roving eye, then I guess it doesn't matter if you're at home or abroad.' She shrugged and gave him a wry smile.

'Oh?' he began, his eyes darkening. 'Emma told you about that, did she?'

'Oh gosh; no, she didn't tell me anything,' Annabel tried to backpedal, anxious that she had said the wrong thing. She shook her head. 'Emma didn't tell me what happened. Sorry James, I didn't mean *you*; I was talking about my own cheating ex. Not that *you're* a cheating ex . . . ' She was gabbling now. 'I just meant that I was talking about my own situation, not yours.' She took a deep breath, feeling flustered for the second time that afternoon.

'I'm sorry to hear that.' His eyes softened and for a moment he gazed at her. 'What man in his right mind would choose someone else over you?' he said quietly.

Surprised, she tried to shrug off the compliment and James returned his attention to his coffee, but the intensity of his gaze had surprised her.

'And for the record,' he added soberly, '*I* wasn't the one with the roving eye; I never have been – nor ever will be – a cheater.'

An hour later, they were back in the archives room. Now that they had the full name of Dorothy's first husband, Annabel was keen to see if they could uncover anything else about him. They worked alongside each other in companionable silence, Annabel searching Singapore's newspapers and business articles from the late 1930s, and James working his way through the death records for the next few years.

'If your grandparents married in 1945, then your grandmother's first marriage could have only lasted a few years,' James mused. 'Divorce was far less common back then, so I would hazard a guess that this Douglas Llewellyn chap must have died.'

'In the war, perhaps?' suggested Annabel.

'Yes, maybe. The timing would be about right; good thinking.' James pulled his laptop out of his satchel and, after logging into the library Wi-Fi, clicked open the website of the Commonwealth War Graves.

'This should be fairly straightforward. All the graves are catalogued online, so we should just be able to do a quick search to see if he's there. Most servicemen were buried at Kranji, up north; there's a huge war memorial there. And even if he wasn't buried there, his name should be in the records if he died in active service.'

A few clicks later and James uttered a sigh of disappointment. 'Nope. Douglas Llewellyn was neither buried nor listed at Kranji. So perhaps not a wartime death after all. Back to the drawing board!'

But Annabel wasn't listening, she was too busy zooming in on the newspaper article on the screen in front of her.

'Look at this, James! Douglas is mentioned in this article about a rubber company.' She pointed to the blurry words of the scanned text and read aloud.

"*Douglas Llewellyn took over as Acting Manager of McKinley's in June 1941. The company continued to go from strength to strength, with rubber demand reaching new heights as the war in Europe raged on. Llewellyn's management of the company was all too brief, however, as he passed away in November of the same year, following a fall at his home in York Road.*"

'A fall?' Annabel's brow wrinkled. 'He can't have been that old, what sort of fall would kill a young man?'

'You're right, that does seem strange. But look' – he pointed to the date – 'November '41, just before the Japanese invasion.'

'Yes, I wonder if there's a connection?' Annabel sat back and rubbed her eyes. They were itchy from staring at the screen for far too long, plus she was still tired from her journey and the jet lag. She closed them briefly, but James kept reading. She was aware of his closeness and the subtle scent of his cologne as he leaned across her to read the screen.

'There's something else here,' he said, scanning an earlier section of the article. 'What did you say your grandmother's maiden name was?'

'Templeton.'

James read aloud, '"*Anthony Templeton took the company to new heights as the start of the Second World War heralded a rapid increase in rubber demand in Europe. Templeton was renowned as a fair and honest manager and was universally respected. He oversaw the next expansion of the company, with the purchase of an additional thousand acres of plantation in Malaysia and a further three go-downs in Singapore to meet the growing supply rates. He took leave to care for his wife when she became ill and sadly died shortly after her, in December 1941.*"'

Annabel leaned in to follow the text as James read. Her eyes pricked with weary tears at the mention of her great-grandparents' passing. Dotty had told her that they had died in London during the war and it had never occurred to Annabel to ask any more than that. Why had Dotty never told her any of this? Annabel felt increasingly uncomfortable. She had adored her grandmother but now she was forced to face the fact that she had blatantly lied to her family. She felt like her foundations had been shaken.

'I'm sorry, Annabel,' James said, noticing her tears. 'I'm guessing you didn't know anything about this? Must be a bit of a shock!'

He gave a sad smile and touched her gently on the shoulder. His proximity suddenly made her feel strange. Despite her earlier misgivings, she had been surprised to find herself actually enjoying spending time with James. He seemed to have relaxed in her company and they were working well together. Why was her stomach now in knots? On the pretext of needing a drink, she pushed her chair back and reached into her bag for her water bottle.

'My great-grandparents died out here? And not in London? That's so strange,' she said after a long slug of water. 'Why on earth did Dotty never tell us anything about any of this? First it was the secret letters and photos, now it turns out that she pretty much rewrote the family history! Why would she do that? What else was she hiding?'

James shook his head and manoeuvred his wheelie chair back to his own computer. 'It does seem pretty strange. Let's see if we can find their death records, now that we know when they died.'

'My great-grandparents, you mean?'

'Yes,' he replied as he set to work tapping on the keyboard. 'And Douglas. We know when he died, so we should be able to find his record now, too.'

Annabel felt a rush of gratitude that James seemed almost as interested in her family research as she was. She was glad that her earlier sense of disquiet had disappeared again. Where had that come from, she wondered? Maybe it was just that she was so tired; far from home, jet-lagged and suddenly feeling very confused about her family.

'Here we go!' James said, pointing at the screen a couple of minutes later. 'Olivia Templeton, died on the thirteenth of November 1941 at Alexandra Military Hospital, Singapore, aged forty-six. Cause of death: cancer.' He scrolled down a little further before continuing, 'Anthony Templeton, died on the twentieth of December 1941 at Alexandra Military Hospital, Singapore, aged fifty-one. Cause of death: heart failure.'

James reached into his satchel again, took out a notebook and pen and began scribbling.

'Oh!' Annabel exclaimed. 'They were both so young. And he died so soon after his wife! But they do say that happens with couples sometimes, don't they? Maybe it's true; maybe you *can* die from a broken heart.' She sighed. 'What an awful Christmas that must have been for Dotty that year, losing both her parents like that as well as her husband!'

'Indeed, it must have been a terrible time,' James agreed. He scribbled one last thing in the notebook and snapped it shut. 'We've made some good progress today.'

'What are you writing there?' Annabel asked, nodding at the notebook.

'I've found where your great-grandparents were buried. Would you like to visit?'

It was late afternoon when they set off towards Bidadari cemetery in James's shiny white BMW. It still had that new-car smell and was immaculately kept, inside and out. He had opened the car door for her, a tiny gesture that had made her smile. The more she got to know James, the more she was warming to him. He was quite traditional, with his old-school manners and classic dress sense, and his neat and tidy car served to emphasise this. Yet at the same time, he had a knack of surprising Annabel with his quick wit. He regularly caught her off guard, making her laugh out loud with his self-deprecation and wry observations.

The BBC World Service was playing on the radio, making Annabel feel slightly more at home in this foreign country. James was a confident but careful driver, expertly navigating the multi-laned highways as they made their way north. Annabel's hand reached instinctively for the door handle a couple of times as drivers pulled out in front of them, with barely a hair's breadth. But she relaxed after a while, feeling safe with James behind the wheel.

James parked the car just off Vernon Road and stepped out of the cool air conditioning into the fierce intensity of the afternoon sun. Annabel looked around and marvelled at how quickly the weather could change here; there was little evidence of the earlier rain. Beads of sweat formed on her forehead as she followed James along the path to the entrance gates.

A pair of imposing white pillars flanked the wrought-iron entrance gates. 'Bidadari Memorial Park,' Annabel read the sign.

They passed through the gates into a lush, green garden. A series of pathways led off in different directions, shaded by lines of tall trees and punctuated by wooden benches at regular intervals. They followed one such path and saw that the area was divided into different sections for different religions: Christian, Muslim and Hindu. There were occasional headstones and memorial plaques, but not the rows of neat gravestones that she had been expecting.

'Where are all the graves?' she asked.

'Good question,' James said, frowning. He stopped in the shade of a large rain tree and took out his phone. He tapped away for a moment, searching the internet for information, then said, 'Damn, this isn't right. I'm sorry. I should have checked before coming out here. This isn't the cemetery, I'm afraid. We're not going to find your great-grandparents' graves after all.'

He continued reading. 'The original cemetery was cleared in the early 2000s, this is just a memorial garden to mark the spot and it's only temporary. This whole area is about to be redeveloped for a new housing project.' He sighed. 'Damn it, I should have checked. Sorry. The cemetery *was* here, so that's something. And the entrance gates are the originals, even if they've been repositioned.' He shrugged and gave a small smile.

'But what about the graves? Exhumed, I suppose?' she asked.

James nodded. 'I'm sure we could find out where they were taken. Let me see what I can find out at the High Commission.'

They turned and started heading back towards the entrance. 'Land in Singapore is at such a premium that this sort of thing happens all the time; buildings are knocked down and land repurposed. Even apartment blocks don't last much longer than twenty years,' James explained.

'I suppose it's all in the name of progress,' Annabel said.

'Yes, the Singaporeans are a rather unsentimental bunch. This country has only got where it is today by constantly moving forward. Progress is key and with a growing population they need more housing. I'm sorry this was a wasted journey.'

'Don't apologise, James, it's OK.' She reached out and touched his arm briefly. Then she stopped and looked around. 'It's a beautiful place and worth a visit. And, like you say, my great-grandparents *were* buried here, even if they're not here now.' She smiled up at him and they continued walking.

'Anyway, it's really kind of you to spend your afternoon helping me. And driving me around, it really does make things so much easier.'

'Even if I am leading you, quite literally, up the garden path?' He raised an eyebrow with a look of self-deprecation that made her feel suddenly fond of him.

She grinned back at him. Sweat had started trickling down her back and Annabel wished she had worn something lighter. But it had been pouring when she had left Emma's apartment and she had been expecting an afternoon indoors. Her friend's advice had been quite clear: 'Wrap up if you're staying inside, it's usually pretty cold with the air con.' She looked down at her jeans and winced.

They walked back to the car in silence, hot and frustrated after a fruitless search. It was a relief to escape the sun as they got back in the car and Annabel was grateful for the bottle of cold water that James offered her. He turned on the ignition and she closed her eyes, enjoying the blast of cold air from the AC.

James was about to start the engine when his phone beeped, announcing a new message. He pulled it from his jeans pocket and his brow furrowed as he read the text. After a moment, his face softened and he turned to Annabel. He raised an eyebrow mysteriously. 'We're not done yet, Watson!'

He handed her the phone and she read the message on the screen,

> Spoke to Julia Chan, she is happy to meet your friend and answer questions. Evenings best. 94218325. Good luck, Alvin.

Annabel grinned. 'Oh James, you found her, that's amazing! Thank you so much!' She looked at her watch: almost 6 p.m. 'Can we call her now?'

James smiled indulgently as he started the car and pulled out of the car park and onto the main road. 'Let's not pounce on the poor woman straight away; why don't we go back to Emma and Tom's and have a cuppa? Give Julia time to get in from work, or whatever it is that keeps her busy in the day. Then you can figure out what you want to say to her, and where and when you want to meet.'

'Yes, you're right.' She nodded, still beaming. She was grateful to have James with her. He was making everything easier, somehow. It wasn't just by playing taxi driver and tour guide for her, or using his contacts to find Julia Chan. It was his calm and steady manner that she most appreciated. She was feeling so excited that, left to her own devices, she would have probably gone in with all guns blazing and terrified the poor woman with her over-exuberance.

'I can't believe I'm actually going to meet her!' She paused and turned to James. 'You'll come with me, won't you?' Her smile faded when he didn't reply straight away, his eyes fixed on the road ahead as if deep in thought. A moment later, he turned to her and smiled. 'Of course. If you'd like me to, then I'll be there.'

She grinned, feeling pleased. 'Great! But there's one thing we need to get clear.' She raised an eyebrow accusingly at him. '*Watson*? Seriously? This is *my* family mystery, I should get to be Sherlock!'

CHAPTER 17

Singapore

WEDNESDAY 25TH DECEMBER, 1940

Dorothy awoke on Christmas Day in her old bedroom at her parents' house in Nassim Road. She looked up and smiled as she saw the perfect blue sky through the gap in the blinds; Christmas had never been this bright and sunny back in London. She winced as she thought of her old home. The past few months had seen London bombed relentlessly by the Germans and every day the news was filled with fresh tales of horror. There was no end in sight for this war, and she worried for her friends and neighbours back there.

Douglas rolled over sleepily towards her. 'Merry Christmas, darling,' he said. He stretched up and kissed her forehead, and Dorothy felt herself relax. She was glad to be here, back in her parents' home with her family, and felt relieved that she had managed to persuade Douglas to accept the invitation.

The first months of married life had not gone as smoothly as Dorothy had hoped. On the outside, the new Mr and Mrs Douglas Llewellyn seemed, to everyone who saw them, the perfect young newlyweds. They made a handsome couple and everyone was delighted for them; none more so than Dorothy's parents, who had been completely charmed by their new son-in-law. They should have been the happiest days of Dorothy's young life. But on the inside, she was feeling miserable.

The wedding night had been an enormous disappointment. Douglas confessed the next morning that he had fallen asleep in his study, having had 'one too many', and didn't want to disturb her by coming to bed in the early hours. But Dorothy knew the truth: he had preferred to spend their wedding night in his study with his old flame, Maria da Costa Pemberton, than with his new bride. She had cried herself to sleep, feeling like an absolute fool.

The next day, they had set off on their honeymoon – a wedding gift from Dorothy's parents – and spent three nights at a beachfront hotel in Changi. Dorothy was determined to put a brave face on and put thoughts of the previous night out of her head. She tried her best to be agreeable and to please her new husband, and determined *not* to ask him why that woman had come to their house on their wedding night. After the way he'd shut her down when she had asked why she had been at their wedding, she was frightened of his reaction.

For his part, Douglas began the honeymoon by being attentive and kind to his new bride, and it had, on the whole, been a pleasant stay. They had spent time swimming in the sea, playing tennis and dining in the restaurant, where other diners smiled and nodded at them, seemingly envying their perfect new marriage. At times, however, Douglas had seemed distracted, his mind clearly far away on other things. But when she asked about it, he just told her that work was 'terribly busy' and that he had lots to do when he got back.

When the moment had finally come, on the second night of their marriage, to consummate their union, Douglas's lovemaking had been decidedly lacklustre, polite even. There was none of the passion or desire of which Clara had spoken, having taken it upon herself to give her friend a pep talk about 'the birds and the bees,' as she put it. And although Dorothy hated torturing herself by remembering it, there was none of the heart-racing passion she had witnessed that fateful night in the tennis shed at the Tanglin Club.

According to Clara, sex could be enjoyable for women as well as men, but it had been anything but that. Dorothy had found the whole experience uncomfortable and stressful. It had all been over rather quickly, too, with Douglas disappearing off to the bathroom as soon as it was over, while she lay there, embarrassed and sore, wondering what had happened. She fretted that Douglas was not attracted to her or that she wasn't doing it right, and it was making her feel miserable.

'Stiff upper lip, my dear!' had been the advice that her mother had given when she hinted that it had been a rocky start. 'It simply doesn't "do" to let the side down. You must try harder to keep Douglas happy and make a success of your marriage.' Dorothy didn't dare confide in Clara about her worries, fearing that, despite their close friendship, she would doubtless feel an element of 'I told you so'.

Once they were back in their new marital home in York Road, it had taken time for Dorothy to adapt to the rhythm of married life. Douglas was an early riser and was usually already on his way to the office before she woke. She would breakfast alone on the veranda, having her morning tea and toast against the backdrop of the lush, green garden. And although Ah Ling was always on hand, becoming more of a confidante and companion than a housekeeper, Dorothy missed her parents and the company she had always enjoyed at their home.

The days were Dorothy's own, to do with as she pleased. Before the wedding, Douglas had encouraged her to end her employment at the newspaper and, despite her reluctance to do so, she had eventually given in to his persuasion. 'Darling, you'll be so busy running the house,' he had cajoled, 'not to mention taking care of the children when they come. I really don't think you'll have time to work.'

She had been disappointed to lose the sense of independence and purpose that she had found in her employment, but supposed that he had been right. None of the married ladies they knew worked for a living; they were all entirely dependent on their husbands. But there was something about that that didn't sit well with Dorothy.

She had been bored to begin with, watching the clock and waiting for Douglas to come home from work. But she wasn't one to sit around twiddling her thumbs. She soon established a weekly routine that involved visiting friends, shopping, going to the club or helping her mother with her various fundraising initiatives.

Douglas would come home in time for dinner and Dorothy made sure to look fresh and pretty and have enough interesting topics ready to keep the conversation alive. After dinner, he would smoke in his study and then join her for coffee on the veranda. They would sometimes dine at the club or invite guests for dinner in the first few months of their marriage, followed by drinks and dancing to records on the gramophone. Douglas was at his best in company and loved nothing more than a party evening of music, cocktails and dancing with lively company and witty conversation. On those evenings, he was more attentive than usual, kind and affectionate with his wife and presenting himself as the doting husband. From the outside, the Llewellyns looked like the perfect couple. But once the guests had gone and it was time for bed, it was different.

Most nights, Dorothy slept alone. Douglas regularly stayed up late, nursing a glass of whisky in his study. He often slept in his dressing room, but from time to time – perhaps more from necessity than desire – he would join his wife in the marital bed. He said he was eager to start a family, but his lovemaking persisted in that same polite, going-through-the-motions style as the first time. Rarely did he stay with Dorothy afterwards, usually kissing her on the forehead before going back to his room, saying, 'I've got an early start, darling, I'll only disturb you when I get up.'

Christmas came and Dorothy was delighted for the chance to return home and spend time with her parents, especially as her brother was there. They arrived in time for dinner on Christmas Eve and, as they sat around the Christmas tree later that evening, singing along to carols playing on the gramophone, Dorothy's heart felt full. She was so happy to be surrounded by her loved ones again, but it made her sad to realise how lonely she had been feeling in her new marital home.

Douglas was on his best behaviour, charming his mother-in-law with compliments and impressing his father-in-law, not to mention boss, with witty repartee. In their presence, he doted on Dorothy, playing the role of the perfect husband with affectionate gestures and constant attention.

The only one who was resistant to his charms was Dorothy's brother, Thomas. Despite Douglas's best attempts, Dorothy could tell that her brother had not warmed to her new husband. She wanted them to get along, but she could tell from Thomas's coolness over dinner on that first evening that he didn't like him.

She was pleased, however, that rather than staying up late as he usually did, Douglas chose to follow her up the stairs and into her bedroom. She was even more pleased by his renewed vigour in their attempts to start a family. Dorothy secretly hoped that this new closeness could be a turning point for them. 'I do love you, Douglas, you do know that?' she told him as he lay on top of her afterwards, breathless and spent. He smiled, then kissed her forehead. 'You are so adorable!' Then he rolled off and turned his back with a cheery 'Goodnight!' Soon, he was snoring.

Christmas Day dawned with clear, blue skies and bright sunshine and the family attended the morning service at St Andrew's Cathedral. It was their third Christmas away from England, but it still felt strange to Dorothy to be going through the old traditions in sunny weather. The words to 'In the Bleak Midwinter' felt so incongruous here, as did the roast turkey dinner which greeted them when they arrived home after the service. It was a jolly meal, with everyone in good spirits, and the festive mood continued as they exchanged gifts around the Christmas tree in the drawing room.

Hanging over the festivities like a cloud, however, was the war back home in England. Life in Singapore had continued in much the same way for the past sixteen months, but back home, seven thousand miles away, friends and family were enduring the most difficult circumstances.

The newspapers and the BBC Empire Service kept them up to date with events back home, and also received occasional letters from Daisy. She always loved receiving these, but dreaded the contents. At the start of the year, food rationing had been introduced and they were having to 'make do and mend' in so many ways. Children had been evacuated from the cities, encouraged by the government to move to safer places in the countryside. Dorothy's eyes teared up at the thought of this; it was all just so awful.

After dinner, Dorothy and Thomas got out the box of family board games, as had been their Christmas tradition since they were children back home in London. They were setting up for a game of Scrabble when a servant arrived with a message for Douglas, saying that he was urgently needed back at the house in York Road.

'Some problem with the damn water pipes, apparently,' he told his hosts with a helpless shrug. Then he bent down to give his wife a farewell kiss on the cheek.

'Oh, but must you go, Douglas?' Dorothy moaned. 'It's getting late; surely whatever it is can wait until the morning?'

'I'm sorry, my love, I wish I didn't have to go, but if it's a burst pipe it could cause absolute chaos! Best get it sorted as soon as possible, eh?'

And with a cheerful wave, he was off.

Christmas evening passed, Olivia Templeton was victorious in the family Scrabble contest and bedtime came. But there was no sign of Douglas. Her parents cheerfully kissed Dorothy goodnight, reassuring her that he would be busy sorting out whatever problem had occurred and he would be back very soon.

Dorothy lay awake, her mind in overdrive. A phone call to the house had revealed that yes, Mr Llewellyn *had* gone home around eight o'clock, but had only stayed for about twenty minutes. She had sat up waiting, but by the time midnight struck on the old grandfather clock in the hallway, she had given up. Feeling confused, not to mention more than a little embarrassed, she had gone to bed, propping her bedroom door open in order to hear the first hint of his return.

When the front door finally clicked open half an hour later, Dorothy tiptoed out onto the landing. She was surprised to hear voices in the hall below and stood quietly in the shadows, looking down through the balustrade. She could make out her brother in the soft lamplight. Reclining in an armchair, he held a glass of whisky in one hand and a cigarette in the other.

When he spoke, Thomas's voice was icy calm. 'So, you finally deign to honour us with your presence?' he mocked.

'Kind of you to wait up for me, Thomas. I didn't know you cared!' Douglas quipped.

'My sister deserves better!' Thomas suddenly snapped, leaping up from his chair. 'She loves you – God only knows why – and this is how you treat her?' Thomas's simmering anger was reaching boiling point.

'I don't know what you're talking about, Tommy!' Douglas raised his hands innocently, his tone placatory.

'Don't "Tommy" me! You might have charmed the rest of them, Llewellyn, but you don't fool me! I *know* what you're up to, where you've been tonight.' Thomas was approaching Douglas now, in a slow but menacing way, like a tiger circling its prey. Dorothy's heart began to pound, the blood thumping in her ears.

'I saw you, Llewellyn; don't lie to me, damn it! The night before your wedding, with *her*! I *saw* you together . . .'

'Now, listen here.' Douglas's tone was quiet but fierce. He squared up to Thomas. 'I don't know what you *think* you saw, but I strongly advise you against making vicious accusations that will only end up upsetting your sister. Do I make myself clear?' He jabbed his brother-in-law hard in the chest with his index finger, causing him to stumble backwards into the sideboard.

Enraged, Thomas gathered himself together and launched himself at Douglas like a wild animal. He caught him around the waist, toppling him to the ground.

Panic coursed through Dorothy then spurred her into action. 'Stop it, both of you!' she yelled from her position at the top of the stairs. The men froze and turned to gaze up at her. Thomas's face remained a picture of fury, but Douglas instantly switched to his 'devoted husband' look. He got up, smoothed down his shirt sleeves and stepped out of the fracas.

'Darling, I'm so sorry I took so long!' he gushed, glossing over the fact that she had almost witnessed a full-on brawl between them. 'Got the water pipe sorted then had a spot of bother with the motorcar on the way back, but it's all fixed now.'

A derisive snort came from Thomas.

Douglas climbed the stairs and, brightly and breezily, called back after him, 'Good night then, Thomas. Do sleep well!' When he reached the top, he took Dorothy by the hand and kissed it. He stank of alcohol with a lingering hint of expensive Chanel perfume. Her stomach churned. But Douglas's fixed smile never wavered. 'Come on, darling, let's go to bed!'

Dorothy was still trembling a few minutes later as she lay there, waiting for him to finish in the bathroom and join her. He had fooled her, she now realised, into thinking that he had ended things with his former lover. And she had been fooling herself that he had ever loved her. She felt utterly wretched.

She sat up and pulled the sheets around herself as he climbed in next to her. He gave her that same, rigid smile as he reached out and touched her shoulder. She could smell the whisky. She flinched.

'Where were you tonight?' she whispered, trying to keep her voice steady.

He sighed dramatically then flopped back onto his pillow. 'Oh darling, don't start that again. I told you; I had to go back to the house, poor old Amir was getting his knickers in a twist over a piddly burst water pipe. I don't know why he felt the need to call me back, all very tedious.' He yawned, as if to emphasise the point. 'It's been a long day and I'm tired. Let's get some sleep.' He reached over to turn out the light, but stopped when Dorothy continued.

'But you weren't at the house.' She trembled as she spoke, knowing that she would need to summon all her courage to say what needed to be said next. 'Ah Ling telephoned and spoke to Amir. He said that you had left. Where have you been all this time?'

Douglas's eyes darkened. 'I told you, darling; the car has been playing up . . . ' he began.

'Don't lie to me, Douglas, I can't bear it!' She turned to face him now, her eyes brimming with tears. 'I *know* where you've been. Thomas *was* right. I smelt her perfume on you.' The tears began to flow and she angrily wiped them away.

He sighed again. 'Oh Dorothy, I don't know why you make such a big fuss, I really don't. Alright, yes; I popped in to see Maria on the way home. Happy now? I didn't say anything as you always seem to blow things out of proportion.'

'You left me here, looking like a complete fool, not knowing where you were, while you were off with your fancy woman?'

'It wasn't like that. Maria has been having a difficult time lately, her husband has been away a lot and she's been feeling lonely.'

'And let me guess,' Dorothy snorted, wild with rage now. 'You were more than happy to keep her company and cheer her up!'

'Oh, for God's sake!' he snapped.

'It's Christmas Day, Douglas; a day for family. *I* am your family, not her! *I* am your wife, not her!'

'Well, stop moaning and be a good wife, then, why don't you?' he sneered. In one swift movement he grabbed her by both arms and pushed her down on the bed, looming over her. The stench of cigarettes and whisky on his breath turned her stomach. He grabbed at her nightdress, tearing the lace as he forced it to the side.

'No! Douglas, stop it, please . . .' she begged, realising what he was about to do. Terror coursed through her as she struggled in vain beneath his grip. 'I'm sorry, Douglas . . . I don't want to . . . Please, no . . .'

But Douglas was in no mood to listen. Ignoring his wife's pleas, he covered her mouth with his hand and forced himself upon her.

CHAPTER 18

Singapore

WEDNESDAY 3RD APRIL, 2019

Annabel's heart was racing as she reached up and knocked on the apartment door. It was the next afternoon and they were high up on the fourteenth floor of an apartment block, standing on the long balcony walkway that ran along the front doors. She looked up and checked the number one more time. Yes, this was the right one.

'Relax, Sherlock, it'll be fine.' James smiled encouragingly and gave her a wink, and she felt suddenly grateful for his presence. The touch of his hand in the small of her back felt strange, yet somehow comforting. For so long, it had been Luke who had stood beside her, supporting her. But not anymore. She felt a brief pang of grief at his absence, but, this time, managed to squash the sensation as quickly as it had arrived. It was definitely progress.

Annabel looked up at James and managed a small smile. 'I hope so,' she whispered back. 'By the way, thanks, James,' she continued. 'I really appreciate you pulling strings to find Julia for me.'

'Well, you've got me there.' He arched an eyebrow. 'It was hardly any great detective work in the end. I happened to mention her name to a colleague in front of one of our admin staff,

Alvin. It turns out Alvin plays tennis with Julia's husband; they were at school together.' He gave a wry smile. 'So, unfortunately, I can't take much praise for my sleuthing skills on this occasion.'

Annabel's face relaxed and she laughed. At that moment, footsteps approached from inside the apartment and she swallowed nervously.

Until this evening, 'Ang Mo Kio' had just been a strange name written as part of a strange address in a strange land. But now she was here, in the place where Dotty's Ah Ling had lived, and it felt unnervingly real. It was all so different from the 'expat' Singapore that Annabel had got to know over the last few days and she felt quite out of her depth. No glitzy condos or shiny rooftop bars here, instead it was a peaceful residential neighbourhood of densely populated, uniform apartment blocks. Some of them were painted in bright colours and many had long poles protruding from their windows, making the most of the afternoon sunshine to dry laundry. On the way there, they had driven past shops and schools, and Annabel had been surprised by the amount of greenery. Singapore was such an urban jungle, but she liked the way that green spaces were protected. This was definitely more of an area for local Singaporeans, and they had drawn curious glances as they'd walked across the car park to the apartment block.

The latch clicked and the door opened to reveal a little old lady with snowy white hair. She was dressed in a pink silk blouse and navy-blue trousers, but it was her smile that caught Annabel's attention. It lit up her whole face and Annabel's nerves instantly ebbed away.

'You are Annabel!' The old lady beamed up at her. She had a slight hunch, but even at full height she would have been at least six inches shorter than Annabel. 'How lovely it is to meet you!'

'Julia?' Annabel smiled back, trying to mask her confusion. She was so much older than Annabel had been expecting and her English was more halting than it had been on the phone. They had only chatted for a couple of minutes, but this was not how she had pictured Julia Chan.

The old lady laughed and reached out to clasp Annabel's hand. Her voice had a birdlike, sing-song quality.

'Aiyoh, better don't let my daughter hear you say that, ah! No lah, I'm Mei, Julia's mummy. Wah, who's this handsome young man? She squinted, looking up at James who was towering over her. Your husband, ah? Wah, so good looking! Come, come!'

Annabel followed Mei across the threshold and into a long, narrow living area, all the while protesting that James was not her husband. But the old lady wasn't listening.

'Julia!' she called through a doorway that opened off the lounge, whilst indicating for the visitors to take a seat. She called again, louder this time and in a different language; Chinese, Annabel supposed.

'Sorry ah,' Mei said, smiling apologetically. 'Is easier for me in Cantonese!'

Annabel looked around the room, taking it all in. It felt like they had stepped back in time; the simple decor and retro furnishings were pure 1970s.

'What a wonderful place!' she said, before sitting next to James on a wooden sofa with olive-green velour cushions. Mei sat next to them in a matching, high-backed armchair.

The old lady nodded approvingly. 'M-goi!' Annabel wasn't sure what the words meant, but figured that she was being thanked. 'This was my mother's home,' Mei continued, 'Ah Ling.'

It all made sense; this apartment, just like its former owner, was from a distant time. The furniture was all made of dark brown wood and the floor was a light brown lino with swirling geometric patterns. A gilded birdcage sparkled where it hung in the far corner of the room and green leafy ferns lent a splash of colour in their large, terracotta pots. Just inside the front door, the small, old-fashioned television was playing something in Chinese. Mei picked up the remote control from the table next to her armchair and turned the volume down.

The slats of the main window were open and a cool breeze drifted through the room. The window looked out onto the covered entrance walkway, which lent shade to the apartment from the fierce Singaporean sun. The whole effect made the room feel a little dark, but pleasantly cool. A small desk sat below the window and old family photos adorned the walls. The whole room could have been displayed in a museum; it was fabulous.

'Annabel, hello!' Julia Chan appeared in the doorway, carrying a tray of cups and saucers. 'I'm so sorry to keep you waiting, I was just making some tea!'

Annabel rose from the sofa and smiled as she stepped forward to greet Julia and introduce James. Like her mother Mei, Julia was petite and smart. Annabel estimated that she was in her early fifties, but her smooth skin made her look much younger. Julia's black hair was cut in a sharp bob and she was dressed in a navy-blue suit as if she'd recently come from work.

Julia set the tray down on the small dining table and introductions were made.

'I am so happy to meet you, Annabel,' she said as she poured the tea. 'Our families have such a long connection, I almost feel like I know you already. In her letters, Dorothy told Po Po all about your family.'

'Po Po?' Annabel asked.

Julia chuckled. 'Sorry, it means Granny in Cantonese. I think our grandmothers would be very happy to know we were meeting, don't you?' She smiled at Annabel and handed her a cup of steaming green tea.

'Yes, I do. Thank you,' she said, taking the cup and putting it on the small coffee table in front of her. 'Although you definitely have a head start on me; as I said on the phone, I'm afraid I only found out about my grandmother's connection to Singapore last week. But it's absolutely fascinating and I'm eager to find out as much as I can.'

'Well I hope you don't mind me dragging you all the way out here to the Heartlands, it's a bit of a trek from town, I'm afraid. But I thought it appropriate to meet here, in my grandmother, Ah Ling's home. Mama lives here now. I live closer to town – Bukit Timah – it's easier for work.' She smiled. 'Call me sentimental, but I thought maybe you might like to come and see where Ah Ling lived and get a sense of who she was. As you can see' – she gestured around the apartment with a wry smile – 'Mama hasn't had the heart to change anything since she passed!'

'That was her writing desk,' Julia said, motioning towards a narrow wooden desk beneath the birdcage at the back of the room. 'She was a great letter writer; always busy keeping in touch with her friends and family.'

Instinctively, Annabel got up and went over to touch the solid wood of the desktop. She looked up at the empty birdcage above and imagined a time gone by when birdsong accompanied Ah Ling's letter writing. She felt a lump form in her throat.

'How strange to think of her letters coming from this very writing desk all the way across the world to Dotty in Cornwall,' Annabel said.

'Dotty? Was that a pet name you had for your grandmother?' Julia asked. 'Ah Ling always called her Miss Dorothy.'

'No; everyone called her Dotty. Always.' Annabel frowned, confused. When had that changed? And why?

Annabel returned to the sofa and smiled at Julia. 'Tell me about Ah Ling. From the letters, it's obvious that she and Dotty were very close. What happened to her after Dotty left Singapore?'

Julia took a sip of tea. 'Ah Ling said goodbye to Miss Dorothy in February 1942. It was the start of a terrible time in Singapore. The Japanese occupation lasted for three and a half years and there were brutal repercussions for anyone who opposed them. Ah Ling struggled for a while. She had no job and not much money. She shared a room with her cousin, Ah Loke, and some other girls who'd been in service and had suddenly found themselves unemployed when the Japanese invaded. Their European employers had all disappeared, you see. They either left Singapore and sailed back to their home countries, or they were rounded up and sent off to internment camps. It was an awful chapter in our country's history.' Julia shook her head sadly.

'Yes of course, I remember reading about it,' Annabel said. 'Changi Jail, wasn't it? A terrible place.'

A look passed between Julia and Mei. Mei started to say something quietly in Cantonese, but Julia stopped her.

Julia turned back to Annabel and continued, 'Yes indeed. Many suffered starvation, torture and even death in that place. There was much fear in Singapore, everyone was terrified of the Japanese. But the human spirit is resilient and Ah Ling was strong.' She smiled proudly at Annabel. 'By day, she found a job working for a tailor in Chinatown. She was an excellent seamstress and she turned those skills to tailoring to help make ends meet during the occupation.'

'But she don't like the customers.' Mei's soft voice cut into Julia's story, her face suddenly turning very serious. 'The tailor work for Japanese, you know. Mama never like them.' She shook her head slowly. 'That time very bad, very bad.'

'You said "by day", Julia, what about by night?' Annabel asked, intrigued.

'Well,' Julia said with a chuckle. 'By night was a whole other story, and one which we are very proud to tell.' She beamed at Annabel then took a sip of tea before she began.

'Ah Ling's older brother, Minghai, was killed when the Japanese invaded Hainan in 1939. He was part of a communist militia called the Hainan Independent Column and carried out missions to undermine and sabotage the Japanese. Ah Ling adored Minghai, they were very close and wrote to each other frequently. But one day, his group was ambushed by a Japanese patrol and Minghai and his collaborators were all shot dead, as a warning to the local villagers against aiding the guerrillas. Ah Ling was heartbroken.'

A look of sorrow fell over Mei's face and she closed her eyes.

'Good grief!' Annabel exclaimed. 'That's awful, I'm so sorry.'

'Ah Ling said it felt like a horrible case of history repeating itself when the Japanese invaded and occupied Singapore. Ah Ling hated them and she vowed to avenge her brother's death.'

Annabel's mouth dropped open, amazed by what she was hearing. From the letters, Ah Ling had seemed a sweet and gentle lady; this was a whole other side of her.

'One day, while working in the tailor's shop, a man from the MPAJA, one of the resistance movements, came to see Ah Ling. He had made enquiries about her and decided that she could be both trustworthy and useful. Chinese workers were largely overlooked by the Kempeitai, you see, and they managed to continue their business without sparking too much interest. Ah Ling became a courier, smuggling resistance materials hidden in bundles of fabric and clothing deliveries from the tailor.'

'Wow! What a brave lady!' Annabel said.

Julia nodded. 'Yes, and she was incredibly successful. Despite a few hairy moments, she was never caught.' Julia smiled at Annabel. 'And in this way, by fighting back against the Japanese, she felt she was getting some revenge, for the sake of her brother.'

Mei, who had been listening quietly, now reached for a small box on the table beside her chair. She opened it and took out a shiny red enamel badge and a yellowing piece of paper. With arthritic fingers, she slowly unfolded the paper and read the Chinese words aloud.

Julia translated, 'For Services to The People. It was awarded to Ah Ling by the local Chinese resistance cell. She was one of their most reliable operatives during the occupation.'

'That's amazing! What happened to her after the war?'

'Well, a whole new chapter started then!' Julia chuckled. 'It was while working at the tailor's shop that Ah Ling met my grandfather, Hsien Lim. He was a hawker, you know what that is?' she asked Annabel, who nodded in reply.

'Hsien Lim was a modest street-food seller. He ran a chicken rice cart with his brother Hsien Long, near the tailor's shop in Chinatown where Ah Ling worked,' Julia explained. 'They were from Hainan, the same island as Ah Ling, and had come to Singapore as teenagers, like so many others, to work for a better life.'

'Aiyoh, love at first sight lah!' Mei continued, a smile on her face. She pointed to the sepia wedding photo in the gold frame on the sideboard. 'But is Papa who love at first sight, not Mama! Every day ah, he greet her, say all the sweet-sweet things. He chase her for so long hor, but she always say no one. But Papa very stubborn, very steady,' She let out a chuckle.

'He was just a humble hawker, you see,' Julia continued. 'And despite his grand plans for opening a restaurant with his brother one day, he had nothing. Ah Ling enjoyed his company; he was cheerful and kind, with a big wide smile, but she wanted more out of life and felt that a lowly hawker was rather beneath her.'

'But then ah, he open restaurant, wah, Mama so happy!' Mei said proudly. 'After that, then open some more! He very determined one.' She nodded, full of pride. 'Got big dreams, you know. In the end, give us good life.'

'Ah Ling and Hsien Lim married and had four children; three sons, then along came Mama,' Julia explained.

'I remember Ah Ling mentioning her children in the letters to Dotty,' Annabel said, smiling, 'as well as the restaurants; what a wonderful story!'

'My uncles run the restaurants these days,' Julia said. 'It's still a family business and still very popular. But you're not here just to find out about my grandmother, are you?' she asked. 'You said on the phone that you want to find out about your grandmother, Dorothy. What exactly do you want to know?'

Annabel put down her teacup and took a moment to consider her response. She took a deep breath before she began.

'You might find it hard to believe, given how close your family obviously is' – Annabel smiled as she gestured between Julia and her mother – 'But none of us ever knew that Dotty had even visited Singapore, never mind lived here. And the fact that she had another husband before she met Grandpa . . . Well . . . ' Annabel shook her head in disbelief. 'We were absolutely stunned.'

'I can imagine.' Julia nodded sympathetically.

'I found the letters and photographs that you returned following Ah Ling's passing in 2010, you see. Dotty had locked them away in a secret drawer in her desk and no one had any idea of their existence. Just after she died, I found them. I was so curious that . . . ' She paused here and shrugged with a coy smile. 'Well, here I am, a week later, hoping that you can shed some light on the subject. You're our only hope, really.'

Julia nodded again then turned to her mother and said something in Cantonese. The old lady nodded and took a sip of tea.

'Of course we want to help. Mother will tell you what she knows. It's easier for her in Cantonese, so I'll translate for you.' Julia said.

'Thank you so much, I would be so grateful for anything she can remember.'

Mei sat back in her chair and closed her eyes for a long moment, as if travelling back to the time when, as a little girl, her mother had told her stories of the English family she had worked for in the big black and white house.

'Do you think it would be alright if I recorded this?' James whispered to Julia, taking out his mobile phone. Annabel was glad of his idea, and pleased when Julia smiled and nodded her consent.

Mei's eyes eventually opened, a new look of concentration transforming her features, and she began, flowing in a rapid fire of Cantonese. Julia began her translation.

'Ah Ling was so happy when the new family and Miss Dorothy arrived. The family before were not so nice. The boss lady would shout and get angry, and Ah Ling was scared of her. So when they left to go back to England and the nice Templeton family came, she was very happy. She was just a little older than Miss Dorothy and they became very close; like good friends, or sisters she used to say. Miss Dorothy was new in Singapore and had a lot of learning to do, and Ah Ling helped her. Ah Ling was very happy.'

Mei closed her eyes. Annabel imagined her picturing her mother as a young woman.

'Then Miss Dorothy got married and everything changed.'

The old lady's face darkened and her brow furrowed as Julia resumed her translation.

'To Douglas Llewellyn?' Annabel asked, after a long pause.

Mei looked directly at her and nodded. Then she answered, but this time in English. 'Yes. He was a bad man.' She shook her head disapprovingly.

Annabel looked at James and raised her eyebrows. Then James spoke up, nudging Mei to continue, 'Did Douglas Llewellyn work for Dorothy's father? We found an article about him in the records office. They both worked for the same company, didn't they?'

Julia relayed this in Cantonese and Mei nodded slowly, before returning to her story and Julia's translation.

'Yes. McKinley's Rubber. Ah Ling thought at first maybe it was true love. Mr Llewellyn was so handsome and came with flowers and gifts for Miss Dorothy. Everyone was so happy.' She stopped and shook her head again. 'But it did not last. He was just using her.'

'How do you mean, "using her"?' Annabel asked. 'To please her father and get ahead in the company, do you mean?'

Julia asked her mother in Cantonese.

'No,' came the reply. 'No, it was not that.' Mei paused again and frowned.

'Then what was he using her for?' Annabel asked, starting to feel concerned by what she was hearing.

Mei sighed and, turning to her daughter, uttered a rapid fire of Cantonese. The old lady grew increasingly agitated and her tone became angrier. Julia stroked her hand, replying with soothing words, but Annabel noticed a steeliness beneath the surface. What were they saying?

Beside her, James fiddled with his phone and Annabel gave him a grateful smile when she realised he was switching off the voice recorder. He gave a brief shake of his head, silently communicating to her that he didn't think it right to record while Mei was upset. The more Annabel saw of James, the more he differed from her previous impression of him. He had always been so quiet and strained around her, so aloof and distant during their university days. Had she read him all wrong, she wondered, or had life altered him? Perhaps a bit of both. But he was a decent guy, Annabel thought to herself, and, in her experience, they were few and far between.

'Mama is worried that you may find it all too upsetting,' Julia explained. 'Douglas Llewellyn did not treat your grandmother well, I'm afraid, and the story does not have a happy ending.' She turned to her mother and spoke in slow, clear English, 'Mama, you want to tell the story or I do it?'

'I do,' the older lady said, with a determined nod. She paused for a moment, then took a deep breath before she began in her accented English.

'Mr Llewellyn, he not nice man lah. Ah Ling don't like him, 'cause he very mean to Miss Dorothy. And Ah Ling really love Miss Dorothy, you know. Like sisters, they so close.' Mei smiled, thinking of her mother.

'That Mr Llewellyn ah, always go and love another woman, but that one already married! But, he don't care, still always go visit her all the time. Ah Ling say some nights he never even come home leh.'

Mei shook her head, tsk-ing softly.

'Aiyoh, that Miss Dorothy, so poor thing. She love him so much, but hor, he treat her so bad.' She picked up her teacup, pausing for a moment.

The pain of Luke's recent infidelity was still raw. Annabel's bruised heart ached at the thought of her cheerful, loving grandmother suffering similar treatment.

'Miss Dorothy she want to have baby, but cannot lor,' Mei continued. 'She got pregnant few times, but every time lose the baby. Wah, so sad, you know. Ah Ling say Mr Llewellyn got angry with her.' Mei scrunched up her face. 'He so cruel one. And always drink whisky.'

Annabel felt a further pang of sadness as she thought back to the conversation she'd had with her grandmother in the hospital, when she'd mentioned not being able to have children. How Annabel wished she'd had the foresight to find out then what it all meant; if she'd known it would be their last conversation, there was so much more that she would have asked her.

'Then war start to come, everyone need to prepare,' Mei went on in her gentle, lilting way. 'Miss Dorothy go train to be nurse, and Mr Llewellyn also go learn to become soldier lor. Ah Ling say that time quite good when he not home; house more peaceful, everybody also more happy right? But hor, good time never last long one.'

Annabel thought back to all the times when she was a small child and her grandmother had patched up injuries and cured ailments. She had a distant memory of her mentioning helping as a nurse during the war, but Annabel had assumed it had been in London. Never would she have dreamed of imagining her grandmother training as a nurse in Singapore.

Mei paused and sipped her tea. Then she turned to Julia and uttered a flurry of Cantonese. Julia sighed, then replied calmly in the same language, seeming to acquiesce to whatever her mother was asking of her. Annabel turned to James with curious eyes. He gave a small shrug in reply; he had spotted it too, the disagreement between mother and daughter.

Mei continued in Cantonese and Julia picked up the translation. 'Then one day, when he came home from training, Mr Llewellyn had an accident. It was very late at night. Ah Ling said he was drinking too much whisky. And he tripped. He fell down the stairs and he broke his neck.'

Annabel gasped. So that was the fall that had killed Douglas Llewellyn: an intoxicated tumble down the stairs. Her initial reaction was sympathy, but then she remembered what she had just heard about Dotty's philandering first husband and couldn't help but feel that he had got his just deserts. She turned to James, who was looking equally surprised.

Meanwhile, Julia was talking to her mother in quick, quiet Cantonese. Although the language was impossible to her, the intention was quite clear to Annabel: Julia seemed to be begging her mother, imploring her even. To do what? Annabel had no idea. But what became fiercely evident was that Mei was not going to give in to her daughter's request. Annabel was shocked as the old lady started shaking and her eyes filled with tears. Mei's voice got louder and louder to the point that she was shouting at her daughter.

Julia did her best to soothe her mother, then turned to their visitors.

'I'm so sorry,' she said calmly. 'But I think Mama needs to rest now. We'll need to finish this another time.'

CHAPTER 19

Singapore

JUNE 1941

Dorothy awoke with a start. It was happening again, the telltale cramps in her lower abdomen and the accompanying warm stickiness between her legs. A rising wave of panic swept over her as she stumbled out of bed and rushed to the bathroom. She looked down at her stained underwear and felt her heart break for the third time. It was so unfair. So bloody unfair. She gave a gut-wrenching moan and sobbed for her loss.

Ah Ling was by her side in seconds, wiping away the tears as she uttered soothing words of comfort. But it was no use, Dorothy thought, there was something wrong with her. It was just over a year since her wedding and this was the third child she had yearned for, and lost. The poor little being that never had a chance to grow, to live, because of her inability to be a mother.

Ah Ling gently led her back to the bedroom. She helped change her underwear and laid towels on the bed beneath her. Once Dorothy was settled, the faithful Ah Ling mopped her face with a cool, damp towel.

'You stay here, ma'am. I call doctor.' She paused, then asked, 'You want call Mr Llewellyn sir?'

That was the last thing Dorothy wanted. She closed her eyes and shook her head, relieved that he had already left early for work. She couldn't face the look he had given her the last two times, that mix of disappointment and disdain. On both those occasions his eyes had asked the silent question 'What's wrong with you?' And the worst part was that she was starting to ask herself the same question. Everyone they knew seemed to be popping out babies left, right and centre, so why couldn't she?

Fresh tears pricked at her eyes and Ah Ling squeezed her hand.

'Is OK ma'am, Ah Ling here.' She nodded encouragingly then continued mopping her brow. 'Everything be OK.' How Dorothy wished that were true.

Since that night last Christmas, Dorothy had slowly come to a place of acceptance about the state of her relationship. She now realised that it was a marriage of convenience – of Douglas's convenience – and she was expected to be terribly British and keep a stiff upper lip for the sake of maintaining appearances. Douglas loved to keep up the image of the perfect newlyweds, especially in front of her parents who were so infuriatingly enamoured of their handsome, clever son-in-law. Even if she had wanted to complain, they could see nothing for her to complain about; everything looked perfect from the outside.

But the reality was quite different. These days, Douglas barely bothered to conceal from her his visits to his mistress; it was an open, unspoken secret between them. At the start of the year, he would come home from the club in the early hours steaming drunk and demand his conjugal rites from his wife. But those drunken sessions ceased after Ah Ling discreetly organised a new door lock to help keep her mistress safe. On other nights, Douglas would come home exhausted from his training with the Straits Settlements Volunteer Force with whom he had recently enlisted. And some nights he wouldn't come home at all.

Silently, Dorothy had resolved to make the best of her lot, for, as her mother regularly reminded her, it simply didn't do to complain. So she kept busy instead, tried to keep her head down and keep the peace with Douglas. There were brief moments of optimism when she felt hopeful that things could change between them. He would give her a kind word, a gentle touch or a compliment on how nicely she kept their home. Those fleeting moments were bittersweet, for it showed her that the man she had fallen in love with was still there, but it broke her heart that she was not – and never had been – his first priority.

The only trump card that Dorothy held was Douglas longed to start a family. Dorothy felt sure that things would be different once she gave him the son he yearned for, that he would love and appreciate her and finally give up his mistress. But with every failed pregnancy, that hope slipped further out of reach.

It was a tense time in Singapore, as talk turned increasingly to war. The fighting in Europe raged on and London was only just catching its breath after eight long months of bombing. British morale was at an all-time low and Dorothy wept as she read Daisy's letters. Their lives in London were full of sirens, air-raid shelters, bombing raids and worlds torn apart by the German Luftwaffe. Every night, she prayed for Daisy and her family and for the safety of her brother Thomas, who was now serving with the Royal Army Medical Corps. The last they had heard, he was heading off to North Africa, but his last letter had arrived several weeks ago.

'But we're still safe here, aren't we?' Dorothy asked her father as the pair of them dined together at the family home one Sunday. She gazed out at the lush, green lawns and the palm trees gently waving in the soft afternoon breeze, and found it impossible to imagine the horrors of war coming to this peaceful island.

'Yes, absolutely; of course we're safe.' Anthony Templeton nodded determinedly. 'But tensions *are* rising between Japan and the West,' he explained. 'Put simply, they want to expand their empire and we're rather in the way.' He gave a wry smile and took a sip of his Claret. 'Strategically, they would love to get their hands on Singapore; it's in a prime location to transport troops and supplies. And they would love to get their greedy mitts on the area's natural resources.'

'Like we Brits did first, with our "greedy mitts", you mean?' Dorothy raised her eyebrows ironically at her father.

'Ha! Yes, you've got me there!' Anthony chuckled.

'It's the rubber they want, isn't it?' Dorothy asked. 'Douglas is always saying how important it is to the war effort.'

'Yes, exactly. Let's face it, that's why we were sent out here in the first place – McKinley's knew that rubber would be the hot commodity during the war, hence my promotion to come out and expand the business. But the Japs will want the oil and tin as well. They'll need us Brits out of the way in order to get them, but it just isn't going to happen. I saw Shenton Thomas at the club the other night, "impregnable fortress" was the phrase he used for Singapore. So the Japs can huff and puff as much as they like; they won't blow our house down!' He chuckled at his joke. 'And don't worry about Douglas, darling, he'll be absolutely fine. I know they're training as if they're actually going to war, but it's highly unlikely that he'll end up in harm's way.'

Dorothy forced a smile and concentrated on her roast chicken. Despite the hero-worship to which he felt his new role entitled him, her husband had been a reluctant volunteer. He'd put it off for months, insisting that he would be far more useful to the war effort if he could concentrate all his efforts on the business. The demand for rubber was rocketing and McKinley's were struggling to keep up with their orders. However, Dorothy had learned early on that keeping up appearances was important to her husband; he had to be seen to be doing the right thing. So, finally, as many of his colleagues and friends had done before him, Douglas had volunteered.

The servants came in and cleared the plates, then brought the dessert. It was pineapple flan, Dorothy's favourite, but she had too much on her mind to enjoy it. She cleared her throat and tried to keep her voice light. 'I do hope I can pop up and see Mummy before I go. She was asleep when I arrived. What did the doctor say?'

Anthony Templeton's face turned serious and he laid down his spoon on the table. 'She's been asleep most of the day, she's just exhausted all the time.' He shook his head sadly. 'She's hardly eating anything. The doctor did some tests and prescribed total bed rest. We should get the results this week.' He sighed. 'I hope to God that she's alright. I don't know what I'd do if . . . ' Anthony's eyes brimmed with unshed tears as his voice broke off.

'She's going to be absolutely fine!' Dorothy interrupted, smiling bravely at her father. She reached across the table to squeeze his hand. 'She's been working so hard lately with all her Red Cross fundraising and it's been so awfully hot! I'm sure it's probably just a combination of the two, it's not surprising that she needs a good rest. Don't worry, Daddy.' The tables had turned and now it was her turn to be the reassuring one. 'Everything will be alright.'

They ate in companionable silence for a few minutes. The only sound was the whirr of the ceiling fan above them, slowly moving the warm air around the dining room. Occasionally, a soft breeze made its way in through the open window and Dorothy enjoyed the cooling sensation against her skin.

'Going back to the Japs,' she pondered aloud as she stirred sugar into the cup of coffee that the servant had poured for her. 'You're absolutely sure there's no way they can invade?' Dorothy's brow creased. She thought back to the newspaper articles she'd read about Japan's invasion of China and of Daisy's war-filled letters. Her friend's tales of the London Blitz had made her blood run cold.

'Oh, they might try.' Her father chuckled. 'I wouldn't put it past them, that Hirohito is a sly old fox! But Singapore is a stronghold; we're untouchable here. Don't you worry, darling, you'll see!'

As time ticked on, however, it seemed that the British government was taking no chances. Singapore's defences were fortified and manpower increased as the Civil Defence recruitment drive upped its pace. People were encouraged to stockpile food and work began on building air-raid shelters, just like they had done in London. But the British insisted it was purely precautionary; nobody believed that a Japanese attack could ever be successful.

A couple of weeks later, Clara called round to Dorothy's house unannounced after breakfast. Dorothy could sense a buzz of excitement in her friend and wondered if it might be anything to do with her blossoming romance with Cyril Cavendish.

'I have some news,' Clara began, as soon as they were seated in the garden, the coffee tray on the table between them. Her face broke into an excited smile and Dorothy got ready to congratulate her friend. Cyril was a thoroughly decent chap and he idolised Clara. But she knew all too well that appearances could be deceptive and she hoped that their marriage would be more successful than her own.

'I've decided to do my bit and help out at the hospital. They're training volunteer nurses in case of an invasion. So I'm going to sign up!'

'Oh!' Dorothy gasped, unable to hide her surprise. 'But Daddy says there isn't going to be a . . . '

'Oh, wake up, Dorothy! Stop burying your head in the sand! Haven't you been listening to the news? The Powers That Be can posture all they like, but it's going to happen. Now that the Japs have a stronghold in French Indochina, they're in prime striking position. And it's been kept hush-hush, but Father said that Japanese planes have been spotted over Singapore, doubtless on reconnaissance missions.'

'But . . . ' Dorothy's brow furrowed.

'But what?' Clara interrupted, her frustration clearly growing. 'You think they just pop over to see if they fancy the look of Singapore's beaches for their holidays?' She gave a wry chuckle and shook her head at her friend. 'They're going to invade, Dorothy, there's no doubt about it, and we need to be ready. So what do you say? Fancy joining me?'

For the second time that morning, Dorothy was wrong-footed. The idea of Clara training as a nurse had been surprising enough, but the fact that she wanted Dorothy to join her was even more unexpected.

'Oh gosh, I don't know,' she blustered. 'I'm not sure what Douglas would think . . . '

'Oh, hang Douglas!' Clara snapped. Although Dorothy had deliberately avoided saying as much to her friend, Clara seemed to know that her marriage was proving a disappointment. She took a breath, then softened her tone. 'I'm worried about you, you haven't been yourself lately. I know how sad you were about losing the baby . . . '

'Babies,' Dorothy whispered, pluralising the word without missing a beat.

Clara nodded solemnly, 'Indeed; babies.' She patted her friend's hand. 'I think a change of focus might be good for you; take you out of yourself, get you out of the house a bit! And let's face it' – she grinned mischievously at her friend – 'what larks we'd have, doing our training together!'

Dorothy rolled her eyes at her friend's enthusiastic persuasion tactics, but couldn't help grinning back. Clara was right, she needed something new in her life. She was in danger of becoming a proverbial bored – and boring – housewife. With Douglas increasingly away on training exercises and no baby to prepare for, there was precious little to keep her at home. And, even if she didn't particularly enjoy the sight of blood, she was sure that she could make herself useful in lots of other ways.

Just three days later, Dorothy found herself standing in line with Clara at the Alexandra Military Hospital. It had seemed like a good idea at the time, but the reality of her decision was now making her stomach do somersaults and her palms feel clammy. The Alexandra was an imposing building in the Queenstown area, on the western side of the city. Built by the British as a military hospital just three years earlier, it housed all the latest equipment and prided itself on keeping up with the very latest medical advances. It was a big place, with over 800 beds and 200 doctors and nurses, and catered for military and civilian patients alike. The hustle and bustle of people going about their business – medical staff, patients and visitors – was overwhelming to Dorothy, and the bitter scent of disinfectant was starting to cloy at the back of her throat.

Today was recruitment day for the nursing school and the two friends were halfway along a queue of ladies, all patiently waiting to hand in their forms to the registrar. Dorothy looked down the line and smiled nervously at a couple of British girls she recognised. But it wasn't just Brits who had come, there were local ladies, too, all keen to come and do their bit.

'Chin up!' Clara had told Dorothy when she'd shared her nerves. 'Worse things happen at sea!' Then she had handed Dorothy a boiled sweet which helped ease the sensation in her stomach. She thought back to Douglas's reaction and her resolve strengthened.

'You, darling? A nurse?' he had asked incredulously, as if the idea were completely alien to him. 'It'd mean hard work and long shifts, plus you'll see some pretty ghastly sights. Are you sure you're up to it?'

Did he think so little of her? That she was so weak? His response had infuriated her. Well, she would show him. Rather than put her off, Douglas had made her even more determined. She didn't want to be a delicate little wife at home, she wanted to make something happen.

Finally, a nurse called Dorothy's name and Clara patted her arm with an affectionate 'Good luck!'

Dorothy was led along the corridor and into a small, white office. The matronly-looking lady behind the desk introduced herself, with a tight Scottish burr, as Sister Jamieson. She fired through the preliminary interview questions in a brusque, no-nonsense sort of way and she gave little reaction to Dorothy's answers. Instead, she scribbled busily on the notepad in front of her in long, spidery handwriting. Dorothy felt as if she were being interviewed for the military. Was this what interrogation was like? Her stomach was in knots and she had no idea how she was holding up. After a while, she breathed in relief when Sister Jamieson concluded her questioning with a curt 'Thank you, Mrs Llewellyn.' Then she nodded to the gentleman on her left, it was his turn.

Doctor Archie, as he introduced himself, was the total opposite of the bustling sister. He spoke in a softer, less hurried way, with a well-spoken English accent that had a slight hint of the West Country. His haystack of sandy-blonde hair fell into his eyes and he had a slightly crooked smile which made his green eyes shine. Dorothy thought him younger than the matronly sister, perhaps in his late thirties. His gentle, easy-going manner reminded her of her brother Thomas and she instantly found herself warming to him.

Instead of firing more questions at her, he asked her about herself; her hobbies, her interests, her life. He explained that he was purely there in a supervisory capacity, that the nursing school was very much the domain of Sister Jamieson and her equally capable colleagues – cue a proud smile from Sister Jamieson – but it was important for him to get a sense of whether or not she would be a good fit. Dorothy found herself hoping that she would.

After the interview, she sat on a wooden bench in the entrance lobby, waiting for Clara. Her stomach fluttered with a combination of nerves and excitement. They would write to her in the next few days, Nurse Jamieson had said, informing her whether or not she had been accepted. The coward in her hoped that they wouldn't want her, that they had been disappointed by her interview answers and felt she wouldn't make a good nurse after all. But she also felt a growing sense of nervous anticipation. To have a role in this place, to be part of a team and to help others was an exciting, if a little daunting, prospect.

Dorothy was jolted out of her reverie by the sharp tap of high heels ricocheting around the lobby like gunfire. She looked up and instantly recognised the owner.

'Mummy!' She smiled and jumped up from her seat, crossing the hallway to embrace her mother. But she stopped short. Her mother had been crying; something was wrong. Fear gripped her stomach like a vice.

'What is it, Mummy? Whatever's happened?' She grasped her mother's hands and ushered her over to sit down on the bench. Dorothy put her arm around her, she was trembling. Olivia Templeton took a handkerchief from her skirt pocket and wiped her moist eyes. Just then, Anthony Templeton appeared, rushing to catch up with his wife. He gave Dorothy the ghost of a smile then sat next to Olivia and wrapped her in his arms.

'Daddy, what's happened? What did the doctor say?' Dorothy whispered, choked with emotion.

'Darling, there's no easy way to say this, I'm afraid,' her father began, his voice cracking as he tried to get the words out. 'Your mother has a tumour.'

CHAPTER 20

Singapore

WEDNESDAY 3RD APRIL, 2019

The drive back to the apartment was a quiet one. As if to match the sombre mood, the late afternoon sky had turned black and the monsoon-like rain had transformed the highway into a sea of blurry red tail lights. The soothing strains of Debussy's 'Clair de Lune' played on the radio, but Annabel was agitated. Next to her, James looked deep in thought, keeping his focus on the road ahead, alert to the unpredictable drivers around them.

She gave a sigh of frustration. 'I just don't get it,' she began. 'Why did Mei get so upset? And why so angry? What on earth was that about?'

'Yes, you're right,' James said. 'Julia was putting a calm front on, but they were clearly disagreeing about something. There's more to this, I'm sure. I guess we'll just have to wait till we can see her again.'

'It all seems to add up, what they were saying, I mean,' Annabel said. 'The last time I saw Dotty, in the hospital, she told me that she couldn't have children. I had no idea she'd suffered recurrent miscarriages, though. She was going to explain everything to me the next time I saw her, but . . . ' Annabel's voice broke and she welled up.

She suddenly felt so tired and so confused, and her grief, still raw, threatened to overwhelm her. She closed her eyes, blinking away hot tears, and was surprised to feel James's warm hand on hers. She turned to look at him but his appearance had not changed; his eyes were still fixed on the road ahead. But his hand was solid and comforting, offering her silent, rock-solid support. It was just what she needed right now.

A moment later, the spell was broken by the buzz of Annabel's phone. She reached down into her handbag and checked it for the first time in several hours. There were four text messages and two missed calls.

'All OK?' James asked.

'Messages from my dad and my brother, checking that I'm still alive and . . . ' She paused as she tapped on the call history, then continued more quietly, 'A couple of missed calls from Luke.'

James looked across at her. 'Your ex?'

Annabel nodded and felt that uncomfortable knot in her stomach again. Seeing his name pop up on her phone felt so normal, so natural, and it had always made her smile. But her heart sank as the pain of his deceit stabbed at her again. Why was he calling her? She could feel her heart start to race as all the anguish of the break-up started to creep over her. She closed her eyes and focused on taking five long, slow breaths, in and out, just as she'd read in some Sunday supplement article.

'Are you alright?' James asked as she finished number five.

Annabel sighed and forced a smile. 'Yes, thanks. I have no idea what he wants. I'll text him back later.'

James slowed the car as they approached a set of traffic lights. The rain had stopped and he turned off the windscreen wipers.

'Have you told your dad what you've found out?' James asked, changing the subject. 'Do you think he had any idea about Dotty's life out here?'

She shook her head. 'No, I haven't told him. And I really don't think he could have known anything; Dotty seems to have done a very good job of keeping all of this top secret. Dad knows I'm here in Singapore, but I guess I was a little economical with the truth. I just said I needed a change of scenery after the break-up and that my friend Jenny had set me up to stay with her cousin out here. It's not exactly a lie.' She shrugged. 'Well, only by omission, I suppose.'

Annabel felt a pang of guilt as she thought of her father and suddenly missed him very much. She wanted to call him, to hear his voice, but was worried she might let something slip about her research. So she tapped a quick reply instead, reassuring him that all was well, that she loved and missed him, then pressed send.

'I don't like keeping secrets from him.' She sighed. 'But he's only just come out of hospital after major surgery and I don't want to bother him with any of this yet. He's got enough on his plate with his recovery and I want to make sure I've done my research and got my facts right before I share any of this with him.'

'Spoken like a true historian!' James turned to her and waggled his eyebrows comically. Annabel rolled her eyes but couldn't mask her smile.

The lights changed to green and James put the car into drive and moved off. 'How do you think he'll react when he finds out? It's pretty amazing that Dotty had a whole other life out here before she married his father.'

Annabel turned and looked at him, her eyes creased in confusion. 'What did you just say?'

'His father,' James repeated. 'Well, you think it's unlikely that Dotty was his biological mother, right? So it could be that he was your grandfather's son from a previous marriage. No?'

'Oh!' Annabel was surprised, but as she thought it through it all made sense to her. 'So you think Grandpa was *also* married before? Maybe his first wife died, too?'

James nodded. 'Maybe. It's one possibility. Is there much of a family resemblance?'

Annabel thought of her dark-haired, dark-eyed father and compared him to the image she had in her mind of her fair grandfather, as she had done several times since finding the secret photographs. She frowned and shook her head. 'No, actually, they didn't look at all alike. Completely different colouring.' She screwed up her face, it didn't make any sense.

'Oh well,' said James lightly. 'Maybe he was more like his biological mother?'

A moment later, it was the turn of James's phone to start buzzing. The car radio screen lit up, showing a call from Tom. James clicked the answer button on the steering wheel to connect it through the car speakers.

'Mate, what's up?' James answered casually.

'Hi James,' Tom began in his usual cheerful manner. 'Don't suppose you're still with Annabel, are you?'

'Yes, she's here, we're in the car, heading back to your place now.'

'Hi Tom!' Annabel added.

'Oh, that's good. Hi Annabel!' He sounded pleased. 'Emma's busy child-wrangling at the moment.' Annabel smiled at his turn of phrase, imagining the busy hubbub of family life. 'So I'm in charge of telling you the plan! Once the little darlings are in bed, we thought it might be fun to do something a bit touristy, show Annabel the bright lights of Singapore! Quite literally, now I think of it!' He chuckled at his own joke. 'We thought Gardens by the Bay. Have a wander, check out the light show, then have some satay and a few beers down there. Pretty casual. Emma mentioned it was on Annabel's list and, well . . . We aim to please!'

James turned to Annabel and raised his eyebrows questioningly. She smiled and nodded her enthusiasm.

'Sounds great, Tom! Thanks for thinking of it!' she said.

'No problem at all! We're both looking forward to hearing how you got on this afternoon, too. Meet you in the car park at 7.30!'

A muffled shout from Emma in the background let them know that he'd got the time wrong.

'Oops sorry, no; eight o'clock apparently!' Tom corrected himself with a chuckle.

'Alright mate, we'll meet you there.' And James clicked off the call. He looked at his watch and spent a moment figuring out timings in his head.

'We'll be too early if we head straight there. Do you mind if we call into my place on the way? I might drop the car off and we can get a cab down there, then I can join Tom on the beers!' He gave her a lopsided grin. There it was again, that fun, carefree side that she hadn't really seen before. She liked it.

'Sounds like a plan!' She grinned back, then checked her watch. It was half past six. What time was it back home? It must be daytime as text messages had started coming through.

'In fact, would it be OK to call my brother from your place? I promised him I'd let him know what we've found out and it feels a bit weird texting all this.'

'Of course,' James said as he turned the car off the highway and onto a tree-lined street. The rain had stopped and the sky had brightened. It looked like it was going to turn into a nice evening. 'No problem at all. You can use the Wi-Fi and curl up in the lounge for a bit.' He noticed her yawn. 'You must be tired.'

'I've actually got a couple of emails I need to send, too, so you can make yourself at home,' he added.

'Thanks, James, that'd be great. And throw a cup of builder's tea into the equation and I'm in!' She smiled back. 'It was nice to try the green tea at Mei's place, but I'm a Tetley's girl at heart!'

'Ha!' he laughed. 'You can take the girl out of England, but . . .'

'She'll still want a decent cup of tea!' Annabel finished for him.

James's apartment in Holland Village had 'bachelor pad' written all over it. It was the total opposite of Emma and Tom's expansive family home – neat and compact, with just two bedrooms.

'Excuse the boxes,' he muttered as he led the way into the open-plan living area. 'I haven't finished unpacking yet.'

Annabel felt a pang of sympathy as she remembered the reason for his new bachelor lifestyle; it was only a few weeks since he'd left the family home and his ex and their daughter had moved back to England. What an adjustment it must be for him.

'It's lovely.' She smiled encouragingly. 'All looks very modern!'

James shrugged in a non-committal way. 'It's OK. Good location and the gym's decent.'

He went through to the kitchen and Annabel heard him running the tap to fill the kettle. She looked around at the open-plan living area, the lounge at one end and the dining table at the other. The furniture, all matching light pine, looked brand new and reminded her of a certain Swedish furniture store. It all felt rather generic and, apart from a solitary framed photograph on the bookcase, it lacked any personal touch.

She went over to the photo and couldn't help but smile at the happy scene. James was at the beach on a perfect, sunny day, looking casual and relaxed in a polo shirt and shorts. On his back was a beautiful little girl of around six years old with long, wavy brown hair. The family similarity was striking; the same fair colouring and goofy, lopsided grin, clearly enjoying happier times together.

'Is that your daughter?' Annabel asked when he came back into the room, nodding towards the photograph. He went over and picked it up, gently caressing the image of his daughter's face as he wiped away some tiny specks of dust. She noticed the sad smile on his face.

'Yes, this is Jessica. That was a few years ago now, though. She'll be nine in a couple of weeks.'

'She's a beautiful girl. You must miss her.' Annabel instantly regretted her comment as she saw the light fade from his eyes. A long, awkward pause followed. James continued to stare at the picture, his eyes full of sorrow. Annabel's heart began to race as she searched desperately for something to say. Something, anything. But the only words that came to mind would have sounded cliched and banal.

'I'm sorry,' she began after an excruciating silence, but James cut her off.

'How do you like your tea?' His face was downcast as he put the photo frame back on the bookcase and made his way towards the kitchen.

'Just milk, please,' she called after him, feeling like a prize idiot for reminding him of his loss. She sighed, then took her phone from her handbag and curled up on the end of the sofa.

She tapped out a quick message to Luke, asking – as politely as she could – what he wanted. Then she messaged her brother, in a much friendlier tone, checking if it was a good time to talk.

The ticks on Luke's message turned blue within seconds and he was quick to reply. His words made her stomach sink.

> I miss you. I messed up. I'm so sorry, Annie. Can we talk?

Annabel sighed and she felt a tug in her stomach. Part of her missed him, too. She would love nothing more than to return home from this trip and get back to their former, happy life together. But she shook herself out of that thinking. She knew that it was impossible; she would never be able to trust him again. Not only had he broken her heart, but he'd humiliated her by advertising himself on dating websites for all the world to see. If Jenny had seen his profile, who else had? Was there any going back from that?

Her phone started vibrating and her brother's name lit up the screen. She was glad to hear his cheerful voice.

'It's great to hear you, Annie!' he said. 'But I haven't got long, I'm afraid. I'm in a cab on my way to a meeting.'

Annabel filled him in on the visit to Julia and Mei and shared what she had learned about Douglas Llewellyn.

William gave a long whistle at the other end of the line as she told her brother of his demise. 'Sounds like the cheating bastard got his comeuppance then!'

'Yes,' Annabel agreed. 'But it was strange, Will. The old lady got quite agitated when Julia was telling us about it. They ended up having an argument in their own language. They speak Cantonese, so we didn't have a clue what was going on.'

'We?' Her brother asked.

'Oh, James came with me. You remember? Emma and Tom's friend, the guy I was at uni with. He's been helping me with my research. And he drove me up to Ang Mo Kio to meet Julia and her mum. To be honest, he's been a real help; he's made all of this so much easier.'

Annabel could hear the relief in her brother's voice. 'He sounds like a good guy.'

As if on cue, James appeared and set down a tea tray on the table in front of her. On it was a mug of steaming tea – just the right colour for her liking – and a plate of biscuits. She smiled up at him and mouthed a 'thank you'. She was glad when he smiled back, the earlier tension gone.

'Oh, James is definitely a good guy,' she continued to her brother on the phone, hamming it up now for his amusement. 'He's just brought me a cuppa and some chocolate Hobnobs, my favourites!' She grinned up at him.

James rolled his eyes self-deprecatingly but she could tell he was trying not to smile. Then he picked up his laptop and indicated that he was going into one of the bedrooms.

'Ha, perfect!' William chuckled at the other end of the line. 'I'm glad someone's looking after you, Annie. I hate to think of you all the way over there doing this on your own, especially after . . . Well, you know.' Her brother paused. 'Come home soon, we miss you.'

Annabel sighed. 'Thanks, Will. I miss you all, too. But there's still more digging to do here. I got the feeling that we didn't get the whole story, that there was more to it. I mean, why did Mei – that's Ah Ling's daughter – get so upset talking about Douglas's death? It was a bit odd, to be honest.'

'Hmm. Can you go back another time, maybe?' William asked. 'Or get Julia on her own?'

'Yes, I hope so. I can't put my finger on it, but I felt that they were holding something back.'

'Listen, Annie, I'm just arriving so I'd better go. But keep in touch and let's chat at the weekend when I've got more time. Sarah sends her love. Come back soon, once you're finished with your sleuthing!'

Annabel's eyes filled with tears as she ended the call; she missed them all, too. To make herself feel better, she picked up a biscuit and dunked it in her cup of tea.

A couple of hours later, Annabel grinned in wonder and pure joy as thousands of dazzling lights above her danced in time with the music.

Emma squeezed her arm. 'Are you enjoying it? It's quite something, isn't it?'

Annabel had seen pictures of Singapore's Supertrees in her guidebook but nothing had prepared her for the magic of the light show. As soon as the music had begun, the enormous metal trees, all covered in greenery and foliage, had come alive in a stunning display of light and sound. The theme for the evening was the waltz and Annabel found herself joining

Emma as they swayed in time to the orchestral music that was playing over the speakers.

'It's amazing!' She grinned back, then set her phone to video mode as she recognised the opening bars of the 'Blue Danube Waltz'. It was one of her dad's favourites; she would send him the clip later.

According to Annabel's guidebook, there were eighteen Supertrees in total. They'd been designed as vertical gardens and ranged in height from twenty-five to fifty metres. High above, an aerial walkway provided a bird's-eye view of the show for those who'd paid the entry fee. Annabel's stomach lurched at the thought of being up so high. She was perfectly happy with her free entry on terra firma, surrounded by hundreds of others. There were tourists, locals, expats and families, all craning their necks skyward, child-like grins on their faces, as they watched the mechanical trees sparkle in the night sky.

The show came to an end with a rousing orchestral finale and applause echoed around them. The pre-recorded voice through the speakers wished everyone a good evening and hoped that they'd enjoyed the show.

'Well that was great!' Emma beamed as they followed the crowds towards the exit.

'Yes, I haven't been down here for ages, I'm glad we came!' Tom agreed. 'I'm glad you enjoyed it, too, Annabel! Nice to tick off a few of the touristy things while you're here. What about you, James?' he asked his friend.

James's brow furrowed. 'To be honest, it's only the second time I've been. We brought Jessica here a couple of years ago for her birthday . . . ' His voice tailed off. After a moment, he cleared his throat. 'It's a bit touristy for me, rather Disneyland-ish, but all very clever and techy. Very Singapore.' He raised an ironic eyebrow.

It was a balmy evening and Annabel enjoyed the occasional wafts of cooling breeze as they made their way through the Gardens by the Bay. It was a huge area, 250 acres of garden all developed on reclaimed land. There were walking paths, ponds, lakes, cafés, children's play areas and individual gardens. It all sat in the shadow of the iconic Marina Bay Sands Hotel, whose three towers were lit up like Christmas trees. High up on top of them, the ship structure proudly sat like the icing on the cake. Annabel could see what James meant, it did have an artificial feeling but it was all so clean, modern and shiny that she couldn't help but be impressed.

They passed an enormous floral clock and two giant glass greenhouses and Annabel made a mental note to come back for another visit while she was here, there was just so much to see. They were heading for the food court where Tom had promised her some of the best satay in Singapore. The sound of a nice cold beer was pretty inviting, too.

Her phone buzzed in her skirt pocket and, as she pulled it out, she was surprised to see Julia's name on the screen. She excused herself from the others and moved away from them to answer the call.

'Hi Annabel,' Julia began. 'I'm so sorry about this afternoon. I hope you didn't feel that you had a wasted journey?'

Annabel did her best to reassure Julia that everything was alright and said that she hoped Mei was feeling better.

'Listen, we need to meet up. Mama didn't want me to tell you – in fact she'll be furious with me if she finds out. She made a promise to Ah Ling, you see. She promised that she'd never repeat what happened to anyone. But now that both Ah Ling has passed and your grandmother has passed, I honestly don't see what difference it makes. In fact, it might actually help explain things for you.'

'Julia, what are you talking about? Explain what?' Annabel asked, feeling that Julia was going round in circles.

There was a sigh at the other end of the phone. 'You deserve to know the truth. So I need to tell you what *really* happened to your grandmother's husband.'

'What do you mean?'

'Well, there's no easy way of saying this, I'm afraid.' Julia paused and took a breath. 'Douglas Llewellyn didn't fall down the stairs. It wasn't an accident.'

CHAPTER 21

Singapore

NOVEMBER 1941

'Dorothy! Dorothy, wake up!' Clara's voice stirred her from the depths of her sleep. Dorothy blinked open her eyes, raised her head from the table where it had been resting and rubbed the crick in her neck.

'You'd better not let Nurse Jamieson catch you napping in your break!' Her friend grinned down at her. 'I'm sure she'd have something to say about it "contravening the Nurse's Code of Conduct" or something!' This last part she delivered in a perfect impression of their boss's lilting Edinburgh accent, making Dorothy smile. They were a month into their nursing training and, along with every other trainee, were rather in awe of the formidable matron.

She checked her watch and sighed in relief; ten more minutes before she was due back on shift. She yawned and rubbed the sleep from her eyes. 'I don't know what happened, I only closed my eyes for a moment.'

'Always the way! Everything alright? You look a bit peaky today.' Clara's eyes filled with concern as she looked at her friend. She poured them each a cup of tea from the large silver urn in the corner, then sat down opposite her.

'I didn't sleep very well last night; I'm worried about Mummy. She's having her surgery this afternoon.'

Clara sighed and gave a sympathetic smile. 'Ah, yes of course. But I'm sure everything will be fine. Your mother is made of stern stuff and she'll make a full recovery, I'm sure of it!' She added a spoonful of sugar to her friend's cup and stirred it. 'I know you don't normally take sugar, but I think you could probably do with some today.'

Dorothy smiled back, glad of her friend's support. The shifts at the hospital were rigorous and she was feeling exhausted from the long days. But despite the physical and emotional demands, she was thoroughly enjoying having an occupation. She loved putting her brain to use in the classroom and the hands-on learning, whether administering medications, caring for critically ill patients or assisting in surgery, made her feel useful. And although they were both tired most of the time and often covered in various bodily fluids, Dorothy had to admit that spending time with Clara was definitely a highlight.

'How is it going with Cyril?' Dorothy asked, keen to talk to lighten the mood.

'Oh, he's a sweet thing.' Clara smiled and gave a little shrug. 'I think he's going to propose soon.' She lifted her teacup to her lips and sipped the steaming drink thoughtfully.

'And?' Dorothy's eyes widened with excitement. 'What will you say? Do you want to marry him?'

Clara looked thoughtful for a moment. 'I think so,' she began noncommittally, 'but the trouble is, Cyril's so awfully traditional and proper about things.' Clara rolled her eyes. 'The most I've got out of him was a mild-mannered kiss after Hugo Dalvey's birthday party at the club last month, after he'd had a bit too much to drink. I was delighted that he was finally getting down to business, but then he stopped himself and kept apologising all the way home. It was *so* disappointing.'

Dorothy smiled at her friend and shook her head fondly.

'That side of things is important to me, you see,' Clara continued. 'But I've no idea how it's going to be with Cyril, if he's going to be any good at it, I mean. I'd just like one night with him to find out. Is that too much to ask? Let's face it, you wouldn't buy a new car without taking it for a test drive first, would you?'

'Oh Clara! You are terrible!' Dorothy burst out laughing, her worries drifting away for a moment. Clara shrugged and started giggling, too.

Their jollity was cut short by the appearance of Sister Jamieson's face around the door. Her mouth was as tight as her brown curls, and her expression severe and unsmiling.

'Ladies, may I remind you that this is a hospital and not a music hall. You will kindly maintain decorum at all times.' They both nodded, looking suitably contrite. 'Nurse Llewellyn,' she continued, checking her fob watch, 'I believe you were due back on shift two minutes ago.' Dorothy nodded again obediently and instantly rose from her seat. 'And as for you, Nurse Davies, you don't have a break for another hour. You will return to the ward immediately.'

Dorothy couldn't help but smile to herself as she left the room, feeling like they'd been caught out like a pair of naughty schoolgirls. She felt lighter after talking to Clara and ready to get back to work.

'Nurse Llewellyn?' Dorothy heard her name as she walked along the corridor. She turned back in the direction of the voice, worrying that she was about to get another telling off, but was relieved to see the tall, willowy figure of Dr Archie approaching.

'I'm glad I caught you,' he began, with an easy smile. 'I understand your mother is in with us for her surgery this afternoon?'

Dorothy felt a lump form in her throat but managed a nod in reply.

'Well, I had a word with Sister Robertson, who'll be on duty this afternoon, and arranged for you to go and see your mother before she goes in.' He looked at his watch. 'Pop along to ward five just before three and you can have a few minutes with her.' He seemed to sense her anxiety. 'And try not to worry; the operation has a good chance of success. Mr Thompson-Wright is a first-rate surgeon, we're lucky to have him here. Try to stay positive.' He put a gentle hand on Dorothy's arm and, with a friendly wink, he continued on his way along the corridor.

Dorothy was overcome by his kindness. The sisters at the hospital were a fierce bunch, regularly reprimanding the trainee nurses and setting such impossibly high standards. But Dr Archie was always so kind and encouraging, so human, and Dorothy was glad that he was the supervisor for her unit. With his ready smile and bright eyes, he was handsome in an 'older man' kind of way, and a couple of the younger trainees admitted to having crushes on him. Dorothy had heard on the grapevine that he was a widower, his wife having died in childbirth a decade earlier. The poor man had lost both his wife and his child in one bitter blow. But he had not let his grief consume him. Instead, he had thrown himself into his work and, with his easy-going, friendly manner, managed to spread a little happiness and comfort wherever he went. Dorothy admired and appreciated him for that.

It was late when Dorothy arrived home after her shift that evening. They had needed all hands on deck when an ambulance had brought in casualties from a motorcar accident. She and Clara had both volunteered to stay on and they had ended up working an extra two hours after their shift ended. Clara had given her a lift home, dropping her at the corner of York Road with a weary 'See you tomorrow!'

The sun was setting on a warm, balmy evening as Dorothy made her way home along the tree-lined avenue. A chorus of tree frogs accompanied the sound of her weary footsteps as she dragged her aching limbs the short distance to the house. She was ready for dinner, a hot bath and bed. It had been a day of ups and downs and she felt physically and emotionally drained. It was a huge relief that her mother's surgery had gone smoothly and the doctor had been optimistic for a full recovery. Dorothy was grateful to Dr Archie that he had arranged some time off to visit and that she had been there to support her father. The sight of him, sitting alone in the waiting room, anxiously awaiting news of his wife's operation, had made her heart ache. It had taken all her last remaining energy to smile and reassure him that everything would be alright.

The heady scent of jasmine filled the air as she turned into the driveway and she breathed it in deeply. A sudden movement up ahead made her pause. She heard voices as the front door opened, revealing Douglas bidding farewell to a visitor. The person had their back to her and it wasn't until they turned around to make their way down the drive that she recognised the dark figure of Maria Pemberton.

Dorothy's stomach sank. What was that woman doing here? She wasn't an idiot, she knew that Douglas still saw her regularly, but how dare she come here, to *her* house? Dorothy wished she could make herself disappear, the last thing she wanted was to have to speak to her. But there was nowhere to hide. There was nothing for it but to continue walking up the drive and hold her head up high. After all, she was not the one doing anything wrong.

Dressed in a long, loose-fitting blue gown Maria was her usual effortlessly-stylish self. As the women approached each other, Dorothy was about to give her customary civil nod when a light breeze caught the fabric of Maria's dress. It swept across to one side in such a way that there was no escaping the sight of her protruding belly.

Dorothy gasped. 'You're pregnant!' The words were out of her mouth before she could stop them. She looked up at Maria and, instead of the usual perfect make-up, her face was red and blotchy with tears.

The Italian's nostrils flared slightly as she breathed in sharply. She looked Dorothy up and down and, with a curt nod, uttered an abrupt 'Si!' Then she brushed past Dorothy and continued down the driveway and onto the main road without a backward glance.

Dorothy's mind raced. Her husband's lover was pregnant. And she had come here, to her husband's house, and left visibly upset. Why? Dorothy added two plus two and came up with a very convincing four.

On cue, the young houseboy, Ravi, opened the door as Dorothy reached the top step. He greeted her with a polite 'Good evening, ma'am,' took her bag and hat, and informed her that Cook was keeping her dinner warm and it would be sent in as soon as she was ready.

'Hello, darling, you're home late! Busy day?' Douglas's voice called cheerfully from the drawing room.

Dorothy was trembling as she made her way through to him; with anger, with jealousy and with an overwhelming sense of bitter injustice. She took a deep breath to steady her nerves, then entered the room.

Douglas laid down his cigar and rose to give his wife the usual, perfunctory kiss on the cheek. She could smell the whisky on his breath. He smiled down at her, taking in her uniform, 'I must say, that little nurse get-up really is rather fetching on you, you know!' He gave her a flirtatious wink then sat down again and picked up his glass. 'Have a seat, darling. Better yet, have a drink!'

Dorothy remained standing, her brow furrowed as she tried to find the right words.

'I've just seen Maria Pemberton,' she began quietly. 'Why was she here, Douglas? To tell you that you're going to be a father?' Unbidden, her eyes filled with tears.

'What?' Douglas's face was the picture of innocence. But Dorothy had seen that look too many times before and it didn't fool her anymore.

'I don't know what you mean, darling.' He reached up to take her hand, but she snatched it out of his reach.

'Yes,' he continued, ignoring her hostility. 'She told me that she was pregnant and that old Fish Face Pemberton was delighted.' He smiled and shrugged with an air of insouciance, 'Nothing to do with me, my love.' He picked up his glass and drank, his eyes never leaving hers, as if gauging her reaction.

Dorothy felt a wave of exhaustion threaten to overcome her. She sank down into a nearby chair and let herself be swallowed up in the comfort of the soft cushions. She was so tired and hungry and longed for her bed. Could she take any reassurance from Douglas's words? He seemed sure that the baby was not his. But how? Dorothy couldn't bear to ask. Her mind was a swirling mist of confusion as she pondered whether or not she could trust her husband.

The ring of the telephone downstairs woke Dorothy from a fitful sleep. She glanced at the clock beside the bed: almost nine o'clock. She had completely overslept. Thank goodness she was on the late shift today, so wouldn't risk incurring the wrath of Sister Jamieson.

Despite the late hour, Dorothy felt like she'd hardly slept a wink. She had tossed and turned into the small hours, alternating between indignant rage in case Douglas *was* the father of Maria's child, and indulgent self-pity at her own inability to produce a child for her husband. They had been married for almost one and a half years and she had now suffered four miscarriages.

'Hello?' Dorothy answered a couple of minutes later, having been summoned down to the telephone by an anxious-faced Ah Ling.

'Nurse Llewellyn, good morning. It's Dr Archie here.' Dorothy smiled as she recognised his soft, lilting accent. 'I won't beat around the bush,' he continued. 'It's bad news regarding your mother, I'm afraid.'

Dorothy's face fell and Ah Ling, who had been standing close by, ushered her into the seat beside the telephone.

'She's running a high fever,' the doctor continued. 'I'm sorry to say that infection has started to set in; it's always a risk after operations such as hers. We've contacted your father and he's coming in straight away, but I wanted to let you know, too. We're doing everything we can, but I think you should come as soon as you can, Dorothy.'

The next twenty minutes passed in a blur as, with the help of Ah Ling, Dorothy dressed and got ready. The driver brought the car round to the door and Ah Ling helped her in, insisting on accompanying her. 'Miss Dorothy, you look so pale. I come with you.'

It was a sombre journey as the car made its way towards the Alexandra Military Hospital. Ah Ling held Dorothy's hand, quietly offering words of reassurance. Everything seemed to have gone wrong in the last twenty-four hours and Dorothy fought back the tidal wave of self-pity that was rising up within her. She must be strong, for her mother and for her father.

After what seemed an eternity, thanks to a traffic jam where an oxen cart had overturned its load, they arrived at the hospital entrance. Dorothy was out of the car before it had completely stopped, on a mission to reach her mother's bedside as soon as possible and reassure herself that all would be well.

But as she took in the haunted look on Anthony Templeton's face, standing outside the ward in grave conversation with Dr Archie, she feared the worst.

'I'm so sorry, my darling girl.' Her father's eyes filled with tears as he looked up and saw his daughter. 'I'm so dreadfully sorry.'

Dorothy's jaw dropped open as she struggled to comprehend what he was saying. 'But . . . ' She stared at him, wide-mouthed, and failed to finish the sentence. For the second time that morning, she sank down into a nearby chair.

'My most sincere condolences, Nurse . . . Dorothy,' came Dr Archie's gentle voice, dropping the formalities for a kinder approach. She felt his warm hand rest on her shoulder. 'It all happened so quickly, I'm afraid, there really wasn't anything we could do. But your mother didn't suffer, if that's any consolation. She wasn't in any pain.'

Dorothy looked up at him and silently nodded her gratitude. She felt numb. None of it made any sense. Her mother had been recovering well when she had left her the previous evening. But then she reminded herself of the perilous nature of surgery; she'd seen patients' fortunes turn on a sixpence, there were no guarantees. The Alexandra Military Hospital was the finest in the East, but even with all its modern equipment and pioneering treatments, they had still lost patients unexpectedly. Human life was fragile and operations were fraught with risk, Dorothy knew this. But how could this have happened to her mother? Her brave, strong, determined mother? Dorothy couldn't believe it.

Father and daughter spent the rest of the day as if in some horrid nightmare. But despite wishing for it to happen, Dorothy didn't wake up. She excused herself from her ward shift and helped her father go through the hospital paperwork and formalities, then took him back to the family home.

She sat with him as he broke the news to the household staff and helped him find the right words for the telegram to her brother, Thomas. The vicar from St Andrew's Cathedral visited mid-afternoon to express his condolences and to start the ball rolling on the funeral arrangements. It was such a busy day that Dorothy didn't have the time to grieve.

All the while, Ah Ling was there in the background, quietly supporting and helping as best she could.

Dorothy returned to her own home at dinner time. Despite numerous phone calls to his office throughout the day, she had not managed to get hold of Douglas. He would be home for dinner though, she thought, so she could break the news to him then.

But dinner time came and went, and there was no sign of her husband. Alone, she sat at the dinner table, pushing her food around her plate. Grief had robbed her of her appetite.

The clock was striking ten when the front door finally opened and Douglas appeared. Dorothy was sitting in the drawing room, trying to concentrate on her latest Agatha Christie novel. Daisy had sent it to her from London and normally she would have devoured it in hours. But with her recent troubles and her raw grief, Dorothy was struggling to get her head around Miss Marple's latest case.

'Hello, darling!' Douglas appeared in the room, swaying and slurring his words in equal measure.

'You're late. Where have you been?' Dorothy fought hard to keep her tone level.

He dropped down into an armchair, sprawled out his arms luxuriantly and kicked off his shoes. He called for Ravi, the young houseboy, and ordered a whisky. The delay in answering her question infuriated Dorothy.

'Awfully busy day, you know,' he finally replied. 'You know how the orders have been recently; and there's so much more to do now that I'm in charge. Stepping in for your father while he's on leave taking care of your mother has been good experience, but don't forget that it's a lot of extra pressure. It's hard work trying to keep up in the office!'

Dorothy winced as he dragged her parents' troubles into his web of deceit.

'But you weren't in the office today.' She stared at him, expressionless. 'I know that because I rang numerous times and was told each time that you weren't there. Where were you?'

Douglas stared at her blankly, momentarily rattled. Then his expression changed to an angry sneer. 'You've been checking up on me, have you?'

'I don't know why you ever married me, when she's the only one you ever wanted!' She fought hard to maintain her dignity, but a sob escaped from her.

Douglas gave the impression of mulling over the question for a moment.

'Well, you were an awfully sweet thing, you know!' he said with a drunken smile. Then he continued, almost to himself, with a sneer, 'And I couldn't let that fool Matthew win!'

'What? Matthew?' Dorothy asked, confused. 'Win how?'

Douglas rolled his eyes and sighed dramatically. 'The idiot was going to propose. And I didn't want him taking what I wanted.' He shrugged. 'So, I beat him to it!'

Dorothy closed her eyes, her face contorting in pain. How different her life would have been if she had married Matthew; kind, good, loyal Matthew. A tidal wave of regret crashed over her.

She took a breath and opened her eyes, staring hard at Douglas. 'Answer me one question. With the truth, for once, Douglas. You owe me that. You were with her today, weren't you?'

The pause was a moment too long. And in that moment, everything became clear.

'Look, Dorothy, Maria was upset, alright?' He sighed and took a deep breath. 'She doesn't know how she's going to tell old Fish Face about the baby.'

Dorothy's pulse thundered in her ears. 'So it *is* yours?' she whispered, closing her eyes against the reality that was engulfing her.

'Put it this way, old Pemberton has been up in Malaya for the past seven months, so it would have to be a bloody immaculate conception for it to be his!' The bawdy cackle at his own joke was the final straw. How dare he make fun of the situation? Of Bernard Pemberton? Of her?

Dorothy leapt to her feet and rushed from the room, desperate to get away from him. All day long, she had fought back her tears of grief, trying to be strong for her father. But now they fell with a vengeance, blinding her vision. In her haste to escape, she nearly collided with Ravi, who was returning with Douglas's whisky. The poor boy had the foresight to duck out of the way and retreat to the alcove until the situation calmed down. Once too often, he had been on the receiving end of the master's drunken temper.

'Oh, come on, Dorothy, don't be like that!' Douglas had dragged himself out of his armchair and was following his wife towards the stairs, up which she was bounding, two at a time.

When she reached the top, Dorothy turned and called down to him between angry, bitter sobs, 'I wasn't ringing to "check up" on you. I was ringing to tell you that my mother died this morning!'

The news had an immediate sobering effect on Douglas and his face registered shock and concern. 'Oh Dorothy!' he called, rushing up the stairs behind her. He moved towards her and grabbed her by the arm.

Dorothy was surprised by his caring gesture, but his touch repelled her now. 'Get off me!' she yelled. And in one swift move, she pushed him away with all her might, turned and ran to her bedroom without a backward glance. It was as she touched the door handle that she heard an awful thumping sound of something landing at the bottom of the stairs.

Ah Ling appeared in the doorway at that same moment, having been preparing the bedroom for Dorothy. Dorothy gasped and grabbed her hand. Together, the two women crept along the corridor and peered over the balcony. There, at the foot of the stairs, lay Douglas's body; silent, unmoving and broken.

CHAPTER 22

Singapore

Thursday 4th April, 2019

Annabel stared at Julia in dumbstruck silence. She couldn't believe what she had just been told: her kind, sweet, loving grandmother had pushed her first husband down the stairs to his death? It just couldn't be true.

They were sitting in a small coffee shop near Julia's office in Raffles Place, where she had suggested they meet during her lunch break. All around them buzzed office workers in smart suits, grabbing a quick bite to eat, a caffeine injection or a moment's respite before continuing with their busy day.

Julia put down her mug and sighed, registering Annabel's reaction. 'I'm sorry, it must be very upsetting to hear all this.'

Annabel shook her head. 'Not upsetting exactly, more confusing. It's so strange that we've never heard any of this before. But maybe this explains why; it's hardly surprising that Granny kept all of this secret, especially if she was responsible for a man's death. When she got back to England I suppose she must have wanted to put all of this behind her, make a fresh start.' Annabel picked up the teapot in front of her and topped up her cup.

'Yes, I'm sure.' Julia gave a sad smile. 'And this is why Mama didn't want me to tell you; she didn't want to tarnish your grandmother's reputation or have anyone thinking badly of her.

She made that promise to Ah Ling, you see. But I felt strongly that you should know. I mean, you've travelled all this way to find out, I thought you deserved to know the truth. I hope it was the right decision?'

Annabel smiled and nodded reassuringly. The worried look on Julia's face eased as she continued, 'Ah Ling maintained that Dorothy acted purely out of self-defence on that night, and not violence. Douglas Llewellyn did not treat her well and they had been arguing right before he fell.' She shrugged. 'You might say he got his just deserts.'

'But what happened next?' Annabel asked, suddenly worrying for her grandmother. 'Was his death considered suspicious? Were the police involved? Did Dorothy face charges?'

She was reassured by Julia's vehement shake of the head. 'No, nothing like that, don't worry! Douglas Llewellyn was incredibly drunk on the night he died – all the household staff could attest to that – and the doctor recorded accidental death. It was assumed that Douglas had tripped at the top of the stairs and was too intoxicated to steady himself as he fell. He landed badly and broke his neck.'

'*All* the household staff?' Annabel asked. 'Who else was there? Did anyone else see?'

Julia shook her head. 'No, no one else saw it happen. But the staff were around and had seen the lead up to it, but Ah Ling said she was the only one who knew the truth because Miss Dorothy told her. She trusted her like a sister, you see, she was her confidante. And even though her husband had been cruel and unkind to her, Dorothy was racked with guilt at what she had done. She was a good woman. Ah Ling worried that she never forgave herself and would live with that guilt until the very end.'

Annabel shook her head sadly, remembering her darling grandmother and the last time she had seen her in the hospital. In those final moments, it consoled her to think that her grandmother had been at peace, thinking of Grandpa and their happy family. But had her mind drifted back to that fateful night in Singapore in 1941? Oh, poor Granny.

'What a terrible time she must have had.' Annabel mused, shaking her head sadly. 'To lose her mother *and* her husband on the same day! How did she bear it?'

'It must have been an awful time, indeed,' Julia agreed. 'Dorothy put all her energy into taking care of her father and, for a while, she and Ah Ling moved back to the family home. Poor Mr Templeton was lost without his wife. He had been devoted to her and had taken leave from his job to stay home and take care of her during her final months.'

Annabel nodded. 'Yes, we read that in the article we found about the history of McKinley's. Douglas Llewellyn had taken over the management of the company.'

'That's right. His wife had become the centre of Mr Templeton's world and his grief overwhelmed him. He wasn't eating, wasn't sleeping and, despite previously being in reasonable health, he deteriorated rapidly. Don't forget, it was also a worrying time in Singapore with the threat of war looming.'

Annabel's brow creased as she pieced together the dates. She opened the notebook that was on the table in front of her and scanned through the notes she had made. 'This was November 1941, right?'

Julia nodded confirmation.

'So, the Japanese invasion was just around the corner. Gosh, what a time it must have been.'

'Yes, they came in February 1942. Unfortunately – or maybe fortunately, who knows – Mr Templeton didn't live to see it. He died just before Christmas.'

'Yes, we found his death record, it said he died of heart failure.'

Julia shrugged sadly. 'Some people don't believe that you can die of a broken heart, but Ah Ling said that's what it was. The poor man was bereft without his wife and his body just gave up. He was reunited with her in Bidadari cemetery.'

Annabel nodded. 'We found that in the Public Records and went to find their graves, but the cemetery is no longer there.'

'No,' Julia agreed. 'There's been so much development in Singapore in the last sixty years. Sadly, even sacred sites have been built on.'

Annabel finished her tea, a pensive look on her face. 'But the big question remains: how on earth do we get from the Dorothy Llewellyn of 1942 Singapore to the Dotty Penrose I knew and loved in Cornwall? And how – and where – does my father fit into the story?'

Julia smiled. 'Well, the story is just beginning. But . . . I've been thinking about it and decided that it's not really my place to tell you what happened next.'

Annabel felt instant disappointment. 'But . . . '

Julia raised a hand to stop her. 'Don't worry, Annabel.' She reached into her bag and pulled out a thick A4-sized brown envelope. She handed it across the table. 'I'm going to let your grandmother tell you in her own words.'

She chuckled softly at Annabel's confusion. 'It will all make sense, I promise.' Then she checked her watch. 'I'm so sorry, but I'm going to have to go; I have a meeting. Read that when you get back later, and give me a ring if there's anything I can help you with.' She sighed. 'Mama didn't want anyone to see it, knowing how protective Ah Ling was over Dorothy. That's why we didn't send it back to Dorothy with all the other letters and photos after Ah Ling's death; She was worried in case the information it contained caused trouble for Dorothy's family. Mama doesn't know I'm giving it to you, but I think you need to see it. Send it back once you've read it, won't you?'

Annabel nodded. 'Of course!'

Julia stood up from the table and lifted her bag up onto her shoulder. She smiled down at Annabel. 'I hope I did the right thing in sharing all of this with you.' She nodded at the brown envelope that Annabel was still holding. 'Prepare yourself – it's quite a story! But I'm pleased to say it has a happy ending.' She patted her new friend's shoulder encouragingly, then left the café.

Annabel remained at the table for a while longer to eat the toasted sandwich that had sat untouched during Julia's narration. She was so tempted to open the brown envelope there and then. But the café was full and new customers were loitering hopefully nearby, so she put it safely in her bag to read back at Emma's later.

She stepped out of the café, into the busy Raffles Place. Skyscrapers towered up to dizzying heights above her and the streets were filled with smartly dressed professionals rushing to and from their offices. Dynamic and modern, it was the beating heart of Singapore's financial district. How different it must have been when Dorothy lived here, Annabel thought, and she made a mental note to research the area's history.

Unlike the dozens of workers rushing around on their lunch hour, Annabel took a leisurely stroll around the large central green. With its lush, green grass and shady trees, it was a mini oasis in the concrete jungle. Locals and tourists alike were enjoying a peaceful lunchtime interlude, relaxing on deckchairs and picnic benches with a takeaway, taking in the sculptures on display, or people-watching from one of the many bars or cafés around the outside.

Annabel was contemplating a stroll down to the river when her phone started vibrating. She smiled when she saw it was James and answered straight away; she had so much to tell him. But despite her pleasure at hearing his voice, her stomach did that uncomfortable lurching thing again, as if something didn't feel right. Why was her body reacting this way?

'How was your meeting?' Annabel asked, once they'd exchanged pleasantries. James hadn't been able to join her to see Julia as he'd had a meeting with his solicitor. She hadn't liked to pry, but assumed it was divorce business.

There was a momentary pause and she heard a sigh before he replied. 'Let's just say it wasn't exactly straightforward. But I think we're making progress.' His voice brightened as he changed the subject. 'How was Julia? Where are you now?'

'All good, thanks, but there's a lot to digest. I've got so much to tell you. I'm still in Raffles Place, but thinking of heading down to Boat Quay for a wander. I'd like to picture where McKinley's warehouse was.'

'Good idea,' James replied. 'Well, I'm just in the car now. How about I come down and join you?'

Annabel felt pleased at the suggestion and agreed. James suggested they meet in half an hour by 'the fat bird' on the Raffles Place side of the river, reassuring her that she couldn't miss it.

It was another bright, sunny day and Annabel was grateful for the gentle breeze that was cooling the beads of perspiration on her forehead. She left the skyscrapers of Raffles Place behind and headed down towards the tranquil Singapore River.

The architecture here was so different from the modern business centre; a mix of imposing colonial buildings and traditional shophouses that evoked Singapore's past. She took out her city map to help orientate herself. On the opposite bank was the elegant cream building of the Asian Civilisations Museum and, further along to her right, she could see the imposing granite facade of the Fullerton Hotel. Following the curve of the river to the left was a long terrace of beautiful, old heritage shophouses with colourful shutters and awnings, and matching terracotta roofs. Today, they were home to bars, cafés and restaurants, but Annabel could picture them as the original shophouses, with the businesses downstairs and living quarters above.

The water sparkled in the bright afternoon sunlight and several old-fashioned wooden boats chugged along, carrying tourists with cameras and mobile phones held aloft, ready to capture the picturesque views. Today, Boat Quay was an enchanting mix of old-world charm and modern vibrancy, but Annabel was curious to imagine how it might have looked back in her grandmother's day. She sat on a bench and took out her phone, then did a quick online search for images of the area in the 1940s.

The sepia pictures that popped up revealed a bustling trading port, with hundreds of small wooden boats crammed side by side along the river. In some pictures, there wasn't much water to be seen due to the sheer number of boats. The area teemed with merchants, traders and locals, all going about their business in this thriving hub. Along the quay, Annabel spotted the same shophouses that still stood today, alongside larger warehouses, or 'go-downs' as they'd been known. This is where McKinley's Rubber Manufacturers must have been, she imagined, and pictured Dorothy's father and Douglas Llewellyn going to and from their office here.

Annabel strolled along the quay, politely declining the numerous attempts from restaurant staff to lure her into their establishments. The aroma of various cuisines filled the air and made her mouth water. Passing a seafood restaurant, she was amazed to see large tanks outside, housing live versions of everything on the menu; from large fish to crabs and lobsters. You didn't get much fresher than that, she thought, smiling to herself.

At the end of the walkway, she crossed over the shiny white Elgin Bridge and made her way back along the opposite side of the river. Along the way, various plaques recounted the area's role as a trading port in Singapore's early days. There was even a white marble statue of the founder of modern Singapore, Sir Stamford Raffles, standing with folded arms, looking pensively out to sea. With his back towards the towering skyscrapers of the central business district, it made for an interesting juxtaposition of the old and new, and a reminder of how far this small island state had come since Raffles landed there two hundred years ago.

She completed her loop of the river by crossing the Cavenagh Bridge and passing by the grande dame of the waterfront, the Fullerton Hotel. From her research on Singapore, she had learned that it was originally built in the late 1920s to house the General Post Office. It was strange to think that it had been here back in her grandmother's day.

The 'fat bird' turned out not to be the name of a pub, as Annabel had predicted, but an enormous bronze sculpture of a squat, dumpy bird on the quayside. James was already there, leaning against it with a frown on his handsome face as he concentrated on typing something into his phone. His features softened into a smile when he looked up and saw her.

'Ah, Botero!' She smiled knowingly, nodding up at the sculpture.

James's brow creased in confusion. 'I'm sorry, what?'

'Botero – you know, the Colombian artist? I bet you it's one of his – it's just his style.' She gazed up at the sculpture. 'Everything he paints, or sculpts, he makes look fat and dumpy! It's a quirky style, but hugely popular.'

James raised an eyebrow. 'I'd take your bet, but you actually sound like you know what you're talking about.'

Annabel laughed. 'OK, we'll keep the stakes low – the loser buys the ice creams.' She nodded over to where an old Singaporean man was selling ice cream from a cart.

'Ice cream? Now you're talking.'

James stood up from where he'd been leaning, uncovering the sculpture's information plaque as he did so.

'Aha! Here we go!' Annabel bent down to look at the inscription, grinning as she read aloud, "Fernando Botero, 1932. Bird, Bronze, 1990." See? I told you so!' She grinned, playing with him.

'Well,' James said, feigning indifference. 'No one likes a show off, Dr Penrose!' He narrowed his eyes playfully as he muttered, 'I bet you read the plaque on your way past!'

She elbowed him in the side and he laughed. 'Mine's a mint Cornetto!' she teased back.

Minutes later, ice creams in hand, Annabel told James what she had found out as they strolled along the quayside.

'I'm sorry this has turned out to be so upsetting,' he said as she finished. 'I guess that's the problem with family history, you never know what skeletons you're going to find in the cupboard. Sorry,' he added with a wry smile. 'Poor choice of metaphor!'

Annabel smiled sadly. Now she'd had time to think about it, the enormity of the situation was overwhelming: her grandmother had killed a man.

'Well, thank goodness, no one ever questioned what happened,' she said, 'but what if they had? What if Dorothy had been found guilty of murder? She would have been hanged!'

'But hang on, let me get this straight,' James said. 'There were no actual witnesses, right? No one else was there?'

'No.' Annabel's brow creased in concentration. 'Well, no, that's not strictly true, some of the household staff were around. Ah Ling was still up. And Julia mentioned a young servant boy, Ravi. He was definitely there, I remember. Julia said that Dorothy nearly crashed into him as she ran upstairs. Poor boy, it sounded like Douglas was as cruel to his servants as he was to his wife and the boy knew to keep his head down.'

Annabel sighed. 'I just can't believe it – I can't believe that dear old Dotty killed a man. It's just so out of character; honestly, she would have never hurt a fly.'

She stopped to drop her ice-cream wrapper in a bin and James finished crunching the last part of his.

'Well, if it's true, it probably *was* in self-defence,' he suggested. 'If Douglas Llewellyn was as cruel as Julia suggested he was, maybe it was the last resort?'

'Oh, poor Dotty, I can't bear to think about what she must have gone through with that horrible man.' Tears sprang, unbidden. 'And was his final act of cruelty pushing her to the point where she became a murderer? It's just too awful to even think about.'

'We need to find Ravi. He must know more about it. Servants talk. Someone must have seen or heard something. Send Julia a text, see if you can find out about him. He was young at the time, so he might still be alive.' James shrugged. 'It's worth a shot, anyway.'

Annabel stopped walking and looked up at him, her eyes damp. 'You really think so?'

James stopped and turned back to her. He reached for her hand. 'Yes, I do. I hate seeing you so sad. I think there could be more to this than meets the eye and, for the sake of your grandmother's memory, we should try our best to get to the bottom of it.' He smiled down at her encouragingly. 'What do you reckon, Sherlock?'

His touch was warm and comforting. Annabel smiled through her tears and thanked him. Then, instinctively, she leaned into him and rested her head against his strong chest. He wrapped his arms around her, steady and warm. She breathed in his now-familiar citrus scent and, for a moment, a sense of calm washed over her.

James was the first to pull away. He cleared his throat with an awkward cough and checked his watch.

'Now come on, it's still early and Emma won't be home from work yet. Why don't we go back to my place? I'll make you a cuppa and you can discover whatever mysteries lie hidden inside that envelope.'

'Sounds like a plan.' Annabel smiled in agreement. 'But I think a glass of wine might be more in order!'

CHAPTER 23

Penrose Farm,
Wincastle
Cornwall

6 June 1946

My dearest Ah Ling,

I cannot tell you how delighted I was to receive your reply to my letter. After all this time, I was at a loss how to contact you, but I had an inkling that dear old Mr Wong at your temple would know where you were. Please send him my deepest gratitude for passing my letter on to you; you have no idea what pleasure your reply brought me. I was so glad to hear that you are well and happy, and settled as a wife and mother.

You must forgive my tardiness in contacting you, dearest friend. As I mentioned in my first, brief note, the past couple of years have been quite a whirlwind. It has taken some time for me to come to terms with the events that led up to my departure from Singapore. As with any tale, it had its ups and downs, but rest assured that I, too, am well and happy.

I feel incredibly fortunate to have had a second chance with a new life — and a new family — here in beautiful Cornwall. I am, indeed, very content with my lot.

How to begin my tale? It is a question that has kept me awake many a night. I suppose I should start at the beginning, or rather the ending, when I bade you farewell at the dock in Singapore. Do you remember that terrible night, Ah Ling? Friday 13th February, 1942. I shudder to think of it. I don't think it matters how much time passes, it remains a vivid memory that just won't fade.

I can close my eyes now and still see the chaos at the docks, where so many of us were trying to escape. The pushing and shoving on the gangplanks, the frightened faces of the children and the fear in their mothers' eyes. I can still hear the drone of the Japanese planes overhead. I can feel the pulsating thump and smell the acrid stench as their bombs exploded around us. These are things I can never forget. I also hear echoes of Shenton Thomas's voice, reassuring us that we were perfectly safe in Singapore. Oh, but how wrong he was! Our world was tipped upside down so quickly and there was nothing to be done about it.

As ever, you were my constant support at that time, calmly and quietly helping me pack, preparing me to leave the country that had been my home for the past four years. I felt so awful leaving you behind, Ah Ling, to an uncertain future and the threat of imminent Japanese invasion. At the time, how I wished I could have taken you with me. But in the end, after everything that happened next, I was so glad that you had stayed behind.

SS Kuala was to be my escape, taking me to Australia, from where I could get a ship home to England. After everything that had happened, first with my parents and then with Douglas, how I longed to go home to cold, rainy England.

I shall never forget saying goodbye to you that night; it was the saddest of farewells. We clung to each other in one last embrace, then both bravely tried to smile through our tears. You were my final link with Singapore, with the family that had disappeared one by one, and it was an utter wrench to leave you.

What happened next came completely out of the blue and you will doubtless be as surprised as I was. I was halfway up the gangplank to board the ship when I heard someone call my name. I turned around and saw her there: Maria da Costa Pemberton. My heart sank. I couldn't face the thought of being stuck on board together for the next few weeks. But what happened next was even more shocking than that.

'Dorothy, you must help me,' she began in that clipped, staccato Italian accent of hers. She sounded like she'd been crying. 'I do not know what else to do. Please take him, I cannot keep him. My husband will kill me.' And, without ceremony, she handed me a bundle of cloth. It felt warm and was moving. I peeled back the cloth and there he was: her baby. Douglas's child. Before I could say anything, she passed me a piece of paper with a scribbled address on it. 'His grandparents, in England. Please take him to them. For Douglas's sake, if not for mine. He was born on Christmas Eve. He is innocent in all of this. Please, take care of him. You must promise me. Please!'

I stood there dumbstruck, desperately trying to keep my balance as I held onto the baby and kept my grip on my suitcase as other passengers hurried up the gangplank past me. But there was little time to respond. What else could I do? There was such desperation in her eyes. I simply nodded my reply and said, 'I promise.'

She disappeared then, dragged back down the gangplank by one of the staff, whom she must have persuaded to let her through. It was time to leave; the ship was ready for departure. And away she went, lost in the crowd of escaping evacuees, leaving me with her child; a tiny scrap of humanity, barely six weeks old.

There are occasions in life when one is denied the luxury of time for careful contemplation and consideration, and this was one such occasion. I had no choice but to follow my instinct. And my instinct at that moment was to protect the helpless babe in my arms. After what had happened to his father – another memory that continues to haunt me to this day – it was the very least I could do.

I moved as if in a trance. The ship was full to bursting, with some five hundred of us evacuees, crammed in like the proverbial sardines. There was nowhere to sit, but everyone was trying to make the best of it, settling in the aisles and stairwells, wherever there was space. No one could move without stepping over or around people. Hot and cramped it may have been, but we were all relieved to be there, away from the pandemonium of the dock and desperate to sail to safer shores. Looking around, it was such an eclectic mix of passengers: Chinese, Europeans, Eurasians, men and women, old and young. I didn't see anyone I knew, which was a relief to me as I might have struggled to explain the baby in my arms.

An elderly Singaporean man in a smart suit nodded at the baby and gave up his seat for me. I accepted it gratefully and settled into it, repositioning the baby as my arm was starting to ache. Despite the chaos going on around him, he was remarkably quiet and, after tucking into milk from the bottle of a helpful mother nearby, he was soon snoozing peacefully.

I took the piece of paper that Maria had handed me from my pocket and recognised the address of Douglas's family home; Highcliffe Manor, Wilton, Salisbury. At that moment, I knew that the only thing to do was to make sure that the baby was safely delivered to his paternal grandparents. In our short marriage, I had never had the opportunity to meet my in-laws. And now I felt rising panic and an overwhelming sense of guilt at the thought of meeting them now, knowing what I'd done to their son. I had sent a telegram and later a letter, informing them of Douglas's death, but no reply had ever come. What must they think?

But safe delivery of the child soon became a distant hope. At 11 a.m. the next morning, SS Kuala, our safe haven and escape route, was bombed by the Japanese.

The chaos at the docks was nothing compared to the chaos on board the ship. We were plunged into darkness, surrounded by terrified screams. But I no longer worried for myself, I had someone else to think about. I found myself shepherded by the kind mother who'd lent me her own baby's bottle – Harriet was her name – and we were among the fortunate few to get onto a lifeboat.

For as long as I live, I shall never forget the sight of those who were left behind. Mothers stood on the side of the ship while bombs continued to rain down, crying out for help that would not come. They faced the most impossible decision; to stay on board the burning vessel or take their chances in the violent waters below. Most could not swim and there were no lifebelts. But, left with no other choice, they jumped in, clutching their babies and toddlers close to them, hanging on to whatever they could reach and desperately trying to keep their heads above water. Sailors were throwing anything that could float down into the water: chairs, tables, rattan baskets, empty packing cases. But few survived, becoming victims of the choppy waters or the barbaric machine-gunning of the approaching Japanese soldiers.

The lifeboat was fit to burst, but the sailors rowed us steadily towards the island. We were packed in, cheek by jowl, but there was some comfort in our being together. Bombs exploded in the water around us, but miraculously we managed to dodge them. I clutched the baby close to me and closed my eyes tight shut against the horrors. But there was no blocking out the sound, the tormented wails of desperation. It was when the baby started to cry that I realised that it was not just my own life that I had to save, but his, too. I couldn't believe what a peaceful little chap he was. Poor little thing, with no milk on offer, he satisfied himself by suckling on the tip of my finger.

And that was the moment, Ah Ling, when I became a mother. Despite everything that was going on, he made me smile. And I realised, quite simply, that he needed me. And, in a strange way, I needed him, too.

We reached the island of Pom Pong and scrambled up the rocks towards the jungle as best we could. But the Japanese were relentless, *cold and callous in their actions, as they pursued innocent people. They shot dead mothers with children in their arms in pure, ruthless cold blood. One of their bullets hit Harriet, who had been so kind to me. I turned to see her lying face down in the sand, a growing pool of blood around her and her infant. Her older child clutched at her body, wailing in horror, until he was silenced by another bullet. It was a living nightmare, Ah Ling, unravelling before my eyes. I felt numb with shock at it all and was grateful to the sailor who came back for me, grabbing my arm and urging me to keep going.*

We made our way up the hill to a clearing in the jungle where the sailors, who were from the British Royal Navy, took charge. The wounded were cared for by a group of British and Australian nurses and those who were healthy scouted about for materials to make shelters. I volunteered my help, but my offer was turned down on account of having the baby. So I sat in the shade with some of the other mothers and their children. One of the women handed me a bag that I recognised as Harriet's, telling me I should have it as it belonged to my friend. Relief flooded through me when I opened it and found packets and packets of powdered baby milk. I hadn't known her long, but Harriet proved to be a real friend to me.

Days passed, turning into weeks as we adapted to this strange existence on Pom Pong

Island, wondering what would become of us. Our number grew as other ships were sunk and survivors scrambled for their lives, just as we had. It became overcrowded and the place soon became dirty and unsanitary.

Our days took on some sort of routine and, little by little, we managed to make our way past the numbing horrors of SS Kuala. We slept under makeshift shelters and ate whatever we could, foraging for food and enjoying the feast when fish were caught or coconuts were found. Fresh water was in limited supply and the mosquitoes drove us crazy. We had only the clothes we'd arrived in and my dress soon resembled a washed-out dish cloth.

It felt like a hopeless situation and I shudder when I think back to those long nights of fear and uncertainty. But the little bundle I was responsible for kept me going. After everything that had happened and everyone I had lost, I suppose I needed a reason not to give up. And that reason was him — I couldn't let him down.

One morning, around three weeks after our arrival on the island, a group of Japanese soldiers arrived at our camp. They barked orders in their limited English and pointed their weapons at us. All the women and children were gathered together in one shelter and told that it was time to leave. We collected our few, meagre belongings and lined up, ready to follow the soldiers.

A new fear took over as we faced an unknown destination. Strange as it might sound, we had become used to our camp at Pom Pong and had found strength in our little community there. We had no idea what would happen next.

CHAPTER 24

Singapore
June 1942

Dorothy grinned. She was back in London with Daisy, laughing with carefree abandon as two handsome young men whirled them around the dance floor of the Hammersmith Palais. The room pulsated to the lively Glenn Miller tune that the band was playing. All around them swirled elegantly dressed couples, a sea of tailored suits and flowing gowns, illuminated by the soft glow of the large central chandelier. It was magical.

Suddenly, the music stopped and Daisy faded into the distance. Dorothy called her name but her friend was gone.

A gnawing ache in her hollowed stomach reminded Dorothy where she was. Reluctantly, she opened her eyes and felt the usual sense of dread creep all over her, the same way it did every morning when she woke. She was not dancing freely in London, but was held captive in Changi Prisoner-of-War Jail.

Dorothy felt the baby stir beside her, nestled snugly against her side. She looked down and saw his dark eyes staring up at her.

'Hello, little one!' she whispered, cautious not to disturb the others in the cell. She smiled at him and felt her heart warm when he smiled back. He gurgled happily and reached out his little fingers to touch her.

She had named him Noel. As a Christmas baby, it seemed appropriate. Plus, it made her smile as it reminded her of a family outing to the West End to see one of Mr Coward's plays before they had moved to Singapore.

The baby was six months old now and, despite the pitiful rations, he was healthy, if a little small for his age. Dorothy had no idea how to judge such things and relied heavily on her cellmate, Pat, for guidance. She was a cheerful, no-nonsense Australian woman from a small town just outside Perth and Dorothy was grateful for her support. Pat's two daughters, Mary and Lizzie, were aged nine and twelve and loved to play with Noel and help take care of him.

The five of them lived in a tiny stone cell that measured six feet by eight. Dorothy and the baby slept on the one raised bed in the middle, with Pat on a mat on the floor on one side and the girls huddled together on the other. A tiny window in the corner gave them some natural light and, on the occasional breezy day, some much-needed fresh air. Facilities were basic and a hole in the floor at the back of the cell was all they had for a toilet. The place was crawling with bugs and there was no escaping the stifling heat. Originally built to accommodate 800 prisoners, Changi Jail was now bursting at the seams with over four times that many.

The first few days had been the hardest. On returning to Singapore from Pom Pong, the women and children had been forced to march across the island to Changi. It was a distance of fourteen miles and they were utterly exhausted before they even began. Their clothes were now barely more than rags and their shoes completely unsuitable for the task. It was a savage undertaking, punctuated by barked orders and violent threats from their Japanese oppressors. The sun had beat down relentlessly and, dehydrated and hungry, many had collapsed. Dorothy soon resisted the urge to help them after receiving a menacing shove in the back from the butt of a Japanese rifle.

Singapore had fallen and the Japanese were now in charge. It had all happened so quickly, the very next day after Dorothy had set off on SS Kuala. So much for Shenton Thomas's resolute belief that the island was impregnable, Dorothy had mused as they were marched past debris left by the Japanese attack. They passed bombed-out buildings and mounds of rubble, occasionally catching sight of a dead body. She had been away from the island for only a few weeks, but everything had changed.

Once they had rested and recovered from the ordeal of their arrival, life in the prison took on a strict, monotonous rhythm. The day began with an early-morning roll call followed by meagre breakfast rations of over-cooked white rice. After that, Pat would set off for her assigned duties in the laundry and the girls, Mary and Lizzie, would go to the makeshift school. There, they spent their mornings in the company of other children their age, having lessons from Mrs Ward, a retired teacher from England.

With a young infant to take care of, Dorothy was not assigned work duties. Instead, she spent her mornings taking care of Noel, often in the company of other mothers and their children. It kept her busy, but she found the long hours tedious. They lived in a constant state of uncertainty, with very little news of what was happening in the outside world and no idea how long they would be held captive.

Early on, Dorothy had realised that the best plan was to keep her body busy and her mind occupied. So when Mary and Lizzie returned from 'school', she left Noel in their care and volunteered her help in the gardens. There was something quite satisfying about tending the vegetable plants and it was good to feel useful, knowing that the food they grew – mainly sweet potatoes, taro and spinach – would help supplement the pathetic rations they were fed by their captors.

One afternoon, Dorothy returned from her garden duties, tired and muddy as usual, to find a screaming baby and two anxious-faced girls. Lizzie, the younger of the two, was sitting on the end of one of the beds, looking as if she was trying not to cry, while Mary was walking up and down the cell, bouncing baby Noel on her shoulder in a desperate attempt to soothe him.

'I don't know what happened,' Mary began in a panic when Dorothy came in. 'He was alright for most of the afternoon, perfectly normal. Then he started to look a bit hot and bothered about half an hour ago. We got him some water but he just won't stop crying! I'm so sorry, Dorothy!'

Dorothy took the baby from the young girl and tried to mask her alarm when she felt how hot he was. She had never seen him like this before and she was worried. But she forced a smile and reassured the girls that they hadn't done anything wrong.

Just as she was wondering how to calm the baby and bring his temperature down, a Japanese guard appeared in the doorway and shouted at them, 'Too loud! You be quiet now! Stop noise!'

'He's sick!' Dorothy showed him the baby. 'Too hot!' she tried to explain in simple words, putting her hand to his forehead to demonstrate.

But the guard shouted, louder now and in Japanese, then slammed the door behind him.

Dorothy fought hard to control the panic that now surged through her. Mary and Lizzie were huddled together on the bed. They looked up at her, their matching brown eyes filled with fear.

Dorothy took a deep breath. 'It's alright, girls,' she managed with a smile, as she bounced Noel on her shoulder. She spoke to him softly, trying to soothe him, but her efforts were in vain and his screaming continued. A passing guard banged on the door outside and Dorothy winced. She had seen first-hand the punishments that these men were capable of exacting for insubordination among the prisoners.

When the door opened again, about half an hour later, Dorothy recognised the uniform of a superior Japanese officer. He was flanked by two other guards, including the one from earlier. The superior looked angry and ready to read her the riot act, but she got in ahead of him.

'Please, help me, sir! My baby is sick! Look, sir!' She showed him Noel's bright-red, angry face.

The guard stared at the child for a moment, then seemed to take pity on Dorothy. He paused, as if considering what to do, then turned to one of his comrades and spoke in a flurry of Japanese.

'You go hospital,' he said, then nodded at Dorothy and beckoned for her to follow him.

Dorothy forced a reassuring smile for the girls and told them not to worry, then followed the guards out along the walkway.

As with everything else in Changi Jail, the 'hospital' was a makeshift facility in a dilapidated wooden hut. Prisoners with medical training volunteered their services as best they could with the pitiful resources available to them. The guard took her inside the hut and pointed at a row of chairs in the corner, then left to wait outside. Opposite the chairs were two dirty white doors labelled 'Doctor' and 'Nurse,' and a cardboard sign on the wall indicated that the corridor down the side of the building led to the ward.

Noel's yelling had eased while they had been walking to the hospital, with the pre-storm breeze cooling him a little. But now that they had stopped and were inside a stuffy building, he began again in full force.

'Oh dear, someone doesn't sound very happy!' a British voice called out cheerfully as the doctor's door opened.

Dorothy looked up from Noel's tear-stained, angry face to see a familiar figure walking towards her. Their eyes met and they both stared in amazement.

'Dorothy?'

'Dr Archie!'

They both spoke at the same time, then laughed at the awkwardness of it. 'It's so good to see you,' he began, then opened his arms to her. Dorothy needed no further encouragement, she got to her feet, shifting the whimpering Noel onto her hip, and let herself be pulled into the doctor's welcoming embrace.

After everything that had happened over the last few weeks, the relief of seeing a friendly face and feeling his supportive arms around her was overwhelming. For so long, she had had to hold everything together and be strong. But the dam burst now and the tears that she had been resisting finally began to flow.

'There now,' Dr Archie soothed, stroking her back. 'It's alright, Dorothy, everything will be alright.'

The doctor led her into his consulting room. He was thinner than when Dorothy had last seen him and, despite his usual cheery smile and manner, she could tell he was exhausted. He had always been so smart at the hospital, but his hair was long and shaggier now and his beard had grown out, making him look older. But one thing had not changed: his calm, caring manner and the sense of peace that Dorothy felt when she was around him. And she needed that now, more than ever.

Dr Archie ushered Dorothy into a chair and took the baby from her. Noel seemed fascinated by the new, bearded face and the distraction seemed to have calmed him. 'Now, tell me,' the doctor asked with a smile, 'who's this handsome little chap?'

And so it all came out. Everything that had happened since Dorothy had said goodbye to Dr Archie some months earlier. He had left the Alexandra Military Hospital back in January, when he'd been called up to accompany a medical team caring for retreating troops in Malaya. But the mission had ended in disaster, with the entire party being captured by the Japanese and marched off to the prisoner-of-war camp.

Never would Dorothy have dreamed of sharing her personal affairs with Dr Archie when they had worked together at the hospital, but everything had changed. She had held it all together for so long, but now it all poured out. She told him all about her husband's infidelity, her miscarriages, Douglas's death, her botched escape from Singapore, surviving on Pom Pong Island and, lastly, the promise she had made to take care of Douglas's child.

Dr Archie listened carefully, all the while tending to the baby. He sat him in a small metal basin on the consultation bed and washed him, wiping him down gently with wet flannels that had seen better days. There was a small electric fan in the room and the soft breeze it created, combined with the water, cooled and calmed Noel. More compliant now, it was easier for Dr Archie to lie him down on the bed and examine him.

'So there we have it,' Dorothy concluded her story with a sad smile. 'Quite alone in the world and stuck here for goodness knows how long, failing miserably at taking care of this poor little chap.' Tears formed in her eyes and Dr Archie came straight over. He put a reassuring hand on her shoulder.

'It is a fine thing you have done, Dorothy. A very fine thing, indeed. I don't know many women who could have done what you have. And . . . ' He paused. 'Please know this,' he continued more softly. 'You are not on your own. Not anymore.' He squeezed her shoulder, then cleared his voice a little awkwardly.

'Anyway, it's good news for this young man; nothing too serious,' he smiled reassuringly at Dorothy, 'Poor little mite was overheating and terribly dehydrated. We just need to keep him cool and make sure he gets plenty of water.'

Dorothy hadn't realised that she was holding her breath until she released it now in a long sigh. She watched as Dr Archie took a bundle of white rags from a box in the corner of the room, tore off a triangle and expertly fashioned a clean nappy for the baby. Then he picked him up and sat him on his knee. He held out the little boy's hand and drew gentle circles on his palm with his finger. *'Round and round the garden, like a teddy bear, One step, two step; tickle you under there!'*

The little boy smiled as the doctor went through the actions of the nursery rhyme, finishing off with a gentle tickle under his armpit. The feeling of relief that he was going to be alright flowed through Dorothy and made her smile, too.

A brief tap on the door and a nurse appeared. 'I'm sorry to bother you, Dr Archie, but you're needed in the ward. Six more have come in and we're running out of beds. I don't know what we're going to do.'

The doctor nodded calmly and told her that he'd be right there. 'No rest for the wicked!' he said with a wry smile, once the nurse had left. 'We are so short staffed here; two of the other doctors are down with malaria and our nurses are dropping like flies, too. I just hope to goodness that it isn't dysentery, as that will spread like wildfire and we've precious little in the way of medication.'

'Let me help!' The words tumbled out of Dorothy's mouth before she'd had time to think. 'I mean, I can help you. I'm a nurse. I want to help you. And I need to keep busy. Please say I can?'

His smile was all the confirmation she needed.

A few days later, once baby Noel was well enough to be left in the care of one of the other mothers, Dorothy made her way to the hospital for her first shift. The pitiful conditions and lack of resources made the work extremely challenging, but it felt good to be useful and to help where she could.

Dysentery had, indeed, started to spread and the ward was overflowing with the pale, gaunt figures of the afflicted prisoners. After months of forced labour, deprivation and malnutrition, they were too weak to fight the disease and many died. With so few medical supplies available, treatment was limited and rudimentary. All they could do was isolate the sick and rehydrate them as best they could with the clean water available. If they were lucky, they would administer quinine which the Red Cross had sent in. Those who were able to eat were fed watery rice and powdered charcoal in a bid to build up their strength.

It was dangerous work, surrounded by highly contagious patients, yet Dorothy found herself looking forward to her shifts. In the prison, she was only allowed to mix with other women and she now enjoyed some male company again. She especially enjoyed working alongside Dr Archie. He had always been such a kind and calm presence in the British Military Hospital and remained so now, even in the face of the horrors they witnessed on a daily basis. He remained cheerful, often daydreaming aloud of a future beyond the camp, back home in England. He told Dorothy all about the place where he had grown up, and where he hoped, one day, to return. He painted the picture of a rural idyll and described it in such detail that when Dorothy closed her eyes she could picture it.

Not that she stayed awake long enough to daydream. Every night, Dorothy fell into bed physically and emotionally exhausted, but it did her good to regain some sense of normality and routine from her work.

Months passed, eventually turning into years. The war rumbled on and life in the camp maintained a strict and predictable routine. To keep their minds occupied and their spirits up, volunteers organised all sorts of social groups – subject, of course, to the approval of the strict prison guards. Sewing bees, singing groups and even musical and dramatic performances took place. The sense of camaraderie was strong. In the face of an uncertain future, everyone pulled together to boost morale wherever they could.

For several months, a group of skilled craftsmen had been working together on the construction of a chapel. Exhausted, malnourished and seriously lacking in materials, it was a testament to their resourcefulness and sheer determination when

Changi Chapel eventually opened. It was a symbol of hope and courage in the face of adversity, not to mention a place of worship and solace. Everyone was welcome, regardless of their faith or lack of, subject only to the whims of the Japanese guards.

On Christmas Eve 1943, Noel's second birthday, Dorothy sat in a pew at the back of the Chapel with the child on her lap. A familiar introduction started on the piano and she joined her fellow women prisoners in a rendition of 'Silent Night'. She snuggled Noel close to her and kissed the top of his dark head, closing her eyes as she enjoyed the beautiful harmonies of some of the more tuneful singers.

The Christmas carol took her back to her life in Fulham, before the war. In her mind, she was sitting next to Daisy's piano, singing with both their families as Daisy entertained them with festive tunes. How things had changed in just a few short years.

'Happy birthday, little man,' she whispered to Noel as tears started to blur her vision. Noel looked up at her, distracted from the toy rabbit she had clumsily fashioned out of an old sock for his gift, and beamed at her. 'Mama! Sing, Mama!'

She smiled through her tears as a wave of bittersweet emotion swept over her. She was his mama. And he was her son. What would happen if – or rather when – they were released from the camp? What would happen to Noel? She would have to take him to his grandparents in Wiltshire, as promised. Wouldn't she? The thought of separation from the child – *her* child – after all this time together felt like a knife through her heart.

For a long time, Dorothy worried how life in the camp would affect baby Noel's development. Every day, she was anxious to make sure he had enough to eat to help keep him healthy. She shared her concerns with Dr Archie while they worked alongside each other. They had grown closer as the months passed and Dorothy was touched that the doctor took such an interest in the child. On the rare occasions when the little boy was ill, Dr Archie made sure that he was the one to treat him and lavished time and attention on him. It warmed Dorothy's heart to see him taking such care of Noel, bouncing him on his knee and playing games with him after a long shift when she knew he was utterly exhausted. Dr Archie reassured her that the little boy was remarkably resilient and she was relieved to hear that he had reached the childhood milestones without too serious a delay.

1944 began and, after eighteen months of relative stability and predictability, things started to change. Fellow prisoners disappeared with little or no warning and those who were left behind started to worry about their fate.

'They go different camp,' was all the explanation that Takashi, the English-speaking guard, would give.

Over the past few months, Dorothy had worked on building a rapport with him in a bid to find out what was going on. Unlike some of the guards who leered at them or were aggressive, Takashi was mild-mannered and polite. He was a family man, he had told Dorothy, with a wife and two young sons back home in Tokyo. He had proudly shown her photographs of them, which he carried in his jacket pocket. And unlike some of the guards, who seemed to relish any opportunity for violence in this war, it seemed that Takashi was only here out of an unwavering sense of duty to his family and devotion to his country.

Early one morning in mid-May, the door banged open and Takashi came into the cell. It was still dark and the children were still asleep. Dorothy and Pat, however, were immediately awake.

'Time you go now, lady,' he announced, nodding at both of them. 'Go different camp. You go today, get ready. Go midday.' And with a nod, he pulled the door closed behind him and he was gone.

'Aw strewth,' Pat drawled in her Australian twang as she rolled over on her mat, 'Midday? I don't think that'll give me long enough to pack!'

Dorothy couldn't help but smile at her friend's irony. In the two years they had been at the camp, they had collected very little in the way of belongings, apart from what they had arrived with and what was donated by the Red Cross.

But the smile faded as reality hit Dorothy like a punch in the stomach. Where were they going? Were they really going to a different camp, or just being taken out to face a firing squad, as she had heard had happened to other prisoners? Her heart began to race.

Later that morning, the women and children lined up for the usual roll call in the central square. There was a buzz of whispered conversations, with everyone wondering what was about to happen. The guards gave nothing away, simply sending the women and children back to their cells, where they were told to await further instructions.

Dorothy knew better than to contradict the guards' instructions, but in a moment of pure recklessness, she passed the baby to Pat and quickly snuck away to the hospital.

Dr Archie looked up in confusion when she burst into his office a few minutes later. 'Dorothy . . . ' he began.

'We're being moved,' she cried. 'We're leaving at lunchtime, going to a new camp. What's going on, Dr Archie? Is it true?' Saying the words out loud filled her with fear and tears welled in her eyes.

The doctor rose from his desk and came over to put an arm around her shoulders. He pulled her to him and held her close. 'There now, shh,' he soothed, stroking her back. 'I heard that there were movements afoot.' He sighed. 'Troops are coming back from the railway in Burma and the Japs are planning on keeping them here. I did hear a rumour that all the civilians would be moved out to make space for them.'

'What about you?' Dorothy asked, a small hope growing that he might be going with her.

Dr Archie shook his head and released her from his arms. 'They want me to stay here. And if the rumours about the poor chaps up in Burma are true, they'll need every bit of medical care we can muster.' He sighed. 'Anyway, let's remain optimistic. Maybe it's a good thing to move to a different camp, this place is so damned overcrowded, it's completely unsanitary. Fingers crossed the next place will be a bit better, ey?'

'En suite bathroom and air-conditioned bedrooms, perhaps?' Dorothy said, giving an ironic smile through tear-stained eyes.

Dr Archie laughed. 'That's the spirit, Dorothy!' He smiled down at her. 'Thank you,' he said.

'For what?' she asked.

'For helping me here?' He looked around the consultation room. 'For laughing at my terrible jokes? For keeping me sane for the past two years? I think that's more than enough reasons, don't you? I'll miss you very much.'

He opened his arms to her and Dorothy was about to go to him when they heard shouting outside. A moment later, the door burst open and a guard came in and grabbed Dorothy by the arm. He barked at her in an angry stream of Japanese, then switched to English.

'Why you here? You bad woman, you go cell. You go now!' Despite her protestations, he dragged Dorothy out of the building. The guard shouted orders to two others who had been waiting outside. She saw them march into Dr Archie's office and the door slammed shut behind them. Panic flooded through her and she begged the guard not to punish the doctor for her misdemeanour. But he ignored her.

Dorothy's worst fears were confirmed when she heard thudding sounds from inside the building, followed by screams of pain.

Tears flowed down her cheeks as she was dragged back to her cell and away from Dr Archie for the last time.

CHAPTER 25

Singapore

Thursday 4th April, 2019

Annabel was so engrossed in her grandmother's story that she didn't hear James come into the room.

'How are you getting on?' he stage whispered, setting down a tray on the table in front of her.

Annabel started, as if woken from a trance. 'Gosh, sorry, I was miles away!' She put the papers down on the table, careful to keep them in the right order. 'Oh lovely, thanks,' she added as James poured her a glass of chilled white wine.

'No problem.' He smiled. He poured his own glass, took a handful of crisps from the plate on the tray and settled in the armchair opposite. 'So, what have you found out so far?'

'It's quite a story,' she sighed. She took a long sip of wine. 'You're not going to believe it, but Dotty was a POW! Her evacuation ship was bombed by the Japanese and she ended up in Changi Jail.'

James stared at her, his mouth dropping open in surprise. 'And she never said anything about it? Wow, that is quite a turn-up for the books!'

'But that's not all. She wasn't on her own in there.' Annabel paused and reached forward for some crisps.

James gave a snort. 'Well no, of course she wasn't – that place was absolutely packed to the rafters! Totally overcrowded and completely unsanitary. Hundreds died, you know. It's a wonder that your grandmother made it out alive!'

'Yes, I know,' Annabel agreed, then took another sip of wine. 'But what I meant was she had company. James, she had a baby in there with her.'

He raised his eyebrows at this. 'A baby? Whose baby? I thought you said she couldn't have children?'

Annabel took a deep breath to steady herself. 'Well, brace yourself. It turns out that the baby was my father, Noel,' she said. Hearing it out loud brought the harsh reality sharply into focus. 'And there's more.' She gave a sad smile. 'My father wasn't Dotty's son. He was the illegitimate son of Douglas Llewellyn and his mistress, an Italian woman called Maria Pemberton, née da Costa.'

James's mouth formed a perfect O and he was momentarily shocked into silence. Then, seeing the tears in her eyes, he came over and sat next to her, putting a comforting arm around her shoulders. Instinctively, Annabel leaned in against him.

James blew out hard. 'Well, that's a lot to take in! How are you feeling?'

She sniffed and was grateful when James handed her a tissue from a box on the table.

'Well, I suppose I'd already started having pretty strong suspicions that Dad wasn't Dotty's biological son. But to have it confirmed like this . . . ' She sniffed. 'To be honest, I don't know how I'm feeling. I was always so close to Dotty. To think that she wasn't *really* my grandmother, well . . . ' Her words trailed as the tears began to stream down her cheeks. She dabbed the soggy tissue at her eyes. 'Sorry . . .

Everything just seems a bit topsy-turvy at the moment,' she managed, in between sobs.

James wrapped his arms around her and held her close. 'Shh, there now,' he soothed, stroking her back. 'Dotty *was* your grandmother, even if not biologically, there's no question about that. This really doesn't change anything, you know. And you might not have inherited her genes, but you certainly inherited her character and her strength. The way you've picked yourself up after everything that's happened recently and come halfway across the world to do this. Honestly, you're pretty amazing, Annabel.'

She gave a watery smile and looked up at him. There was such intensity in his dark brown eyes. She was suddenly aware of his body, up close against hers, warm and firm. She breathed in his cologne and her pulse quickened.

'I know everything feels hard right now,' he continued, gently wiping the tears from her cheek. 'You're still grieving, but you *will* get through this. If Dotty's tale is anything to go by, it's clear that you Penrose ladies are made of strong stuff!'

He smiled down at her, his hand still caressing her face. Overcome with emotion and a sudden, urgent longing, she reached up and touched his cheek. Their eyes locked and, after a brief nod of encouragement from Annabel, his lips were on hers. Gently at first, then with increasing intensity, as he explored her. She wrapped her arms tightly around him and melted against him, savouring every sensation. He tasted of wine and minty freshness and, wrapped in his strong arms, she felt safe.

After a few minutes, Annabel pulled him down so they were lying together on the sofa. He nuzzled her neck and she chuckled softly. 'Who would have thought it, all those years ago, back at uni?'

James paused and looked at her. 'What do you mean?'

'Well, us . . . being like this. You barely had the time of day for me back then; I was sure that you hated me!' She laughed.

James turned serious and Annabel worried that she had clumsily killed the mood that she'd been so enjoying. He looked her straight in the eye.

'Hated you? You're kidding, right? Don't tell me you didn't know?'

'Know what?' Annabel propped herself up on an elbow, her brow furrowing. James mirrored her position, so they were now facing each other.

'The reason I couldn't talk to you. The reason I turned into such an absolute mess whenever you were around?' He screwed up his eyes. 'You *must* have been able to see it?'

Annabel shook her head. 'See what? You were so standoffish whenever I tried to talk to you,' she said with a shrug, 'I just assumed you didn't like me!'

James groaned and buried his face in his hands. Then he looked at her again. Annabel saw that his colour was up, he seemed uncomfortable. He moved away from her and sat on the edge of the sofa.

'You turned me into a bag of nerves, Annabel! You were so beautiful and so damn cool! From the moment I first saw you in the quad at Trinity during Freshers' Week, I was well and truly smitten. Head over the proverbial heels.' He sighed as Annabel's eyes grew wide in surprise. 'For the first two years I tried to work up the courage to ask you out. But I gave up on the idea when I overheard you talking with your oh-so-cool mates at the Valentine's Ball in the second year. If I remember correctly, that Hugo Sotheby-Waugh was holding court with you and a few of his other female friends. He was working his way round all the guys in our corridor, asking how interested you were in dating them. What was it you said to him when he asked about me? You could never date someone who "swam like a fish and had the personality to match," I think that was it.'

Annabel closed her eyes and cringed as she remembered that drunken night, so many years ago. She felt ashamed that she had cared so much about impressing the 'cool' gang with her witty, snide comments. That wasn't who she was. Dating Hugo had been a big mistake and she had soon come to her senses. But it seemed the damage had been done.

'Oh James,' she whispered.

He cleared his throat awkwardly. 'Well, there we go. Nothing to worry about, it's no big deal.' He shrugged. 'It's all in the past. Ancient history!' He tried to force a smile but she wasn't convinced.

'Anyway, are you hungry? I could make us something to eat?' His tone was overly bright and he seemed keen to change the subject. He started to get up, but Annabel put her hand on his thigh to stop him.

'Don't go, James.' She pushed herself up and sat next to him. Then she reached out and touched his cheek. 'I had no idea,' she whispered. 'I'm sorry. I was a bitch around that time, I wasn't myself. Call it a serious lapse in judgement, but I was desperately trying to impress the wrong people. I'm not proud of it.'

Hesitantly, she leaned in against him and rested her head against his chest. Relief flowed through her when she felt his arm move around her shoulders. She looked up at him and whispered, 'I'm so sorry.' She smiled coyly. 'I had no idea that you liked me. But I'm quite glad that you did. And hope that maybe you still do?'

James bent down and gently touched his lips against hers. She held the back of his neck and pulled him closer. Between kisses she murmured, 'I'm not missing out a second time around. We've got a bit of catching up to do, don't you think?'

He pulled back and gave her a questioning look. 'Are you sure?'

She nodded her reply with a smile, then kissed him deeply, her hands in his hair while he stroked her neck. His fingers were gentle but decisive as they made their way along her collar bone then down her chest. Carefully, he undid the first couple of buttons on her top. Every touch made her tingle with pleasure and she moaned when, at last, his hand slipped under the fabric and caressed her breasts.

At that moment, James's phone started buzzing. He pulled away with an apologetic smile and checked the screen. 'Ugh, lousy timing! I'm so sorry, do you mind if I take this? It's Jessica.' He checked his watch. 'I promised to speak to her before school, she'll be heading off shortly. I'll keep it brief.'

Annabel smiled and nodded, and was surprised that James stayed on the sofa to take the call. She discreetly edged further away from him, ran a hand through her hair and quickly did up the buttons on her top. James clicked the 'answer' button on his phone and Jessica appeared, dressed in her blue gingham school dress.

'Hi, Pumpkin! How are you today?' he began, a smile lighting up his face.

'Hi, Daddy.' The little girl beamed back with a gap-toothed smile. 'Look!' She pointed to the missing front tooth. 'It came out!'

James laughed, a happy, carefree laugh that made Annabel smile. It was lovely to see this relaxed side of him.

'Well that's great news, congratulations!' He chuckled. 'Did the Tooth Fairy come?'

Jessica nodded and excitedly told him that she had earned two whole pounds for her tooth, which was double what she'd got last time.

Annabel reached forward for the crisps on the coffee table, but her efforts to be discreet were in vain and, before she knew it, she'd knocked over her wine glass. The sound was clearly audible on the other end of the call.

'What's that noise, Daddy?' The little girl's forehead creased. 'Is there someone there?'

'Um, well, yes actually.' Suddenly put on the spot, James's tone became awkward as he passed Annabel the box of tissues to mop up the spillage. 'My friend Annabel came round to visit.'

'Annabel? Who's that?' Jessica looked confused.

'Just my friend. She's visiting Singapore because her granny used to live here a long time ago, during the Second World War. Amazing, hey? Annabel wants to find out more about her granny's time here and I'm helping her. It's very interesting actually, and you know how much I love history!' James chuckled. He was gabbling now and Annabel could feel the awkwardness of the moment. Jessica did not seem impressed.

'Anyway,' he continued, changing the topic, 'how's everything going at your new school? Have you made some nice friends?'

But Jessica wasn't interested in talking anymore. Annabel could detect the signs of jealousy and betrayal. The little girl couldn't hide her upset that her father was spending time with a female that wasn't her or her mum. With a face like thunder, she said that she had to go. Seconds later, ignoring her dad's protestations, she ended the call.

James looked crestfallen. He put his phone on the table and, with his elbows on his knees, dropped his head into his hands. He looked defeated. 'I can't seem to get anything right.'

Annabel sighed. 'I'm so sorry,' she began.

He shook his head. 'It wasn't your fault. Jess has really struggled with the separation and it's hardly surprising, really. Her seemingly perfect, happy life has been turned completely upside down.' He sighed.

'It'll get easier, just give it time. Kids are resilient, she'll bounce back, I'm sure.' Annabel reached out to touch his back but he edged slightly away and didn't respond.

'Maybe I'll make a move,' she said quietly. 'And you could try calling back?' She glanced at her watch. 'Emma will be home soon, I can read the rest of this at her place.' She nodded to the stack of papers from the coffee table and got to her feet. Something sank inside her when James did not protest.

'OK, sure,' he said, getting up from the sofa. 'Sorry, I don't think I'll be much company now. I need some time on my own. Shall I book you a cab?'

Annabel demurred and, feeling awkward, made a swift exit. She made her way out to the bus stop and used the transport app that Emma had recommended. Three minutes later, the right bus pulled up. She was glad to get out of the late afternoon sun and into the coolness of the air-conditioned bus.

What had she been thinking? Annabel sighed as she settled into a vacant seat. There was a chemistry between them and after a couple of glasses of wine she had let herself get carried away. But neither of them was in any position to be rushing into something new. They weren't at university now, all footloose and fancy free; she was still getting over a break-up and James had his ex-wife and daughter to consider. It was all just too complicated. She wished she could turn the clock back and start things all over again.

But for now, she just wanted to get safely back to Emma's and read the rest of her grandmother's story.

CHAPTER 26

Sime Road Camp, Singapore
May 1944

It was a vain hope that living conditions would be better at the new camp. Sime Road was far worse than Changi and, with overcrowded huts and inadequate facilities for the number of inmates, malnutrition and disease were rampant.

Before the war, the Sime Road site had been the headquarters of the RAF. When the war began, it had become the Combined Army & Air Force Operations HQ. It was located in the centre of Singapore, in what had been a pleasant green, leafy area, on the road leading to the Royal Singapore Golf Club. It looked very different now, with a series of long, attap prison huts lining the road.

The golf club had become unrecognisable, too, since the start of the occupation. The Japanese had taken over the clubhouse and now used it as their office. Roads had been built across the greens, and fairways had been dug over to grow sweet potato and tapioca. And the green of the third hole now boasted a large Japanese shrine.

Dorothy's heart had sunk on arrival. They had been forced to march all the way there from Changi, a distance of nearly fifteen miles, in the sweltering midday sun. Although small for his age, the now two-and-a-half-year-old Noel had weighed heavily in Dorothy's arms as she had trudged along the dusty road. She had been grateful not to be separated from Pat and her girls, who not only helped her carry and take care of Noel, but who also kept her spirits up.

For the first week at Sime Road, those spirits had plummeted to an all-time low. She barely ate, instead giving most of her food to Noel, and was quiet and listless. With no news from Changi Jail, Dorothy had no idea what had happened to Dr Archie. The sound of his pained cries on that final day continued to haunt her and she was racked with guilt that he had been punished because of her. What had they done to him? She had written to him numerous times but she had not yet received any reply. All correspondence was heavily monitored and strictly censored so she had purposely kept the letters mild and brief. She had also tried writing to one of the other nurses, Margaret, with whom she had become friendly while working at the hospital, but there was no reply from her yet, either.

Pat was worried about Dorothy and told her as much. In the end, it was her Aussie friend's no-nonsense, tough-love approach that had finally bucked Dorothy out of her torpor.

'Now come on, I can't stand by and let you give up. We've come too bloody far for that! And besides, you've got the little fella to think about.' She had nodded towards Noel who was, at that moment, trying to catch a drowsy cockroach that had crawled under the door of the cell. 'Who's gonna take care of him if you cark it? He needs you, Dozza.' Her tone softened as she used the Aussie-style nickname she had given Dorothy. 'Come on, love, we've just got to keep on keeping on. Stick a smile on it and she'll be right!'

Dorothy knew that Pat was right. She also knew that the only way to get through each day was to do as she was told and keep busy. By now, she had perfected the ninety-degree bow expected by the Japanese guards, and was mild and obedient in all her interactions with them. In this way, she avoided the slaps that were regularly meted out for any hint of insubordination.

Leaving Noel with the playgroup, a gathering of similar-aged children organised by Mrs Fossett, Dorothy's days were filled with an assortment of jobs. She worked in the tapioca fields, knitted socks for the Japanese and did shifts in the match factory that the Japanese had set up in the camp. They were long hours, but she was glad of the opportunity to earn slightly larger portions of rice for her son. As a growing toddler, Noel needed all the nourishment he could get and Dorothy's maternal instinct to protect him had never been stronger.

Life in Hut Fourteen was grim. The only saving grace was that Dorothy still had Pat and her daughters for company. Noel adored the girls and she loved to watch them playing together. Their cell was smaller than the Changi one, but the layout was different, with enough space for the five of them to sleep side by side on wooden platforms, which somehow made it feel more spacious.

As before, the camp was infested with cockroaches and mosquitoes and there was always much hullabaloo when the children spotted one of the many rats. It amazed Dorothy how easily they had all adjusted to their new environment. While it would have appalled the mothers back in their former lives, watching the children play 'chase the rat' had now become something of an entertainment.

The prisoners survived on minimal rations and Dorothy sorely missed the relief packages that the Red Cross had managed to deliver to Changi Jail. Those parcels contained much-needed canned food, medical supplies and welcome toiletries such as soap and toothpaste. But more than that, they had also been a symbol of hope and support that had helped them keep going. Without them, life in this camp felt a lot harder.

One afternoon, a few weeks after her arrival, Dorothy was returning to her hut from the tapioca field when she saw a group of women and children arriving at the camp. She winced as she recognised the scene, remembering her own arrival some weeks earlier. Had they also come from Changi, she wondered?

Dehydrated and exhausted, they were a raggle-taggle bunch who certainly looked as though they had endured that arduous walk. Children were crying and tired mothers had little energy to comfort them. Her heart went out to them.

Dorothy paused behind a palm tree and watched as the guards lined them up and began the routine roll call. Then they announced which huts they would be going to. Dorothy heard her own hut, number fourteen, being called and she groaned inwardly. How on earth were they going to fit anyone else in? It was already full to bursting.

The guards organised the women into their hut groups and then led them off to their new accommodation. A small group of women with several young children between them filed along the path to Hut Fourteen and Dorothy followed behind.

One of the women dropped back from the group, red-faced and harassed. She was struggling to manage a bag with a broken strap and two young children, both of whom were crying. Dorothy caught up with her.

'Hello, can I help?' she began with a smile. She picked up the bag by its one remaining strap and hefted it up onto her shoulder.

The woman looked her up and down, clearly exhausted and fed up. 'And who are you? The bleedin' welcoming committee?'

she asked in a familiar London accent. 'What a place!' she spat, nodding at the state of the huts.

'Well, the Ritz it certainly isn't!' Dorothy gave a wry smile. 'I'm Dorothy Llewellyn, I just got here a few weeks ago from Changi.'

The other woman looked at her and sighed. 'Sorry, I'm forgetting myself, it's been a hell of a day.' She wiped her hand on her dirty dress then reached it out to Dorothy. 'Maureen. Maureen Thompson, that is. And this here's Susie and Billy.' She indicated each of the children then picked up the youngest, Billy, with a tired sigh. She peered more closely at Dorothy. 'Hang on a minute, don't I know you from somewhere? I'm sure I've seen you before.'

A guard had noticed Maureen lagging behind and came to chivvy her with a string of angry Japanese. He pointed his gun menacingly.

'Alright, alright, keep your hair on!' Maureen muttered, while Dorothy instinctively bowed low and apologised.

'A word of warning; the guards here are stricter than the ones at Changi,' Dorothy whispered as they set off to follow the others. 'It really doesn't do to make them angry. I presume you've come from Changi, too?'

'Yes, out of the frying pan and into the bleedin' fire, by the looks of things!'

Dorothy gave a sad smile. 'I'm afraid so. But we've come this far and hopefully we won't be here too much longer.' Her voice brightened as she continued, 'You heard about the Normandy invasion? "D-Day" they're calling it.'

Maureen nodded. 'Yes, we heard about that in the Red Cross messages. How do you get your news here?' Maureen asked.

'Some of the chaps have built a radio and have managed to tune in to the BBC. Highly risky if the guards were to find it, obviously, but it hasn't half boosted morale! The Jerries are on the back foot now, it can't go on for too much longer.'

'Let's hope you're right!' Maureen said. 'I can't bear the thought of another Christmas dinner of bleedin' hard rice and watery porridge!'

Dorothy smiled. 'Maureen, I need to ask you something. I've been trying to get in touch with a friend of mine back at Changi, one of the doctors I worked with at the hospital there.'

'That's where I've seen you before!' Maureen said. 'You were in the hospital when I took young Billy in!'

'Yes, that would be right. I was working there until we moved here in May. Well, I'm anxious to find out about a colleague of mine, Dr Archie,' she began. 'I haven't heard from him and I just want to know that he's alright.'

'Dr Archie?' Maureen nodded slowly. 'Tall chap, blondish hair?'

Dorothy nodded.

'Yes, I remember him, he was good with Billy. Nice chap and a good doctor.' She was quiet for a moment and looked thoughtful. Then she shook her head and continued, 'Listen love, I'm not sure I can help you. My friend Brenda was in the hospital just last week, her chest was bad. She said the doctor was a young Scottish chap.'

Dorothy nodded at the description. 'Dr Mackay,' she confirmed. 'But no Dr Archie?'

Maureen stopped and turned to look Dorothy straight in the eye. She paused for a moment, as if considering what to say. 'Well, she didn't mention him.' She shrugged. 'Maybe he was just off duty. Or maybe he was moved to another camp, too?'

It made no sense. Dr Archie had said that he was needed at Changi and that he wasn't going to be moved. So why wasn't he there? She feared the worst. What had they done to him? Her pulse quickened as her mind went into overdrive.

They stopped outside Hut Fourteen and, after shouted instructions from the guard, Maureen put young Billy down on the ground. Then she motioned to take back the bag from Dorothy.

'Thanks for helping with this, I appreciate it. See you around, I suppose.'

Dorothy watched as Maureen and her children were led into a cell within the hut. Then she made her way back to her own cell at the far end, her hollow stomach a knot of anxiety.

The days passed and life at Sime Road Camp took on the same, monotonous routine that it had at Changi. But routine was important, as was the sense of purpose that Dorothy achieved from her various jobs. Keeping busy helped her make it through the days and helped her sleep at night.

News from the outside was sparse as communications were highly censored. But the radio broadcasts continued to spread hope. And that hope was rewarded in May of the following year, when the news came that they had all been waiting for: the war in Europe was over.

Word spread like wildfire through the camp, whispered conversations passing on the wonderful news. The collective relief and joy was muted though, for it would be dangerous to let the guards know their source of information.

Dorothy breathed a huge sigh of relief and sent up a silent prayer for her brother, Thomas. With every fibre of her being she willed that he had made it through alive. Several times she had tried writing to his Cambridge address, in the hope that he might have returned there on leave, but the lack of reply had left her worried.

She thought, too, of her other loved ones, of Daisy and her family back in London and Clara and her family. She knew that they had booked tickets on a ship to leave Singapore just a couple of days before her own ill-fated evacuation. Had they made it away safely? She had no way of finding out, but prayed that they were now safely back in England.

One sunny morning, Dorothy was on her knees in the paddock, pulling the weeds from the long lines of tapioca. She had now been a prisoner of war for two and a half years and her clothing was threadbare. Her once pretty, pink sun hat was faded and stained and offered little protection from the relentless heat. But, better sun than rain, Dorothy thought. The monsoon-like rain storms turned the gardens into a quagmire and the work became even more muddy and miserable. Given the lack of washing facilities, the mud stuck for days.

Dorothy hummed while she worked. The previous night there had been a musical evening in Hut Twelve which had put everyone in a good mood. Spirits were high after the recent news from Europe and three of the girls from her hut had given a splendid rendition of the Andrews Sisters 'Boogie Woogie Bugle Boy'. It had brought back happy memories as Dorothy remembered the first time she had listened to it with Clara, drinking their own, home-made versions of the Singapore Sling at her friend's house, just a few months before the island had fallen to the Japanese.

The tune had stuck with her and she smiled as she hummed, pulling the weeds out with ease and dropping them into the bamboo basket at her side. It was hot work and her back ached. She had torn a strip of fabric from around the bottom of her dress and folded it up to make tiny pads to protect her knees from the stony ground.

She heard footsteps approaching and she looked up. A guard was bringing another woman over to weed the line with her.

'You show her how do weeding!' he barked.

Dorothy nodded obediently and looked up at the newcomer. She was a bit older than Dorothy, her dark hair greying at the temples. Her collarbones stuck out unnaturally above the neckline of her thin blue cotton dress. All the prisoners had lost weight to an unhealthy degree during their time in the camps, but this woman looked seriously unwell.

'I'm not sure there's much to show.' Dorothy gave a wry smile after the guard had left. 'You pull the weeds out like this.' She demonstrated, holding up a spindly green plant. 'Then pop them in the basket like this.' She dropped it into the bamboo basket. 'And that's pretty much it!'

'Alright, thanks.' The woman coughed, a nasty, hacking cough, then turned away to spit phlegm on the ground.

'Sorry,' she muttered, sounding embarrassed. 'Chest's bad again. It's this bleedin' humidity.'

Dorothy offered her sympathy and indicated for the woman to work opposite her. Then she put the basket between them and got to work. The basket soon started to fill up as they made their way along the row of young plants.

They worked in silence for a few minutes, then Dorothy started humming the song again and smiled when the other woman joined in. But it was short lived as another coughing fit took hold of her. Again, she turned away and spat. Dorothy saw the phlegm on the ground and noticed that it contained blood. She tried not to show her alarm.

'I'm Dorothy, by the way,' she said with a smile. 'I haven't seen you before, what's your name?'

'Brenda,' the other woman said.

Dorothy recognised the name immediately. 'Oh! Are you Maureen's friend? With the two little ones, Susie and Billy?'

Brenda nodded. 'Yes, we shared a cell over in Changi. Haven't seen much of her since we were moved here, though. I'm in Hut Eight but I've not been out and about much; haven't been too well.' As if on cue, she coughed again, a deep, rattling sound that made Dorothy wince. 'But now the Japs seem to think I'm well enough to make myself useful, so here I am.' She shrugged.

'Stop talking! Must work!' A guard came over and shouted at them.

'I'm sorry,' Dorothy muttered once the guard was out of earshot. 'Listen, I know you spent time at the hospital in Changi Jail. Did you see anything of Dr Archie while you were there? I worked with him in the hospital, you see. I just wanted to find out if he was alright.'

'Oh!' A look of recognition spread across Brenda's face. 'That's where I've seen you before!'

'Yes.' Dorothy felt a strange sense of déjà vu. 'I worked there as a nurse. I knew Dr Archie from before, though. We worked together at the Alexandra Military Hospital.'

Brenda shook her head sadly. 'Poor chap!'

Dorothy dropped a handful of weeds into the basket and looked at Brenda. 'What do you mean?'

'You mean you didn't hear what happened to him?'

Dorothy shook her head, her pulse quickening.

'Well, it was all a bit hush-hush.' Brenda frowned. 'But a while back, we heard that he was given one hell of a beating by the guards. Then he just disappeared, no sign of him. And that's it, that's all.' She shrugged. 'No one really had a clue what became of him. The other hospital staff didn't know. But I think everyone feared the worst. Such a shame, he was a good doctor and such a nice man.'

Tears sprang to Dorothy's eyes. 'Oh God!' she cried, her face creasing in misery.

'You, stop talking!' The guard had returned. He shoved Dorothy hard in the back with the butt of his rifle and she tumbled face first into the sticky brown mud.

She tried to regain her composure as she pushed herself back up, bowing low in apology to the guard.

'I'm sorry.' Brenda whispered as the guard moved off. Her face was full of concern. 'Friend of yours, was he? The doctor?'

Dorothy nodded and wiped a mess of mud and tears from her face. She swallowed hard and fought to compose herself. She was to blame. Whatever they had done to Dr Archie, it was all her fault. He had been the kindest and best of men, her rock during the hardest time of her life. And now he was gone.

'I'm sorry' Brenda repeated with a long sigh. 'Too many lives have been lost in this bloody war. I'm glad it's finished in Europe, but when will it ever end for us?'

The answer to Brenda's question finally came a couple of months later. In early August, tiny seeds of hope began to flourish for the starved and exhausted prisoners when news came that the Allied troops had bombed two key Japanese cities. Dorothy had never heard of Hiroshima or Nagasaki, but suddenly those names were on everyone's lips as the key to ending the war. Dorothy found herself facing conflicting emotions as she thought of the cities that had been decimated and the innocent lives that had been lost. Thousands of women and children who, like her, had not chosen this war, had had their lives cut short.

As the days passed, there was an increasing mood of optimism around the camp. Encouraging rumours buzzed around that the Japanese surrender was imminent. As if to confirm this, the prison guards became distracted, increasingly preoccupied by what was to come. There were no more physical punishments for prisoners who stepped out of line and their manner was much less hostile, verging on cordial, as if fearful of the retribution that could come. The tide was on the turn and Dorothy finally let herself dream of a life beyond Sime Road Camp.

Eventually, on the 15th of August, 1945, the news came that everyone had been waiting for. After six long, gruelling years, the war was finally over.

CHAPTER 27

Penrose Farm, 6 June 1946

The end of the war brought with it a tumult of emotions. We were overcome with joy at our newfound freedom, naturally, but it was tempered by a sense of uncertainty. The world was a very different place from the one we had been taken from in 1942 and, institutionalised as we had become, there was an apprehension about what would happen next.

We didn't leave the camp straight away, but had to stay for a few more days of voluntary incarceration. The Allies had dropped leaflets into the camp after the surrender, advising us to stay put for our own safety. We didn't know what awaited us outside the camp and we had no papers, no money and nowhere to go. So we stayed at the camp and awaited the arrival of the Allied troops to take charge and help us.

We all hoped and prayed that we would soon be repatriated and that family and friends had made it through the war for us to return to. We yearned to go back to our normal lives, but after almost six years of world war, we had to face the stark reality that those lives didn't exist anymore.

It was a rainy day when a bunch of cheerful British soldiers helped us up onto the back of a pick-up truck and drove us away from the camp for the final time. 'Good riddance,' we all cried as we set off.

I was glad to still be with Pat and her daughters. They had been my one constant in the past few years of chaos. We were taken to a temporary holding camp where our details were processed and we underwent medical assessments. After years of malnutrition and starvation diets, we were reduced to skin and bone. Our bodies were unaccustomed to eating normal amounts so a careful refeeding process was required. The temptation when one has been starving is to dive in and eat one's fill, but this ended in tragedy in some cases.

Looking in the mirror for the first time, I cried. I instantly felt ashamed of my vain tears; I was alive, after all, and so many others were not. I didn't recognise who I was anymore. I didn't know the old woman who looked back at me from the pane of glass. She had dull, haunted eyes and skin like tanned leather from days working under a relentless sun. Emaciated and malnourished, her hair was lank and unkempt. She was at least a decade – if not two – older than me. She couldn't be me. But she was who I had become.

My appearance was, however, the last of my worries. Uppermost in my mind was Noel. When we left Sime Road in August 1945, he was three and a half years old. Despite the ordeal, he was a happy little chap, if a little shy. He was small for his age but the medics deemed him healthy and his speech and physical development were progressing well.

It had been three and a half years since I had promised Noel's mother to deliver him to his paternal grandparents in England, but how could I give him up now? He was my son and I was his mother, bonded by the worst of experiences and a deep and unwavering love. Sleep proved elusive those first few nights in the holding camp; our bodies unaccustomed to even the slightest of comforts, the canvas camp beds felt like five-star luxury! But what kept me awake most was the thought of my parting from Noel.

After just over three weeks in the holding camp, it was time for another parting. Pat and her girls had been issued berths on a ship bound for Perth; they were finally going home. They had received the wonderful news that her husband, Joe, had made it through the brutal ordeal of working on the Thai-Burma Railway. He was safely back on the family farm in Fremantle, being taken care of by his mother and waiting for his girls to come home.

Not only would I miss Pat terribly, but I envied her joy and comfort of returning to her family. If I did make it back to England, I had no idea who or what awaited me. But I was happy for her, too. Mary and Lizzie were now aged thirteen and sixteen and, despite everything that they had endured, they had become the most delightful young ladies. They were bright and intelligent, both keen to finish their school studies and apply to university. But, most importantly of all, they were immeasurably caring and kind. They had been like sisters to Noel and he adored them. On that last morning, I hugged them both close, kissing each of them on the cheek, then watched as they picked up Noel for one last cuddle.

I hugged Pat one final time and the tears flowed. For three and a half years, she had been my rock. We had been through so much together and had made it through. We had shared the good times and the bad, the laughter as well as the tears.

'Strewth, Dozza, don't get all emotional on me now!' she said, exaggerating her Australian drawl to lighten the mood, whilst blinking back her own tears. 'Keep your pecker up and remember: it'll all be alright in the end. And if you're ever over in our neck of the woods, you be sure to look us up!'

Just a few days later, it was my turn to receive a precious white envelope from the desk staff at the camp. It contained two tickets for passage on the Royal Mail Line ship SS Almanzora, bound for Southampton. I read the names on the tickets and wept. I couldn't believe it was finally happening. 'Mrs Dorothy Llewellyn and Master Noel Llewellyn,' I read out loud. It was strange to hear Noel's full name. Of course it was biologically correct; Douglas had been his father, after all. But that connection was gone and his only remaining link was to me, his mother.

On the morning of Saturday the 15th of September, 1945, a date I will never forget, I packed our meagre belongings and we set off to the docks. It was hard to explain to Noel what was about to happen and how our lives would change as we left Singapore. But he was excited at the prospect of going on a big boat.

A strange feeling of déjà vu washed over me as we boarded the ship. I remembered walking up the gangplank on that fateful night three and a half years earlier. But everything was different now. Instead of a tiny baby in my arms, I carried a wriggling three-year-old. And instead of the deep sense of anxiety that filled the ship that night, the mood was lively and cheerful.

We found our cabin and settled in for the journey with our cabin mates, an older British lady called Nora and her quiet teenage son, Peter. Noel was curious about our new surroundings and, after a thorough exploration of every nook and cranny, he soon snuggled into the soft pillow on the bed and was fast asleep. I watched him for a while, he was so content and I envied his peacefulness. Inside, I was in a real quandary over what to do with him when we arrived in England. I wanted to put that moment off for as long as possible, but at the same time I couldn't wait to set foot back on British soil.

It was on the third morning of the voyage that the most marvellous thing happened. Noel and I had just finished our breakfast and were making our way out along the deck and back to our cabin, when I heard someone call my name. Until now, I had recognised a few women from the camp on board the ship, but I had chosen to keep myself to myself. This voice belonged to a man. It was deep and familiar to me.

'Nurse Llewellyn? Is that you? Dorothy?'

I stopped and turned to see a figure behind us. The sun was behind him and he was a dark silhouette against the light. He was tall but his shoulders were hunched, leaning heavily on a walking stick as he approached us. I looked closely at his features and although the thick beard was a new addition, I recognised the shaggy blonde hair and easy smile.

'Dr Archie!' I cried. Tears filled my eyes and a huge wave of relief flooded through me. For so long, I had feared him dead and had blamed myself for what had happened to him. I rushed towards him and reached up to embrace him in a tight hug.

'You're alive!' I said, smiling as I held him close.

'It would seem so.' He laughed. His eyes softened as he looked down at me. 'Hello again, Dorothy.' He kissed the top of my head. 'And hello, young man,' he added, looking down at Noel, who, confused by the excitement, was clinging on to my leg. Dr Archie reached down and ruffled his hair. 'Look at you, Noel, you're getting so big now!'

Noel looked up and studied the newcomer's features for a moment. Then he reached up and held out his hand. Dr Archie smiled and began to trace a circle on Noel's open palm with his finger. 'Round and round the garden, like a teddy bear . . .'

A shy smile slowly spread across my son's face. 'Doctor,' he whispered, making us both laugh. He was a shy little boy, so it was marvellous to see that he not only remembered, but was pleased to see our old friend.

'But your leg,' I began, conscious that he was standing awkwardly. 'Come, please sit down and tell me everything.'

I ushered the doctor over to a bench on the deck and Noel climbed up onto his lap, fascinated by his beard. As we sat there, looking out at the tranquil waters of the Malacca Strait, he told me what had happened to him since we had last met.

On that last, fateful morning, he had been on the receiving end of an angry guard's frustration. The swift verbal reprimand that he should have been given for seemingly encouraging my insubordination soon descended into a brutal beating. I winced as he told me how it had taken two other guards to pull his attacker off him. It had left him broken, bleeding and unconscious.

The Japanese leaders of the camp respected Dr Archie. He had proved himself useful at the camp and they recognised his unwavering devotion to duty. Now, thousands of prisoners were returning from the Burma Railway, many of whom were in desperate need of medical attention, and Dr Archie's skill was urgently needed. But before he could help others, the doctor needed to heal himself.

The vicious attack had left him with a black eye, a fractured collarbone, two cracked ribs and a broken leg. Ashamed of how one of their men had treated the respectable doctor, the Japanese Major in charge of the camp had come to personally issue a formal apology and assure him that his attacker was being punished for overstepping the mark. Dr Archie was then transferred to a solitary room, far away from the hospital and his colleagues, where one of the Japanese doctors nursed him back to health.

'And I made a pretty good recovery,' he concluded. 'Apart from the leg, that still gives me a bit of gyp.' He gave a wry smile, which fell when he noticed me wiping away silent tears. 'What's this?' he asked, touching my wet cheek.

'I thought they had killed you!' It all tumbled out in a sob. 'I heard you had been beaten and then disappeared. I thought you were dead and I blamed myself. I'm so sorry that I got you in trouble that day. All this' — I indicated his leg and his walking stick — 'It's my fault!'

Dr Archie shuffled closer along the bench and put his arm around me, pulling me close to him.

'Shhh, there now, Dorothy,' he soothed as I cried against his shoulder. 'Everything is alright. The war is over and we're both here and alive. I'd say that's something to be thankful for. Don't cry, my dear, I can't bear to see you cry.'

He reached into his pocket and pulled out a handkerchief. Noel reached up and took it from him, then proceeded to wipe my tears away, which made us both smile.

I cannot describe the relief that I felt on seeing Dr Archie alive and well. The fear that I had been responsible for his death had hung over me like a black cloud for over a year. But it wasn't only relief that I felt, it was that old feeling of calm reassurance that I had always felt in his presence. It was exactly what I needed.

Over the next couple of weeks of the voyage, Noel and I spent most of our time with Dr Archie and we grew close. We shared our tales of the last few years in captivity as well as stories from our former lives. He was so good with Noel and it was wonderful to see my little boy's confidence grow as they played together. And, truth be told, it was wonderful to have someone to take care of me. He was the kindest of men and spending time with him made me feel happier than I could remember being for quite some time.

One evening, we were sitting on the deck after dinner, watching the sun set. Noel was safely tucked up asleep in bed, watched by our cabin-mate, Nora.

'Tell me, what are your plans when we get back to England?' he asked.

I sighed, knowing what lay ahead. 'I have to visit Noel's grandparents in Wiltshire. I promised his mother that I would take him there.' Even though the thought of it broke my heart, I knew that I had to keep my promise.

'And then? After that, where will you go?'

I shrugged. 'London, I suppose. I need to find my brother and visit my best friend, Daisy, in Fulham. What about you?'

'I'm going home, Dorothy, to Cornwall.' Dr Archie considered me thoughtfully for a moment. 'Would you like to come with me?'

I smiled at his kind offer. 'For a visit? Why yes, that would be lovely. Perhaps in a few weeks, once I've found Thomas and spent some time in London?'

But the doctor was shaking his head. 'No, that's not what I meant. Dorothy, I know I'm a lot older than you and this is probably rather sudden, but I was wondering . . .'

He rose from the seat and sank, rather clumsily, down onto the deck. I thought for a moment that he'd dropped something and was looking for it, but he continued.

'Dorothy, I didn't mean for you to come to Cornwall as a visitor. I was wondering, well, hoping, that you might do me the very great honour of coming with me as my wife?'

I gave a gasp of surprise. Dr Archie took my small, cold hand in his warm, soft one. It was the strangest sensation, Ah Ling, but his touch had the most wonderfully reassuring effect and I instantly felt safe.

'You see, I've always been so terribly fond of you,' he continued, his voice catching a little. 'Ever since you started your training at the Alexandra Military Hospital. And now, more than ever, I can't bear the thought of our parting when we reach Southampton. I hope it's not too arrogant to say that I think I could make you happy. And after everything we've been through, I think we both deserve a little happiness. Wouldn't you agree?'

Then he gave a shy smile. 'Truth be told, I've fallen hopelessly in love with you. I do believe I can make you happy, Dorothy, if you would give me the chance. I want to take care of you. Please say you'll consider it?'

It was not the head over heels romance of my first engagement, far from it. I was older and wiser now, battle-scarred from both my marriage to Douglas and years as a prisoner of war. But it had not left me cynical. I knew what mattered and what was important to me now, and Dr Archie was offering it all: respect, kindness, loyalty and affection. I had grown so fond of him and knew that Noel adored him, too.

My heart felt full and tears blurred my vision as I stroked his hand in mine. 'Will we live by the sea?' I asked.

His face broke into the widest grin. 'We will live wherever you choose, my darling! Does that mean what I think it means?'

I was so choked with emotion that all I could do was nod my agreement and smile through tears of joy. I pulled him back onto the bench beside me and he wrapped his arms around me and kissed me, slowly and gently. And I felt like I had come home.

We were married by the ship's captain, a few days off the coast of Portugal, the day before we docked in Southampton; Tuesday the 16th of October, 1945. It was the second time around for both of us and it could not have been more different from the first. Instead of a full church and a fancy dress, it was just us with the captain and two of his crew as witnesses. Our cabin-mate Nora had proved a good friend; not only did she offer to take care of Noel for me, but she also gave me a pretty pink dress to wear for the occasion – a third-hand donation from the Red Cross, no less. Archie had shaved off his beard and looked handsome in a smart white shirt and navy-blue tie.

The captain arranged a simple wedding breakfast for us and played a Glenn Miller record on the gramophone. It was the first time I had heard 'In the Mood' and it became an instant favourite. Archie couldn't dance because of his injured leg, but the music was so cheerful and uplifting that I couldn't help myself and I enjoyed being twirled around by the first mate. The whole event was nothing like our first weddings, but it was full of joy and hope for our future together.

Autumn welcomed us home to England with her overcast skies and crisp morning air as we docked in Southampton. But nothing could spoil the joy I felt at being back in my home country. I had been away for a little over seven years and so much had changed. All around us, we saw the scars of war, wounds that were yet to heal, but the mood was optimistic and cheerful. In true British spirit, everyone was looking ahead to the future and striving to get their lives back on track.

Noel stared out at this foreign, grey place and his forehead wrinkled. He shivered inside his new woollen sweater, whose scratchy collar had been bothering him all morning. 'It's so cold, Mama!' were his first words as he stepped off the gangplank and onto British soil for the first time. I smiled, but felt an ache in my heart as I wondered; for how much longer would I be his mama?

After much agonising, Archie and I decided that our first stop must be Wiltshire. My promise had been to deliver Noel to his grandparents so that they could take care of him, so that was what I must do. Over the past few months, I had allowed myself to daydream that there would be some reason that they could not take him. Perhaps they would be too elderly, too infirm, or just plain unwilling to take care of a small, lively three-year-old who would disrupt their peaceful lives. Or maybe, just maybe, they would understand that I was his mother now and he belonged with me. I had many sleepless nights before we arrived in Wiltshire.

Our first morning in the pretty village of Wilton was spent trying to find Highcliffe Manor, the home of the Llewellyn family. But it was a fruitless task. We asked everywhere, at the post office, the church and even the local public house, but no one could help. And what's more, no one had heard of a family named Llewellyn living in the area. It was the strangest thing.

In the end, we gave up searching and caught the bus into the county town of

Salisbury. There, we were able to visit the town hall and spoke to a very helpful man in the public records office. He obligingly took all the details and promised to look into it while we found somewhere for lunch, for we were exhausted and hungry. I'm sure you can imagine my complete and utter shock when we returned a few hours later to learn that neither Highcliffe Manor, nor the Llewellyns, existed.

I was utterly dumbfounded. Gradually, I reached the awful realisation that Douglas simply had not been who he said he was. That suspicion was confirmed when Archie contacted the Dean of Oxford University and learned that there had never been a student named Douglas Llewellyn. Ah Ling, that man had lied about everything. He was a fraudster and a fake.

Years had passed, but the grief of his lies and infidelity hit me again, and I wept. I wept for the naive young girl I had been, so easily taken in by his charm and smooth talking, and I wept for Noel, to have such a man for a father. Perhaps it was fortunate that he was no longer alive to influence the little boy.

It was a terrible shock, but there was a silver lining: Noel would stay with me, with us. I felt uncomfortable about it at first, aware that he might still have paternal grandparents who were alive and would love to take care of him. Would he be better off with blood relatives? I agonised over it for some time and

Archie promised to make further enquiries when we reached London, but he didn't hold much hope. Without knowing Douglas's real name, it would be like looking for a needle in a haystack. But worse than that, it was a haystack that had been set alight. During the war years, many public record offices had been damaged and documents destroyed. I felt duty bound to at least try, but to be honest I felt more than a little half-hearted. Ultimately, I had become Noel's mother and he was my son, and our separation would break my heart.

London was a sorry sight when we arrived there by train a couple of days later. Efforts to repair and rebuild were well under way, but it would take years to recover from the aftermath of the war. How strange it was to be back there after being away for so long. Not only had the city changed, but I had changed. Despite Archie's careful dietary plan for us to slowly regain the weight we had lost, we were still horribly thin. We looked so different, with our tanned skin and skeletal frames, and drew curious glances wherever we went.

Archie's first stop was to visit an old friend and colleague, who kindly gave us a loan to tide us over for a while. We took a room in a small guest house near Waterloo Station and planned to spend the next few days making enquiries, organising paperwork and contacting loved ones. For my part, I was next to useless as the cold English weather got the better of my tired, weakened body. I woke on the first morning with a horrible cold and ended up bed bound for a couple of days. I was so exhausted and floated about between sleep and wakefulness, gripped by fever. Archie was completely wonderful. Not only did he take care of me in his usual gentle, loving way, but he arranged for the guest house manager, a war widow called Mrs Sutton, to watch Noel when he needed to go out. I was in such a daze that I didn't follow what Archie was up to. All I knew was that he was my rock and I thanked God for him.

On our third morning in London I awoke feeling so much better, my fever had broken and the pounding in my head had eased. Around mid-morning, Mrs Sutton brought me tea and toast and reassured me that Noel was behaving himself, playing with her son who was a few years older than him. She was so kind. She told me that Archie had returned from his appointments and was in the sitting room downstairs with a 'very handsome feller' in tow. Still a little dazed, I didn't follow what she was talking about, but a few minutes after she left, there was a knock on the door and Archie came in.

'Hello, darling, I'm so glad you're looking a bit brighter. I've brought someone to see you.' He smiled at me and stood back as another man entered the bedroom. I worried that I was having a relapse as I could not believe my eyes: it was Thomas! My darling brother was alive and was standing there in front of me, a big grin on his face.

'Hi, sis! Long time no see!' He chuckled. Then, before I knew it, he was sitting beside me on the bed, wrapping his arms around me. How I had missed him! I had needed him so much over the last few years, through my ordeal with Douglas, the deaths of our parents, then three and a half years of prison hell.

Laughter and tears flowed freely as we caught up, a mixture of relief and joy and a release of all the pain we had been through. I had lost many loved ones and feared that I may have lost Thomas, too. I looked up at Archie, my wonderful husband, still standing by the door and smiling at me with such love in his eyes, and thanked him for finding my brother.

Mrs Sutton kindly offered us the sitting room for our private use and, swept along by our happiness, joined us with a plate of sandwiches and pot of tea for lunch. Post-war rationing continued to make catering a challenge, but the fish paste sandwiches and tea with powdered milk made for the finest meal I could remember.

It was the most wonderful reunion and my heart felt fit to burst when my brother introduced himself to Noel as his Uncle Thomas.

The little boy took to him immediately and the pair were soon on the floor, playing with the building blocks that Mrs Sutton's son had kindly given him.

We shared our news from the past few years and tears were shed when I described our parents' funerals. Thomas shared his wartime tales, including a brief stay in a German prisoner-of-war camp followed by a death-defying escape that had our hearts racing. He told us all about his new job at Great Ormond Street Hospital for Children and how he was engaged to be married to a lovely girl called Marie. She worked as a curator at the nearby British Museum and was the sister of one of his new medical colleagues.

I felt the need to come clean to my brother and explain Noel's origin. Thomas must have been able to calculate that the dates didn't allow for Archie to be his father. But something rather wonderful happened that stopped me. Noel reached his arms up to Archie to be picked up and called him 'Daddy'. Maybe it was because Mrs Sutton had often referred to Archie as Noel's daddy that the little boy had picked up on it, but from that moment on, the deal was sealed. Archie smiled fondly as he picked him up and kissed the top of his head. Then he gave me a wink and a silent pact was made, we both felt it would be easier that way.

And so our little family was formed. Archie had been busy while I was unwell and, with the emergency papers that we had been issued in Singapore, together with our new marriage certificate, he had managed to get new identity documents for us. We were now officially Dr and Mrs Arthur Penrose. I hadn't realised until that moment that Archie was not his official name, but I liked Arthur, it sounded so distinguished and it suited him well.

The clerk had taken pity on Archie, given our rather exceptional circumstances, and helpfully stretched a few rules to process Noel's adoption and change of name at the same time. It felt only right and proper that, with our new start, he should take Archie's family name and that we both shed Douglas's fabricated one.

On that note, Archie had also been to visit the Head Office of McKinley's Rubber to enquire about Douglas Llewellyn. Explaining that his wife was the daughter of one of their former senior managers in Singapore had opened doors, but yet again the trail ran cold. The company secretary was able to share a copy of Douglas's application to the company several years earlier, plus a form containing the details from his passport. But all the paperwork was in the only name we knew: Douglas James Llewellyn. We realised then that it was time to draw a line and give up; we would never find out where Douglas's parents were, or who indeed the real Douglas had been.

Our final visit before we left London was one that filled me with the greatest joy. On Sunday afternoon we caught the underground train out to Putney Bridge and walked along the river, past Fulham Palace and the football ground at Craven Cottage, as I had done so many times in my former life. It was all so familiar but, scarred by the war, it all looked so different.

We turned into Queensmill Road and I was overcome with emotion. There I was, back in my old neighbourhood for the first time in seven long years. Curious faces pressed up against the bay window as we walked up the path to the black front door of number twenty-six. Daisy opened the door with the brightest of smiles and I fell into her welcoming arms. We held each other for a good few minutes, sobbing tears of joy and relief, while our husbands and children made their introductions around us.

It was the happiest of afternoons, being reunited with my friend and meeting her loved ones. Daisy's mother, Averil, kept us supplied with pots of tea and trays of sandwiches and home-baked cakes, all made from hard-saved ration coupons. It was so wonderful to see Averil and she sat listening to every detail as Daisy and I talked nineteen to the dozen about the past few years.

Daisy's husband, Bert, was quite the life and soul of the party and delighted Noel with various games and magic tricks. Their children, Vera and Eddie, were mini versions of them; Vera having Daisy's kind and thoughtful manner, and Eddie being another born entertainer. Both were so good with Noel, whom everyone assumed was my and Archie's son.

It turned out that Daisy had not received the letters I had sent her from the prisoner-of-war camp. It was hardly surprising, given the conditions at the time, but it made things easier when it came to explaining my new family. We were starting a new life and both Archie and I felt that, for the sake of the child, it would be easier to let people believe what they already assumed; that we had married after Douglas died and I'd given birth to Noel soon after. Although it felt wrong to let my oldest friend believe a falsehood, we wanted to start afresh and I had Noel's best interest in mind.

The afternoon wrapped up in its usual fashion, with a good old sing-song around the piano. Daisy played as beautifully as ever and we worked our way through a medley of wartime songs and Vera Lynn classics, singing with gusto as we belted out that there would always be an England and we would meet again.

The lyrics were apt as we made promises to keep in touch and to visit the next time we were in London. And Archie, who had got on like a house on fire with Bert, invited them to visit us in Cornwall. When the time arrived to say farewell, there were tears in our eyes. Daisy pulled me close in a warm hug.

'I can't tell you how glad I am that you made it back here in one piece! I was so dreadfully worried about you.' Then she stepped back and looked me up and down, her forehead furrowing as she took in my thin frame. 'Truth be told, I'm still worried about you — please promise me you'll eat up and put some weight on! I know that Archie will take care of you, he's such a lovely man and you just seem so natural together, like you were made for each other. I'm so happy you met him!'

My heart was full as we left Queensmill Road and walked back along the night-time streets to the tube station. I felt safe with my hand tucked in my husband's, while he carried the sleeping Noel in his other arm. I looked up at him and smiled; I, too, was so happy that I had met him.

The next morning, a damp and chilly Monday in late September, we caught the train from Paddington Station to Cornwall and arrived at Bodmin Parkway as the sun was setting. Noel was fascinated by the changing scenery, leaving behind the suburban sprawl of London and passing through picturesque meadows, pretty villages, leafy green woods and finally the rugged beauty of Bodmin Moor.

We stayed a couple of nights in Bodmin to visit Archie's father in his nursing home.

The poor man was in his early eighties and suffering from senile dementia. After the death of his mother, a couple of years before he had left for Singapore, Archie had found a tenant to take over the running of the family farm and had arranged for his father to move to a nursing home in Bodmin.

It was a bittersweet reunion between father and son. There was a flicker of recognition in Mr Penrose senior's eyes, but he could not remember his son's name, nor that he even was his son. He was a pleasant, cheerful old man and very good with Noel, but his conversation was extremely limited. He made repetitive comments about the weather and told us how busy he'd been on the farm during the recent harvest. We smiled and nodded along, but I could tell it pained Archie not to be known by his father. It wasn't until we were leaving that he addressed his son by name.

'Goodbye, Arthur. Tell your mother that I'll be home soon.'

Archie's eyes misted over as we left and I squeezed his hand in mine. So often Archie had supported me and it pleased me to be able to offer him comfort when he needed it.

Mr Penrose's parting message at the end of that visit was strangely foreboding, for he was soon home and reunited with Archie's mother. The dear man died just six weeks after our return.

By that time, we had moved into the family home, Penrose Farm, and had been working all hours of the day and night to make it habitable before the winter set in. It had been empty for nearly four years as the tenant farmer had been called up and his wife and children had moved in with her mother. The place had fallen into such disrepair and there was even evidence of squatters at some point. Windows and doors were broken, vines and plant roots had taken hold and animals had made their nests within the four walls. It was a sorry sight. We had our work cut out for us, but every Saturday we made time to travel to Bodmin to visit Archie's father. Noel and I would stay to say hello and have a cup of tea, then we would leave Archie holding his father's hand, listening to his wandering stories, while we went round the shops.

It is six months now since Mr Penrose's funeral, how time has flown, and Penrose Farm has well and truly become our home. Our plan had been to smarten it up ready for a new tenant, then move to one of the bigger towns, Bodmin or Truro, for Archie to join a medical practice. But after all our hard work, we both felt such a strong connection to the place that neither of us could bear to leave. Archie — or should I say Arthur, for that is the name he has chosen to use now — found that farming his family land gave him such a sense of satisfaction that, for the time being at least, he has decided not to return to his medical work.

Talking of names, it seems that Arthur's pet name for me has stuck and I have become Dotty! It was a playful name that he first used on the ship returning to England and I rather like it. It seems fitting that we have fresh names for our fresh start.

There was some curiosity when we first arrived in Cornwall, but that was only to be expected. We were so tanned and, despite our best efforts, still very thin, so naturally we stuck out. Neighbours who remembered Archie were curious, especially as they knew that he had been abroad at some point. We told everyone the same story and stuck to it, that we had met in London during the war, married and had our son.

Ah Ling, Penrose Farm really is the most perfect place that I have ever known and Noel is so happy here — we all are. The gentle pace of life suits us well and the area is so picturesque and serene. The balmy Cornish summer has arrived and it is wonderful to see our little boy thriving. Noel spends his days running and playing with the dogs in the meadows, helping his father with the animals on the farm, or building sandcastles down on the beach. Perhaps he was young enough that his mind has cast off the horrors of the prison camps. I sincerely hope he was.

My memories, however, have continued to haunt me for some time. After Douglas's death

I suppose I felt guilty for feeling such happiness. I felt that after what I'd done, I somehow owed him. Should I have searched harder for his parents to hand over his child, or even returned Noel to his mother? But the latter would have been impossible, as I discovered on a chance reading of a newspaper article in the new year. It announced Bernard Pemberton's inheritance of his family title and castle in Berkshire. There was a photograph of him with his wife. The caption read: 'Sir Bernard Pemberton with his second wife, Lucille. Sir Bernard's first wife, Maria, was killed in the bombing of Singapore in February 1942.'

My guilt at keeping Noel eased after that, for he is now, technically, an orphan. But he is not parentless, for he has the two of us and we adore him.

Your friend, as always,
Dotty x

CHAPTER 28

Singapore
Friday 5th April, 2019

Annabel yawned. She stirred a spoonful of sugar into her coffee cup then took a long, reviving sip. Around her, the family morning routine was in full flow. Tom was long gone, having left early for the office. Above the hum of the radio, she could hear Emma in her daughter's room, patiently explaining to Leila that she couldn't wear her Moana costume because it was a school day and she had to wear her school uniform. Daniel was finishing his homework sheet at the other end of the dining table, while around him Gloria tidied up the remnants of breakfast. It was busy and chaotic, but Annabel had enjoyed fitting into family life with the Nortons and she would miss it.

It was her last day in Singapore, the next morning she would be flying home. To where and to whom, she wasn't exactly sure yet and her stomach sank as she thought about her return to England. She felt a pull to go straight to Cornwall, back to her grandmother's home, but she knew she really should see Luke first. He had texted her on a daily basis, switching his tone between carefree nonchalance, to begging for reconciliation, to downright anger and accusations. None of it had done anything to help his cause; it was well and truly over for Annabel. She just had to make him understand and accept that. Her mind drifted back to the previous afternoon on the sofa with James and she felt a twinge of guilt, coupled with a confusing stirring in her stomach.

It was ironic, she mused as she sipped her coffee, that after a week in Singapore her body was finally adjusting to the seven-hour time difference just as it was time to go home again. But despite overcoming the jet lag, sleep had proven elusive last night. Annabel's dreams had been haunted by Dotty's story, filled with images of war and prison camps, torture and bombing, starvation and desperation. She was glad when the morning came and she could join the family at the breakfast table. Emma had been such a good friend to her over the past week and Annabel would miss her.

Emma appeared, her battle over the costume apparently won as little Leila followed behind her mother, looking sulky in her uniform. Emma sat opposite Annabel and sighed dramatically, 'Honestly, mornings in this household never get any easier!'

Gloria came over and put a fresh cup of coffee in front of Emma and she smiled up gratefully. 'You are a godsend, Gloria, thank you!'

'So how are you feeling this morning, Annie?' Emma asked. 'That was a hell of a lot to take in last night!'

Annabel nodded slowly. 'Yes, I think it will all take a while to process, that's for sure!'

'Have you told your family yet?'

'No.' Annabel's brow furrowed. 'I'll call my brother later and let him know, I think. But it definitely needs to be a face-to-face conversation with my dad.'

'How will he take it, do you think?' Emma asked.

Annabel smiled. 'Oh, dear old Dad is quite unflappable. It'll be a shock, I'm sure, but deep down, I don't think it will change anything for him. Dotty was his mum and they adored each other. And Grandpa was a wonderful father to him. His childhood on the farm really was idyllic.'

'But he moved away years ago, you were saying? What made him leave if he loved it there so much?'

Annabel rolled her eyes. 'Mum,' she said with a shrug. 'And work, I suppose. He was in the military and they moved around a lot. I think he would have liked to have gone back to Cornwall but Mum had her heart set on a sunny expat retirement with plenty of beaches and golf courses. And Portugal fitted the bill!'

Emma glanced at her watch and pulled a face. 'Damn, we'd better make a move, sorry! Don't forget we've got dinner tonight, our treat and we're going to a classic Singapore landmark. You'll love it!' She gulped down the last of her coffee then continued, 'Tom invited James but he's not sure if he'll make it. I think he's had a tough few days on the family front.'

Annabel winced and butterflies twisted and turned in her stomach. What was she feeling? Relief? Disappointment? Yearning?

Emma got up, called the children to gather their school bags and slipped her shoes on. 'I do wish I could come with you today.' She reached down and patted Annabel's shoulder. 'Changi Museum isn't the most uplifting of places, I'm afraid, but I can see why you want to go. I still can't believe your granny was a prisoner of war there, it's just incredible!'

Annabel couldn't believe it either. Try as she might, she could not reconcile her sweet, soft grandmother with the determined, resilient woman who had made it through internment in one of the most notorious camps with a tiny baby that was not her own. It was, as Emma had summed up, incredible.

A couple of hours later, Annabel found herself on the other side of the island, engrossed in the information boards in the Changi Museum. As an historian, she found the exhibits fascinating, but as the granddaughter of a former internee, they were especially poignant. There were artefacts, diaries, photographs and paintings, all of which documented the daily lives of the prisoners and the horrors they had faced. Entering the recreated jail cell and listening to recordings of the internees sent a shiver down Annabel's spine. She imagined what life must have been like in these cramped confines and this brief glimpse was more than enough for her; how had her grandmother endured it for three and a half years?

What shone through most in the museum, however, was the immense fortitude and tenacity of the human spirit. The internees had gone through hell, yet they had not given up. Time after time, day after day, they had rallied themselves and supported each other in order to survive. Annabel smiled as she read about the clubs and societies that had been organised in the camp and gasped in wonder when she saw the Changi Quilts.

The quilts had been the idea of one Mrs Mulvany in 1942, Annabel read, and were intended for the wounded in Changi Hospital. Their real purpose, however, was to keep the women busy with a sense of purpose and to boost morale. The women were asked to put something of themselves into their square of embroidery and their combined patchwork piece was a poignant collection of these remarkable individuals. Annabel spotted a map of Australia, a love heart, a four-leaf clover and a patriotic British flag.

In one of the museum rooms there was a computer with records of the prisoners who had been kept at Changi. Her pulse quickened as she typed 'Dorothy Llewellyn' into the search box. The computer thought about it for a few moments, then loaded a page showing all her grandmother's details. Annabel gasped. Right before her were Dotty's – or rather, Dorothy's – nationality, year of birth, profession and cell room number. The last field, year of death, was left blank. Annabel's eyes teared up as she realised that this needed to be updated. She should probably inform someone of her grandmother's passing. It was suddenly all so official, so real.

After visiting the museum, Annabel made her way through to the chapel. It was in the open air, with prison-high white walls but no roof. Only the altar was undercover, with a simple A-frame roof structure made of wood. She read that this was a 1988 replica of the original chapel, which had been made from any salvageable materials that the prisoners could get their hands on.

Annabel sat on the last bench, closed her eyes and took a deep breath. She found herself drifting back in time and imagining her grandmother. A devout Christian, Dotty was bound to have knelt here, praying for her family and for an end to her internment. As a child, Annabel had especially loved visiting Dotty at Christmastime and singing carols together in the local church. 'Silent Night' had been her granny's favourite, she remembered now. Had she sung it here? For a moment, Annabel had the strangest sensation of her grandmother's reassuring presence beside her and it made her smile.

Before she left, Annabel spoke to the receptionist and got the contact details of the museum curator. The receptionist was interested to hear about Dotty's story and Annabel promised that she would be in touch soon. As an historian, she knew only too well the importance of sharing individual stories.

Annabel was sipping a cold glass of iced lemon tea in the café beside the museum when her phone started vibrating. She winced, worried that it would be Luke pestering her again. There had been four messages from him when she had woken that morning, asking her to call him. She really couldn't face speaking to him.

She tapped on the screen and was relieved to see that it wasn't Luke calling, but James.

'Annabel, it's good news!' he began. 'I've found him! Ravi Chowdhury, your grandmother's former houseboy. He's in a nursing home in Queenstown and has agreed to see us. He's ninety-two now, but still has all his marbles. Where are you now? Have you got time this afternoon?'

Annabel's pulse quickened and she felt her heart begin to race. She wasn't sure if it was the prospect of meeting someone who had actually known her grandmother during her time in Singapore, or the thought of spending time with James. She took a deep breath to calm herself and made a plan to meet him.

Ravi Chowdhury was a small, wiry man with fine white hair and deep brown eyes. He was sitting peacefully in an armchair in the corner of his room, overlooking the nursing home's lush garden of palm trees and bougainvillea. A ceiling fan whirred above, breaking the silence. There was a glass of water and a book on the table beside him, face down but open at his last page.

'Mrs Llewellyn, you say?' he asked with a deep Indian accent after Annabel had made their introductions. She was relieved to hear that his English was excellent.

She nodded and was pleased when Ravi's studious face broke into a smile of remembrance.

'I remember her well; a most pleasant lady. Always so kind. I was much younger than the other staff, you see, and far away from my family. But Mrs Llewellyn was always so good to me.

She arranged for my lessons, you know, so that I could learn to read and write. For that, I will forever be grateful to her. She opened up a whole new world to me. Suddenly, I was travelling all over; Egypt, Venice and often a pretty English village called St Mary Mead.' He pointed to the book on the table and Annabel grinned when she saw the author's name.

'Oh, Agatha Christie!' She chuckled. 'One of her favourites!'

Ravi's face beamed in a wide smile. 'Yes, yes! It was your grandmother who introduced me to Hercule Poirot and that funny little old lady, Miss Marple!'

Annabel smiled as she remembered watching adaptations on TV with her grandmother when she was young. Although Dotty declared every time, the books were far superior to the television versions.

'What can you tell us about *Mister* Llewellyn, Mr Chowdhury?' James asked.

A shadow fell across the old man's face and his jaw tightened.

'He was a bad man. A very bad man.' Ravi shook his head slowly and closed his eyes, wincing as he seemed to take himself back in time.

'What did he do to you, Mr Chowdhury?' Annabel asked gently after a long pause.

Ravi opened his eyes and turned to look directly at her. 'He used to beat me. Usually when he was three sheets to the wind.' The old man spotted Annabel's surprise at the colloquialism and smiled. 'Ah, that was how Mrs Llewellyn described it, you see; I learned all my English from my employers.' He nodded proudly before continuing. 'Mr Llewellyn was an angry drunk. When he was under the influence he would become so impatient with us. I was the youngest and the lowest rank in the house and he would usually take out his frustration on me.'

Ravi paused in his narration and reached out to touch Annabel's arm. He continued confidentially, 'I hope I do not speak out of turn when I say that the Llewellyns' marriage was not a happy one?'

Annabel smiled kindly at the old man and reassured him that she wanted him to speak plainly. She had warmed to him instantly and was enjoying the sound of his lilting, sing-song Indian accent.

'Poor Mrs Llewellyn,' he continued. 'She put up with so much from that man. Drinking, gambling and even – forgive me ma'am – other women.' He shook his head, a look of disgust on his face.

'As I said before, he was a bad man. And I am sorry if I sound callous, but when he fell down the stairs, part of me felt relief. Relief for poor Mrs Llewellyn that he could not continue his cruelty towards her and relief for myself and the other staff that he could not beat us anymore.'

Ravi closed his eyes again and shook his head. The old memories seemed to pain him and Annabel returned his previous gesture and gently put her hand on his arm.

'I'm sorry to drag up bad memories, Mr Chowdhury, I really am. You said that Mr Llewellyn *fell* down the stairs. Do you think that's what really happened?' Annabel could feel her heart racing as she braced herself for his answer. 'I know that Mrs Llewellyn and he had been arguing beforehand. You don't think there might have been some sort of tussle before he fell, do you?'

'Yes ma'am.' Ravi nodded in agreement. 'There was a tussle and Mrs Llewellyn pushed him off her. Then she turned and ran to her bedroom. Mr Llewellyn turned to go back down the stairs but the rug had moved over the edge of the top step and he slipped. He was completely blotto, you see. He slipped on the step and he fell; it was as simple as that.'

'I hope you don't mind my asking, Mr Chowdhury, but how can you be so sure of what happened?'

'Because, ma'am, I was standing in the alcove in the hallway downstairs, hiding ma'am. I saw it all happen with my own two eyes.'

Relief flooded Annabel as she and James drove away from the nursing home a short while later. She felt giddy with delight.

'I knew that Dotty couldn't be a murderer!' she told James as he drove. 'I just knew it couldn't have been true. I'm just so glad that we now know the truth for sure. Thank you so much for finding Ravi, James, you have no idea how much it means to me to have been able to talk to him and know for sure.'

James smiled and nodded thoughtfully, eyes fixed on the road ahead. 'But your grandmother didn't know, did she? The poor lady blamed herself and had to live with the guilt, thinking that she'd killed him.'

'Oh Lord, yes.' Annabel sighed as realisation dawned. 'Poor Dotty! She must have had that on her conscience for the rest of her life. How awful that after everything he did and everything he put her through, it seems that Douglas Llewellyn didn't even stop troubling her after his death. He had to have the final say, didn't he, to win in the end.'

'But he didn't win, did he?'

Annabel frowned. 'What do you mean? Dotty spent the rest of her life thinking herself a murderer. I'd say for a man who seemed hellbent on making her life a misery, he'd clock that up as a victory.'

James shook his head. 'Your grandmother had a long and happy life. She had a devoted husband, a loving son and, from how you've described it, a beautiful home.'

He turned and gave her a wry smile. 'I'd call that a win, wouldn't you?'

The taxi pulled up outside the hotel later that evening and Annabel gasped. The Raffles Hotel really was like something out of a movie, with all the opulence and elegance of a bygone era. She was instantly captivated by its beautiful, whitewashed facade and its classic colonial design spoke of sophisticated, old-world charm.

A very tall Sikh doorman dressed in a turban and full, extravagant livery opened the car door and welcomed them to the hotel. He ushered them up the steps and through the main door. Tom gave their reservation details to the receptionist while Emma and Annabel explored the lobby.

It was an oasis in the heart of the city, Annabel mused as she looked around. She felt instantly soothed by the calming atmosphere, her senses delighted on every level. Delicate music was coming from a harp in the corner and she breathed in the intoxicating scent of lilies in an enormous display of fresh flowers. She looked up and took in the beautiful galleried landings that surrounded the central atrium. White pillars rose from floor to high ceiling and, in the middle, a magnificent chandelier sparkled with hundreds of twinkling lights.

Ceiling fans and potted palms added to the air of old-world colonial refinement. The greenery continued through the glass doors at the side, which led to lush, tropical gardens beyond. Rich, opulent decor adorned the lobby, with antique furniture and intricately designed carpets. Raffles Hotel really was the last word in timeless elegance and sophistication.

'What do you think? It's quite something, isn't it?' Emma asked with a wide grin. 'I thought you'd like it!'

Annabel returned the grin and linked arms with her friend. For a moment, she was lost for words, overwhelmed by the hotel's beauty and charm. 'I love it! It's absolutely stunning,' she finally managed. 'And thank you for the dress, you're a lifesaver!' She looked down at the cornflower-blue shift dress that her friend had lent her.

Emma chuckled. 'You look gorgeous in it, that colour really suits you! And, to be honest, since the twins, I'm afraid I've struggled to fit into it!'

The hotel staff were courteous, attentive and impeccably dressed. They showed the trio to their table in the Tiffin Room, named after the old colonial tradition, and Tom ordered a round of Singapore Slings.

The design of the Tiffin Room was similar to the lobby with its high ceilings, white pillars and ornamental lighting. Displays of blue and white porcelain adorned the shelves around the room and diners sat on old colonial-style rattan chairs. It was stylish and elegant and the soft music playing further enhanced the mood.

'Cheers!' Tom called as they raised their glasses.

Annabel was soon feeling mellow and happy with Emma and Tom. Conversation flowed easily, with Tom sharing tales from the office and Emma describing an amusing music lesson with her year one students earlier in the day.

The waiter came to take their order and Annabel looked at her watch. There was no sign of James. She found herself feeling disappointed. It was her last night in Singapore and he had been such an enormous help that it didn't feel right to leave without a proper goodbye. He had mentioned that he had an important call to make this evening, but had hoped that he would have it wrapped up in time for dinner.

A short while later, the waiter arrived with the first two plates and Annabel breathed in the delicious aroma of the Singapore Laksa they had ordered, spicy and fragrant. After a couple of minutes, she felt him approach behind her again, presumably with the third and final plate, but it was a different, deeper voice that spoke.

'I'm so sorry I'm late!'

Annabel turned and beamed when she saw that it was James. He forced a smile, but beneath it she could see that he was tense and agitated. She suspected that his meeting had not gone well.

'Ah, you made it! Good on you, mate!' Tom cheered, before calling over the waiter and ordering a beer and a menu for his friend.

Annabel tried to steady her heart rate as James made his greetings. What was happening to her? She felt like a nervous teenager. He was looking handsome in beige chinos and a navy-blue shirt, open at the collar. He bent down to kiss Emma on the cheek and then came over to Annabel. She breathed in his scent and felt herself colour when he whispered in her ear, 'You look beautiful.'

James caught them up with the drinks and soon seemed more relaxed. Emma and Tom were keen to hear about their explorations earlier in the day and Annabel told them all about her trip to Changi Museum, the visit to Ravi Chowdhury and their final stops of the day.

'You won't believe it, but we visited the street where Dotty lived. Her family home, I mean, where she lived with her parents when they first moved here, on Nassim Road.'

'Oh, I know where that is, near the Botanic Gardens.' Tom nodded.

'That's amazing! What was it like?' Emma asked.

'The street is absolutely gorgeous!' Annabel replied. 'It's got those old colonial black and white houses and in such a beautiful spot, surrounded by trees and lush gardens. It's so quiet up there, you feel a million miles away from the city. Sadly, the house no longer exists; number twelve is now a shiny, modern apartment block.'

'Ah, shame! How did you find out where your granny lived, though?' Tom asked.

'Well, it was a bit of a surprise to be honest. Dotty's letters never mentioned the address and it didn't occur to me to ask Julia if she knew,' Annabel explained, her words tumbling out in a heady mix of enthusiasm and alcohol. 'But clever old James, here, texted Julia to ask and she knew exactly where the house was. I didn't know where we were going, he kept it as a surprise for today,' Annabel explained with a grin. 'He's so good at all this detective work, he's not a bad Watson to my Holmes.' She beamed at James and instinctively found herself reaching out to touch his arm.

He raised an eyebrow with mock sternness and put his own hand on top of hers. 'I think you mean Holmes to your Watson,' he corrected. The usual bickering ensued over who was which character and neither of them noticed the grin that passed between Emma and Tom.

Moments later, Emma yawned loudly and looked at her watch. 'Well, I hate to be the party-pooper, but I've got an infant choir recital tomorrow morning that is going to need all my energy and enthusiasm, so I'd better make a move.' She looked pointedly at her husband. 'Come on then, Tom, shall we book a cab?'

But Tom was clearly enjoying himself and had no intention of leaving so early. He wrinkled his nose in confusion then checked his watch. 'It's not even ten, Ems, I was thinking I might have another . . . ' Then he stopped as he felt his wife's eyes boring into his, suddenly cottoning on to her meaning. 'Oh, right, I see!' he bumbled. He gave an ostentatious yawn. 'Come to think of it, I am pretty tired. Big day tomorrow, too!'

Farewells were made and they beat a hasty retreat, leaving an amused James and Annabel laughing at their not so subtle attempt to leave them alone.

The alcohol had worked its magic and it was lovely for Annabel to see James so relaxed. He reached across and took her hand in his. He gazed into her eyes. 'God, you look lovely tonight.'

Annabel smiled shyly as the butterflies returned. 'You don't scrub up too badly yourself!' she quipped.

He rubbed his thumb across the back of her hand, his eyes fixed on hers. 'What do you say we get out of here and head home for a nightcap?'

CHAPTER 29

Singapore

Friday 5th April, 2019

Annabel was feeling a swirling mix of nerves and excitement by the time they reached James's apartment. He had been the perfect gentleman in the taxi, calm and composed as always. But the way he had looked at her earlier and held her hand throughout the journey had left her in no doubt of his intentions. She couldn't help her mind drifting back to her last visit, and the thought of his kisses sent her pulse racing again.

It had been a fun evening and, after drinking more than she usually did, she was enjoying the relaxed, carefree sensation that was flowing through her. It was her last night in Singapore; tomorrow she was going back to the real world. So for now, she intended to banish all thoughts of exes and complications and live for the moment.

They got back to James's apartment and Annabel settled herself on the sofa while he switched on the lamps and put on some soft music. Then he went through to the kitchen and reappeared moments later with two glasses. He handed one to her then sat next to her on the sofa.

'Cheers!' she said, raising her glass to clink against his. She swirled the smooth, coffee-coloured liquid around the glass, then breathed in its sweet, creamy aroma. 'Mmm, Baileys, my favourite.' She took a sip.

James nodded. 'Yes, I had a vague memory from years ago that you liked it.'

'It's been a lovely evening,' she began. 'And a lovely week. I'm so grateful for everything you've done to help me, James, I really am. You've been so kind and generous with your time, not to mention incredibly helpful.'

He shook his head, deflecting the compliment. 'It's been my pleasure, Annie, you don't need to thank me.'

'Well it's been a pleasure for me, too, James. I've really enjoyed spending time with you. I've enjoyed getting to know the real James. It's made me realise how much I missed out on all those years ago at uni.'

She reached out and put her hand on his knee but he didn't respond. Instantly, she withdrew it, sensing that something was wrong.

'Is everything alright?'

'I'm sorry.' He sighed. 'I've spent the last week longing for this, but now that we're here it all feels a little . . . '

Annabel tensed as she waited for him to finish.

'Overwhelming, I suppose,' he eventually said.

'Oh,' she said softly. 'Do you want to talk about it?'

James put his glass on the coffee table and leaned forward, elbows on his knees and his head in his hands.

'I've been married for the last ten years. But it's over. Emily told me today that she wants a divorce. And I don't know how to feel about that. I always believed that marriage was forever, that we would stick at it and make it work. Till death do us part, in sickness and in health, for better or worse. Apparently

Emily's new man has moved to England to be with her and she wants to marry him.'

Annabel let out a long sigh. 'That's a lot to process. I'm so sorry, James.' She reached across and rubbed his arm.

'And I can't help but feel like a failure,' he continued. 'Because I couldn't make my marriage work. Apparently, the affair has been going on for years and I was the last to know. What kind of idiot doesn't even notice?'

She moved closer to him and put her arm around his shoulders.

'It takes two to make a relationship work, James, you can't make it happen on your own. Trust me, I know all about that. Please don't be so hard on yourself. I'm right here and I don't see anything idiotic about you whatsoever. I think you're amazing.'

'I don't know about that . . . ' he began. 'What I do know is that I hate how she's made me feel, so stupid and worthless.' He gave a bitter laugh. 'Here we are, you and me, on the brink of something that could be truly wonderful, something I longed for for years, but I'm suddenly feeling completely useless, like I'm damaged goods.'

Annabel wrapped her arms around him and pulled him against her. 'We're not eighteen anymore, James, we all have baggage. We've all been through the mill, made mistakes, had our hearts broken. We've just got to make the best of it and try to find happiness where we can. It's a cliché, but time *will* help things start to feel less painful. You've had a hell of a knock, but you'll pick yourself up again and things will get better. I promise. And please never forget, you *do* deserve to be happy.'

'Thanks.' He rubbed his hands over his face. 'Ugh, I'm sorry.' He sighed and turned to look at her. 'I think all the alcohol has made me a little maudlin.'

'There's no need to apologise, I'm here.' she smiled and reached out to stroke his hand.

He stared intently at her, as if committing every feature to memory. 'God, you're beautiful, Annie.' Then he took her face in his hands and gently kissed her.

Annabel felt her insides melt at his touch, a deep heat flowing through her. She wrapped her arms around him and pulled him close. His kiss was passionate and full of longing.

After a minute, he pulled back, doubt clouding his face. 'Annie, are you sure—'

But she stopped him. 'Shh, James, please stop worrying. This is where I want to be, right here, right now, with you. OK?'

His face eased into a smile and she leaned forward to kiss him again. His lips were soft and tender, and his kisses tasted of whisky and cream. She breathed in the scent of him, an intoxicating combination of male musk, alcohol and cologne.

Annabel stood up from the sofa and, with a flirty smile, reached down for his hand. 'Come on,' she whispered.

Without a moment's hesitation, James took her hand and went with her. Then he led the way to his bedroom. He flicked on the bedside lamp, set his phone to play through the speakers and quickly tidied away the clothes that were on the bed.

Annabel sat on the end of the bed and looked around. The room continued the bachelor pad theme of the apartment, with minimalist furniture and simple decor in muted tones. On the chest of drawers was a collection of photographs; James holding a baby Jessica, James with an older couple who she took to be his parents and a more recent photo of James with his daughter. The smiles in the pictures spoke of simpler times, when he had been happy.

James came and stood in front of her, the soft lamplight making his eyes shine. He cupped her face in one hand, then gently traced a finger down her cheek and neck. His touch was electric and Annabel could feel her heart pounding in anticipation. He continued to trace a path down to her collarbone then followed around the neckline of her dress. He smiled down at her, his gaze soft and warm.

The music changed to a romantic love song. 'This is one of my favourites,' she whispered.

'Well in that case, we'd better make the most of it.' He grinned, adopting a more formal stance. 'May I have the pleasure?' He held out a hand, inviting her to dance and she laughed.

'You're full of surprises!' She stood up from the end of the bed and let herself be swept up in his arms. He held her close and they swayed to the music. Annabel relaxed into him, resting her head against his shoulder and wrapping her arms around his waist. He was humming along with the song and she enjoyed this more carefree side of him. She closed her eyes and breathed in deeply, taking in the freshly laundered scent of his shirt. It was a wonder to her how she could feel simultaneously so relaxed and so electrified in this man's presence.

The song came to an end. He bent down and kissed her softly on the lips, then led her over to the bed. They sat side by side, their fingers intertwined, hearts racing. The air was filled with a heady mix of anticipation and excitement.

Annabel looked at James in the lamplight. A five o'clock shadow was starting to spread across his jaw. She reached out and ran a finger across the stubble. She noticed a small scar on his chin and a mole on his neck that she'd never seen before. She was taking it all in. His handsome face, normally so composed and confident, gave a flicker of hesitation. To reassure him, she leaned over and kissed him full on the lips, then lay back on the duvet, pulling him down beside her.

Leaning on an elbow, James looked down at her and smiled. Then he bent down and kissed her neck, slowly running his hand all the way down from her shoulder to the tips of her fingers. She shivered at his touch. Then, checking that she was happy for him to do so, he stroked her stomach and ran his hand down to her inner thigh.

His touch was electrifying and Annabel was overtaken by desire. She reached to undo his buttons and soon he was taking off his shirt. The sight of his bare chest made her grin with delight. He was tanned and muscular, with broad shoulders and well-defined abs.

'Well someone clearly takes care of himself!' she teased, before reaching up to finger the patch of dark hair at his breastbone. 'You are so gorgeous,' she added, enjoying the feel of strong muscle under her fingertips.

James smiled bashfully then leaned down to kiss her again. Annabel wrapped her arms around him, enjoying the feel of his warm skin against her.

'I think you've got a bit of catching up to do, Dr Penrose,' he said in between kisses. 'Much as I love this dress . . . ' He reached around and unzipped it. Seconds later, the dress was on the floor.

'Is that better?' Annabel asked coyly, feeling a little shy as she sat there in nothing but her black satin underwear.

James gave a low growl of appreciation and wrapped her in his strong arms, rolling over on top of her and kissing her, more passionately now. She could feel his arousal and the heat of desire coursed through her. She tugged at his belt and, his eyes never leaving hers, he obliged her by standing up and taking off his remaining clothes.

She gasped at the sight of him fully naked, muscular and firm, and felt a growing ache inside her. She pulled him down beside her and he unclipped her bra. He moaned at the sight of her soft breasts, then bent down to brush his lips against them. Then he made a trail of kisses all the way down her stomach and stopped to slip off her underwear. He kissed her inner thigh and slowly, teasingly, worked his way up to explore the place that made her moan in delight.

Eventually, she could bear it no longer and pulled him up close to her. 'I want you,' she whispered in between kisses. She reached down to stroke him and his deep, guttural groan made it clear that he felt the same way. Fears and inhibitions were forgotten and their bodies melted together in a blissful union.

After, they lay entwined in each other's arms, both happy and deeply satisfied.

'It's been a wonderful evening, thank you, Annie, the perfect way to say goodbye.' He kissed her cheek then pulled her onto him as he settled into his pillow. With her head on his chest, she didn't see the sad look in his eyes as he spoke the words.

Within moments his breathing had deepened and he was asleep. But Annabel lay there, wide awake, for some time, reflecting on what he had said. Goodbye. Had part of her hoped that there was some way that this could have continued?

Yes, perhaps it had. She was not naive enough to think that straight out of the ashes of two recently failed relationships a long-distance romance could have kindled, but the finality of goodbye made a part of her ache.

Annabel woke early. Her mouth was dry and her head was thumping. She checked her watch: 5.27 a.m. She looked down at James, sleeping peacefully beside her. His brow smooth, he looked younger and so carefree. Memories of the previous night flooded back and her stomach flipped as she remembered his touch and his kisses. How she wished things could have been different, that they could have met under more straightforward circumstances.

She slipped out of bed and quietly got dressed. Her flight was at eleven and she needed to get back to Emma's to finish packing and say goodbye to the family. Without disturbing James, she gathered up her things and scribbled a note to leave on the kitchen table.

She hated goodbyes. It had been lovely while it lasted, but now it was time to go home.

CHAPTER 30

Cornwall

THREE WEEKS LATER

The sun was shining as Annabel and her brother William greeted guests at the door of All Saints' Church in Wincastle. It was early summer and the weather was obligingly warm and pleasant for the morning of their grandmother's funeral. Annabel looked around the churchyard and smiled at the magnolia tree in full bloom and the magnificent carpet of bluebells under the trees.

'Dotty would have loved this!' she said, her eyes shining with unshed emotion.

William put an arm around his sister. 'I know. But she's here, sis, I'm sure of that.' He squeezed her shoulder. 'You know she was never one to miss a good party!' He gave her a cheerful wink.

Inside the church, their father Noel was handing out the orders of service, perched on a stool to rest his hip, as per his wife's instructions. His recovery had been slow and steady, but a minor setback had delayed their trip to Cornwall – and, consequently the funeral – by a couple of weeks. Jeanette, looking chic and elegant in a navy-blue coat dress, was chatting to the vicar, Reverend Pascoe. The beautiful strains of 'Ave Maria' came from the organ and the scent of lilies filled the air. The church was packed. In a bittersweet echo of her one hundredth birthday party, Dotty's nearest and dearest had turned out in their masses for her. But this time it was to bid farewell.

It had been three weeks since Annabel's return from Singapore and, once she had recovered from the jet lag, she had kept herself busy. Her first task had been to meet Luke for a coffee and spell out, in no uncertain terms, that it was over between them. She ignored his pleas for forgiveness and reminded him that apart from wanting different things out of life, ultimately, he had lost her trust and respect.

'There's someone else, isn't there?' he had asked, bitterness and accusation in his voice.

Annabel's stomach had twisted as her mind had drifted back to James. Was there someone else? She wasn't sure. She had fought hard to push him out of her mind, but hadn't yet managed to make it through a day without him interrupting her thoughts. They had exchanged occasional messages since her return to England, but at such distance and in different time zones, their former intimacy had turned into polite chit-chat.

Annabel decided that it was for the best to draw a line and move on. He lived on the other side of the world, for goodness' sake, never mind the fact that he was also reeling from an unfaithful wife and trying to cope with what sounded like an acrimonious divorce. He was trying to be a good dad to his daughter and carve out some sort of new life for himself. As for her, she needed time to figure things out for herself after her break-up, too. It was all just too complicated. It had been a holiday romance, fun while it lasted.

'No, of course not,' she had replied, somewhat defensively. She could feel the colour rise in her cheeks. 'But even if there was, Luke, I don't think you're exactly in a position to accuse me of infidelity!'

She had ripped off the proverbial Band Aid and left Luke in the café, looking dejected and miserable. His time alone while she'd been away had not done him any good. She could tell that he'd been drinking more than usual and having too many late nights. His face, usually so handsome, looked pale and puffy. He was unshaven and she could smell that he'd started smoking again. His whole aura was unkempt and unhealthy and did nothing to change Annabel's mind.

Her next visits were to her Head of Faculty at Bristol University and her estate agent in Bath. For a while, she had been mulling over the idea of taking some time off work to focus on the book she was writing and now seemed like the right moment. Her request for a one-year sabbatical was approved and arrangements were made for her house in Oldfield Park to be rented out.

Since Dotty's death she had been feeling such a strong pull to Cornwall and, for a while at least, she planned to make Penrose Farm her home. She had given Luke two weeks' notice to move out of her house, then had packed up her things and headed off down the M5 without a backward glance.

She couldn't wait to get back to the farm. After everything she had found out in Singapore, it was almost like she needed to get to know her grandmother again, through this new lens. She had volunteered to sort Dotty's belongings during her stay, for which her father was grateful, and the sea air, endless beaches and wide, open countryside would be the perfect tonic to get herself back on track after Luke.

'It's Annabel, isn't it?' Her thoughts were interrupted by a lilting Cornish voice.

Annabel took in the smiling face and blonde curly hair of the lady approaching the church door and smiled. 'Hello, Sue!' she said, recognising the nurse who had taken care of Dotty in her final days. The older woman beamed and wrapped her in a warm hug.

'I'm so sorry, again, for your loss, my love. You must miss her very much. Your grandmother was a wonderful lady, I felt I had to come and pay my respects.'

Annabel thanked her for coming, then introduced her to William. When the next guests arrived and William started chatting to them, Annabel saw an opportunity and took Sue to one side.

'Sue, you said something in the hospital that has been playing on my mind. After she died, you said that Dotty was a very brave lady. Do you remember?'

Sue nodded, her smiling face becoming serious.

'At the time, I just thought you meant she'd been brave after her fall, coping with being in hospital and so on. But that wasn't what you meant, was it?'

Slowly, Sue shook her head.

'She told you about Singapore, didn't she? And about my father?'

'Yes, my love.' Sue sighed and gave a sad smile. 'And that's why I'm here.' Her tone became hushed and confidential. 'While she was in hospital, your granny told me that she had something to get off her chest, something that she'd never told anyone. She said she was going to tell you when you came in the next day, but . . . ' She trailed off and gave a sigh.

'She never got the opportunity,' Annabel finished for her.

The older lady's brow furrowed in thought. 'I don't know if she knew her time was nearly up, but I could tell it was important to her to share whatever it was. She asked me if I would listen and I said I would.' Sue gave a little shrug. 'Dotty was such a sweet old thing that I was happy to. So I stayed on after my shift that afternoon, made us both a nice cup of tea and she told me her story. But to be honest, it all sounded so fantastical that I wasn't sure if she was making it up, losing her marbles, maybe?'

Annabel chuckled. 'I think Dotty kept every one of her marbles right up until the very end!'

'But it wasn't all true, was it? All that about living in Singapore with that good-for-nothing husband, the war, the baby, the prison camp?'

Annabel gave a wry smile and nodded.

'Well, blow me!' Nurse Sue said, her face a picture of surprise. 'She said she hadn't told any of the family,' she continued. 'Made me swear to keep it secret until she'd passed, but then to let *you* know. She was quite insistent about that. "Tell Annabel," she kept saying. "She'll understand". She loved you so much, my dear.' The nurse reached out and squeezed Annabel's hand. 'So that's why I came today, to see you again. Dotty wanted me to tell you everything.' She gestured to the church and the guests, 'Not now, obviously, but maybe we could have a cup of tea one day and I could tell you what she said. But it sounds like you already know a lot of it?'

Annabel smiled fondly and nodded. 'Thank you, Sue, I'd like that. And thank you for being there for Dotty. She hadn't told us anything. But I found some old letters and photographs in her desk and curiosity got the better of me. I went out to Singapore a few weeks ago and managed to piece together her story.'

Sue's mouth dropped open. 'Oh lovey, you went all that way, halfway around the world? You needn't have gone on a plane, you could have just come over to Bodmin and I would have told you everything!'

Annabel burst out laughing at the irony and gave her a spontaneous hug. They swapped phone numbers and agreed to meet soon.

'Before I go in, I just want to tell you two things that Dotty kept saying, over and over,' Sue said. 'First, she told me that taking your father as a baby was the best thing that ever happened to her.'

Annabel felt a lump in her throat and fresh tears pricked at her eyes.

'Second, she asked for forgiveness for what she did. I think you probably know what I mean. It's sad to think that she carried that guilt and shame with her until the very end.'

Annabel's face fell as she thought of the suffering her grandmother had gone through.

'Oh, poor Dotty,' she sighed. 'The guilt wasn't hers, Sue. It wasn't her fault, I found that out while I was in Singapore.'

'Oh, really? Well that's marvellous!' Sue chuckled, her face breaking into a wide smile. 'What a relief! Well, you'd better tell her that, my love, then your grandmother can rest in peace!' Sue looked up at the blue sky and smiled. 'Look, a skylark!' she said, pointing to a small bird high above them. 'Don't often see them around these parts. Now, that's a good sign!' She squeezed Annabel's hand encouragingly one last time, then made her way into the church.

Left alone, Annabel looked up at the skylark hovering above. 'Rest easy, Dotty, you don't need any forgiveness. We love you,' she whispered. And at that moment, the skylark began to sing.

'What was that all about?' William asked, coming over.

'I'll tell you later.' she smiled, wiping her eyes.

He pulled her close in a hug. 'I think it's time to get this show on the road. Everyone's here.' Then he looked up, over her shoulder. 'Oh, I spoke too soon; one last straggler cutting it a bit fine! Who's this?' His brow furrowed. 'I don't recognise him.'

Annabel stepped out of his embrace and turned to see who was coming up the path towards them. Dressed in a smart, black suit, the tall, dark figure was instantly familiar. But it couldn't be. Could it?

'Oh!' she gasped, her face a picture of confusion and surprise. 'What are . . . How did . . . ?' but she didn't manage to finish any of her questions.

'Hello, Annabel,' James said, a nervous smile on his lips.

'Hi!' she managed to croak, staring at him. Her heart was thumping and she seemed to have momentarily lost the ability to speak.

William eased the tension with a cheerful introduction. He shook James's hand, told him it was good to meet him, and thanked him for helping Annabel with her research in Singapore. Annabel was grateful for her brother's easy, relaxed manner as, at that moment, she was feeling anything but relaxed.

Introductions made, William excused himself and went to join the pall-bearers in the car park, where the hearse was arriving. It was almost time for Dotty's final journey. Annabel's heart felt heavy at the prospect.

She continued to stare at James. What on earth was he doing here? She had briefly mentioned the date of the funeral to him in a text, but had no idea that he would come. She was surprised and confused, but strangely pleased.

Annabel took a deep breath to steady herself and smiled up at him. 'I'm sorry, I'm just so surprised to see you.' She paused and gave a sigh. 'But it's so good to see you, James, it really is.'

A smile replaced the hesitation that had shadowed his eyes. 'Well, I'm glad to hear that. It's very good to see you too, Annie. I've missed you.'

Annabel's insides somersaulted.

'I really hope I'm not intruding. I hope you don't mind me coming?'

She smiled at him and shook her head.

James sighed. 'I just wanted to be here for you, Annie, that's all. That is, if you'd like me to be?' The uncertain look was back.

'Yes.' She beamed, reaching for his hand. 'I'd like you to be here, very much indeed.'

The relief in his face was visible and he stepped forward and wrapped her in his arms, holding her close. Annabel breathed in the scent of his cologne and felt the usual sense of peaceful calm wash over her. This was where she wanted to be, safe in his arms.

'It was awful not saying a proper goodbye,' he said, breathing into her hair. 'I've spent the past three weeks trying to put you out of my mind, but failing miserably. I landed in London last night and drove down first thing this morning. It's Jessica's birthday on Tuesday, so I'll head up to Oxford to see her in a couple of days. But I've been having a long, hard look at things and I think it's time to make some changes.'

She stepped back from him and looked up into his dark eyes. 'Oh? What are you thinking?'

'I don't want to be a long-distance dad, only seeing my daughter a handful of times a year. She deserves more than that. I need to be closer. So I've decided it's time to move back to the UK.'

Annabel smiled. 'Oh!' was all she managed.

James tilted his head and continued mysteriously, 'And the thing is, there's another special lady I'd like to spend more time with.'

'Oh really?' she asked, feigning innocence. 'She must be pretty special to make you move halfway around the world?'

He wrapped his arms around her waist, pulled her close so that they were face to face, and chuckled. 'Oh yes, she is *very* special indeed!' He stroked her cheek then bent down to kiss her lightly on the lips. Her insides melted at his touch.

'So what's the plan?' she asked.

'Well, I put in for a transfer back to London,' he said. 'And it's been approved. Hopefully in the next couple of months.'

'That's great news.' Annabel beamed up at him, a warm feeling spreading through her.

'It's not going to be without its complications, Annie. But someone very wise reminded me recently that we're not eighteen anymore. We all have our baggage, but we deserve to be happy.'

Annabel grinned, remembering the words she had spoken back in Singapore.

'And I think that spending more time with you would make me very happy.' He smiled shyly. 'If you'd like to, that is?'

'Yes James, I would like that very much.' She reached up and kissed him.

'Oh, I nearly forgot, I have something for you.' He rummaged in his pocket and pulled out a small, purple artificial flower.

'An orchid?' Annabel said, taking it from him. 'From Singapore? It's beautiful! Is it for me?'

'For Dotty,' he said.

'Thank you, James.' She smiled through her tears. 'It's perfect.'

Then he gave her his arm and escorted her into the church. It was time to say goodbye to her grandmother.

Epilogue

Cornwall

ONE WEEK LATER

Seagulls squawked overhead as Annabel and James walked hand in hand across the golden sand of Smugglers Cove. It was a perfect summer's day; the sky was the deep, Cornish blue that Annabel so loved and the sun felt warm on her skin. She enjoyed the feel of the soft sand between her toes and the scent of the salty sea air. Monty trotted along beside them, barking his reply to the noisy birds above.

It had been an idyllic few days at the farmhouse. After his trip to visit Jessica for her birthday, James had returned to spend time with Annabel. Her parents had taken themselves off to visit friends in Exeter for a few days, so they'd had the place to themselves. And they had spent it in a bubble of blissful happiness, savouring each other's company and exploring each other as they made love morning, noon and night. They had fallen into a routine of breakfasts in bed, long leisurely walks on the beach, bubble baths and cooking dinner together. It had been perfect.

Annabel glanced at her watch. 'Time to head back up, I think,' she told James.

He nodded and squeezed her hand. 'How are you feeling?'

She gave him a smile. 'Ready as I'll ever be!'

James wrapped an arm around her shoulder, pulling her close against him.

'I'm glad you're here,' she said.

'Me too,' he replied, before bending down to kiss her softly.

They left the beach and made their way back up the winding track. Ahead of them, further along the clifftop path, they made out the familiar figures who were waving at them and waved back. Noel and Jeanette, and William and Sarah greeted them with kisses and handshakes. Annabel was pleased at how easily James had fitted into being with the family.

They were gathered around a brown wooden bench that had been delivered that morning and placed in the spot that Dotty had declared 'the finest view on the North Cornwall coastline.' The bench had been Noel's idea, feeling that he wanted a special place to come and sit peacefully and remember his 'dear old mum'.

Annabel read the engraved inscription: 'For Dotty, who loved this place.' It was simple, but perfect.

'Well, everyone, I think it's about time,' Noel said to them. He took out a silver-plated urn from his bag.

William tapped on his phone and within seconds the rousing introduction of Glenn Miller's 'In the Mood' filled the air, making them all smile.

James turned to Annabel, looking surprised. She grinned at him, her eyes sparkling with tears as she explained, 'It was one of Dotty's favourites.'

Noel took the lid off the urn. 'Goodbye, darling Mum,' he said, a catch in his voice as he lifted it and began to shake it out over the edge of the cliff. 'Thank you for everything.'

'Goodbye, Dotty,' Annabel whispered as the breeze carried the tiny fragments away over the beach and towards the sea. 'We love you.'

She felt James take her hand in his.

The family stood watching the ashes float away, listening to the music and deep in thought as they each remembered Dotty in their own way. The music finished and Noel thanked them all for coming.

'We were lucky the wind was blowing in the right direction!' William quipped.

His mother raised her eyebrows at him, 'Oh, for goodness' sake, William! Must you ruin the atmosphere?'

Annabel chuckled, glad that, for once, it was her brother's turn to get their mother's reproach.

'What?' William replied, feigning innocence. 'Much as we all loved Dotty, we didn't want to end up wearing her!'

Everyone chuckled at his irreverent humour, apart from Jeanette who tutted at her son and shook her head. 'I think it's time for a cup of tea, shall we head back?' she asked.

'You all go.' Annabel nodded at her. 'I'd like a few minutes with Dad.'

James bent down to kiss her and William gave her a supportive wink. They both knew what was coming and managed to deflect Jeanette's curiosity with the promise of freshly-baked scones back at the house.

'Fancy a little walk, Dad? It's such a lovely day.' Annabel took her father's hand and led him away from the others.

'James is a nice chap, Annie, I like him very much.' Noel nodded his approval as they walked along the clifftop. 'I'm sorry to say that there was something about Luke that I could never quite get on with. I always felt that you deserved better. And I'm glad that you seem to have found it in James.' He bent down and kissed his daughter's cheek. 'I hope things work out for you two.'

'Me too, Dad,' she replied with a smile. 'It's complicated, but there's no rush. We'll just take it one step at a time.'

'I'm glad I've got you on your own, actually,' Noel said. 'You never told us much about your trip. I know you said you stayed with a friend, but what made you go to Singapore?'

Annabel chuckled. 'Well, it's funny you should ask that, Dad, as that's exactly what I wanted to talk to you about.'

'Oh?' Noel replied.

She hooked her arm through her father's and they walked side by side along the path, enjoying the invigorating salty breeze and the sight of the wildflowers in full bloom. This had been Dotty's home for over seventy years and it was Annabel's home now. She loved this place, there was nowhere else she would rather be.

Above them, a skylark soared, singing its distinctive melody. Annabel smiled.

'Let me tell you a story, Dad. It's the story of a very brave lady, a promise that she made and a secret that she kept for many, many years.'

Historical Note

The events that took place in Singapore in February 1942 were unprecedented. Defeat to the invading Japanese seemed numerically impossible, with the Allied forces outnumbering the enemy by almost three to one. Everyone believed that the city-state was invincible. Yet within one short week, due to a combination of overconfidence and inadequate preparation, the unthinkable happened and Singapore fell. Winston Churchill called it the 'worst disaster' and 'largest capitulation' in British military history.

The Japanese occupation of Singapore - or 'Syonan-to' as it was renamed - lasted three years and eight months. It was a time of extreme hardship and brutality for everyone living here, but none more so than those who were imprisoned. Changi Jail became synonymous with the suffering and inhumane treatment of Allied prisoners of war. Its overcrowded conditions led to widespread disease, malnutrition, starvation and death. Many prisoners were also subjected to forced labour projects like the Thai-Burma Railway, or Death Railway as it was later dubbed. Throughout the Japanese occupation, it is estimated that around eighty-five thousand prisoners passed through the gates of Changi Jail, many of whom were forced to march there - like Dorothy in the story - from other parts of the island.

Despite the hardship and conditions they endured, the Changi prisoners of war showed remarkable courage and resilience. It was a daily struggle for survival, battling against the effects of malnutrition and the constant risk of injury or disease. The prisoners grew ever more resourceful, turning to ingenuity and improvisation to meet their needs. They also kept busy, organising groups and activities to keep up morale. Educational classes, concerts, sports and literary arts gave them a break from the daily monotony of prison life, and they never gave up hope. They truly were a testament to the fortitude of the human spirit, prevailing both physically and mentally throughout such extraordinary times.

Anyone who has visited Raffles Hotel in the past thirty-five years may be surprised to learn that there was, indeed, a ballroom at the front of the main hotel entrance, where the driveway is today. It was added to the original building in 1920 and had a reputation as 'the finest ballroom in the East.' It was demolished during the 1989-91 renovation. Hainanese bartender Ngiam Tong Boon was the man credited with mixing the first Singapore Sling, as per Clara's story, in around 1915 in the hotel's Long Bar. These days, the iconic drink still attracts visitors to the hotel and they serve around one thousand glasses of the gin-based cocktail each day! It does seem strange that Beach Road, where Raffles Hotel is situated, no longer runs along a beach. When the Sarkies Brothers first opened their hotel as a modest ten-roomed establishment in 1887, it did have direct beach access. However, due to land reclamation and urban redevelopment, the hotel is now just over a kilometre (as the crow flies) from the sea.

These days, Raffles Place is at the heart of the country's Central Business District and it is hard to imagine it full of cars and rickshaws as it was in the first half of the twentieth century. John Little was the oldest department store in Singapore, opening its doors in Raffles Place in 1842 and operating there until the 1950s. The building no longer exists (the site is now occupied by the Singapore Land Tower), but a replica of the shop's white triangular gable can still be seen today at the entrances of Raffles Place Mass Rapid Transport (MRT) station, as a nod to the iconic store.

The rubber industry is the reason in the story for Dorothy's family emigrating to Singapore. Before the Second World War, Singapore was one of the world's most important hubs. Natural rubber was grown mainly in neighbouring Malaya and Singapore's role was more about being the commercial, processing and shipping centre. Its output of natural rubber fuelled industries worldwide, in particular the entire motor industry and many military applications. Singapore was strategically extremely important to the Allied powers and, consequently, to the Axis.

In the story, Dorothy lives in two black and white bungalows, firstly in the prestigious Nassim Road with her parents, then in York Road with Douglas Llewellyn. The 'black and whites' are an iconic legacy of Singapore's colonial past and around five to six hundred still remain standing today. They were built between 1903 and 1941 for high-ranking colonial officers, military personnel and their families, as well as wealthy expatriates. These days they are mainly owned by the Singapore Government and are used for residential, commercial or hospitality purposes. Typically situated in lush, wooded areas, these beautiful, historic buildings take you back in time, to a world far away from the skyscrapers and apartment blocks of modern Singapore.

One of my favourite characters in this story is Ah Ling. Not only is she a loyal companion and friend to Dorothy, but she has an inner strength and devotion to her family and country that is admirable. Many civilians like Ah Ling risked their lives by joining resistance groups during the Japanese occupation. In the story, Ah Ling joins the Malayan People's Anti-Japanese Army, but other groups also operated at the time, such as the Oriental Mission, Dalforce, Chinese Communists and Force 136.

The SS Kuala that Dorothy boarded really did leave Singapore on 13th February 1942 and was bombed by the Japanese the following day. There are several eye-witness accounts online and details vary between sources. However, the one thing they all have in common is the sheer horror and barbarism of the events that took place.

It is estimated that around 75 - 80 million people were killed during the Second World War. As Laurence Binyon wrote in his poem 'For the Fallen', composed on the cliffs in north Cornwall, *we will remember them.*

Author's Note

When I moved to Singapore in 2016 to teach at an international school (much like Emma in the story), I really didn't know very much about the history of the island city-state. Visits to heritage sites such as The Battlebox, Kranji War Memorial and Changi Chapel & Museum sparked a deep fascination in me and I soon found myself drawn into the country's wartime past. Looking at the modern city today, it's hard to imagine the place under invasion then occupation. I was captivated by novels like Noel Barber's 'Tanamera' and Jenny Ashcroft's 'Island in the East', which really conveyed the human cost of war and showed how Singapore was changed irrevocably.

Researching for this novel has been a fascinating experience and I have tried my best to keep the story as historically accurate as possible. Most of the wartime experiences were based on firsthand accounts, either documented online or in print. Some artistic license has, naturally, been used, either when detailed information was unavailable or in order to shape the narrative more effectively. Any mistakes or oversights are entirely my own.

'The Fall of Malaya and Singapore' by Jon Diamond (Pen & Sword Military), was a great starting-point and introduction to the history of wartime Singapore. 'Life and Death in Changi - The War and Internment Diary of Thomas Kitching, 1942-44' (Landmark Books) and 'Diary of a Girl in Changi' by Sheila Allan (Simon & Schuster Australia), both gave a real insight into the daily routines of the Changi prisoners of war. Further research was carried out at The Battlebox and also at Changi Museum & Chapel when it reopened in 2021 after extensive renovation. The museum shares so many incredible firsthand accounts, as well as personal objects from the former internees, and was an excellent source of information. For general background information on Singapore, 'One More Story to Tell: Memories of Singapore, 1930s-1980s' by Chan Kwee Sung (Landmark Books), was a very interesting and informative read. To find out more about the iconic hotel, I read 'Raffles Hotel' by Gretchen Liu (Oxford University Press).

This book is dedicated to my grandmother who passed away in 2020 at the age of 101. She lived in London during the war and, like Daisy in the story, took part in night-time fire-watching duties. As with so many of her generation, she was incredibly stoic and resilient, and I was always intrigued to hear her talk about her wartime experiences. She is much missed.

Acknowledgements

If writing a novel is like climbing a mountain, getting it published is like reaching the top of Everest. It has been a long journey; immensely satisfying but not without its challenges. I am so grateful to everyone who has encouraged and supported me to get to the summit.

Firstly, to my friends and family who have read my work over the years. Thank you for taking the time to read my early scribblings and for being kind and enthusiastic with your feedback. Thank you to my writing buddies at the Inverness Novel Writing Group back in the early days: Rivka, Caroline and Joe. Not only did they offer invaluable feedback and guidance, but they gave me the encouragement to believe I could do this.

A lot of research went into the writing of this book and I am extremely grateful to several key sources in Singapore: the National Library Board for their excellent online resources, the National Archives Centre for their research advice, and the National Heritage Board for their fascinating interactive portal. The new Changi Museum & Chapel also provided so much inspiration, with its amazing artefacts and firsthand accounts of the internees' experiences. Thank you, also, to my Singaporean friends, April and Jon, for checking my local references and - most importantly - my Singlish. Thanks lah!

To my agent, Sara Keane of Keane Kataria Literary Agency, a huge thank you for your belief in me and my writing. From the very beginning, I have really appreciated all your support and encouragement, and it's a privilege to work with you. Thank you to the team at Hodder & Stoughton who have also been brilliant: Annie Ku, Laura Oliver and Charlea Charlton. Thank you to Lisa Brewster for the beautiful cover design, and a very special thank you to my lovely editor, Cara Chimirri, who has just been fabulous.

The biggest thank you of all goes to my husband, Chris. When we first met, I shared with you my dream to one day become a published author; thank you for believing in me and for your constant support and encouragement to make that dream - and so many others - come true. Thank you for all the cups of tea, for keeping me company while I write, and for your endless patience and faith in me. Thank you for listening to every single word of my stories, for discussing characters and plotlines, and for spotting mistakes and suggesting improvements. You are the best sounding board I could wish for, thank you for being my biggest fan.

Lastly, thank you to my readers for picking up this book and taking a chance on a debut author. My aim is to write the sort of books that I would enjoy reading, I really hope that you enjoyed it, too.